# Walking the Shadows

Also by Donald James

Monstrum
The Fortune Teller
Vadim

# WALKING THE SHADOWS

## Donald James

CENTURY · LONDON

Published by Century in 2003

1 3 5 7 9 10 8 6 4 2

First published in the United Kingdom in 2002 by Century
The Random House Group Limited
20 Vauxhall Bridge Road,
London SW1V 2SA

Random House Australia (Pty) Limited
20 Alfred Street, Milsons Point, Sydney,
New South Wales 2061, Australia

Random House New Zealand Limited
18 Poland Road, Glenfield,
Auckland 10, New Zealand

Random House (Pty) Limited
Endulini, 5A Jubilee Road, Parktown 2193, South Africa

The Random House Group Limited Reg. No. 954009

www.randomhouse.co.uk

A CIP catalogue record for this book
is available from the British Library

Papers used by Random House are natural,
recyclable products made from wood grown in sustainable forests;
the manufacturing processes conform to the environmental
regulations of the country of origin

ISBN 0 7126 8447 6 – Hardback
ISBN 0 7126 8424 7 – Paperback

Typeset by
Palimpsest Book Production Ltd, Polmont, Stirlingshire

Printed and bound in Great Britain by
Clays Ltd, St Ives plc

Marie-France Aries
Born 9, rue Gustave Doré, Paris,
October 7th, 1941.

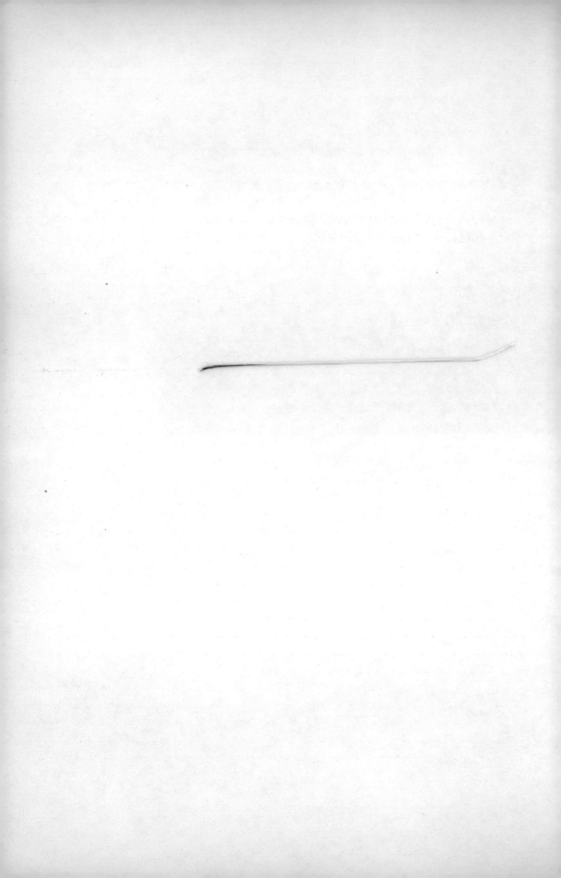

*Où sont les neiges d'antan?*

*Where are the snows of yesteryear?*

François Villon, 1431–1470, priest, womaniser,
murderer – and the greatest poet of medieval France.

# Walking the Shadows

# I

*July, 1985 – San Francisco.*

ONE HOUR TO live affects us all in different ways. Of course there was panic. But other reactions too. The three Jamaican women in the seats in front of me were praying, quiet, confident prayers; across the aisle, a young couple clutched each other, their hands moving intimately under a blanket. There were a lot of silent people, staring ahead, white-faced, lip-licking.

My mother was not among them. She sat upright and New England in her seat, sixty-nine years old, her face distorted by last year's stroke but her steel-grey hair perfectly in shape, her suit a matching steel grey. Her head was slightly turned to the window watching the rain gathering over the Pacific – or, a few minutes later, the play of single shafts of sunlight across the city as we circled San Francisco Bay. When enough fuel was burnt off or dumped over the ocean we would go for our no-undercarriage, no-hope emergency landing.

An engine coughed. A thin trail of smoke fled past the window and was gone, a signal that we were near the end of our fuel. We would be going for a landing in minutes. Our pilot had put the problem succinctly. On take-off our undercarriage had jammed three feet short of full retraction. From this position it refused to move.

My mother turned from her survey of the Golden Gate, its towers a sullen, magnificent orange in the late afternoon sun. 'Well, Sonny . . .' she said as the bridge passed beneath us, 'Your father believed in facing facts. I believe he would have put our chances of survival at zero.' Her lips were like soft rubber, no longer capable of holding the lines of spite, anger or contempt, emotions that had shaped them for forty years, but there was now an undisguised satisfaction in her tone.

'He wouldn't have given up hope,' I said.

'What do you know?' She stared challengingly at me. 'You two weren't exactly close.'

I turned away from her. I marvelled furiously at the way she had succeeded again, even in these circumstances, in reducing me to schoolboy petulance. It was a thin, badly frayed thread that joined me to my father, but even that she had always tried to break. Since his death, she had claimed to possess his memory as she had once possessed the man.

The pilot was reducing the circumference of the circles we were flying. Engines screamed. The jet banked steeply, steeply enough to elicit a collective gasp from the hundred or more passengers. I sat sick and silent beside my mother, her face cast in indifference to her fate, to mine, to the fate of all of us, men, women and children on the plane.

'Sonny,' she said. 'To choose this moment to sit there sulking is absurd. Say something,' she commanded.

I fought off the images of huge, crumpled piles of airframe rolling the length of a runway, exploding black smoke and fierce flame, of scattered suitcases bursting their locks as they struck the concrete, of bodies bouncing like dolls. 'I'll say something,' I said. With engines howling in my ears I felt reckless. I couldn't remember ever challenging my mother. But this was a chance to say something that had riled me since I was a teenager. It's at times like this, I guess, that important trivia surface. 'You christened me Thomas Bannerman Chapel,' I said. 'I'm forty years old. Do you *have* to go on calling me by that ridiculous preppy name. I'm *not* Sonny. I'm Thomas, for Christ's sake. Tom.'

She glared at me in genuine shock. 'Your father always called you Sonny. It was his favourite name for you.'

For her, that closed the matter. Around us there were muted screams, squealing intakes of breath as the captain gave ominous orders to the cabin staff about overhead baggage and exit clearance. The plane banked sharp right and the Golden Gate once again disappeared beneath the wing. I glanced quickly at my mother. She pursed her carnival rubber lips. She had no fear of death. More than that, she welcomed it as the gate to pass through to rejoin her husband. My father, General J. Dwight Chapel, US Army.

I was afraid, of course. But fear wasn't how I'd imagined it would feel. No awful panic. No uncontrollable sweating. Perhaps I was helped by years of feeling numb. A sort of deadness was my emotional condition. If it didn't sound too pretentiously literary I'd say what I was suffering was *ennui, Weltschmerz,* terminal boredom. However hard I pushed I just couldn't seem to burst through to life. Why else had I been making love to my sister for the last seven years?

My mother was speaking but nothing much was registering. I watched a teenage girl unstrap herself and run down the aisle screaming in panic. Two cabin staff caught her and led her back. None too gently. One of them was herself shaking visibly.

How could my mother go on speaking calmly through this? She had gone back almost forty years and was talking about the satisfaction my father *might* have had raising me. Had it not been nullified by the disappointments of later years. By that she meant my long addiction to white powder and the two short spells I'd spent in the Franklin County House of Correction at Greenfield, Mass. But, to me, all that seemed a thousand years away. As we began another tour of San Francisco Harbour, my mind drifted, exhausted by fear of the next ten minutes. Where in the wide world had I started to fail him? When we lived on post in Heidelberg? In Seoul? Or when he'd served with NATO at Fontainebleau and my mother had sent me to a fierce, French lycée as punishment for failing to make my grades in French at the American School?

'Perhaps you were given too much as a child,' my mother was saying. 'Perhaps, after all, it was our fault that you turned out the way you are. We tried to maintain a balance between too much and too little. But it's not easy, of course.'

A balance . . . My mother's favourite form of punishment was a leather belt applied to the back of my bare legs. I could still remember the frightening hysteria of those sessions, her frequent and complete loss of control. But it was the injustice that hurt most or perhaps, more truthfully, hurt longest. I could never understand why I was being punished like this, especially while my sister was hardly more than reprimanded for the same offence. Against these sessions with my mother, punishment from my father seemed to have a rationale. It would take the form of occasional sallies of harsh discipline in which I'd be forced to run, carrying a log on my shoulders, round and round a gravel track behind the house while, on his stop-watch, my father checked that each circuit had been completed in the allotted number of minutes. Many times my knees had buckled onto the sharp gravel.

I'm not pretending it happened every week but when it did, it was a heart-bursting ritual. My mother would watch from the garden doors, her lips, handsomely bowed in those days, pursed with determination, urging my father to award an extra circuit. The blonde head of my sister Margot would glint from the curtain's edge of one of the upper windows. She, I knew, would be laughing.

Final preparations were being made in the aircraft. Shoes had been removed. Cabin crew were hurrying along the aisles with last minute instructions. Did I say I was more numbed than fearful? Then why are my hands shaking, my whole body shaking? But I'm not allowed to be afraid, not plain, simple terrified, for Christ's sake. I'm General Chapel's boy.

Flight attendants were working their way down the plane showing passengers the head down, crash position. I'm not sure, as a child, how much I had loved my father – perhaps it was proportionate to my fear of my mother. But whatever it was I felt for him, I wanted to separate it from her. So I said it. 'He didn't belong just to you, you know,' I said. 'There was something left for Margot and me. Maybe even, that part was more real.'

The lips struggled into a twist of contempt. 'For your sister there was real feeling, yes. But what do you really think he thought of you? He saw you as you are, Sonny. A failure, a self-pitying addict. A wasted life.' She was not afraid of death, since her stroke she had made that clear, but she couldn't let go of life without a final outpouring of spite.

'A wasted life doesn't just happen, for Christ's sake,' I said. I'd never said it before. Thought it often about my life, though. 'A wasted life gets *caused*!'

Spittle shone at the corner of her mouth. She dabbed an embroidered handkerchief to her lips. 'You're accusing *me*?'

'You bet,' I said. 'You have to take some responsibility for what happened to me. Nature *and* nurture. Every half-way decent element in me came from Dad. Everything else came from you and the way you raised me. He just wasn't strong enough to stand up to your bile.'

'My God . . .' she said. Her eyes glittered. 'You ungrateful wretch.'

The madness of it was exciting me, exhilarating me almost. Here I was bawling out my mother as the plane sliced down with

4

every chance of becoming a ball of smoke and flame on the runway.

'If I look back,' I was shouting over the engine noise, the passenger screams, the flight attendants' pleas for calm. The final words of mad Tom Chapel. 'If I look back there were a dozen times when I can see that he was apologising. Apologising for not being able to stand up for his son.'

She turned fully toward me now. I swear the thought of a crashing plane was far from uppermost in her mind. Her face, despite the stroke, had that icily composed quality that still scared me. 'And what would you say if I told you . . .' she said, spitting saliva, '. . . if I told you he wasn't your father at all?'

I stared at her. 'You don't mean that.'

But she did. I could see it in the fury on her face. She'd gone too far, as she always did in anger. Her mouth pressed closed.

The engines whined in my ears. The plane dipped sickeningly.

I suppose a few seconds elapsed. Maybe not. She had turned away as I shrieked out loud. A sound unnoticeable among the screams and sobs around me.

Don't ask me to tell you why I shrieked. I may have been laughing. At that moment, minutes from almost certain death, experience was so compacted, I was unable to identify any reaction. I simply shrieked. Was it relief? Some sort of demonic glee that my oh-so-proper mother, a true descendant of her seventeenth-century Massachusetts ancestor, Margaret Flee-from-Adultery Smith, yes that was the name she had adopted during the Salem Reverencing Week of 1636 . . . Was it uncontainable delight that my mother had actually committed the sin of sins? Jesus!

A flight attendant yelled to me to get my head down. Head on my knees awaiting my Maker, I made swift calculations. I was born in November, 1944. Sometime in early 1942 my mother, a newly married woman, was sent to London with military rank as a civilian medical adviser to a US aid organisation for European children. In early 1944 my father had arrived in the UK, an infantry colonel training for the landings in France. She and my father had managed a few weeks together at an apartment building in Chelsea called Whitelands House. I'd always delicately assumed these were the conceptual weeks. Despite her pregnancy, she had followed Allied troops across France and ministered to sick French children in the last months of 1944. Always one to put duty first, she had left it too late to get back to London before I made an appearance on stage. I was born in a US Field Hospital in an obscure village in north-east France.

That's the story. But was she now telling me that she had been impregnated by someone else during one of those wild, pre-invasion, martini nights in London? Or became pregnant even, as an unlooked-for result of a knee-trembler in the fog by Westminster Bridge as the Luftwaffe growled overhead? Surely not the direct descendant of Margaret Flee-from-Adultery Smith!

I was thinking these thoughts when suddenly, there was a heavy and terrifying creaking thud beneath me. My mouth opened in horror. The noise from the other passengers was indescribable. I lifted my head. We were still in the air, the wings rolling, flying south into the inlet, about two hundred feet above the water. Fisherman's Wharf was on our starboard . . . Telegraph Hill . . . the Transamerica Pyramid . . . but we were going down.

Now the terror was real – and final. The passengers' screams had faded. From all around me came a soft whimpering. I closed my eyes.

The co-pilot was speaking. An accent from somewhere south of the Mason-Dixon line. 'Ladies and gentlemen . . .' His voice sounded truly strange. High pitched, almost choking: 'I'm here to tell you that the great clunk you just heard was our . . . son-of-a-bitch undercarriage finally dropping into place.' And with a long exhalation of breath, 'God be praised!'

All around me people were crying, tears of relief streaming down their cheeks. I looked at my mother. Eyes, mouth and fists were tight closed in fury.

We came off the plane to a ring of yellow and red emergency service vehicles, bubble lights still flashing. Drivers leaned out of their cabs. Paramedics stood beside their ambulances. Two big unmarked trucks painted an inconspicuous dark green had give-away refrigeration vents on the roof of the cab: mobile morgues. The guys in emergency gear were clapping and whistling. We felt as if we, the passengers, had personally done wonders to achieve our own deliverance. We waved back. We felt great.

Everybody except my mother. She walked stiffly, leaning heavily on her stick, towards the line of blue airport buses that were already piling in behind the fire trucks. Three or four TV vans, nose to tail, came racing along the runway, sliding to a halt at the edge of a sea of emergency landing foam. A young woman in a dark business suit got out of the leading van, adjusting her hair with a mirror held in her free hand. Men with equipment tumbled out the back. Stepping carefully on three-inch heels round the edge of the foam, chance brought the reporter to my mother as the first interviewee. A microphone was exchanged for the reporter's mirror. She gave a quick nod to the cameraman. I missed her question but I heard my mother's answer: 'I have absolutely no comment to make on what happened. And I never will have.' She swiped at the microphone and knocked it from the young woman's hand.

I was ecstatic. I ran forward to help my mother onto the bus. Among the gasps of relief as our fellow passengers tumbled in around us, I pressed her to tell me who it was, who had fathered me. I kept my eyes narrowed with concern. Maybe even the tearful glint of something more. I wanted to communicate to her that I suffered, I felt her shame. The best moment of my life or what?

Her face blanched with fury. 'I should never have spoken,' she said. 'Be sure of this. I have uttered my very last words on the subject. May your father, looking down on us today, forgive me my stupidity.'

Which father was that?

# 2

## 1985, St Juste, South of France.

MARTY PEARSON DROVE his hire car through the sharp cut in the limestone ridge that carried the road forward, south to the village of St Juste. With all windows rolled down the intense, dusty-sweet scents of Provence were beginning to turn his head. Turn his head again, as they had forty years ago.

He stopped the car at the next crossroad. He was sure he remembered it. He ran his hand back and forth across his cropped grey, grizzled hair. Surely there used to be a sign here, *St Juste 0.5 km*. But, for some reason, no longer. He got out of the car and walked the few paces to the top of the ridge. From here, he would be able to look down on the village, cupped in the valley, the ancient church with its later steeple, the village square, the yellow ochre, pale-tiled houses straggling either side of it. Would there be new buildings scattered through the valley, the modern holiday villas of the English, Dutch and Germans?

The road flattened out. Back then it had been surfaced with pounded rock. Today it had a thin skin of asphalt. So . . . he shrugged. If a strip of blacktop was the limit of the late twentieth century's incursion on the parish of St Juste, so what?

He reached the high point in the road and looked down. In the heat his head was swimming. His gasp of surprise was audible, a groan almost. Below him, there was no village to be seen. No valley to be seen. Instead, a fat finger of sparkling water reached right out to the next ridge, a lake, a reservoir four or five kilometres long. He felt his legs tremble, his eyes mist over. So much, that at first he failed to see the church steeple rising ten, fifteen feet above the blue-green waters and the waving outline of rooftops somewhere below the surface. *Lac St Juste*, said a sign just below him, the sign he had been looking for, *constructed with contributions by the European Community.*

An anger seized him. For a moment he stood there fighting it, recovering control of his breathing, restoring himself to some sort of sanity. Much of what he'd hoped to learn from his visit to Provence was going to be drowned below the waters of that lake. The families of the village of St Juste were no doubt scattered, the secrets of forty years ago irrecoverable.

His eye followed the shoreline. The château was still there, a few dozen feet above the lapping waters. A monstrous stone pile, empty now in all probability, abandoned by everyone and everything but the pigeons in the turrets and the rats in the cellars. Marty Pearson had travelled a long road to bring him to this point. Over the years of searching and tracing, the long hours spent in libraries smelling of floor polish and record rooms across the world, he had never really faced the question why. Or rather what. What would he do if his researches put together the past in something like the shape he was beginning to expect it to form? What if he were *right*? But in this moment of bitterness and rage that fate, and the need for ever more water for the tourist industry along the coast, had almost certainly deprived him of the chance to find the answers he sought, he realised all too clearly what his object was. Someone must suffer. In all probability, someone must die. The sins of the past, the greed and gain must be faced and atoned for. If the pieces of his past fell as he believed they would, he could no longer disguise why he had finally come back here. Research, yes. Confirmation, yes. But, in the last resort, he had come back to St Juste for vengeance.

The harsh limestone hills reeked dust and sunlight. Marcel Coultard couldn't really be sure but it might have been twenty years, even more, since he was last up here in this concertina of low rock ridges and shallow canyons. He knew he must be careful. Bones broke easily enough at his age. To think at one time he used to negotiate these broken trails by moonlight, a file of women behind him, burdened by heavy suitcases and rolls of bedding.

An old man now, in a linen suit and a straw hat with club-striped band around the crown, he sat alone in the deep shade of a jutting rock, waving the insects away with a yellow bandanna, using his atrophied left arm despite the dull ache it brought. He smiled at his own vanity. He'd always been concerned that his many ladies never quite realised the extent of his mild deformity. But within seconds his mind swung back to the much more important point that he had come up here to be alone and to think about.

9

'It's the right thing,' he said out loud. 'It was the right thing to do.' Then he paused, flicking with his yellow bandanna, yet again wondering.

He had made many hard decisions in his life. Illegal frequently, immoral often enough. And they had passed into silence, forgotten or undiscovered. But on this last great decision, he had done what he knew was right. It would stir a hornet's nest of opposition. Opposition from friends, from neighbours and hardest of all, his close family. His son Sébastien, especially. He didn't look forward to telling him. Or, alternatively, he could tell nobody. And when the bombshell exploded he would, of course, be dead.

On the other hand, if he had made his will to his two children, Claire and Sébastien, nobody would oppose. Nobody would say that it was anything but right. The past was well buried in this corner of France. Buried by common consent. And for forty years Marcel had lived as though it were buried with his consent, too. But that had never been entirely true. In all those years he had justified his wealth and success by the promise to himself that he would put it all right in the end. That he would do this.

He had not come up here to decide. That decision was taken and confirmed with papers already signed in the local *notaire*'s office, although it was true that he hadn't really spent a good night since. The thought of telling his daughter, Claire, of telling Sébastien, his son, made his stomach turn. But it had to be done. He had no right to delay.

He had come up here because he had decided to take the step today. He had come up here, climbing too hard and too high for an old man, because this spot, in these hills, was the place where he had made the original promise to himself, the promise to make amends for wrongs he had done, for evil he had profited from.

Perhaps memory was playing tricks now but it seemed to him that on those freezing winter nights in 1942 this was the same jutting rock he had always stopped at to looked back and count the women struggling in line along the frosted path behind him. Anonymous shapes, bundled against the cold, recognisable as women only by their gasps or cries as they slipped and scrambled between the rocks. He would raise his arm to decree a halt and would point down to the Château St Juste, the vast sprawling ruin poised above the village where they would rest and spend the next day. The bundled women would gather round him, tears freezing on the scarves wrapped round their mouths. And they would shake his hand or try to throw their arms round him and kiss him.

For him, a sense of triumph. He had avoided the French Special Police. He had succeeded in another 'transfer': the frightening and draining task of bringing five or six Jewish women eighty kilometres on foot over four long nights, from Brignac in the mountains to St Juste, a staging post on their escape route to Spain or Italy.

But that was over forty years ago. And with the triumph there had also been disaster.

Marcel Coultard got to his feet and stepped out from the shade of the rock into the jutting sunlight. Crickets and *cigales* trilled and stopped as a golden oriole hunted from branch to branch. In the silence his old man's voice spoke again. He wanted to shout it to the pine tops but the words came out coated with a thick wheezing, as little more than a whisper. 'The right thing, Marcel! You've always known it was.'

The right thing. But, of course, he would have to live with it.

With a final flick of his bandanna he gestured goodbye to his past and began the dangerous descent. White dust coated his pale blue espadrilles and his brown, bare instep. The path here was no more than a track made by wild boar and running water, following the natural slopes of the land down to the Lac St Juste. He lifted a hand to shade his eyes.

Below him, on the edge of the lake, stood his home, a timeless pile of stones with square towers and battlements standing more or less as they'd stood for close to nine hundred years. True one turret, the Saracen Tower, and large parts of the enclosing wall had been brought down by canon-fire centuries before. But when exactly, and in what conflict, he never really knew. His daughter, Claire, was the family historian.

He shifted his eyes to the blue-green, almost incandescent surface of the lake. It was about five kilometres long and less than a kilometre wide, its far end sealed by a low, grey concrete dam. A sailboat made slow headway in the heavy air. Three or four fishermen crouched over their rods in flat-bottomed punts. Around the shoreline, distant speckles of colour, just discernible to his fading eyesight: a family spreading a picnic lunch; children in bright swimming costumes running for the water.

There had been no lake for most of the château's life. Instead, a long shallow valley had run down from its walls. The village it had once cradled, St Juste, had been drowned by a departmental decision, in 1973, to build what they called a feeder lake for some much larger reservoir to the east. Now only the tip of the church spire was left.

And the château. Positioned as it was above the level of the waters, the Château St Juste was now a fortress without a village to defend, but perfectly placed by God and man in Gothic splendour on the edge of the new lake.

Marcel Coultard loved the place, had loved it since he was a boy when he'd first entered the great cool kitchen as a village lad hired to carry out the barrels of scraps for pig food. Loved it long before he'd ever dreamt of owning it.

He took a few more steps down. The path twisted here between two walls of rock and he knew he must be careful. At seventy-nine he had a finite number of months or years to go. He accepted that, prepared himself for it. But why hasten God's plans?

He moved on, concentrating on the path before him. But it was a rougher terrain than he remembered. The path, from now on down to the château was no more than a narrow gully of dust and pebbles. He should have brought a stick. Pride, he said to himself, comes before a fall.

It was steep here. He remembered the difficulty he'd had getting past this point. Marcel placed one pale blue espadrille on a rock, testing it for support. Carefully he let it take his weight as he stepped down with the other foot. When the rock gave, he rolled, neatly compact, from hip to shoulder like a trained parachutist landing. He lay on his back, breathing hard. He'd lost his hat and one espadrille, but nothing *felt* broken. He moved each leg and flexed his feet from the ankle. He did the same with his arms and hands. Pain free. An old man's luck.

The scents of rosemary and wild lavender had an almost physical presence. He took deep breaths before he felt ready to haul himself up. He was, he acknowledged, greatly overweight. He was gathering the resolution for what he knew would be an immense effort, when a stone thudded down beside him, rolled off the path and stopped in his eye line. A small boulder several kilos in weight, fallen from the ledge above him. He turned his head and tried to squint up but it was into the sun.

Marcel Coultard's life had been conspicuously lucky. He had slept with beautiful women, he had drunk fine wines, he had enjoyed good friendships and he had been blessed with a wonderful wife. More than that, he might have been beaten or tortured or indeed killed on a dozen occasions during the war. But he had survived and prospered. Luck was something he took for granted, but this was a close call. No doubt about it. Weeks of drought had cracked and shrivelled the earth, loosening the old bindings of root and grasses. A stone could fall anytime.

He smiled to himself. With my luck, he thought, I could easily live to be a hundred. Still lying on his back, he turned his eyes upwards as he heard a rustle among the rocks above him. He missed the flight of the second stone but it was bigger, a rough-shaped piece that landed rock on rock and rang as it bounced away downhill.

He saw the third as a falling shadow. And felt the first dead pain as it thundered on his chest. He had lived long enough in these hills to know that a natural fall of rock brought showers of earth and small stones with it. He knew what it meant when the earth and stones were absent. There was a man up there.

A shadow fell across the sun. He made to duck another rock when he saw the dark outline. The man, ten metres above him on the edge of the limestone cliff stood, legs braced apart, holding out a piece of rock half a metre across. In panic now, shouting to him not to do it, Marcel tried to push himself up. A rock struck him between the shoulder blades, deadening his arms. He slipped, grasped a handful of grass and slithered to a stop, looking up. His head fell back. It rested comfortably in the soft grasses by the track as the last rock fell.

This time, heavier and more carefully aimed, it dropped towards his eyes. He saw it as an ever-growing shadow, black against the sky.

The man who found him told the police his skull was crushed like a gull's egg.

# 3

BOSTON, MASSACHUSETTS. MY mother's driver was there to meet us when, eight hours later but only seven P.M. Eastern Standard Time, we made it to Boston's Logan Airport.

I've landed a hundred times at Logan but that day the landing approach low across the sea had my whole body shaking, discreetly enough, but shaking all the same, a muted orgasmic quiver. Not too surprising, I suppose, having just survived an air emergency. But then why didn't it affect my mother the same way? Anger is my guess. We had flown the three thousand miles from San Francisco in as close an approximation to silence as two consenting adults can get. Three or four times I had pressed her to tell me more but she hit me with a look of such pure venom that I finally gave up and dozed and drifted through some of the weirdest dreams I'd ever had. Don't worry. No details. Other people's dreams are as fascinating as a dripping tap.

You want to hear more about me? It wouldn't surprise me if you didn't. But this could be your only chance. Thomas Bannerman Chapel, newly revealed as the bastard son of an unknown father, five eleven and pseudo-athletic of build. Tennis, you'd say, is his game, or squash. To look at me, I mean. In fact, I haven't played either for years. A good, unthreatening appearance: short, dark hair running to curly, blue eyes and good teeth but no natural, glad-to-meet-you smile. Reserved with men, nervous of those slow, thoughtful French philosophy students or Oxford dons or clever New York Jews. With women I'm more at ease. Flirty, even. A conventional dresser, pretty surface-conventional altogether as a matter of fact. But underneath, as you already know, the sort of smudge who'd sleep with his sister – a dark side to his character is what I'm confessing to. It's a side I've certainly tried to run away from, but always so far with weighted legs like little boys in dreams.

Did I say I was a writer? Perhaps not. I seldom push it forward. I write small, slice-of-life literary volumes. Life among the east coast American rich. Sub-Fitzgerald for the 1980s. Sub-Tom Wolfe, come to that. My books seldom earn out their advance, but my allowance from my mother handles any short-fall in my accounts. Truth to tell, my mother's allowance also shapes my literary efforts. She makes sure of that. Through *my* keyhole on Boston life, I am allowed to see no violence, no angst, no aberrant sex, no sex at all much beyond a little polite adultery. I write about the world as my mother sees it, self-centred, self-censored as it is. Which is okay, because my small Boston Common publisher, my mother's cousin, Alice Marchant, doesn't believe in the existence of the Boston of George V. Higgins either.

Beyond pretending to be a writer, women are the most impor-tant feature of my life. My sister heads the list. Margot is one of those free spirits you hear about. Or perhaps she just spends a great deal of her life making people think of her as a free spirit. Whatever, she does it wonderfully well.

I know now, of course—, learnt it a few hours back in that plane over San Francisco Bay—, that Margot isn't my full sister. If I'm not my father's son, Margot is no more than my half-sister. I suppose that should make me feel less screwed up about things but, strangely enough, I'm not sure I'm so happy about that aspect of my mother's revelation. It seems to loose one of the bonds that binds Margot and me together.

What I'm saying, I suppose, is that I don't think a woman like Margot would have an affair with someone like me if there weren't an extra incestuous jolt in it for her somewhere. There's a thought.

How did it all come about, Margot and me? I'll make it quick. We grew up as senior officers' children do, in cold corners of northern Europe, in Korea, the Philippines and at half a dozen army posts up and down the United States. Most of our lives, there were servants around of one sort or another. Devoted, mostly plump women of darker skin colour who aroused more affection in Margot and myself than our mother ever had.

Margot is younger by just over two years but by the time she was eight or nine her leadership of our duo was pretty firmly fixed. She was blonde and pretty, like our mother, and shaping to be tall and slim. Her commanding role was based quite simply on her willingness to tackle our father – General John Chapel, US Army. What would earn me ten circuits with the log on my shoulders, earned Margot an indulgent smile. General John (her name for him) really liked her impudence. 'Your sister's got spunk, Sonny,' he'd say. 'She knows that in this world you don't git if you don't try. Isn't that right?'

'That's right, sir,' I'd say. But I knew exactly what I'd *git* if the trying came from me. He thought she was cute and sassy. And he thought his son was in danger of becoming a wimp. In his way I think he loved me. But he felt it was his duty to me to ride my ass over every trivial item. Not surprisingly I grew up nervous of his huge, uniformed presence.

If I grew up a wimp, it was in part of his making. I was scared of facing him, scared of that hatchet face and glare that he had developed over the years as a commanding officer. Around about the age of seven I developed the habit of blinking when he questioned me and this particularly infuriated him. In the beginning, the log-run was devised as a cure for the blinking. There's parental psychology for you. But General John was not a brute. He was misguided. He was pushed further than his genuine good nature really wanted by the ice-hard principles of my mother, and he realised, I'm sure, that frightening an already frightened small boy was not going to take me far along the road of sturdy independence that he aimed at for me.

What effect these parental pressures had on Margot and me, I'm not at all sure. Throughout childhood and even late into adolescence as far as I'm aware, Margot and myself had been a pretty normal brother and sister. Okay, she ruled the roost but that isn't at all exceptional. She just had that sort of brick wall personality. If she said no to something, you accepted it. At least I did. And most of her friends did.

But as children we played together. We exchanged smutty jokes together. We grew out of childhood together and took the road to adolescence together. We talked a lot about sex, as most young people do. We exchanged information, boy to girl, girl to boy. Quite a lot about masturbation, I remember, how boys did it, how girls did it. What it felt like.

Did I actually believe she'd slept with someone at this time, around sixteen, seventeen? I don't know. In that clever way she had, she claimed to have done it and claimed not to have. She kept this up for over a year. She was like that, Margot. She could make me look a fool for even asking the question, on the assumption that of course she'd had sex – or equally on the reverse assumption that it was an insult to ask her. Maybe you don't remember how much we all talk round the whole issue at that age. Likely as not pretending to what hadn't yet happened, denying what had.

But for me it was all natural, normal stuff. Talk, talk, talk . . . You have a sister so you get an inside track into how girls think about sex. Until the night of the Souza party on Martha's Vineyard, I don't think I'd ever thought of Margot as anything but a sister.

Senhor Emilio Souza, the Brazilian *chargé d'affaires* in Washington at the time, was the father of two good-looking sons and a sumptuously pretty daughter. For that summer, he'd rented for Senhora Souza and the children a fine house in its own compound with servants, secretaries and a handsome native-American driver-bodyguard from the tribal lands up at Gay Head.

Senhor Emilio himself, overweight but I guess handsome enough, was seldom to be seen at the house and the impeccably beautiful madam, cool and distant with her own children as much as with us, had her own adult preoccupations, dinner parties and the like, leaving the field clear for the Souza kids and their newly acquired friends. This was the sixties when experiment with drink and drugs and sex was in the air. Beach parties, where parents could be relied on not to interfere with the proceedings, were a great attraction to the American summer young.

I had lost a year of my life to the desire of the draft board to submit me to several rigorous psychological examinations (which had ended in my rejection by the Army), so I was comfortably into my twenties when I returned from England having just completed my first year at King's College, Cambridge. Margot was planning the next stage of her life and we were really back together again after the first big separation of our lives. So we'd sat around in the dunes and drunk punch and smoked dope and talked as the ocean rolled in towards us.

Further down the beach the music, the sudden flare of steaks on a barbecue, the shadowy figures of girls dancing in bikinis, provided a rich background to the senses. I was giving Margot a detailed rundown of my feelings for Elaine, the English girl I'd

17

met at Cambridge. But I could see she was less than intrigued. Even at the distance of twenty years, I remember how often she looked at her watch until, irritated, I began pressing her about who her date was . . . what time had she fixed to meet him. Was it one of the Souza boys? The elder, Martin, had a big reputation with the girls, I warned her unnecessarily.

I stayed on it too long. Until she jumped up, flicking her cigarette ash over my bare chest. While I yelped and brushed at the embers, she was off running down the beach, barefoot, her red Hawaiian skirt fluttering in the breeze. In seconds she had disappeared into the darkness.

I got to my feet. The dancing was behind me. To the new Beatles song, *A Hard Day's Night*. I was still thinking of the girl in Cambridge. I took a pack of cigarettes from my jeans pocket, tapped one out, lit it and strolled toward the deserted end of the beach.

I wasn't consciously following Margot. Perhaps I walked for a few minutes, trailing my bare feet in the soft white sand. I'd finished the cigarette and was thinking of turning back when I heard her voice. Just talking, it floated from somewhere among the dunes. But the tone was special. She'd linked up with her date. That, at least I could tell from the tone. None of that icy acidity she could spill over you as easily as cigarette embers. No. Something soft, laughing occasionally. A word of what sounded like Spanish but I guess was Portuguese. She was in the sand there with one of the Souza brothers.

It seemed natural to drop down on my knees, to start edging my way forward. If I had a plan, it was to rise out of the dune grass, arms waving and throw a big scare into them. It was the sort of thing Margot would have done to me. I know it was.

I crawled forward. I was wearing cut-offs. Dune grass scratched at my bare knees. There was no light from the beach party here but a moon had slid silently from behind the strings of pale summer cloud lacing the night sky.

Margot's voice was muffled now and the gasps and theatrical groanings indicated a fairly advanced stage of adolescent petting had been reached. I wondered which of the Souza boys she'd chosen. Jamie was young, younger than Margot, but darkly handsome. Martin the elder was too sure of himself but good-looking enough not to have to dip for dates. My money was on Martin.

I was very close now. On my belly I slid up a low mound of sand and stopped. Grasses waved in my face. Ahead of me was a hollow, ten feet by ten, like a great king-sized bed. No sound but the rustling of grass and bodies squirming in the sand. I reached forward and parted the clump of coarse dune grass. What I saw jolted an electric shock through me.

I was twenty years old, sexually barely experienced. Like most young men in the mid-sixties, I had never seen a man and woman making love. Certainly never seen what I was watching now. Never dreamed it possible of my sister. Even less so of the elegant and haughty Senhora Letitia Souza.

They lay on their sides, clothes scattered around them. Margot naked but for her red skirt peeled back to expose her to the older woman – Madam Souza propped on one hand, her bare breasts falling across Margot's mouth. I watched, completely transfixed, as the Brazilian woman's hand, those be-ringed fingers, moved up and down Margot's body, *into* Margot's body. I watched the expression on her face as she bent to kiss my sister, mouth open, tongue moving over her lips and teeth.

But it was the image of Margot that transfixed and dominated me, on her back, her legs thrashing wildly as those glittering fingers worked her. I don't know how long it was before I reeled back down the beach. All thoughts of the girl in England had been wiped clean from my imagination. What had replaced them, I wasn't entirely sure. Constantly leaping into my mind was picture after picture of Margot, twisting, flailing, hissing with pleasure. I'd seen her fooling with boys at parties before and her nonchalant arrogance had done nothing to me. Perhaps, tonight, it was the sheer commitment of her lust. It moved me sideways. Sideways to where exactly, I didn't know. But I knew I would never look at Margot in the same way again.

I got drunk that night and slept on the beach. I dragged myself back to our house and stood on the porch steps fiddling for my keys. Every time I thought of what I had seen on the beach, it set a whole bunch of nerves jangling in my head. I felt . . . infinitely disturbed.

General John greeted my overnight absence with back-slapping congratulation and a wink of comradely understanding. Margot, tan and fresh in a white polo shirt and a gingham skirt, was just about to leave for a couple of weeks stay with some friends in

Kentucky. I scuttled upstairs, hoping to avoid seeing her alone. But she came to my room to say goodbye.

I was just out of the shower, wearing only a pair of jeans. I grabbed up a tee-shirt as if I needed to cover myself in her presence.

She came in and sat on my work table, legs dangling. She had that cat's smile, the lips turned up at the edges. 'Enjoy the party?' she asked me.

'Sure,' I said.

'Get laid?'

'Too drunk. You?' I made it sixties-casual. But I was terrified of her answer.

'Why d'you ask? You think I'm too young? You want to go out and beat the brains out of the guy.'

I shrugged into my tee-shirt. 'Buy him a beer, maybe.'

'Cool,' she said. 'Except you already know there's no guy involved.'

I looked round in panic for my cigarettes but she got there first, tossing the pack to me. 'How long d'you stay? Watching?'

'Watching?' I frowned and tore open the pack of cigarettes.

'Peepo-ing.' She projected it like Lucille Ball.

I could feel the fire in my cheeks. 'What d'you think I am?' I said. 'I heard you with some guy. I beat it. End of story.'

She slipped off the table. 'Ten minutes,' she said. 'I'd say you had your beady little eyes on us for the best part of ten minutes.' She stopped, her hand on the door. 'You crept up thinking I was fooling with Martin or Jamie, uh? Well, I tell you. It's a big, big world out there, brother Tom. I've just discovered it's not just us kids. The grown-ups like to play too. They're all hot for it.'

'Senhora Souza . . .' I croaked out her name.

She smiled. 'For openers. Senhor Emilio rang me this morning.'

'Christ! He knows?' I said, dry-mouthed with horror. 'Somebody told him?'

'*She* did. Who else? I told you, there's a big world out there to play in. I don't understand it yet, Tom. But I'm going to, damn right I am.'

'Listen, you could be in real trouble.'

'I don't think so. Emilio invited me to lunch when I get back from Kentucky. A deux.'

'You going?'

'What do you think?'

I nodded, puffing my cheeks. She crossed to the door, opened it and pointed a pink varnished nail at me. 'Ten minutes, Tom. What were you thinking about all that time? That's what I want to know.' And she slid through the narrow opening of the door and closed it quietly behind her.

That autumn I went back to England to continue my studies at Cambridge. Margot and I spoke on the phone a lot, of course, mostly about our love lives – Margot with the son of the current French or Italian ambassador, and sometimes with the ambassador himself. I was still seeing Elaine, a very bright, very English, Natural Sciences scholar from Girton College, the great blue-stocking institution of Cambridge, more or less equivalent of Radcliffe.

Elaine and I stayed together for nearly two years but strains were showing as I came to the end of my time in England. I enjoyed being with her and the sex and everything but she really was too serious-minded for me. It didn't occur to me that it followed that I was too fundamentally un-serious for *her*. And at our last May Ball, walking at dawn on the banks of the River Cam with King's College Chapel rising like a cathedral to our right and stone bridges and lawns speckled with exhausted graduates-to-be, the men in white tie and tails, the girls in ball gowns, Elaine delivered her own verbal Dear John.

She did it nicely enough and, before we went for a final punt down river to Grantchester, I told her I saw her point. 'Hm,' she huffed, 'most girls would have hoped for at least a token fightback. On May Ball night too.'

'Does that mean you want to . . . I mean before we split up?'

She laughed. 'Why not? The sex has always been great. But I despair, Tom. You're sod-all good for anything else.'

I tied up the punt under an overhanging willow. We were, neither of us, dressed for this. I ripped off my white tie and boiled shirt. Elaine unzipped her ball gown and let it float down her body. A passing boatload of undergraduates and their girls cheered lustily.

A half hour of a final, fine, careless rapture marked our parting. Only later would I discover how careless it was.

I returned to Boston before Margot was through with Sarah Lawrence and her ambassadors and settled down to an existence based pretty firmly on nightly, and soon daily, use of the white powder. I had no plans, no particular inclinations and relations with my family were abysmal. I'm sure nobody was surprised when I was awarded my first short spell at the Franklin County House of Correction.

It was there I met a man who was going to have an important background influence on my life. Walter Strummer was a financial con man. A fraudster with a mind so quick he could spot a fraudulent possibility in a nunnery. His problem was that he *looked* like a fraudster. Amiable and good company, he was nevertheless big, mean-eyed and dark jowled. No, you certainly wouldn't buy a used car from a man like Walter. And he knew it. He got someone else to do the marketing.

So what he saw in the smooth-cheeked preppie he was sharing a cell with was a front. A perfect front man, what's called 'painfully honest' (to look at). In the years after Franklin County I worked sporadically for Walt, attending meetings with the rest of his team, never knowing the whole story, but well coached in when to put in a disapproving word or a nod of approbation. You understand this was not great money I was getting. But what Walt Strummer paid was enough to rent my (pretty seedy) apartment just down from Quincy Market, and, more important, was enough to keep my mother off my back. I was, she told her family, a financial services adviser.

Margot was back from Sarah Lawrence by then and highly diverted by stories of my colourful employment with Walt Strummer. Her men friends, all rich, mostly older, tumbled across her bed at a truly impressive rate. Their habits, demands, preferences, she would recount to me. When we'd had a bottle or two of champagne between us she would get what I thought of as flirty, throwing her legs around, coming into my room in her underwear. Brother and sister stuff if you're twelve maybe – but with a strange, exciting sense of something more if you're approaching thirty.

For a few years after General John died I even moved to New York to be closer to Margot. During that time, she gave me innumerable messages in word and gesture that any man would have said were impossible to misinterpret. But they were always delivered with one of her enigmatic cat-like smiles. Even sometimes with an erotic flicker of a long pink tongue. I suppose we might have come together any of those New York nights. I think we didn't because I was scared of her. Terrified of her ridicule if I had got things totally wrong, if I was misinterpreting what she meant as no more than a high camp joke.

I envied the glitz of her lifestyle. From time to time I earned pretty good money (and one mercifully short jail sentence) from Walt Strummer's scams, but my lifestyle never even began to compare with hers. Magazines showed her relaxing on yachts in the Mediterranean, skiing in Switzerland or flying in for aristocratic country house parties in England. Her income came in 'presents'. She never tried to deny that. Margot was one of those women at the beginning of the Reagan years, constantly photographed and gossiped about, an open, unapologetic courtesan.

I was held in thrall by her. Every girlfriend I ever had during my time in New York City told me that. It's what broke every relationship I thought might go somewhere. And it's why Elaine, Cambridge Elaine, when she came back into my life in New York City years after Grantchester, was totally and sweepingly different.

Different, first and foremost because she had a child, *my child*, a cute seven-year-old little blonde girl named Romilly, conceived, it appears, in our farewell coupling in a punt on the Cam that last May Ball dawn.

But Elaine was different in other ways too. Physically very different from Margot, not as tall or as slender, brunette rather than blonde, well-dressed rather than stylish, competent rather than commanding. Yet as attractive, even more attractive than I'd remembered her. Too sexy to be called homely, but veering that way with her girl-next-door smile.

She was an administrator. And because her own sense of self was constructed on a variety of jobs ranging from children's charities to five years' service as an administrator at the BBC, she was confident enough to genuinely like Margot. Thought she was fun. Liked her sense of style and her parties and her mad stories of the roustabout playboys she serviced (Elaine's word). The difference between Elaine and every other woman I'd ever met was that she wasn't one iota scared of my sister.

Elaine was in the US to attend interviews at a number of big TV outfits in New York and New England. She calculated the whole process of getting the job she wanted might well take seven or eight weeks what with re-calls and green card problems. I kept in touch throughout all this and at the end of that first month

Elaine and I began to go places, in a mild, slightly awkward way, not sure whether we were dating or not. We had, after all, a child together in common, a child I was just getting to know and like. Perhaps I should have been angry that Elaine had never told me about Romilly but I couldn't feel angry about missing a relationship I never even knew existed. Or losing a chance for fatherly love that I couldn't imagine. Some men would have felt bad about it. Maybe I should have. But I didn't.

What was positive was that every time I spent a day with them at the house of the friends she was staying with on Long Island, I seemed to get on better and better with Romilly. I'd take her out for long walks along the beach and we'd hunt for clues to the treasure that the English pirates had buried in the days when they had made Long Island Sound their own. We never found treasure, but we once did find the curved butt and part of the firing mechanism of an early pistol and the excitement we both felt was the beginning of a serious bond. Elaine, I saw, got real pleasure out of seeing Romilly and me together.

What maybe wasn't so positive was that I was beginning to hold back on information Margot was constantly pressing me to reveal. Had I slept with Elaine? Not since Cambridge (the truth). Had I even kissed her? Well, no. Not really. In fact, Elaine and I had kissed as we left the Bosun's Bar on Bleecker Street two days earlier. It had been a warm kiss, no tongues down throats. But no lack of feeling either. Margot had smirked knowingly at my denial.

That weekend we went, Elaine, Romilly, and myself, sailing with Elaine's friends at Oyster Bay. Sunday night, looking out over the Sound, shoulder to shoulder leaning on the rail, Elaine told me flat: Margot was all style and no substance. Great to spend an evening with, but that was it. Fun, yes – but a bad, bad influence on a growing boy. Time I woke up to the fact.

Nobody had ever said that about my sister.

There was more. Next week, back in Manhattan, Elaine quite literally set it up. In a forthright but non-combative way she told Margot that unless she stopped hanging weights round her brother's neck, he'd never stand a chance of a real relationship with any woman. Asked Margot straight, was that what she wanted? I was standing there in the room. I thought there was going to be a godawful explosion. I looked at Margot, I looked at Elaine. Waiting.

Metaphorically, I put my fingers in my ears. I watched Margot's face. I was convinced she was about to hit the button. But Elaine was right. She didn't. Amazingly, Margot took it like a pussycat.

It was liberating. And when Elaine told me that she was taking an administrative post at WGBH and asked me to leave New York and marry her in Boston, I said yes.

# 4

ELAINE AND ROMILLY and I lived in Newton in a pale blue clapboard house on tree-lined Homer Street and had lunch at my mother's house in Boston alternate Sundays.

On second thoughts, maybe that's not a fair way of describing our life. When Elaine took time off from her work there were good times. We visited Louisiana and heard the Beale Street Blues played in New Orleans. One summer we drove up to Toronto and saw the falls and went on to stay a week in Montreal. But it was an organised life. Elaine had a talent for organisation. It was her job. Irregular work hours didn't faze her. Sleep, food and work were taken care of. Romilly was whisked off every morning to school. I, as a writer, was expected to write.

Except I wasn't in the least interested in what I was writing. Each year in the fall I would go into Boston and talk about a new book with my Aunt Alice Marchant at her office at Marchant Books. Her enthusiasm couldn't sustain me past the title and after that it was a lot of hours peering at the magnificent golden leaves dropping from the beech tree outside my window, or, come winter, the drifts of snow banked against the chestnut hedge.

I make no complaints about my family. Romilly was great to be with, a blonde-haired little girl with lots of sober, serious charm. I learned to become a fond father. I felt fond, although I suppose even the term *fond* implies a certain remoteness short of love. Love was a territory I couldn't quite enter, although what exactly held me back I don't know. Certainly not Romilly herself. I'd think a lot about General John at this time, a limited man for sure but totally lacking the authentic viciousness of my mother. I'd think about my mother too, and wondered if she really did fit the category of evil.

Elaine and I lived on good terms, friendly, civilised. But we had faded quickly to a point when there was very little physical in our relationship. I kissed her when she came home from work but we seldom drew warmth from having our arms about each other. I didn't really want to talk about it although both of us, I know, were uncomfortably aware of it. It didn't need Romilly to push Elaine towards me urging, 'Love Daddy,' to make us realise.

On another level, Elaine couldn't be faulted. She was a crisp achiever, prepared for me to drop the security of Marchant Books and write the book I wanted to write. Problem was, I don't think there *was* a book I wanted to write. That's what nobody understood. Nobody except Margot. By this time I had begun to call her again in New York, getting carried away, confiding more intimate details about life in Newton than I knew I should.

Romilly was coming up to eleven when I told Elaine I was planning to write a very different sort of book, hard-edged, New York based – and began to shuttle down to New York once a week to do my research.

I think at first I really planned a book. I even thought of drawing on my experience in the House of Correction for the opening chapter. How my mother would have loved that! But at some point in the next month or two my enthusiasm waned and whether or not it was what I'd planned from the beginning, my visits to New York turned into a simple opportunity to see Margot.

Her own situation had changed by then. She was married to a member of the New York State Senate, a rich and puffy fifty year old named George Layton. She gave the sort of parties my mother would have been proud of and lunched with other political wives while George was away legislating in Albany. No lovers as far as I knew. Talk (just talk) of adopting a Vietnamese child next year. Charity dinners, exhibitions, lectures. Not at all the woman she used to be.

I was soon asking her about it.

'Nobody gets a straight run through life, Tom,' she said with a lazy flick of her cigarette. 'What's important is to know when to change pace. When to change direction, duck, weave, zigzag a little even.'

'And that's now.'

'Listen darling,' she said. 'I'm *ageing*. I bear in mind that in Hugh Heffner's Chicago mansion, there's no such thing as a thirty-something playmate.'

'You're still looking great,' I told her.

She grunted. 'I need to do something Tommy, but it doesn't include leaving George.'

'For Christ's sake,' I said. 'The world's your oyster.' I'd grown up believing it. I meant it.

For a moment she looked at me, lips pursed, tongue in cheek. 'As long as you think so, Tommy darling.' She patted my ass as she walked over to freshen her drink.


The times I spent in Manhattan with Margot were easy, companionable, unpressured. She had told me long ago she thought I was a lousy writer. She would read my stuff and hurl herself backwards on the sofa, kicking her legs, whooping her undisguised contempt. If I tried to talk seriously to her about what I was to do next, she recommended a year in a seminary or the City Sanitation Department for a life of adventure. She very seldom mentioned Romilly or Elaine.

Every two or three weeks I would stay over. There was plenty of room in the five-bedroom apartment and as often as not Margot would be up and out before I woke up.

In Manhattan I slept late. I got up around noon. I had a few acquaintances in the city who would occasionally suffer me for lunch. But most of my friends were powering on towards becoming leading figures in advertising or on Wall Street. Walter Strummer approached me a few times and I would get dressed in my three-piece suit and borrowed briefcase and sit in on a couple of incomprehensible meetings. I was arrested after one of them and questioned by two FBI agents for six hours non-stop. But Walt was as good as his word and I was out of Police Plaza that evening, never (so far) to return. That fee, from Strummer's accountant, was particularly fat – 25,000 dollars. But dollars so earned don't add to a man's sense of his worth. I was a father, a husband, but I felt my presence as no more substantial than a light shadow in the lives of my wife and child. You're right. Self-pity was beginning to strangle me.

In later years I've thought that maybe Margot understood this. I wonder. I never had the chance to ask.


It was the day after Romilly's eleventh birthday party. Elaine had organised things as only she can. There were twenty-five kids, all ready for the Boston History Mime Company which had been hired. The table in the garden under the great leafless beech was piled with presents. Inside, there were make-up bars and dress-up bars and a good mystery present for each of the guests. My mother thought it was wonderful – and in most ways it was. I just felt I needed more to do. To be more in the centre of things. Romilly looked stunning and about fourteen. Elaine beamed with pride and even, briefly, hugged me as the mime company made their entrance in eighteenth century costume.

When it was over and my mother and Romilly and our Czech au pair were bagging up the thousand pieces of glittering wrapping I told Elaine I had to take the late shuttle down to New York. Held up by the need for some research. Necessary to do it before the weekend.

I remember she looked at me for a long time. Not smiling, not scowling. 'Okay, Tom,' she said. 'If you're sure you have to.'

Do women have a sixth sense?

I arrived early evening at La Guardia and took a twenty-dollar cab ride into the city. It was beginning to snow from a dark, clouded sky, the flakes whirling madcap against the buildings. With no time to settle the snow was blown like pale dust across the streets. In more settled parts, walkers, bundled in heavy coats, left long grey trails behind them on the sidewalk. It was Thursday. I knew George was in Albany. I wouldn't have come down if he'd been at home.

Margot was on her way out. But she kissed me hallo. Full on the mouth, paused briefly and slipped out her tongue to flick across my lips. Sort of sisterly. 'Get yourself a glass of wine and a sandwich and watch TV. I'll be back before midnight.' She stopped, checked herself in the hall mirror, cursed at something that displeased her and headed for her bedroom. I poured a glass from an opened bottle of Bordeaux and followed.

She stood before a mirror, enjoying me in reflection. 'You look really down,' she said as she brushed on another lipstick before one of six bedroom mirrors. 'Anyway I thought it was Romilly's birthday. What's a fond father doing in New York on a night like this?'

She was hitting me below the belt, of course. It was part of our unique relationship. She punched and I didn't duck.

I took a mouthful of the wine. A good château Bordeaux, 1982. Margot never drank anything less than the best. 'I needed to get away to the adult world,' I said. 'I've had enough of birthdays and plans to take a cabin in the Adirondacks and next year's visit to the maternal grandparents in Piddle Trenthyde, Dorsetshire. Sounds like something out of Agatha Christie, for Christ's sake.'

'It's also called family life,' Margot said with a last flexing of the lips to examine the results of her brushwork. Then she stepped back, pulled open her coat to reconfirm she was wearing just the right dress, ran a hand down below the waist, taking a crease out, rebuttoned and turned to pass me.

'Family life. How would you know?' I said.

'Naughty,' she said, grabbing up her purse. 'Was my oaf of a driver waiting outside?'

'There was a dark blue Jaguar. I didn't see a driver.'

'I'll have him emasculated on the block if he's gone off to get coffee when I need him.' She flashed past me. 'Listen for his screams.' She stopped at the front door, swinging back a shoulder in an elegant musical comedy gesture. 'You got a girl for tonight? A hump?'

I couldn't take my eyes off her. 'If I want one,' I said. I could feel my heart beating. She stood, hand on the door handle, hip jutting. 'And you do, don't you, Tommy?'

Suddenly I could see this wasn't adolescent jousting. With a hot rush I was reminded of the morning at Martha's Vineyard when she had faced me down over my Peeping Tom act on the beach.

'Don't you, Tommy?' she repeated.

I looked away. 'Maybe.'

'I won't be late,' she said. 'Midnight, not later. Wait up for me?'

During the evening I finished the Bordeaux and started on a bottle of Glenmorangie. I was feeling agitated, fretful, pushing thoughts from my mind. How many times, between gulps of Scotch, did that image of Margot on the beach with Senhora Souza come back to me . . . I tell you this because I'm not trying to claim innocence. I know I should have called a cab and grabbed my bag and made for La Guardia. I know that.

But I didn't.

Slumped on the sofa, I watched a ten-year-old re-run of *Mission Impossible*, a neat fake submarine trick. I dozed and woke and finally struggled to my feet. In the spare bedroom I stripped off my clothes and poured myself a drink and enjoyed that strangely sensuous feeling of wandering naked through someone else's apartment. Try it. I promise you, it could move a bishop.

The apartment had four bathrooms and I chose Margot's. I liked the outrageous, excessive tile-work, a recreation of an Egyptian temple. I liked the scent of oils and soaps and unguents from the most expensive stores in the world. Powders from Harrods, pastes from the Rue de Rivoli, creams from Milan or Rome. I liked being in Margot's bathroom.

I ran hot water into the big onyx bath and climbed in, balancing a half-full glass of Glenmorangie in one hand, mindful of General John's dictum: there's no bigger faux-pas for a house-guest than to shatter a Scotch tumbler in the tub.

I settled carefully in the perfumed water. I let my head fall back against the padded rest. I let those two female ivy-twined bodies on the beach run and re-run through my mind. I drank and placed the glass on the side table. I was asleep before I could reach for it again.

I woke up to find someone in the bathroom with me. Margot was standing in the middle of the Egyptian tiled room in her floor length robe. Silky, pale green, almost art deco in style. She had a glass of white wine in her hand.

'I didn't hear you come in. How long have you been back?'

'I came straight in to see you.' She gestured to the silk robe. 'More or less.'

'A good evening?' I asked.

She shrugged. 'As good as they get.'

It didn't sound like Margot. I could see life with George hadn't a lot to offer in the way of pizazz but I always guessed Margot had her own ways of making up for it. I said so.

'Monday,' she said. 'The Van Gogh exhibition at the Museum of Modern Art. Dinner with Mary Anne and her mother. Tuesday the gym, lunch with the book club, dinner alone. Wednesday – children's charity performance for African orphans. Lunch peanuts and mealy cake. Evening, a poor performance of *Otello* which even Katia Ricciarelli singing Desdemona failed to elevate. Return to apartment. Brother, probably drunk. Certainly asleep in the bath.'

'Hey, don't hand me responsibility for your life.'

'No. George shapes my life. Or rather I've decided to shape it round George.'

'You haven't done bad,' I said, rolling my eyes round the Egyptian fittings.

'Is that what you think?' Her voice was draining of vigour. '*I* think . . .' the vigour returned with her smile. 'I think it's time. . .' She lifted her bare foot and placed it on the bath-stool. A long tanned leg split the join of her robe. I could see right up to her pale blonde crotch. She knew it.

'Dammit . . .' she said, and took a thoughtful sip of her wine. 'I'm sure it is.'

The robe fell from her knee. She did nothing to twitch it back in place. I lay, staring. I knew what I wanted to do. Did I dare reach out and slide my hand up the inside of her leg? But so many times I'd been to this point, an invitation that was perhaps no invitation at all. Would I pull back once again, snivelling with fear of ridicule. Would I? My tongue was sticking to the roof of my mouth. I was transfixed by the smoothness of her knee extended towards me.

But I knew, once again, I wasn't going to move.

She was looking down at me, not smiling, grave-faced. 'Time, I've decided, for one of life's zigzags, Tommy. Existence with George is becoming just that. Flat, dull and unprofitable.'

'You're bored.'

'I'm bored,' she agreed.

'Take a lover,' I said, my mouth dry to cracking.

She put down her drink. 'That was my thinking too, Tommy,' she said, slipping off the robe and stepping into the bath with me.

# 5

I TOOK THE shuttle back in the early afternoon. La Guardia was already crowded with Friday commuters. I bought *The New Yorker,* knowing as I paid for it that I would never get past the first couple of paragraphs.

It was as if I'd swallowed a handful of amphetamine. I needed something to slow me down. I had not stopped shaking since Margot had left the apartment for some lunch date. I could hardly concentrate enough to buy a ticket and get myself onto the plane. I was suddenly living on the dangerous edge of life. My emotions were as turbulent as the worst or best times of my teenage years. I was aghast with guilt at what I'd done. And, simultaneously it seemed, aflame with exhilaration.

The intensity of the one feeling created the other. In my perpetual re-run of the evening, I'd reached the image, somehow in black and white like the softcore photos boys sold to each other at school, of Margot twisting in the bath to hurl herself on top of me, the image, the sensation even, of her breasts sliding up my body. I'd reached the image of the arm hooked around my neck and that first amazing kiss while her free hand circulated soapily between my legs . . . when someone took the seat beside me.

'A penny for your thoughts,' said an overweight engineer I knew simply as Jack from a dozen encounters in the shuttle.

A penny for my thoughts! Thoughts of leaving the bath for the bedroom; of penetrating her for the first time as we reached the hallway, as her wet sliding body moved with me. Thoughts of champagne bubbling between her legs as I drank Dom Perignon from her and words . . . 'People do it all the time,' her mouth murmuring, as she enclosed my penis.

'Not brothers and sisters,' I groaned.

She had laughed, lifting her head, her eyes with that mad sparkle of sapphires. 'It just makes it that much more fun,

Tommy.' She tapped me with an index finger. 'Whaddya think, honeystick?'

I paid off the cab outside our house at Newton and fumbled undone the latch on the picket fence gate, my eyes scanning the upper floor windows, feeling sure Elaine was watching me. But there was no shadow standing there, no movement of the curtains. Guilt can get to you in all sorts of ways I told myself, but nevertheless managed to drop my overnight bag between the gate and the front door. And nearly drop it again as I let myself in.

No music. But the pleasant scent of a fresh baking floating through from the kitchen. Romilly was visiting with friends after school – everything in the house seemed normal. The books, mostly Elaine's, still occupied the high bookshelves. Her favourite nineteenth-century Chinese carving of Shou-hsing, the god of Long Life, still stood on his ebony plinth. There were no cases packed beside the front door or cabs waiting outside. Yet somehow I couldn't believe that everything was this normal. I looked around. Hell, something must be different, I'd just slept with my sister, hadn't I?

I heard footsteps across the polished board floors and Elaine came in from her study. I took in her sombre face, the way she stopped four or five paces from me and stood, tall and composed, a sheaf of papers in one hand. She knew.

'All okay?' I said, tentatively.

She did smile then. But it was wry, regretful, terminal. 'No, Tom,' she said. 'All is not okay.' She paused and looked at me for longer than I was comfortable with, forcing me to speak. I knew this was unwise. Never ask a woman what's wrong. She'll tell you.

'What is it, Elaine? Something wrong?'

'I'd like to do this in a friendly civilised way,' she said slowly. 'You're a nice man, Tom. Weak and useless, but good at heart. I think you'll want to do the same.'

I stood in the middle of the room, cold with fear. 'I'll want to do the same? About what?'

'About us.' She said it so calmly, in an almost neutral way, as if she were in fact proposing we discuss the grocery list.

I said it, what people always say in these circumstances, that old first line of pretence. 'What about us?'

'About us splitting up, Tom. Separating. Getting a divorce eventually.'

34

I couldn't speak. I couldn't begin to guess what to say. What I should say. What I wanted to say.

'You look shocked. And I'm even prepared to believe you are.' She placed one finger in the middle of my chest and pushed gently backwards. 'Sit down,' she said. 'I'll get you a drink.'

She walked towards the kitchen and turned in the doorway. 'You have to admit, Tom, we don't really have that much worth preserving, worth fighting for. If it had been a different kind of marriage, I would have started fighting months ago, years ago even. But it isn't, is it?'

So fucking reasonable. What can a man do against that? I suppose, in the end, it really depends what he *wants* to do about it. I didn't answer and she took that for answer enough. She turned into the kitchen.

Sangfroid.

'I'm not going to play games with you,' she said, 'and I don't expect you to play games with me. You've been going down to New York at least once a week for months now. I don't believe it's research. I don't think you even expect me to believe that. Am I right?'

'What d'you mean, it's not research?'

'I'm only keeping calm about this on condition you treat me with respect. I said it's not research. I'm right?'

That look left me no choice. 'Maybe not entirely research,' I said. I took a long gulp of my drink.

'I believe you've been seeing a woman there. Well, let's be late twentieth century about this, fucking a woman there. Yes or no?'

I felt skewered. I liked Elaine. As long as we could stay on generalities, no mention of Margot, I didn't want to lie to her.

'Yes or no, Tom?'

'Yes,' I said. 'Yes.'

'I believe that woman's Margot.'

The highball glass, half full, seemed to slip through my fingers. It rolled across my lap leaving a big dark stain as if I'd wet myself. 'No,' I said. 'Not Margot.'

Elaine looked at me. It was all so obvious to her, I suppose. She has clear grey eyes that make her difficult to lie to. She looked down at her nails, then up at me. 'You fucking wimp,' she said softly. 'I think you've been having sex with your sister. I am *owed* an answer. It's your sister. Am I right?'

I could have tried to lie on a technicality but those eyes below sharply lifted eyebrows allowed no squirming. 'Yes,' I said. 'But it's no big thing. Just once.'

'Sex with your sister, no big thing? God save us . . . Just the once.'

'I promise.'

'Then it was last night?'

I nodded and looked down at the damp patch.

'If it started last night, it's clearly got the chance of a future.'

'I swear Elaine . . .'

'Don't . . .'

'Elaine . . .'

'Pack your things,' she said. The words rattled out. 'Move in with your mother or Margot or whoever. I'll make arrangements to leave here within a month. I'll go back to England. With Romilly, of course. Distasteful as it'll be, I'll stay in touch. You can come over to see her any reasonable time you want. I'll get the divorce moving here in Boston before I leave.'

'You've got everything thought out,' I said. Was I bitter? Relieved? I don't know.

'I've had time,' she said and drained her drink.

'Jesus Christ! Had time. What time? This was a drunken blunder. It only happened last night.'

'Don't kid yourself, Tom,' she said, getting to her feet. 'This started back in your teens. My mistake was to believe I could do something to divert it.'

She walked into the kitchen. I think I had the hope she had gone in to cry a little, alone. I stood hesitantly until, after a few moments, she called to me. She'd put on her snow coat and a pair of rubber boots.

'I have to go out now, Tom,' she said. She stood, swinging her car keys in her left hand. 'I'll be an hour or more. Maybe you can arrange to be packed and out by then. The things you need for the next few days. As soon as you let me know where to send them, I'll crate up the rest of your stuff.'

She wasn't looking at me. She just swung her keys, waiting for my answer.

'Okay,' is what I said. 'If you think that's best,' I managed to add.

'I'll talk to Romilly when she gets back,' Elaine said. 'Carefully. I'm not going to blast her with it. I'll make sure I let you know what I've told her so you can keep your end up.'

There it was. All incredibly English. No shouting match, no recriminations. No underpants on the lawn – she was going to crate them for me, for God's sake.

'Just in case you think our parting begins to look a little blood-less . . .' she said.

She had turned her back on me. I saw her free hand move towards something on her left.

'You're not the sort of man a woman knifes or shoots, Tom. You're too soft for that. But I'd still like to say goodbye with a little flourish.'

I hadn't seen her lift the plate. Perhaps I saw it coming up at me in that second before the cream cake exploded full in my face.

That cream cake rankles. I really would have preferred it if she'd tried to hit me with something. Maybe not a poker but some-thing all the same that showed she felt that what I'd done deserved a few bruises. The cream cake was plain humiliating. It said I couldn't seriously be blamed for what had happened, I didn't have the stature, the substance for real blame. The cream cake proclaimed I was helpless in the face of Margot's wishes.

The last years have been a kind of desert. Elaine left for England and has now found herself a job in the South of France. Romilly goes to an international school down there on the Riviera. The first year after they moved out, Elaine allowed her to visit here in Boston and that worked out pretty well. I felt close to her, but something in me, maybe my own upbringing, kept me or her at a distance. We were polite to each other, considerate, although it wasn't difficult to see that I'd quickly become a paper father again. She tolerated this not unamiable man in her life – but she had no intention of letting him play an important role. At first I made several efforts to break out of this emotional cage, to show her that I really did love her. But I was deeply disturbed by the idea that I was just doing this for self-show. That maybe I didn't love her that much. That what I saw as an emotional cage didn't exist. That there was nothing to break out of. Maybe I was as close to my daughter as I wanted to be.

All this constituted a rough status quo that was easy enough to maintain – until the disaster of Romilly's visit last year.

She was fifteen, a pretty grown-up fifteen, a tall blonde girl already shapely enough to attract the covert stares in Jourdans or any one of the other Boston stores she loved hanging out in. She had looked up a couple of friends from her childhood here and was never short of company. I insisted she should call in a couple of times every day and she was happy enough to do that. It allowed me to place a parental imprimatur on her activities. Again no problems, perhaps because I never dared to say no.

The last time Romilly was over from Europe, Margot had tried to pressurise me to bring her down to New York. This time she moved directly in on Romilly and called her with an invitation for the two of us to take the shuttle down and stay with her for the weekend. For Romilly it was a powerful image: her mysterious and only vaguely remembered aunt in Manhattan, holding out a promise of glitz and glamour. I was powerless to refuse her. That weekend we flew down to New York.

It was the sort of challenge Margot could rise to beyond anybody I knew. From the beginning, she treated Romilly not only as the adult she was desperate to become but as some sort of special friend with secrets and feminine intimacies from which I was excluded. I had a miserable time, reading *The New Yorker* and watching TV while they went shopping in SoHo and followed it up with a work-out at Carrie's, the in-gym where you positively had to be seen.

Was it all set up? I've thought of this a thousand times. But it's never been a thought I've been willing to pursue. Romilly had been left down at the gym to be escorted back by the eighteen-year-old son of Margot's neighbour in the same apartment building.

Margot came back, dumped her gym bag and looked at me as I switched off the TV. 'Jesus, you poor old thing, Tom. Give you a pipe and cardigan and you'd be a dead ringer for Walter Pidgeon in *Mrs Miniver*.'

'I don't need a cardigan,' I said.

'No . . .' She smiled. 'I know what you need, little brother.' She looked at her watch. 'It'll be an hour before Romilly's back.'

Why didn't I say no? Damn fool question. Because I was desperate for attention, surly and jealous of my own daughter.

We ran into Margot's bedroom. Nothing kinky this time. We raced each other to pull off our clothes. Ten seconds later I plunged into her. We were rolling across the bed, sweat-covered, grunting mindlessly, when the front door slammed and Romilly's voice floated: 'Margot . . . Dad? Is anybody at home?'

I lay there, scared to draw breath. The bedroom door, I noticed for the first time, was open about two inches. I could just see into the hall where Romilly was moving back and forth across the opening. 'Listen,' she said to the boy with her, very grown-up. 'Can I get you something? There's beer in the fridge.' That English usage for refrigerator touched me to the quick.

Margot was easing back the duvet, swinging her legs to the floor when Romilly decided on another check. 'Margot,' she called, the width of her body filling the crack. 'Margot?'

The door eased slowly open. Romilly's face appeared round it, suddenly looking only twelve or thirteen. In the curtained room she at first saw nothing. She was actually withdrawing her head when Margot moved, stood naked beside the bed.

Romilly's head turned. She perhaps took a few seconds to register what she was seeing. I think she whimpered like a small child. Then the door slammed shut.

'She hadn't seen us, for Christ's sake,' I hissed. 'If you'd stayed still it would have been okay.'

I know contempt when I see it on a woman's face. What I didn't know was the cause for it. Silently, in the darkened room we got dressed.

The boy had gone by the time we emerged. Romilly was in her room. I knocked and walked into a stream of words. Not hysterical, screaming words. Not bloodless, calculated words either. Elaine, she told me, had said that we had split up because of another woman. For years Romilly had tried to imagine the other woman, the woman who could compete with her mother. Now she knew. 'In a way,' she said, 'I'm glad I know. I wouldn't like to have grown closer and closer to someone like you. I think you're weird, right? I think you're the pits.'

I could think of nothing to say. No rebuttal, because it was what I believed about myself.

'I've asked Danny, the boy next door, to drive me to the airport. I'm not staying here with a pair of perverts.'

All that was a year ago. Since then I've heard nothing from Romilly. A note or two from Elaine giving me change of address details in France. That was all. I tried writing to Elaine in her new home near Nice but when I read the letter through it was such a pathetic, squeaky attempt at apology, I had to abandon it. Instead I called and spoke three stumbling sentences to Elaine before she cut in. 'If at any time in the future,' she said, 'Romilly wants to contact you, I've made sure she knows where to find you. Goodbye Tom.'

Back here on the home front, I've long ago abandoned my breakout plans from my mother's financial stranglehold. I've just completed my eighth slim volume of scenes from a Boston half-life. The New York novel was never real anyway. It was an excuse to take the shuttle down to see Margot. Of course it was. And do I still? On and off. That's to say Margot takes lovers and drops me – or drops lovers and takes up with me. There has sometimes been as much as six months between my last sex with Margot and one of those phone calls where somehow I can tell the lover's on his way out. And I'm back in for a month or two. Those brief times when I'm summoned back to favour are what I live for.

Games play a big part in the sexual experience we share; dominant and dominatrix, we take turns. Sometimes the cruelty is the actual, physical infliction of pain on one another. Mostly it's the cruelty that perhaps only a brother or sister can inflict on the other, revealing our weaknesses, our fears. Early on, I perceived Margot's awareness of the narrow line she trod, a fear that could be dramatised as some sort of descent from her role as high courtesan-wife to cheap fifty dollar hooker. Whenever I am dominant in our games I play on this, forcing her to dress like a street-walker, even paying her money to submit to being cuffed to the bed while I abuse her. Then after perhaps an hour or two of the most complete submission, she'll metamorphose into a tigress and the roles are reversed and insults will be hurled at me like salt grinding into the deep wounds of childhood.

Exhaustion follows these sessions, exhaustion for both of us. But no tenderness. Afterwards we will lie together on the bed among the tacky trivia of our addiction, sated, in silence and maybe even shame.

Do I love Margot, am I in love with her? No, is the answer. Categorically no. I don't have any of those feelings of tenderness for her and I'm sure she has none for me. But I need her. I have an irresistible physical need to possess, to wallow in her body. And what does she get from me? God only knows. I submit to her needs without knowing or understanding what they are. She can go without me for long periods while I am incapable of going without her. Our games play both ways, but I have no doubt who, in the end, is the dependant among the two of us. I would like to know more. But I know it would be dangerous to ask.

Don't tell me I have to stand up and start living. Like any addict, I know that. I know I have to walk out on my addiction, on Margot. Like any addict I persuade myself that that's something I'll have to address with all urgency – but not tonight, for God's sake. Just give me until tomorrow.

In the meantime I wait for Margot to call for me – and I do things like escort my mother to San Francisco where we attend the funeral of one of her many cousins. Of course, it all went badly wrong when we were circling a few thousand feet over San Francisco, but normally these little attentions I pay her dispose her well enough to the idea of keeping my allowance up to the rate of inflation. And since I am too scared to play as much as a bit part in Walt Strummer's operations after six hours of FBI hospitality, I make every effort to at least appear to do what I'm told. Oh yes, who says I don't live a life to be proud of?

# 6

THE FUNERAL OF Marcel Coultard was held on the first
Thursday in July. Since the graveyard at St Juste was now
below the waters of the lake, he had asked to be buried in the
cemetery of Villefranche. The funeral service, however, would be
held in the bare Crusader chapel in the château crypt.

Messieurs Mantel, Bouchier, Jonquard and Beste, four former
wartime Resistance comrades of Coultard, took the four corners
of the coffin. They were supported by Gendarme Philippe Rodinet
in dress uniform and Notaire Luc Rolin, the sons of two equally
notable dead Resistants. With Coultard himself these names had
made up the Committee of Seven, the most celebrated Resistance
group in these hill villages behind the Mediterranean coast of
France during the later stages of World War II.

After mass had been said, Maître Hercule Mantel, Mayor of
Villefrance and the aged senior partner of Mantel, Rolin, the only
law firm in the town, stood before the coffin on its plinth and
addressed the mourners crowded into the Crusader chapel.
Marcel's two children, Claire Coultard, heavily veiled, and her
brother Sébastien, were seated in the half circle of more distant
relatives of the dead man and the aged survivors of the Committee.

'We're here today,' Mantel said, one hand taking the weight
of his big, heavy body on an ivory handled stick, 'to bid goodbye
to our leader and comrade in arms, the father of Claire and
Sébastien . . .' He nodded towards the two younger figures in
the centre of the half circle. 'No words I can say can celebrate
his life more than the personal recognition Marcel Coultard
received by no less than three Presidents of France. He was the
holder, as you know, of the *Légion d'honneur*, the *Médaille
Militaire* with palms, and of decorations from the Israeli,
American and British governments. But there is some small piece
of his life that I'm able to offer to you today.' He smiled and
nodded to himself, content to have intrigued his audience.

'We're fortunate that Marcel's business was in film-making,' Mantel continued. 'In the last week since his death, one or two pieces of film taken of Marcel himself, probably by his brother Pierre, have surfaced and, before they go to join the rest of the film archive in the museum, I believe it would be appropriate to show these fragments here today.'

He signalled to someone at the back of the chapel and the lights were lowered. A small screen had been drawn down between folds of red curtaining. The projector began to click; scratched white numbers jerked up on the black screen to be replaced by footage of a bleak hillside in winter. Heavy mist clung to the tops of umbrella pines; pockets of snow had settled among the rocks. As the projector whirred, dark figures moved in the far background, lower down the hill. The camera swept back and forth, inexplicably panning the hillside on either side of the path, then settled again on the figures struggling upwards.

They were much clearer now, six or seven people bundled against the cold and burdened with bags or sacks or sometimes suitcases tied to their backs. The leading figure seemed much more agile, less burdened by his alpine rucksack or, as he got closer, the Sten gun that could be seen hanging round his neck.

'I shall check the records with the few clues we have in the film,' Mantel said, 'to try to establish the exact date of this operation. The Sten gun Marcel is carrying was supplied in a British drop in October 1942. You can see now that they were all women in the party. And if you look at the amount of luggage they were carrying, I think it suggests they were all *young* women. This could easily be the convoy of six that you'll find recorded in the museum, that Marcel brought through the mountains in the first week of November 1942.'

The group were labouring upwards towards the camera now. Marcel Coultard's hand went up to tighten his scarf round the bottom part of his face until, under the rim of the thick black beret, only his eyes were visible. He lifted his hand to greet the man operating the camera, then he stood aside to help the women the last few yards up to the glade encircled by pine trees. The women had no need to hide their faces. They were already stateless citizens, hunted as Jews by the French special police. In a matter of days now they would be moving on by truck or train into Italy where anti-Semitism had no government backing or, along the coast of Southern France, to cross the Pyrenees into

43

neutral Spain. With one more short sequence of the women one by one embracing Marcel, the light faded and the makeshift screen went blank.

Leaving the small Crusader church, Claire and Sébastien Coultard, daughter and son of Marcel Coultard, followed the coffin to the hearse in the château courtyard from where it would be transported down the mountain road to the graveyard at Villefranche sur Bol.

Over three hundred people were by now present at the gates of the Villefranche graveyard. Villagers from Villefranche and the former village of St Juste joined with representatives of the film business drawn by the Coultard name. From what had been a minuscule distributor handling locally made travel fillers, Marcel Coultard had built the business into one of the biggest exhibitors along the Mediterranean coast. Elaine Chapel was assigned a special place as one of the most senior Ciné-Coultard executives. Her daughter, Romilly, had left school a day early to be present.

The local headquarters of the 327th Infantry provided a guard of honour and a unit of blue uniformed CRS crowd control police were there to supervise parking and the movement of mourners in the small walled village cemetery.

Romilly Chapel, still no more than a few months past her seventeenth birthday, wearing black (borrowed, like the high heels, from her mother), attracted covert looks from villagers who'd never seen her in anything but jeans or tennis clothes. Elegant as a model, they said. As the line of mourners followed the hearse into the graveyard, Romilly leaned close to her mother. 'Sad, isn't it?' she said. 'A war hero and everything.' She dropped her voice. 'You know, in the village, they're saying it wasn't an accident.'

Elaine turned her head towards her daughter, her black straw hat brushing Romilly's cheek. 'Don't talk nonsense, Rom. More important – don't *spread* nonsense. You've lived down here long enough to know how rumours take off.'

'It's not necessarily nonsense,' Romilly said stubbornly. 'Why couldn't he have been killed for his money? People are every day.'

'You know about these things, do you?' Her mother smiled indulgently. 'Marcel fell on a walk up in the hills. He brought down a shower of rock with him. Simple enough.'

'*Too* simple perhaps,' Romilly said heavily.

The long line of mourners had come to a temporary halt. The

heat rolled over them in waves. The coffin had been removed from the hearse by the pall bearers. Claire and Sébastien Coultard, the woman taller than her thickset brother, followed the pall bearers through the gates of the Villefranche graveyard towards the stone Coultard family vault. The coffin was placed on rollers at the opening of the black velvet draped vault and the bearers, their work done, withdrew into the crowd.

'There,' Romilly whispered to her mother. 'I'm serious. The prime suspects. Sébastien Coultard and his sister. Terrified that old Marcel was planning to leave the money to someone else.'

'And who else was he planning to leave it to?' Elaine asked.

'You, perhaps. You may be forty but you're very fanciable. Anyway that's what the boys say at the café. Makes me writhe with jealousy. Come on, Mom, tell me. Did he ever hint you'd be a rich woman someday? I know he was old but did you like him?'

'I *did* like him,' Elaine said, hugging her daughter with one arm. 'But not in the way you're so grossly suggesting. And no, he never hinted I'd be a rich woman someday. We had a business relationship, Rom.'

Romilly looked at her mother, her expression serious. 'That true? About him never hinting he was going to leave you something?'

'Your imagination's running away with you,' Elaine said in a tone to drop the subject. She was looking round. 'You know we have close to one hundred percent of the Festival organisation up from Cannes and nearly every major American distributor represented. Very impressive.'

'Very,' Romilly said absently. Her mother glanced at her. Her attention was already elsewhere, on the young lawyer Luc Rolin, who had returned from Paris to help out at *notaires* Mantel, Rolin when Luc's father had died.

'Be back,' Romilly said to her mother. She eased her way through the crowd and reached Luc who gave her an exaggerated bow and kissed her on both cheeks. 'You're looking all of twenty five,' he said.

'You think black suits me?'

He smiled. 'The way you look, everything suits you. And I think you know it very well.'

'Have you read the will yet?'

'Marcel's! How do you know I'm looking after that?'

'Everybody knows you're taking over your father's work,' she said. 'Have you read it?'

He shook his head. 'For your information, Romilly, it's still sealed. There's to be a meeting tomorrow morning. It's a formality that country lawyers like to observe.'

'Who'll be there?'

'Just the family. Claire and Sébastien.'

'And you read it out? Like Agatha Christie?'

'Your mother's signalling to you. Listen Romilly, are you free this weekend? Saturday night perhaps? There's a new restaurant in Nice . . .'

She was immensely flattered. 'Perhaps,' she said. 'Call me.'

Romilly got back and stood beside her mother. The line moved forward. Colourful handkerchiefs were produced to mop peasant brows. Madame Odille Beste, notorious in her youth as the only divorced woman in Villefranche, fainted and was helped away by her son, Tancrède the baker, and a second man, Jo-Jo, the game show host, a face well-known throughout France. Afterwards in the cafés on the market place they would say Odille had fainted on purpose. Meanwhile, the more middle-class local mourners strove hard to pretend it wasn't nearly ninety-five degrees. The line continued its slow shuffle forward. The CRS saluted and waved directions until the whole assembly of people, village folk and film folk alike, were standing in a wide half circle round Marcel Coultard's vault.

Minutes later the ceremony of the interment began.

Among the mourners, several men indulged in a covert glance at Romilly, though none watched her with the same protracted attention as the priest by the cemetery gate. A grizzled grey-haired man in late middle-age, he attracted no attention here at the funeral in his heavy soutane. His black beret announced what was in any case obvious – he was not a young, fashionable member of the priesthood, one of those who might turn up in jeans to a baptism perhaps and slyly apologise for having forgotten his robes. Very clearly, and the beret underlined it, he was of the old school. Then with a final glance at Romilly, as if, perhaps, he were trying to fix her in his memory, he turned away and walked rapidly along the path through the wood to where, an hour earlier, he had been directed to park his blue Citroën van.

# 7

I HAD THOUGHT, feared, that my mother's revelation during the San Francisco air emergency would have an impact on my relationship with Margot. What worried me was that, if we weren't full-blooded brother and sister, the spice might have gone out of things for her. So as soon as I'd dropped my mother off into the care of her nurse, I went back to my apartment and called Margot.

She was jubilant. 'I saw you on TV, Tom. Striding off that plane with what they call, God knows why, studied nonchalance. And waving to all the air emergency crews. Great! The general's lady didn't look so happy with things.'

'No. Listen, I can tell you why. She confided a big, big secret to me while we were at death's door. Or so we thought.' I paused to get the right effect. 'It appears I am not—you hear me—*not* of the general's loins. But whose loins I am of remains a mystery.'

There was silence at the other end.

'What do you think?' I asked anxiously.

'What do I think?' To my relief Margot's voice was completely upbeat. 'I think it's exciting as all get out. I'm just running through half a dozen names of their old friends trying to guess who the hell it could have been. It must have been in wartime London, of course. So who? Who would have dared to have copped a feel in Pall Mall, put his hand up her skirt at a Buckingham Palace reception, shove his tongue down her throat in the lobby of the Ritz?'

'Stop it, Margot,' I said.

'I have to call her. Can't let this one by. Demand she swears a solemn oath that I am my father's daughter. I'll insist on her word of honour as if I were all caught up about it. Quiet anguish, you know the thing. Sniff and sob. Long thoughtful silences. Force her to give her word she hadn't been screwing anybody else when I was conceived. Boy, will she hate me for that!'

'Or me, for telling you. You're a bitch, Margot,' I said, well pleased with her reaction.

'Listen,' she came back suddenly angry. 'I owe her nothing. Every drop of her own peculiar brand of love went to General John. No leftovers for us. Why should we feel sorry for her?'

'That's what's so strange,' I said. 'Crazy even.'

'What is?'

'She was mad about him. Do you see her as much as looking at some other guy? You just think of her in London during the war for a minute or two. Twenty-seven years old. Married three or four years. I just don't see it.'

'So she's done you a favour. She's given you the mission in life you've always needed. This could be the making of you, Tommy. The hunt for the mysterious father. Tell you how you start. You send her nurse out for the afternoon and when she's taking her nap, you ransack the house for clues.'

'I tell you honestly Margot, I don't plan to spend the next years of my life looking for my biological father. Especially knowing that, when I did find him, he'd probably be a *Boys from Brazil* clone of General John.'

'I don't know,' she said. 'Maybe you could hope for something really shabby. Like an affair with the Duke of Windsor.'

'True enough, I just don't see her lunging at the pinks of one of the General's junior officers.'

'Me neither.' She'd lost interest in the subject in the sudden way she had. 'Listen, I'm bored,' she said. 'My Wall Street whizz-kid can talk about nothing but himself. Himself and his fears that his wife will find out about us and start divorce proceedings which will cost him the house and the dog.'

'Too bad.' I couldn't have felt better about it. He was on the way out. I sensed it.

'You doing anything this coming weekend?'

'Not a lot. Why?'

'What d'you feel about a weekend in the big city?'

'Good,' I said. Then tentatively, 'George . . .'

'He'll be here . . .'

My heart sank.

'Unless he takes up some fact-finding offer to visit Amsterdam's museums.'

'And will he?' I tried to keep it casual.

'Oh for Christ's sake Tom. I've asked you down for the

weekend. Lunch, dinner somewhere new. A show, an exhibition, a party even. We don't need my husband out of the way for what we're going to be doing.'

'Of course not,' I said. But I could sense something in her voice, tone, intonation . . . Whatever it was, I knew she already knew for sure that George was going to Amsterdam this weekend.

I'd told Margot I wasn't prepared to spend my life searching for my biological father. But I can't deny some curiosity. The crisis over San Francisco and the long flight back to Boston had exhausted my mother. Her nurse had consulted her doctor and a sedative and an absolute confinement to bed until tomorrow midday was the result.

I thought immediately of Margot's suggestion and I told Maria, the nurse, that I would be quite happy to take charge of things while she took a break. She'd often mentioned a man friend who worked in the deli down the street.

My mother lives in a big old house, one we lived in as a family whenever my father, or I should more accurately say simply General John, was posted in the eastern half of the United States. Perhaps because it had spent so many of the last forty years only intermittently occupied, the house had become a museum of the family's life. There were desks and cupboards and credenzas full of dusty papers, military, personal and scholastic. There were shelves of bound photographs, mostly military records of operations the general had planned or taken part in. There was an extensive loft with moth-eaten uniforms and boots and piled dusty suitcases with damaged hinges and solid, leather-belted World War II trunks.

As Maria left with a freshly made-up face and black heels to replace her white rubber soled shoes, I saw the extent of the task, even its hopelessness. But that curiosity wouldn't go away and I knew my mother well enough to know that she meant it when she said that there was no more to say on the subject.

I started in the loft.

It was slow work: looking back over your past life always is. Like looking up a word in a dictionary. You linger on old photographs. You read letters you can no longer remember having received. In one file, the corners nibbled by mice, General John had kept all the reprimand notes he had written to me from the age I could read, onwards. It was a sad catalogue of boyish offences. Yet strangely, I was able to detect a real affection under-lying his comments. It was my mother's added short remark at the end of most of the notes that contained the real sting.

I sat for perhaps a half hour reading the file and I gradually drew out of it a picture of my mother as the real bully of the pair. My father – the man I had believed to be my father – was certainly something of a military disciplinarian. But the real bullying tone was hers. I can't understand why I had not seen before that any increase in the punishment set in these sadly formal reprimands was always in her handwriting: a week's loss of pocket money scored through in her hand and changed to a month plus beating with the paddiwack, a loofah like instrument of torture which she had preferred to the belt as I got older.

So was she punishing me for her own transgressions? Was the way she had tormented me through childhood plucked straight from the flight from adultery preoccupations of the Bannerman family? A bit glib maybe, but it fitted neatly enough.

Downstairs my mother was impatient for attention. Her stick thumped hard on her bedroom floor and almost automatically I rose to go down. Then I stopped myself with thoughts of all the times I had cried for her as a kid, and I turned back to the papers.

All my mother's family stuff was packed into these trunks and cracked leather valises up here too. The Bannerman nineteenth century photographic portraits were an astonishingly depressing series of grim women in black bombazine and men in cravats and cutaway coats. They were bankers mainly. Or politicians. Others posed in uniform: a Navy captain from the War of 1812, several Civil War Unionist officers and a World War I general. Perhaps this military strain had been what brought her into the arms of General John. The Chapels had been soldiers, and mostly generals, since the Civil War.

Curiously I had always been indifferent to this background story. Perhaps because the US Army is essentially a meritocracy, and army children absorb that very quickly, it never cut any ice with my friends that my mother's family were Pilgrim or just post-Pilgrim stock. Piled and stacked and boxed, the history of the Chapels and Bannermans remained untouched. My interest was in the more recent past.

From the loft I went down to the living room floor and searched through some of the desks stuffed with papers. The variety of the paperwork they had kept was astonishing. One of them, probably him originally, had had real problems with the idea of letting go anything. But there was still nothing there that cast any light on my own background.

One box-file tied with string was bursting with legal documents carrying seals and fluttering red tape. I looked quickly through the terms of family trusts and deeds but none of it added anything to what I already knew. Most of the money had come from my mother's side of the family. General John's Chapel parents and grandparents had provided him with little more than an education and entry to West Point. Meanwhile, the thudding of my mother's stick was now right above me. And was joined by her voice calling, insistent and baffled that no one answered. She didn't like being ignored. She was capable of coming down to look for me. I didn't want to be caught searching her private papers. Time I moved on.

The general's office looked more promising. There was a lot of material here on his war service. He seemed to have assembled it in files for a book of memoirs he was never able to write. I sat down in his leather swing chair. All the major facts seemed to be as I had heard them. Dates for his going to London. His work on the early cross-channel invasion plans in a planning team under General Sir Frederick Morgan. D-Day itself and the horrors of the beaches. It was all there. And strangely it brought a lump to my throat.

I was leaving his office to the rhythmic thumping of my mother's stick in the room above, when I noticed a framed picture I had not seen before. It was of Margot and me when we were kids, probably not more than four and six, playing on a beach somewhere. The General was there watching, a tall, impressive man physically, a wry, fond expression on his face. Strange how an hour with a bundle of memories can subtly change your view of a man I'd thought of all my life as my martinet of a father. Someone else had taken the picture because my mother stood in the background, bending forward holding a black Labrador by the collar as it tugged forward to join the children. She was a good-looking woman in her thirties, blonde and shapely. But there was something sour about her features even then. Something eternally disapproving.

I dropped the picture back in the desk drawer, a little too hard perhaps, because the rusting clips on the back of the leather frame sprung and frame, glass, photograph and backing parted company. I was about to push the drawer closed when I noticed the edge of a faded envelope sticking out a fraction of an inch from between the backing and the picture of us on the beach.

I drew out the envelope. It was old and unsealed. I opened it. It contained a single small photograph no more than two inches by one and a half with a white scalloped edge. It was of me, a small boy running hard down a quayside, running towards the camera. Sunshine and boats in the background. There were dozens of such pictures about in the office but none, as far as I remember, showing me quite as young as this. I held it close, examining it with the care and admiration we reserve for ourselves alone. The sheer exuberance struck me. The energy . . . I turned the picture. On the back there was no caption, but the palest of blue stamps of the company who had developed the print had survived the thumbwear of time. Hamley's Photographic, Barnstable, Cape Cod, Jul. 47.

So we had spent a summer holiday on Cape Cod in July, 1947. The war over, General John back in the US, Margot just a month from being born. But wait a moment. There was something strange about that little boy. His exuberance, his energy, the very running action, was not that of a boy born in November 1944. Not that of a child of two and a half. My mother had very often talked of how physically advanced I was as a child. People, she said, remarked upon it. Suddenly I knew why. Surely the child I was looking at was, at the very least, a four year old.

What was I doing here? Manufacturing a mystery? Searching old documents and letters, you expect to come up with a mystery. You want one, you come up with one. Is that what was happening? I held the picture up. I could take it to a paediatrician. He or she would confirm it. But I didn't need a doctor. I knew that boy was not two and a half years old.

So I now had two mysteries. An unknown father and a birthdate at least two years earlier than the date recorded on my passport.

I was sitting in the chair beside my mother's bed. In the silence between us I could hear Maria come in from her visit to the deli.

'I won't ask you again, Thomas,' my mother said. 'I demand you give me that photograph. It simply does not bear the interpretation you put upon it.'

'I think you're going to destroy it,' I said. 'And I don't want it destroyed.' I don't think I would have ever spoken to her like this before the air emergency over San Francisco.

She tossed her head. She cast around for a threat, found none that might work and snarled her frustration, the left side of her mouth becoming even more distorted. 'The picture is my property. Hand it back.'

'I want you to tell me what it's all about first. When we thought the plane was about to crash you told me that I was not my father's child – or rather the child of the man I'd always thought was my father.'

'I've no more to say about that. I told you at the time.'

'Dammit, I've a right to know,' I said. 'I've a right to know who my father was.'

'I want you to leave now,' she said. 'What you've done is indefensible, breaking into his office and going through his papers like a common thief . . .'

'Like a common thief? This picture is me. This is who I am, for God's sake, not the fake you made of me. This is the real boy.'

Her mouth twisted. 'Don't you ever think what it was like for him to have a child like you? To have had to acknowledge you as his son. Don't you ever think how much he wanted a real boy . . .'

'Then perhaps you should have let him have one,' I said.

She stared at me in disbelief. She'd certainly never expected to hear anything like that from Sonny Boy.

'I've a right to know my father's name. I've a right to know my age,' I said. 'I don't think I was born in 1944. I was born a year, two years earlier. So sometime late in 1942. Is that right?'

She stared at me like a reptile. 'You're talking arrant nonsense. Give me the photograph. And call the nurse on your way out.'

That imperiousness in her tone, totally indifferent to my feelings, caused the anger to flare into my cheeks. I could feel the heat there. 'Do you want me to take this to a paediatrician? Because I can. I can do it this afternoon. I can get a professional opinion, within parameters, of how old that child is. How old I am, for Christ's sake!'

She stared at me, sloe-eyed. 'Call the nurse,' she said calmly. 'It's time for my lunch.'

\*　　\*　　\*

Maria was waiting, quite close I thought, to the door. As I gave her my mother's message about lunch she squeezed my wrist. It was the hand still carrying the photograph. 'Thank you,' she said.

'What for?'

'You gave me the break. The hour to go down to the deli.'

'Big deal.'

'Yes, big deal.' She smiled her brilliant, middle-aged, Hispanic smile. 'Jack just asked me to marry him.'

Hard to remember sometimes that life is something that happens to other people, too.

# 8

THE DAY AFTER Marcel Coultard's funeral, in the square of Villefranche sur Bol, the midday klaxon, decreeing the end of the Friday market, was just minutes away from being sounded. The market square, the Place Mistral, was beginning to empty. This close to midday, most of the women of the village had completed their shopping and were already in their kitchens. The travelling butchers and fishmongers who sold their produce from big white trucks with let-down sides were already cleaning the counters and locking them upright. At the roadside stalls, unsold vegetables were being re-crated and stacked in the all-purpose Citroën vans with the corrugated sides.

At the cafés around the square, their tables set out on the dusty gravel, workmen in overalls drank an aperitif before making their way home to lunch. A few people stopped and talked, swinging shopping bags or feathered chickens by the neck. In the centre of the *place*, the old men had finished their last game of *pétanque* and were dusting off their metal *boules* with chamois leather cloths. Half a dozen younger ones stood around watching, drinking from cans of beer. It was an entirely unremarkable Friday morning end of market in the South of France.

When Romilly entered the Place Mistral from the east end beside the church, she was forced to stop half a dozen times to shake hands with neighbours and wish them, *Bonjour Madame, Bonjour Monsieur.* With her own age group she'd stop for a kiss on both cheeks from boys and girls she had known since she and her mother had moved to Villefranche.

In something of a hurry to get home from her tennis match to make a call to Anne-Marie, the German girl who was her best friend at the international school down on the coast, Romilly avoided the big café where she would have to stop for more greetings and offers of a coffee or a kir, and slipped into the deep shade between the produce trucks and vans.

55

The waiter at the Café de la Paix Faite, the Café of Peace at Last, remembered seeing her pass. He didn't include it in his statement at the gendarmerie later that afternoon, but, as he told his colleague at the café, any man would have remembered seeing her pass with legs like that and her tennis skirt flicking from side to side as she walked. But once she disappeared among the jumble of vans, clothes racks and piled produce crates not sixty metres from the arched exit to the village, nobody seemed to recall seeing her emerge and pass under the watch-tower for which she was heading.

At her house just beyond the olive grove on the edge of the village, Elaine sat on her terrace working on the draft of a letter to Los Angeles. She badly needed the vice-president of Paramount to commit his two major spring productions to next year's Cannes Festival. It used to be automatic, but things were changing. Cannes did not always have quite the pull it used to have for American distributors. She glanced quickly at her watch and whistled silently. She had a meeting in Cannes at the Negresco at three o'clock. Romilly had promised to be back from tennis by twelve-thirty at the very latest. It was now just before one. Elaine made a decision. She would tell Madame Garrigues she would have lunch alone. Romilly could have it when she got back.

By one thirty she had finished lunch and a knot of anxiety had settled in her stomach. For a moment she sat with a glass of mineral water and told herself she was worrying unnecessarily. Romilly was an hour late. She'd stopped for a soda in the square. Except . . . except that she'd promised to be back straight after tennis. So, a teenager's promise. She was getting upset about a broken teenage promise.

Elaine went up to her bedroom and began to change for her meeting but found it difficult to decide what to wear. Her bedside clock now showed one fifty. She stood for a second in the middle of the room, tapping a bare foot, trying to decide. Then she pulled on a robe, ran downstairs and looked up the home number of Jacqueline Beste who taught tennis at the village courts. Three long rings and Jacqueline picked up. Without preliminaries, Elaine asked her what time Romilly's lesson had ended.

'Before midday,' Jacqueline said.

'You're sure of that.'

'Sure. I remember the market klaxon sounding as I packed my

tennis bag. Romilly had already left. She told me at the beginning of the lesson that you had an important meeting in Cannes
this afternoon and she didn't want to be late for lunch. Why?
Isn't she back yet?'

'Not yet,' Elaine said briefly.

She thanked Jacqueline, ran upstairs again and pulled on jeans,
sweater and espadrilles. Calling to Madame Garrigues that she
would be back in a few minutes, she took the dirt track past the
olive grove and into the village.

It was less than half a mile. She walked briskly, sometimes
breaking into a half-run, so that she was already brushing the
sweat from her temples with the back of her hand when she came
upon the Commandant of the local gendarmerie, Lucien Duval,
returning to his office after lunch. He had stopped to examine
the strip of lawn outside the stone building with the barred downstairs windows. The lawn made it look less forbidding. The lawn
and the flower beds had been Duval's own idea and the Inspector-
General had commented favourably on the effect when he was
in Villefranche last year.

He was aware of someone hurrying along behind him. He
looked over his bulky shoulder. He was a man still in his middle
years, but far from fit. He touched his hand to his kepi. 'You've
taken up jogging, Madame Chapel. I should join you.' He indicated the bulge of his blue uniformed shirt.

Elaine shook her head. 'I'm looking for Romilly. She's late
home. Very late,' she added in a tone close to desperation.

'Ah . . . Duval spread his heavy hands. 'These young ones.
Stopped in the *place* for a coca with her friends . . .'

'You saw her there?'

'No . . . no. But it's what they do, isn't it?'

Elaine was already moving on. 'No, it's not like that. She knew
she had to be back . . .'

Lucien Duval turned back to the door of the gendarmerie.
Friday afternoon there wasn't a lot to do. He'd had a good lunch.
Now a hour's doze in his new chair perhaps, then an early game
of *boules* . . .

# 9

I ARRIVED AT La Guardia on a Friday mid-morning shuttle. Margot had hinted George would not be out of the apartment until late afternoon, not, she added, that it would make any difference. I had just one errand to run downtown, a meeting at two o'clock, so I bought myself an early sandwich and a couple of glasses of Bordeaux at the French Bar in the Village, said hello to a few acquaintances and presented myself at the grand twenty-sixth floor offices of Roddam, Spurling, Jones at a few minutes before the appointed time.

I wasn't really dressed for a visit to a Manhattan law firm but I didn't really care what they thought of my jeans and sports shirt. I'm a rebel – at least that's what I like to think. I was here for a weekend with Margot – Roddam, Spurling, Jones were lucky I could fit them in.

A young woman deliberately chosen for her considerable powers of sexual intimidation checked me out with evident dubiety then led me through thick mahogany double doors that looked frankly ridiculous in these square-cornered functional rooms. We entered a broad corner office with a young-middle-aged man standing behind more mahogany, and the assistant said 'Mr Chapel. Mr Spurling.' and withdrew. I shook hands as he introduced himself as Rod Spurling, declined his offer of coffee and took the seat he indicated with a view out across the Hudson to New Jersey.

'You must be wondering what this is about,' Spurling began, as he had probably begun a thousand interviews before.

The truth was I sat there with a low curiosity threshold. Since my mother's stroke I had visited and been summoned by a dozen lawyers and bank managers and investment advisers in Boston and New York. It wasn't that her fortune was so large (although it wasn't inconsiderable) but more that she preferred to have it handled in penny packets, with half a dozen signatures on each transaction. This way, she felt, it was less likely to fall into the hands of financial predators. Like me.

I didn't have a view. I just visited these various advisers, nodded sagely to their suggestions and signed if they asked me to. Stroke or not, my mother could have done better herself.

'I don't recall my mother mentioning Roddam, Spurling, Jones,' I said in response to his tired opening gambit. 'I thought I'd been in touch with all her financial people by now.'

'Your mother . . . ?' He looked puzzled.

'I take it you handle some of her financial affairs. You want me to sign some papers.'

He frowned. 'No . . . No, this meeting has nothing to do with your mother, Mr Chapel.'

We eyed each other silently across the desk. Did he intend to tell me what it *was* about? It was my turn for a tired gambit. 'Let's say you start at the beginning, Mr Spurling?'

'Very well.' He stood up. 'Might I ask you for some kind of identification, Mr Chapel. I regret this – but in the circumstances, since you're not one of our clients . . .'

He proffered a thinly apologetic smile. I handed him my driving licence.

'Yes. Thank you.' He handed it back and sat down again behind the mahogany. 'You are separated from your wife, a British citizen named Elaine Chapel. And you have a daughter, now aged seventeen, Romilly Anne.'

'That's correct.' Neither Elaine nor I had pushed for a divorce. I always imagined she'd ask for one when she met someone she liked enough to consider marrying. Was this it? Maybe she was still so pissed at me, she preferred to pass the news through a lawyer. But that was unlike Elaine. I would find out.

'Your wife and daughter live in France.'

'They do.'

'Roddam, Spurling, Jones has been retained by a French law firm, Mantel, Rolin in the department of the Alpes Maritimes, the Riviera, to make initial contact with you.'

The Riviera. Where Elaine lived. So she had met someone else and wanted to set the ball rolling. Well, I couldn't blame her. 'Okay, Mr Spurling,' I said. 'We're talking divorce, are we? Let me say now, I have no problems about that.'

He didn't like that. He smiled his thin smile and gave me effortless superiority. 'We are not the sort of firm that handles divorce, Mr Chapel. Except for a limited number of established clients

If we'd been talking about a divorce we would have contacted your own lawyers.'

The guy was definitely supercilious. Unhappy in his work. 'Ah . . .' I opened my eyes wide. 'We're not talking about divorce? So what am I doing here . . .' I looked around me, 'in your expensive corner office with the breathtaking views, Mr Spurling?'

'I asked you here today to discuss your position vis-à-vis your daughter, Romilly.'

'Why? Has it changed?'

'It's changed in the sense that she has just been named sole beneficiary of a considerable estate.'

I got there immediately. I was being cut out of my mother's will. Instead it would go to Romilly when she was eighteen or twenty-one or whatever. Well, I couldn't claim I liked it, but I wasn't really surprised. 'This is money my mother's leaving Romilly. Right?' I said.

'Wrong. As I said, it has nothing to do with your mother's affairs, Mr Chapel, of which I am totally ignorant.'

Our eyes met. 'Okay,' I said, taking it slowly now as I should have from the beginning. 'Romilly has been left some money. So who by? How much?'

'The estate has yet to be valued.' He placed his hands flat down on his desk 'But I'm informed it will come out, after taxes, in the region of one hundred and ninety million francs – say twenty-eight million dollars.'

This did take my breath away. 'For Romilly?' I said. 'Twenty-eight million dollars? All of it?'

'She is the principal beneficiary.' He paused. 'You are to receive an income of half a million francs, approximately seventy-five thousand dollars a year, for life.'

I stared at him dumbfounded. What was going on here? Seventy-five thousand dollars. I could give up writing. And Romilly twenty-eight million!

'Any questions so far?' the idiot asked.

My reply was equally idiotic. Shock, I guess. 'Why did you quote it in francs?'

'Because this is an entirely French matter.' He stopped himself. 'That's to say the estate in France, and the corporation that goes with it, are registered as a limited company in London. English law is, like ours, more flexible. The London registration is a formality. Essentially you can ignore that. The property is French.'

I sat back in my chair. 'You won't mind if I say, Mr Spurling, that you're not putting this over too clearly. So could I have some straight answers? Who is it? Who left my daughter twenty-eight million dollars?'

He smiled. I think it was a smile.

'I have a right to know that, don't I?'

'Of course. Especially as the point of this meeting is that you will be, as French law requires, one of the trustees for the money until your daughter's twenty-first birthday. A French lawyer is the other.'

'So who was it? Who left the money if it wasn't someone in my mother's family?'

'The benefactor is French.'

'You're sure there's not been a mistake here,' I said cautiously.

'I can assure you there has been no mistake. Many years of investigative work, I believe, went into tracing yourself and your daughter. Many thousands of dollars were spent.'

I shook my head like a tired old nag. 'Who commissioned this work?'

'The benefactor is a French citizen, I'm allowed to say that.'

'For Christ's sake, who is it?'

'The French lawyers would prefer to supply that information themselves. My role is simply to inform you of the existence of the will and an important condition attached. Beyond that I am a facilitator.'

'Condition?'

He hesitated, looked down at his hands, then up again . . . 'Should any unfortunate accident occur . . .' He looked at me, shrugged, and got it out: 'Should Romilly Anne die before her twenty-first birthday, the estate would pass back to the direct line of descent of the benefactor.'

'What about Romilly's mother, Elaine? Does she figure in all this largesse?'

'No. Romilly's mother has not been appointed a trustee. Nor would she be a beneficiary in the event that your daughter . . .'

'Died before the age of twenty-one.'

'Correct.'

'I don't understand this at all. When do I find out who left the money?'

'The French have their own way of doing things. They, the lawyers for the benefactor, wish to inform you themselves of the extent of your rights and responsibilities.'

'Okay. How is that to be done?'

'In this office. A Maître Luc Rolin, that's what they call them-selves, Maître, Master . . . it's a lawyer's title . . .'

I nodded. 'Sure. I went to a French school, Mr Spurling. Very tough. Too tough for me. So Rolin is due here – when, today?'

'Next week. Tuesday afternoon. Will that be convenient to you?'

'I'll make it. Romilly knows about all this, of course.'

'Not yet.'

'My ex-wife . . . separated wife – does she know?'

'No. There's no need for her to know. She's not in the loop.'

These lawyers.

'I'd say she'll be bang in the middle of the loop if her daughter has just inherited twenty-eight million dollars.'

He glanced at a leather clock on his desk and stood up. I stayed sitting. 'When did he die?'

'What?'

'The benefactor. The Frenchman who's leaving Romilly the money.'

'Earlier this month,' Spurling said. 'He was a very old man.'

'What was his business? Is this twenty-eight million dollars money he made?'

'There is a business involved.'

'What sort of business?'

'He owned local cinemas. He was a motion picture exhibitor.'

'That's the business Elaine, my one-time wife, works in. Is there a connection?'

'There might well be.'

Lawyers are infuriating. 'Could this be my wife's boss we're talking about?'

'I haven't been informed.'

In the long silence, I stood up. 'In this hundred-dollar-a-minute game we're playing, am I getting warm?'

'Please, Mr Chapel. My instructions are clear. Only the essen-tial details are to be communicated.' He crossed the room and opened the door. 'You live in Boston?'

'I do.'

'From now on all travelling and hotel expenses will be covered by the estate, of course. In the meantime, if you'll undertake not to talk about our meeting . . .'

'Not to talk about it? Who to?'

'To anyone.'

'If you're asking me not to tell Romilly and her mother? Forget it. The first thing I'm going to do when I leave here is put in a call to France. The way I see it, and the way I'm going to do it – they have a right to know.'

'Yes,' he said reluctantly, 'Yes, I suppose they do. But please . . . I understand a number of people are affected in one way or another by this news . . .'

'People who missed a handout in his will, you mean?'

'Yes.'

'Members of this Frenchman's family?'

'I've told you all I know.'

'Mr Spurling, you don't mind me saying you're being excessively secretive about all this.'

'I'm telling you all I was asked to pass on to you. That and the request to ask your wife and Romilly to be discreet when they receive the news.'

Discreet. That was going to be hard for a seventeen-year-old heiress.

It was raining in New York. Hot and raining. Even in daylight, the sidewalks glittered with neon reflecting from every direction. But I felt good. Like a kid I splashed the puddles. My daughter had just inherited twenty eight million dollars. And I was free forever from the old witch in Boston.

My first thoughts as I had left the Spurling office had been that I'd keep this piece of information from Margot for the time being. Why? I'm not sure. I'd choose a time to let her have it with maximum impact. Both barrels. I wasn't going to throw away a piece of news like this. I had too few items I could use to excite, astonish or amaze her. And I'd needed to do that of course, had needed to all my life.

My second thought, or set of thoughts, made me feel really good. Passing this news on to Elaine and Romilly was an opportunity, an excuse for contact with them which I hadn't had for two years. More than that it seemed to open up a new connection with them, something totally unrelated to the unhappy past.

Even more than that, I would have to fly to France. Things would have to be discussed. Papers would have to be examined. I would have a function in their lives.

I might even be able to manoeuvre myself into being forgiven.

On his way out of Villefranche, old Auguste Martin always considered that when he reached the stone monument to the Resistance fighter, Pierre Coultard, shot on the roadside here by fascist fanatics in the winter of 1942, that he had reached halfway up the steep road to the Château St Juste where his sister, Bernadette, worked. Nearly eighty years old, he found the five kilometres by bicycle from Villefranche more and more wearing on his aged muscles. But the flat few hundred metres passing Pierre's monument were always welcome. Somehow, playfully, he liked to imagine that he owed the respite to Pierre and he never failed to lift his beret as he cycled past.

For a moment, as so often these days, he found himself lost in memories. Memories of the seventeen-year-old Resistance hero. After the war, Marcel Coultard had been presented with his brother's posthumous *Légion d'Honneur* by the Prefect of the Alpes Maritimes himself in a ceremony at the spot where young Pierre was gunned down in 1942.

That winter of 1942 . . . the most exciting days in Auguste's life. A Resistance fighter working under Marcel Coultard's Committee of Seven. Danger everywhere . . . Not from the Germans of course. They were still ruling northern France from Paris as they had since their lightning victory in 1940. It was not till the end of 1942 that Hitler had decided he needed to occupy the rest of France, the so called Free Zone, from more or less the mid-point of France all the way down to the Riviera coast.

No, there had been no Germans down here to shoot Pierre Coultard. He was shot by Frenchmen, by young anti-Semitic fanatics. Auguste spat into the roadside dust. Pierre had been ambushed by a squad of the special police of the French Commission for Jews, caught leading a column of Jewish women through the forest to safety. The young fascists had dragged his body to a tree by the side of the road and bound it upright to

64

the trunk. The Jews, mostly women and children, had scattered in the thick woods. Some of them were believed to have escaped. The rest were captured and beaten and shipped to the East under the new French anti-Semitic laws. The Free Zone was far from free if you were a Jew.

It was hours before anyone had been able to go up to recover Pierre's body. Auguste had been appointed lookout on the road not yards from where he was passing now. It was early dawn, the hills surrounded in November mists. Maître Jean Rolin, the lawyer, and Marcel, Pierre's brother, had formed the burial party. You can't leave a body up here. Pierre had, by then, been torn to shreds by forest animals, by rodents and the wild boar that roamed the area. When Marcel and Jean Rolin arrived to bury him they reported two enormous buzzards were at work. But Pierre's face was clearly recognisable. On it, something approaching a smile, Rolin always swore in his cups. But Marcel had freely admitted being close to breaking as he removed his brother's crucifix.

Taking advantage of the short stretch of flat, Auguste took one hand from the handlebars and snatched off his beret as he passed the limestone monument. The young ones drove past without noticing, but the senior citizens of the village still refused to miss an opportunity to salute, not just Pierre Coultard, but those days of high excitement, of dangerous endeavour. They were saluting their youth. As the road became steeper again and he pressed harder on his pedals, old Auguste Martin felt that special kick of pride at his own part in those years when resisters were simply those who believed that what the new French government at Vichy was doing to the Jews was un-French. Just sing the *Marseillaise* once through, Marcel used to say, and you'll know the arrest and internment of Jews is wrong.

This was a ferociously steep section of the road and Auguste had acquired the habit, in the last year or two, of getting off his bicycle and pushing it for the next hundred metres. Passing a group of young Scandinavian hikers as they branched into the woods, Auguste found it difficult not to think that in a few minutes these tall brown bodies – the girls he was thinking about, of course – would be swimming naked in the lake below. No shame, these Scandinavian girls.

He let the bicycle slow to a halt and laboriously dismounted. Breathing hard, he pushed on the handlebars. A car, a vehicle of some sort passed him. His head down, tongue out, Auguste counted the steps until the road would flatten out again. He had reached forty when he heard the cry. His hearing was too distorted to be able to locate it. A woman's cry, one of the Scandinavian girls perhaps, who'd slipped on the path down to the lake. He pressed on.

The woods came tight up to the roadside here, trees hanging like trailing garden plants from the white limestone rocks that seemed to want to reach out to form an arch overhead. Even on a good day, there was never more than a thin slot of sunlight on the road.

For a moment he thought the sudden change of light was deceiving him. Fifty metres ahead something seemed to be blocking his way. A *sanglier*, a wild male boar perhaps. He blinked. Certainly it had the shape of a boar and was moving, humping its back as if ready to attack. He stood there uncertainly. Mostly, wild boar he had seen had thudded away into the woods but he had heard stories of wounded animals, crazed with pain, a hundred kilos of violent power . . .

He was ready to swing his bicycle round, get on and pedal fast down the mountain when a sound made him hesitate. A human sound.

The old man moved forward cautiously. When he was thirty metres away, the light changed, lost its sharpness and he saw it all differently. A young woman lay on the roadway. She was moving, struggling to get up and falling forward onto her face. He dropped the bicycle and stumbled forward. He could see the blood now, trickling among the dust and stones of the road. Reaching her, he saw it was a young girl, in a tennis skirt and bloodstained shirt. Her face was torn and her blonde hair matted with blood.

He looked down helplessly at her. He would have to get her off the road. Again she humped her back in an attempt to bring herself upright. Sounds were coming from her, like an animal whimpering in pain. Auguste leaned down and took her under the arms. Dragging her, aware of the harsh road surface tearing at her bare knees, he got her to the roadside before he let her slip from his trembling arms.

He knelt beside her. The face was turned towards him, the eyes seemed to be looking at him but there was so much blood he couldn't be sure. And yet he knew her. He forced his racing mind to slow down. That American girl who lived beyond the olive grove.

'I'll get help,' he said. 'You understand? I'm going to get help.'

He got to his feet. His head was swimming. It was fewer kilometres up to the château, but far easier to ride back down to Villefranche. With a last glance at the girl, lying there, her eyes open in her bloodied face, he got onto his bicycle and pushed off down the hill.

Elaine ran across the stone bridge over the River Bol and only slowed as she came through the arch below the watchtower. For a moment she stopped, her eyes raking the Place Mistral for a girl in a white tennis skirt. The square was almost empty. Three men were cleaning up after the market, their wide brooms sweeping in slow rhythmic movements, bringing up clouds of pale, sunlit dust. She moved quickly forward through the dust. She was looking for a familiar face, any familiar face. The café tables around the square were full of tourists, bereft of anyone she recognised. A moment's thought would have told her. Lunchtime, Friday. Most of the local workmen would be eating at home. She fought to remain calm, but instead panic seized her. Dread. Then she saw Emile, the waiter at the Café de la Paix.

She threaded her way through the tables at a pace that made him turn towards her.

'Emile,' she said. 'You haven't seen Romilly, have you?'

'Not since she came back from tennis.'

'She passed through the *place*?'

'She was in a hurry, I think.'

'But she crossed the square, heading for home?'

'The stalls were packing up. Produce everywhere. The usual mess. Romilly was dodging between the vans.'

Somewhere distantly, down towards the coast they both heard sirens. Their heads came up at the same moment, listening until the sound faded. But the idea had been planted.

'I must see Sergeant Duval,' Elaine said, her voice shaking. 'I want the police involved.'

Lucien Duval came awake quickly when he heard Elaine Chapel in the outer office. The panic was there, clear in the pitch of her voice. He heard her daughter's name spoken: Romilly.

He opened his office door. Elaine Chapel stood against the

67

counter, one hand to her face, the other slapping the woodwork. 'What is it, Madame?'

Before she could answer the door swung open and Auguste Martin almost fell into the narrow lobby. 'Lucien,' he said breathlessly. 'Quickly, *mon vieux*. There's a girl in the road.'

In that second of quiet as everybody absorbed the meaning of Auguste's words, Duval heard the intake of breath hiss through Elaine's clenched teeth.

'On the way up to St Juste,' the old man said. He was waving his arms, urging Duval and the two duty gendarmes to move. 'She's hurt.'

'You left her?' Elaine swayed in the middle of the sweltering reception.

'I moved her to the side of the road. I moved her to safety, Madame.'

'Hurt you say. How badly?'

'She'll be all right,' Auguste said. 'But I had to leave her. I had to get help, Madame.'

Duval turned towards the two men behind the counter. 'Get an ambulance up to the St Juste road.' As the young gendarme picked up the phone Duval turned back to Auguste. 'Where is she?' The sergeant gripped Auguste's wrists to support him. 'How far up?'

For a moment the old man fought for breath. 'Say half-way. Just past the monument.'

'Look after Auguste,' Duval said to one of the gendarmes. 'Find him a chair and a glass of something from the medicine cabinet.' He placed both the old man's hands flat on the counter and turned to Elaine. 'Perhaps you'd like to come with me, Madame?'

# 11

'LISTEN TOM,' MARGOT was saying, almost as I stepped through the door. 'I'm for a wild weekend. Add a little spice to our dull lives. Things are slow, you know?'

This was a more carefully presented Margot than she would have been for a casual evening with just the two of us together. She wore a dark blue cocktail dress and heels and a generally soigné look that hadn't fallen into place in five minutes.

'Spice?' I said, dropping my duffel bag down in the hall. 'I thought your life never lacked spice. Never allowed to.'

'Which is why, just now, I feel the need for something special.' She whirled like a blonde Liza Minnelli and stopped dead with a double thumb-click. 'Something different. That's what I need.'

I needed to use the phone to call Elaine in France. I wanted to tell her about my extraordinary interview with Roddam, Spurling. I wanted to tell Margot too but I knew her in this mood. Times like this she wouldn't brook an interest in anyone or anything else. My news would have been shoved aside with a few not even very polite expressions of interest. And we would have very quickly gone back to what was concerning Margot.

I gestured to her dress and tried to produce an upbeat, Manhattan all-fun weekend tone. 'Hey,' I said. 'I didn't know you planned a party.'

'Maybe.'

I was wearing jeans, loafers and a sports shirt. 'We going somewhere needs a jacket?'

She shook her head. 'You're fine as you are.'

'No party.' I was baffled but not displeased. 'That spells a quiet evening in.'

She walked into the big living room and began pouring herself a glass of white wine. I'd introduced her to St Veran and it had quickly become a must-have favourite. 'Did you hear me, Tom, for God's sake? That's what the last few months have been. Too many quiet evenings in. This weekend I'm looking for something different.'

'Sure.'

'So how does wild sound to you?'

'Well okay,' I said. 'How wild?'

She stepped back from the table. 'Pour yourself something. You know where everything is. I was thinking of asking May Palmer over.'

May Palmer was the recently married wife of the owner of a bunch of Canadian technical magazines, none of them big enough to challenge the big names, but profitable enough to make Billy Palmer a millionaire several times over. May herself was short but shapely and sharp tongued. Her friendship with Margot went back to when they were at Sarah Lawrence together. So had she told May about us? Christ, surely she wouldn't be that reckless. May was a talker. More than that she was a drinker. The two combined was dangerous to any friend who handed her a secret. Margot must know that.

I played it frowning, slightly bewildered. 'How does May make for a wild weekend?' I said slowly.

Margot stuck her tongue out at me.

'I'm being nice to you, Tom. May's knocked out about you and me. She wants to get in on the act.'

A threesome. I walked over and poured myself a drink. 'You told her?' I said.

'In strictest confidence. Why not?'

'Her husband knows George, is why not. They do lunch together when George is looking for election funds.'

'Darling, do you really imagine that May would say anything?'

'I've seen her when she's had a few drinks. She's not the soul of discretion, is she?'

'But nobody takes what she says seriously. Anyway, she's one of my closest friends. I trust her.' She waved a hand, irritated. 'More than that, she is really turned on by you.'

'If she is, it went right past.'

'Oh, she's turned on by you, Tom, don't doubt it. You're lusted after. Except I told her: *taste if you dare*, so she's been holding back from the too obvious advance. But she likes you, Tommy. She's hot to come over and see us.'

There was no point in fighting it. Margot had already made

up her mind that it would be that kind of weekend. I could have said no. I could have turned round and gone straight back to Boston. But to what? Instead . . .

'Three-cornered,' I said. 'Well, good. I guess . . .'

But good was not at all what I was thinking. I hadn't been close to Margot for months. The last thing I wanted was to share her. Tonight or any night.

I wanted off the subject of May. I wanted to engage Margot with our *own* concerns. 'Listen,' I said. 'I've been taking your advice. *If the old lady won't tell . . . find out.* Wasn't that what you said.?'

The fine line of her eyebrows rose. She was still leaning against the door jamb, but upright, alert, arms folded. 'Been sneaking through the family papers, have you?'

'I sent the nurse out and ransacked the house. Went through the attic, the study, the general's desk. Everywhere.'

'Tommy!' She was excited now all right. 'D'you get anything? Your real father's name? Who was he? Someone known, I wouldn't mind betting.'

I held the photograph of the little boy running down the quay in my inside pocket. 'I didn't get a name,' I said. 'But I'm getting there.' I was about to produce the photograph but she turned away. I'd failed to keep up the pace.

'Listen Tom,' she said. 'No need to say anything to May when she gets here, about you *not* being General John's firstborn.'

'Why is that?'

'Just don't.'

'Not so much fun if I'm just the half brother? Not quite the same if she finds out she's not taking part in a fully incestuous threesome. Is that it?'

'Just don't mention it, Tom. Okay?' Her mouth was set hard.

My fears rushed to the surface. 'Okay. But does that go for us too?'

'What are you talking about?'

I walked up and down, hands deep in my trouser pockets. 'Are you still interested in someone who turns out not to be your brother? Just half kosher, so to speak.'

'Interested?' She turned her lips down.

'I mean being your brother is a big part of the hit, isn't it?'

She looked at me strangely. An expression I couldn't fathom, one I didn't like. 'Will it be the same, you're asking.' She pursed her lips, a half smile. 'We'll see, won't we? Anyway I'm bored with all this. Let's get May over here.'

I wanted to press on. I wanted to know how she really felt. I knew it was a mistake to push her – it always was. But I had to know. 'Margot,' I said . . .

Her eyes took on that steeliness that had made me pull back even when she was a small girl.

'Don't push it, Tom,' she said. 'I don't care what she told you in that plane. To me, you're still my brother. I don't want to think about anything else. For Christ's sake I wish I'd never known.'

The phone saved me. She wheeled quickly and walked out into the hall.

She was back in seconds, waving her hands dismissively. The mood change was complete. 'Strange alien clicks and whistles,' she said. 'Someone calling from Baffin Island I'd say at an educated guess.'

The phone rang again.

'Shall I leave it?' Margot asked herself, pose dramatic. 'No . . . but, on the other hand, who do I know marooned on Baffin Island?'

She disappeared and came back again in a matter of seconds.

'Alien clicks and whistles repeated? ' I said. Then I saw her white face.

'It's for you, Tom.' Her normally light voice cracked. 'Elaine.'

I don't remember going to the phone, or lifting it. I just remember the awfulness of Elaine's voice.

'It's Romilly,' she said. 'She's had an accident. A terrible accident.' She was sobbing. 'Tom, she's lying here in a coma.'

# I 2

IT WAS LATE afternoon when the British Airways flight dropped towards Nice Airport. I'd done Kennedy–London, London–Nice as the quickest option across the Atlantic. I didn't see the Bay of Angels; I didn't see the Alps, ragged and dark-edged to the north or the rolling smoke of a forest fire along the ridge of foothills to the west; I didn't see the colour washed buildings of the old town or the great hotels along the Promenade des Anglais. Not this time anyway. Instead, the knowledge that I'd be with Romilly within an hour made the few sentences that Elaine had got over to me on the phone buzz like insects in my head. A coma. None of the doctors was prepared to say when she might come out of it, although a scan showed her brain operating undamaged. She had been taken by helicopter to a specialist unit in the *Centre médical* at Nice. The French do these things well. They also have one of the most highly skilled medical sectors in the world. So far, as good as could be hoped for.

What had happened? Well, that was a great deal more confused. Most likely, a hit-and-run driver. But there were unanswered questions. I think that's what Elaine was trying to say on the phone.

I knew I'd learn more soon but, meanwhile the mind needs something to feed on. On the long flight, I let images float through my mind. Images of Romilly as a very serious minded seven year old, blonde hair in a pony-tail, her accent for the first months in the US quite strongly English, then as juvenile conformity took over, a gradual move to American English. She was an Anglo-American in the best sense, feeling no great tugs in either direction. She had grown up in both countries, had made friends in both places. When I last saw her on that disastrous visit to New York, she still spoke like an American. I wondered how she sounded now — if she could speak. But more than that I wondered what sort of young woman she was growing into. Was she direct, briskly competent in handling life like her mother; or was she, God forbid, more of a reflection of my own haunting uncertainties?

It was thinking about her like this, for a longer sustained period than I had ever thought about her, that I began to get some ideas about the sense of distance I had always felt from her, the veil as I sometimes thought of it, between us. Even before that appalling afternoon when she had found Margot and me together.

And now, high over the Atlantic, I thought I began to see something, some chink of light. Those images of Romilly when young were in fact matched against a shadowy figure in the background. The shadow of Margot as a nine, eleven, thirteen, fifteen year old. And once I saw that, I realised how desperately I didn't want Romilly to be like Margot, even to look like Margot. I couldn't take it farther than that, not at this one sitting anyway, but I felt my muddled feelings of guilt sufficiently strongly to call Margot during the short wait at London.

'I called the hospital in Nice,' Margot told me before I could say anything. 'She's stable, better than stable . . .'

I wanted to scream at her to keep out of it. To keep out of Romilly's life because I didn't trust her in it, but I didn't have the courage. I had the courage to say what I'd been thinking about though. That was something I had to say. 'Margot,' I began. 'I wasn't calling about Romilly.'

'Okay . . .' she drawled.

'I was calling about you. About me and you.' I swallowed hard. 'I wanted to say that I think any relationship between us had better end. I think maybe that's better.' Formal, but firm. Well . . . pretty firm.

'Any relationship? Don't be crazy, Tom. We might not be real bio brother and sister – but we've grown up believing we are. That's what counts.'

I took a deep breath. 'I was talking about . . . between us, you know. I meant sex.'

'Oh, *that*, darling. I shouldn't get yourself worked up about that. That's just fun.'

'I mean it, Margot. I've been thinking a lot on the plane . . .'

'You're hysterical, Tommy. Schoolboy guilt. You think if you swear to the good Lord to stop humping your sister, Romilly will be all right. Well, you know it won't make any difference, darling. Romilly will get better without your self-sacrifice. I told you, I called the hospital in Nice after you left. She's reacting to the

74

spoken word. Not speaking yet but reacting to Elaine. It's a first step, the vital one.'

I didn't want to speak to Margot about Romilly's condition, didn't even want to hear good news from her. If there was good news, Elaine would give it to me. 'Margot,' I said, 'I'm not blaming you . . .'

'Terrific,' she said.

'You know what I mean. We got into this as kids. We didn't understand.'

'You're spinning myths,' Margot said. 'We weren't kids. We were adults when this started, bored or randy or just scared of relationships with the outside world. You decide which. But we weren't kids.'

'Okay,' I said. 'Either way, the time's come. It's time to break loose. I mean it.'

'I can hear that.'

'So, as from now . . . it's . . . over.'

There was a long silence.

'We'll stay friends, of course,' I added.

'I expect.'

'But that's all. Like, nothing more.'

'As you choose, brother,' she said huskily. 'Except you're not of course, any longer. My full brother, I mean.' Then she switched wave bands. 'Hey, when you get to Nice, give Romilly a big hug for me, okay? And give yourself one from me, too. If you dare.'

That made me flinch.

I hired a car at the airport, a good, comfortable dark green Renault Laguna. There was a clear, no-frills map provided in the information pack that came with it. It was a straight twenty minute run into Nice, the Mediterranean on my right, then a sharp turn away from the beach restaurants and ten minutes in heavy traffic with every crossing blocked by milling, well-dressed crowds making their way home from work. In the half hour I heard three separate versions of local news on the car radio: National Front departmental election successes in the south, the continuing drought and forest fires and the record number of visitors to the Côte d'Azur this summer.

They were starting on a fourth snap news broadcast, had just made it to the drought of droughts and were about to cover the forest fires again when I swung into the *parking* at the *Centre médical,* a clutch of modern white buildings on the heights above Nice. I moved out of the near hundred degree heat and into the air-conditioned entrance lobby. For a second I stood dazed at the bustle of visitors and staff in white coats and the proliferation of signs. Then I moved forward. I didn't need the reception desk. I took the green signs to intensive care, the glass elevator lifting me to the fourth floor.

I emerged in a quiet, bare, pale grey corridor. Sunlight filtered coolly through smoked glass. Three floors below me people, mostly in white coats or uniforms moved purposefully up staircases and along interior walkways. Their movement had that stilted balletic quality of an old science fiction film. Ahead, my way was blocked by two middle-aged nurses at a white desk. A portly French cop, hatless, in short-sleeved blue shirt and leather cross band came forward, but let the nurses handle it.

I was explaining who I was when Elaine came out of a room on the right and closed the door carefully behind her. For a moment she didn't see me. She had stopped, her eyes cast down as if examining the polished diamond pattern of the terracotta floor.

She looked terrible. Desperate and utterly alone. The slightly bent eyeglasses she wore, having had no time I guess for her contact lenses, added to the effect. She was wearing jeans and a yellow shirt. I hadn't seen her for over two years but the time alone would never account for the drawn pallor of her tear-smudged face. There was a rip in the knee of the jeans and a big rusty blood stain down the right bosom of the shirt.

She looked up. I was suddenly scared at how she was going to react. But I needn't have been. 'Tom,' she said and put her hands out to me.

I stepped past the nurses' desk and put my arms around her. For a few moments she just rocked back and forth in my arms. I didn't look down but I think her eyes were closed. I was terrified there'd been some further news. I had to say it. 'How is she? Any change?'

'She's alive,' Elaine said into my shoulder. 'At this moment, that's all that counts.' She broke free, but kept one arm round my waist. 'The doctors are with her,' she said. 'We can get a cup of coffee in the canteen.'

I shook my head. 'I want to see her first,' I told her. 'I couldn't sit drinking coffee without seeing her. Is she out of the coma?'

She shuddered. 'She surfaced for a few seconds . . . mumbled one or two words, then slipped away again. Just go and look at her. You'll understand.'

She moved to the door she had just left, knocked briefly and went in. Seconds later the door opened again and Elaine held it wide for me to enter.

Two young men in white coats were standing back from a high white medical bed. I don't know what I expected, but I had never thought she would be lying there bandaged like a mummy. One foot, one arm and a centre section of her face were uncovered. Her eyes were closed and an oxygen feed was taped to her nose. Wires and leads connected her to monitors on a side shelf. She was being drip fed.

I stood over her. Every time she breathed out a small bubble of saliva formed on her lips. No expression, no movement, no sign of life except that small fragile bubble of air on her lip.

I've felt useless in my life, worthless, supernumerary – but never anything like this. I leaned forward and touched her unbandaged hand. Two tiny drops of liquid exploded on her wrist and I realised the tears were mine.

Outside the room Elaine and I stood together in silence. We'd sometimes half-turn and look at each other, then turn away. We were both fighting to get some control back. I was fighting with the idea of the coma. How could the doctors have reported the brain activity was normal. Normal for what? For the most profound, dreamless sleep?

Yet, looking at her, that's not the way it seemed. Perhaps it was a straight translation of my fears but as I looked for something behind those closed eyes, I saw her mind as a black space dead to the life that flowed through her veins and arteries. Dead to words spoken to her, to kisses, to tears dropping on her hand.

The anguish I felt was not just a new level of pain. For me, it was a new level of feeling anything, joy or misery. I didn't understand it, but it was as if, through the anguish, I had reached a new sense of being alive.

I was aware Elaine was looking at me. 'Hard to take, uh?' She closed her eyes and shook her head, then opened them. 'It gets no easier.'

'She'll come through,' I said. 'She'll come through.'

'Let's get some coffee,' she said. 'The doctors say they need half an hour.'

We took the elevator to the ground floor. Just inside the main doors a green on white sign pointed to the cafeteria. There were no more than a dozen or so people there, mostly nurses and very young student doctors in white coats. The *plats du jour* for dinner that evening were written on a large blackboard beside the self-service counter: quail or boeuf bourguignon. Johnny Halliday played low on the stereo. Every now and again he was interrupted by a whispery female voice making a call for one of the staff and someone stubbed out their cigarette in a blue *Loterie Nationale* ashtray, pushed their chair away from the table and hurried out.

Elaine and I sat opposite each other. Across the table I stretched out and held her hand. She didn't pull back.

'I'd gone up to the village,' Elaine was saying. 'I was in the gendarmerie when this old man almost fell through the front door. He was yelling something. It took me a minute or two to realise he was saying there was a girl lying in the road.'

'She'd been on her way home . . .'

'Yes . . . No.' She took a deep breath. 'I don't understand any of it, Tom. I think I'm too dazed or exhausted to be thinking clearly. But she was found on a road on the other side of the village. Two, two and a half miles away at least. The road leads up to the lake and the old flooded village. She definitely wasn't on her way home.'

'Home would be in the other direction . . . ?' Elaine nodded and I was engulfed by a sense of loss. A sharp awareness that I couldn't even envisage where my daughter had lived the last six years. A sense of shame that my daughter was a stranger to me. Might now remain a stranger for ever.

'The mystery,' Elaine said, 'is that we know she *was* on her way home at midday. Someone had actually seen her walking across the market square. How in God's name did she get knocked down three kilometres away on a mountain road minutes later?'

'What do the police say?'

'I don't know. Somebody asked me a few questions, local police – I don't remember my answers. I just got into the ambulance with Romilly. When they realised at the local hospital how serious it was, I stayed with her in the helicopter that brought her here. I've been here overnight.' She looked down at the stain on her shirt. 'As you can see.' Slowly she lifted her head. 'Thanks for coming, Tom.'

'You don't have to say that.' I hesitated. 'Or maybe you're saying something else. Thanks for coming alone.'

She paused, then nodded. 'You know she phoned?'

'Don't worry,' I said. 'There was no chance of me bringing Margot.'

We both looked up as a shadow fell across the table. A man of slightly more than medium height was standing there, slender, about forty-five-years old. He wore a well cut pale grey suit. He had something of an egg shaped bald head, tanned brown, and with thick dark hair curling at the sides. His face was long and sallow. A wide, well-shaped mouth just stopped the general impression short of morose. As I half turned towards him, I saw a second figure, taller, older than the other, about fifty-five, a man with tight, African hair with a light surface fuzz of grey, a mid-brown complexion, a sharp European nose and a fine sweep of African lips. From Somalia perhaps.

Two young uniformed gendarmes waited just inside the doorway.

The first man extended his hand to Elaine. 'Madame Chapel?' There was a faint interrogative in there somewhere. 'Jean-Claude Fabius,' he said in English. 'I am the *juge d'instruction* appointed in this matter.'

'Judge?'

He nodded. 'In serious cases, the French practice is always to have a judge directing the investigation.' He turned to me. The interrogative was in his eyebrows this time.

'I'm Romilly's father,' I told him. 'Tom Chapel. I just flew in from the United States.'

'Bien,' he murmured. We shook hands and turned to the tall, slender man beside him. 'This is special investigator, Lieutenant Polydore Bisset, based at gendarmerie headquarters at Nice. He will be conducting the investigation into your daughter's accident.'

Elaine nodded without speaking.

'Accident?' I said. 'You mean someone's been to the police. Someone's reported an accident?'

The lieutenant leaned across and shook hands with Elaine, then me. 'It's terminology, Monsieur Chapel. It'll be recorded as an accident until it's proved not to be,' he said, also in English, but this one had learned to speak with an American instructor.

I could see Elaine was looking distressed. 'But she was nowhere near where she was supposed to be. It just couldn't have been an accident . . . She was *taken* to where she was found.'

Maybe it was plain exhaustion but I was already confused. Or maybe we were just behaving like all parents in circumstances like these. I turned to Fabius. 'In serious cases, you said, Monsieur. Doesn't that mean you have already decided that there was a serious crime committed here? That *you* think Romilly was attacked?'

'No,' Fabius said formally. 'It's a serious case if it's a hit-and-run. We start with the most obvious, the most likely scenario. A case of a young man taking a girl for a ride on the back of a motor-bike, a little too much showing off, a little too much speed, an accident at a stretch of road with loose gravel . . . Afterwards the boy is too afraid to admit it.' He raised his shoulders. 'You have to admit it happens every day.'

'Not to our daughter it doesn't,' Elaine said.

'I didn't mean to imply it was an event of no consequence.'

I felt my anger rising. 'So do you have the name of this young man with the motorbike?' I asked. 'His description.'

Fabius looked at me. 'It was a hypothesis, Monsieur, as I'm sure you're aware.'

'Look, Romilly was expected home for lunch,' Elaine said firmly. 'She'd made a point of telling me she'd be back. There was no way that she was going to go riding on the back of a friend's motorbike while I was waiting for her at home. As a matter of fact she has a horror of motorbikes. You'll simply be wasting your time pursuing the accident theory.'

Fabius nodded gravely. 'Very well. I'm sure that will be noted. The point I'm making Madame Chapel, is this. Your daughter was last seen that day in the market place. Crossing the market place. We have the deposition of the waiter, Emile. But she was not seen at the town gate. She was not seen passing through the gate. She was not seen on the road on the far side of the gate – or on the bridge over the Bol. Immediately, those are the moments we need to fill in. Please excuse me now. I'll leave Lieutenant Bisset to take over.'

Very politely, but coolly, he shook hands with us both and turned towards the door, then paused and turned back. His expression was thoughtful. 'It will perhaps be helpful to remind you that this is a French investigation. Not English, not American. Of course the object is the same in each case.' He addressed himself to Elaine. 'It is possible we shall find we can rule out an accident, Madame Chapel,' he said. 'But please understand our procedures, please appreciate that they have a logical basis: what happened to your daughter is technically an accident until we have forensic evidence of anything more. Lieutenant Bisset is investigating that accident.'

I wasn't sure of this man. He seemed to be unnecessarily playing with words, ideas. And somehow his clothes seemed too good, his cologne too subtly expensive. I bet the pale yellow shirt was handmade in Paris. It didn't help that I was unshaven, haggard from a long flight, shabby, in tired jeans and a leather jacket. But I'd read just enough about French investigations to know that the supervising judge, perhaps close to our District Attorney in this context, could make or break a case.

'May I join you?' Bisset, who had been standing slightly away from us while Fabius held the stage, now came forward as the judge turned for the door.

'Of course,' I said. I watched him lean over to take a chair from an adjoining table. The physical dexterity was impressive. He seemed to swing the chair into place, sit and draw out a note-book all in one single fluid movement. For a moment he sat staring at the blank page. He was an unusually good-looking man, confident with unhurried movements. Dark eyes folded deep below his brows made for an unsettling steadiness in his regard, a continuous assessment, calculation, even.

Judge Fabius had reached the canteen door. I got up quickly and called after him. He stopped while I caught up with him, looking slightly put out at my unseemly shout across the canteen. Well, to hell with him.

'Monsieur Fabius,' I said, trying to organise my thoughts as I crossed the room to stand next to him. I glanced back to see that Elaine was absorbed, talking to Bisset. 'There's something you should know,' I said to Fabius. 'Something I haven't even had a chance to mention to my wife . . . to Romilly's mother yet.'

His chin lifted a centimetre or two. 'Something you should have told me?'

I ignored that. 'In the last week, my daughter has been willed a very large sum of money,' I said.

'And why are you telling me this?'

I looked at him, baffled. 'Why . . . ?'

'Yes.'

'For Christ's sake,' I said, 'because I think you ought to know. A very large sum.'

'You're suggesting there is a link with the accident?'

'I don't know. But it's possible, isn't it?'

'On what grounds?'

I was going to get nowhere with this man. The lieutenant with Elaine had to be more sympathetic. 'I just thought you ought to know. That's not so fucking unreasonable, is it? You might even want to follow it up.'

He looked at me, steely-eyed. 'Thank you, Mr Chapel. In fact, I'm well aware of the situation.'

That really surprised me. 'You are? You are? How?'

He took a deep breath, exasperated himself. 'This investigation began the moment your daughter was found, Monsieur. I immediately ordered the compilation of a dossier with all relevant facts. That information emerged among them. I have no reason to believe it is significant.'

'You looked into the question?'

Slowly: 'I don't believe it's significant. I informed Lieutenant Bisset of my view.'

'Great.' I nodded abruptly and walked away. I was close to the end of my tether. But I knew who had the upper hand here. In the coming days we, Elaine and I, were going to need Monsieur Fabius a lot more than he was going to need us.

'Mr Chapel . . .'

I slowed and half turned back to him.

'I did point out that this was a French investigation. But be sure we'll call on you should we require your help.'

I should equally have pointed out that it might have been a French investigation, but the victim was my Anglo-American daughter. And that gave Elaine and me certain rights of involvement. But I didn't. I nodded to Fabius and turned away to where Elaine and Bisset were sitting. The lieutenant was leaning toward her, the right degree of concern on his face. I liked this better.

'Let me ask you first,' Bisset was saying, 'about how your daughter might have got nearly three kilometres up on the road to St Juste if she was *not* given a lift on a friend's motorbike. Did she have transport of her own? A car? A bicycle? Does your daughter have a bicycle, or a Solex perhaps, Madame?'

Elaine raised her head. She had obviously been miles away. Or more likely a few dozen yards away, upstairs in intensive care with Romilly. 'A bicycle? No, no bicycle.'

The lieutenant made a note. Then looked up, holding a long pause, the dark eyes shadowed by the brows. 'Madame Chapel, have you any reason to believe Romilly was afraid of something? Of someone?'

She shook her head, baffled. 'Afraid of someone? Not at all. Why do you ask?'

'This morning I went to see her tennis instructor at the little sports centre they have at Villefranche. I wanted to check times – when the lesson ended, how long Mademoiselle Chapel, Romilly, took to collect up her things and leave the tennis courts. While the instructor was giving me the information I wanted, she mentioned a man Romilly said had been following her. Not a young man. Romilly had laughed about it, as some young women do. A flasher, she'd called him, although I don't believe she meant he had actually exposed himself to her.'

'A stalker?' I looked at Elaine.

Bisset nodded. 'A stalker. Yes, that would be the word.'

She grimaced. 'She said nothing to me.'

'Does Fabius know about this?' I said.

Bisset nodded and concentrated on writing in his notebook. 'She must have friends at school I could check with,' he said without looking up. 'Friends she would have talked to, about any fears of a stalker.'

'Her closest friend is a German girl named Anne-Marie Schiff,' Elaine told him.

'And her school is?'

'The International School at Sophia Antipolis.'

He made another note. 'Let's think about the time she took to get her tennis things together and cross to the market square. The tennis instructor said she left on time, early even, three, four minutes before midday. In which case the waiter's story, that she was crossing the square as the midday klaxon sounded the end of the market, that checks out.'

He moved in the slender, splay legged chair, pulling it forward towards the table. 'Then,' he said, 'there's the old man's story. Auguste Martin. Do you know him?' Again to Elaine.

'Everybody in Villefranche knows Auguste. He used to be the blacksmith. He's a good man. A *Légion d'honneur* for resistance during the war.'

'But he's old. Can we trust the times he gives us?'

'What does he say?' I asked, to get into the exchange.

'He says that he delivered some haricot beans to Madame . . .' he checked his notebook. 'Madame Noyer . . .'

'A widow who lives on the other side of the village,' Elaine said.

Bisset nodded, ran a hand across his grey hair. 'He claims he had already left Madame Noyer when he heard the market klaxon.'

'What's the importance of that?' I said.

He turned and lifted his hand. One of the young gendarmes came forward. 'Get me a coffee, will you? And something for yourselves.' He handed the gendarme a hundred franc note.

The confidence was easy. The accent when he spoke French, I noticed, was not local. Parisian. He watched the gendarme order his coffee at the counter, then turned back to me.

'The importance of the timing is this, Monsieur Chapel. If the waiter was right about the klaxon. And Monsieur Martin was equally right, it seems certain that your daughter was invited, enticed or forced into a vehicle within minutes, even seconds of having started to cross the crowded square. Where exactly that happened we don't know. As Monsieur Fabius has pointed out, nobody saw her leave the far side of the market place, pass under the arch or cross the bridge.'

'Oh God . . .' Elaine said with an exhausted, terrified shake of her head. 'So she *was* abducted?'

'Unless . . .' He waited while the gendarme placed the espresso on the table, his change next to it. 'Unless she accepted this ride willingly?'

She shook her head in distress. 'No, no I'm sure she didn't. Whether she knew him or not, if someone took her up there then it must have been against her will.'

He nodded. 'That's my impression too, Madame.'

'As I understand it, that's not what Monsieur Fabius thinks,' I said.

Bisset drank his small espresso in two quick gulps and stood up. 'At this stage it would be too early to guess what the impressions of Monsieur Fabius are,' he said expressionlessly.

As he was leaving Bisset gave me a quick movement of his head which seemed to mean he wanted speak to me alone. I told Elaine

I'd walk him to the lobby. She nodded, too distracted to attach any significance to what I was doing.

We passed through the swing doors and stopped just inside the broad lobby. His eyes tracked lazily from side to side. I wondered if he were thinking the same as me, that, despite the white coats, the lobby looked more like a five star hotel. But there was a air of efficiency and restraint about the building, no cheap 'in house' modern art decorating the walls. No welded sculpture presented by a local exhibitionist. Instead a few Picasso reproductions, a Miró, a Kandinsky, *La Place du Marché à Murnau*. A reassuring severity. A level of taste which was more than modern municipal.

'Will you be staying at Madame Chapel's house?' he asked.

'We haven't talked about it, but I'm sure I will. If I need to, how do I get in touch with you?' I asked him.

'My office is here in Nice.' He handed me a blue card: *Lieutenant Polydore Bisset, gendarmerie Nationale, Rue de la gendarmerie, Nice.* 'You can get in touch with me here.'

'Thank you.' I took the card. 'You had something to say to me.'

He dropped his notebook into his inside jacket pocket. His jacket moved back with the movement. I could see the gun strapped underneath his arm. 'I wondered if you had any questions you wished to ask me that you would have preferred not to ask with your wife present.'

I thought for a moment. 'We've thrown out the accident theory. So there was a purpose. A motive.'

He inclined his head like a teacher approving a smart pupil's question. For a moment that was as far as I could go. In these circumstances the mind of the victim, even a secondary victim as I was, works in heavy, cumbersome movements. A protective mechanism, I suppose. Bisset seemed to understand this. He was giving me time.

Ugly thoughts edged their way into my mind. 'Tell me,' I said.

He hesitated, then looked me in the eye. 'If you haven't thought of it already, you will. I've checked with the doctors, there's no evidence of sexual assault.'

'Thank God . . .'

He held up his hand. 'I didn't want to say this before your wife, but it's likely that it was only a matter of time.'

'You mean that's what he was planning. That, whoever it was, just didn't have time?' I leaned back against the wall. I'd never dealt with ideas like this in my life. 'The arrival of the old man, Auguste Martin, saved her?'

'No . . .' he said thoughtfully. 'My guess would be that the group of Norwegian hikers saved her.'

I frowned.

'There was a group of young Scandinavians going down to the lake. Monsieur Martin passed them. I've spoken to them. Nobody can describe the vehicle that passed, but most of them are sure there was one.'

'So whoever abducted Romilly drove past them?'

'But didn't realise they were about to turn off the road. He thought they'd be coming round the bend in seconds.'

'And that saved her. From rape.' I felt a sour nausea rise in me.

'We're still speculating, Monsieur Chapel, but it fits with your daughter's conversation with the tennis coach about a stalker. Street thieves don't spend days following potential victims.'

He was looking past my shoulder at the men passing between the main doors and the elevators. 'You always ask yourself, what sort of man?' he said, almost musing to himself. 'What sort of man might be responsible for something like this?'

*The man responsible.* In the flood of concern about Romilly, I had hardly thought of the man who had done this to her. I had thought of her, not him. Until now.

'She would have put up a fight,' I said. That seemed to be important to me. The idea of her lying passive while she was pawed by this creature was intolerable.

'There were what could be defence bruises and cuts on her forearms.'

I took a step away from him towards one of the lobby windows. In the rear courtyard two men were reloading an ambulance with portable oxygen cylinders. When I turned back to him I'd formulated my question. 'If it's a stalker, will he be back?'

'Here at the hospital? Highly unlikely, but not something we should take for granted. The city police have a man there, but I'll arrange for our people to take over, the gendarmerie.'

'And afterwards? When she's recovered? When she's back home?'

'Far too early to say, Monsieur. And no point in speculating that far ahead.'

'They're obsessives, aren't they? Isn't that the way it goes?'

He lifted his shoulders. 'If it's as we think. If it was the stalker.' He held out a long brown hand and shook mine. 'Any time you want to talk . . . you have the number.'

'You mean that?'

'I mean it, Monsieur.'

I turned to make my way back to the canteen, but I found myself incapable of moving. I'm not sure how long I stood in the centre of the lobby, lost in thought. A few minutes ago, I had seen what was happening to Romilly in terms of her alone – when would she emerge from the coma? How deep would be the trauma she would suffer? How long would it take her to recover from the physical damage?

I had rejected any idea of an accident but it had not, until a few moments ago, really penetrated my confused and scrambled consciousness that that meant a man, a man with an age, a shape, a job, a man with a motive, with the intent to do evil, maybe the worst evil, murder, to my daughter.

I was breathless. I knew I should go back to the canteen. I knew Elaine was waiting. I looked for something to focus my thoughts on, to take them off the man who had done this. All around me people were moving purposefully across the lobby. The glass elevators slid past each other in a silent pattern of movement. The two gendarmes were already outside in the fore-court, catching up with Bisset.

I couldn't go back to Elaine feeling like this. Feeling so full of pent-up anger, I could not behave in a manner that passed for normal even in these totally abnormal circumstances.

Instead I walked back and forth across the wide lobby, trying to concentrate on Elaine and what I could do to relieve her burden. My immediate problem was how much to tell her. Should I tell her that the police thought Romilly had narrowly escaped being raped? That somehow her struggles had deterred him? Or perhaps she was already way ahead of me. She didn't believe it was an accident, either. She didn't believe Romilly had got into a car willingly. Okay, as Lieutenant Bisset was saying, it wasn't any big jump to guess what he wanted her for.

Then suddenly I was no longer thinking sequentially. Thoughts circulated bizarrely in my head, coloured images zoomed like alien ships in a cheap space movie. I had stopped in the middle of the lobby. I was attracting glances from the security men in the grey uniform near the door. One of them was actually coming forward. What was happening to me? Was this shock? Was this what it did to you?

I began again, walking back and forth across the lobby. Somehow this attracted less attention. The security man dropped back. But, passing the central reception desk each time, I still collected a glance from the duty receptionist. After a minute or two I could feel some normality returning. With an effort I redirected my thoughts to Bisset, trying to assess him as an investigator. That helped. Lieutenant Bisset might well be right for this job. But I was thinking that I was distinctly unimpressed with Fabius when I heard my name spoken over at the desk.

# 13

A FRENCHWOMAN IN a dark suit with dark chestnut hair held back by a black ribbon, was leaning forward, talking to the receptionist behind the desk. She was gesturing with her sunglasses in one hand and held a briefcase in the other. From this angle I couldn't see the woman's face and couldn't be sure of her age. But I had heard the words clearly. She was asking if a Monsieur Chapel had arrived to see his daughter in Intensive Care?

The receptionist was offering to call up to the unit and ask, when I came forward and gave my name.

The woman turned.

She was in her early thirties, about five-eight in heels. She had a Mediterranean darkness of skin and eyebrows but the eyes themselves were surprisingly light hazel providing her features with a particularly strong focus. 'I'm Claire Coultard,' she said in English. 'Or I was before my marriage. Claire du Roc now, officially. But I still use my unmarried name.'

I waited for her to go on.

She looked at me, puzzled. 'Coultard,' she said again. Then after a moment. 'Impossible! The name Coultard means nothing to you?'

'No. I'm sorry, Madame,' I said. 'Nothing at all. It's clear that it should.'

'My father was Marcel Coultard from St Juste. The Château de St Juste, a few kilometres outside the village of Villefranche.'

When this further piece of information clearly meant nothing to me she shook her head in bafflement or irritation, I wasn't sure. The eyes widened. She tapped her teeth with her sunglasses, then tried again. 'My father owned Ciné-Coultard, the company your ex-wife works for. He died earlier this month,' she said.

I felt that buzz of tired incomprehension behind my eyes.

She took a deep breath. Speaking slowly, she said: 'My father left his entire estate to your daughter . . .' a movement of her head in the direction of the main body of the hospital, '. . . Romilly.'

Oh, Christ. 'It was your father . . .'

'Yes.'

'I'm sorry, I'm really sorry. The name meant nothing.'

Irritation flickered across her face. 'You *do* know about the will?'

There was something too sharp for me about the tone. I answered, similarly brusque. 'Of course. But the New York lawyer I talked to gave me no details. Not empowered to, he said. Or something of that sort.'

'I see.' She paused. 'You haven't yet seen my father's lawyer, Maître Rolin?'

'There was a meeting arranged in New York.' I gestured. 'Obviously I couldn't make it. Look, I have a thousand questions to ask you, but . . .'

'But just now you have a daughter in a serious condition in Intensive Care.'

'Right.'

'I understand.' She smiled briefly and her teeth showed bright white against her tan southern skin. 'But I'm sure you understand, we do need to talk, Monsieur.'

'I'm sure we do. This just isn't the best time.' We had walked away from the desk and now stopped before the revolving doors. 'You haven't had a long drive over here to see me, I hope?'

'No,' she lifted her leather briefcase. 'My office is here in Nice. I came straight from work.'

'But how did you know I was in France?'

'Word travels down here in the South, Monsieur Chapel.' She paused, her face tightening. 'Are you prepared to talk to me?'

I found myself surprised at the question. 'Of course. Why shouldn't I be?'

'Did he owe you money?'

'What?'

'Did my father owe you money? It's the obvious answer. That he'd mortgaged everything to you.'

I held up my hands. 'Please . . .' I said. 'If you knew the state of my finances . . . Let's start over. I said I'm prepared to speak about all this. But not yet. Not at this moment.'

'Then say we arranged for you to come to the house at the end of the week. Friday perhaps. I'll be there from just after midday.'

Jet lag had shot my reactions to pieces.

'The house?'

'My father's house. The one he left . . .'

'Of course.'

'Château St Juste. It's five or six kilometres above Villefranche – well before you get into the mountains. Anybody in Villefranche will direct you.'

'Villefranche is the village my ex-wife and daughter live in.'

'Correct,' she said, her eyes on me.

'Okay, I'll be there,' I said. 'Château St Juste. Friday.'

'Your daughter . . . I phoned as soon as I heard. Is her condition stable?' The hard look around the mouth had softened.

'That's about it,' I said. 'No more than that.'

'I'm sorry, Monsieur. It's a terrible thing to have happened.'

It's hard to explain how the normal thought processes dissolve at a time like this. I never thought for a moment how Claire Coultard really felt. She had, after all, presumably been deprived of a fortune by her father's bequest to Romilly. Glibly, I assumed her sympathy because she looked and sounded sympathetic.

'Yes, terrible,' I said. She shook hands quickly and her heels were clicking across the tiled floor as Elaine came out of the canteen.

I glanced once more at the Frenchwoman passing through the revolving doors, then turned back to Elaine as she crossed the lobby towards me.

'I couldn't wait any longer,' she said. 'I must get back to Romilly. Who was that?' She peered short-sightedly towards the revolving doors. She hadn't recognised Claire Coultard. She must have known her but Elaine's sight didn't work at that distance in a crowded lobby.

'The woman? . . .' I was about to tell her when I suddenly realised that it was somehow out of the question for me to explain Coultard's bequest now when everything needed to be focused on Romilly. 'Someone from hospital administration,' I said quickly. 'She needed a few details.'

'Let's get back, Tom. We have to keep talking, talking, talking to her. Day and night. It's what the doctors say. It's the only way we can help.'

I looked at her exhausted face, her sweat-runnelled hair, her blood-stained shirt. 'Listen, Elly,' I said. 'Do this for Romilly. Get a cab. Go home. Take a shower and a couple of Lorezepam. I'll take tonight.'

She began to shake her head.

'Elly,' I said. 'This could go on for days. You've got to learn to pace yourself.'

'And what about you?'

'Me,' I said, 'I haven't paced myself for twenty-five years. But I'll learn, too. I promise.'

I spent the night reading to Romilly's blank face from a *Guide to Provence,* all the reading matter that could be found for me at that hour.

It was seven o'clock, a clear, perfect South of France morning. I drove up towards Villefranche sur Bol along twisting roads lined with olive groves, their leaf-bloom a hazy silver green in the early sunlight. Churches across the valleys rang out the bells that had once called workers to mass. Nice fell away behind me, and before me rose the foothills of the French Alps. In the Ancient World, Greeks had been here my *Guide* had said, and, inevitably, Romans, their legions on passage to Spain or northern Gaul. Saracens had been here too, no more welcome in the tenth century than North African Muslims are today. And then, in the early Middle Ages, Provence had blossomed. Its own special language and the luxury of its living had produced the troubadours, the wandering poets who had spread the word of courtly love throughout Europe.

Lack of sleep carried my thoughts, and my head snapped up as I came close to missing the sharp bend in the road ahead. It was a moment that brought me back to the present. Apart from an hour or two during the flight over and catnaps beside Romilly's bed, I had not slept for two nights. I was dog-tired. Yet, much as I needed it, I still didn't want to sleep.

Ahead I glimpsed red roof tiles as the road reared like an angry serpent and within a few hundred yards a red and white roadside sign signalled Villefranche sur Bol. Villefranche is, of course, a common enough name for a French town. The Bol river which distinguishes this Villefranche from a hundred others was now not much more than a trickling summer stream, different I imagined from when the spring snows melted and the water came rushing down from the mountains. I slowed to cross a narrow stone bridge. The village stood above me. On this side at least, the ramparts were still more or less standing and pierced by a narrow stone arched gate with a squat tower above it.

Passing under the gatehouse I found myself quite suddenly among the plane trees and pastel-washed houses of the market square. At first sight Villefranche seemed to me to be more than the village that Elaine had talked about. Maybe less than a town but in the market place there looked to be a good range of shops below the balconied upper windows and even a few offices and a bank among the dominant restaurants and café-bars.

Even at this early hour there was a lot activity, street cleaning, deliveries, café tables being washed down in the Place Frédéric Mistral. If I stayed here long enough I'd no doubt find out who Mistral was, apart from a cool wind that blew down the Rhone valley and across these hills in spring and early summer.

I stopped at the Café de la Paix for coffee. Heavy-eyed, I watched the procession of village women to the baker's shop. Most of them were dark haired, solidly built. A sleeveless flowered apron was standard dress, a square black plastic bag flapping around short legs. Then one of the women would betray some very different racial ancestry, fair-haired and taller from far north of here, harking back perhaps to the times when Provence was a great base for the northern crusading knights.

At the table next to me a man with a small sack across his shoulder began some negotiation with the woman who owned the café. The contents of the sack were at stake. Finally the man swung the sack onto the table in front of him. It rattled as if full of pebbles as the woman delved inside. Handfuls of big pale snail shells were lifted, examined and dropped back into the sack before she agreed the price. Snails, I noticed, figured prominently on the menu-board beside the door.

I finished my coffee and regained the car. But I didn't take the road to Elaine's house. She had given me a key and directions to her house on the edge of the town but the idea of sleep seemed absurd when there was still so much unresolved about what had happened to Romilly. I drove on through the village. It wasn't difficult to get onto the road where Romilly had been found. There was only one way out of town.

I drove slowly. A couple of kilometres or so out of Villefranche, on a steep climb through great pockmarked rocks and umbrella pines, there was a monument to a wartime Resistance fighter on the right and a little further on a gendarmerie jeep with a single driver, his head slumped forward, dozing or listening to a jazz station as the sun came over the high hills

I pulled up well before the jeep. I didn't want to spring any surprises on the gendarme if he was asleep. I slammed my door hard and I saw his head come up. Seeing the Laguna, he quickly put on his kepi and jumped out of the jeep, adjusting his dark blue Eisenhower jacket. Today's gendarmerie is a well turned out, well trained outfit. My former father, General John, would have approved the sharp salute for the stranger.

I introduced myself.

'Romilly's father,' the young man said.

So much for believing you can be a stranger in these parts. 'You know Romilly?'

'Of course. I'm sorry, Monsieur Chapel. In the village, we're all shocked at what happened. I'm Philippe Rodinet,' he said and we shook hands.

I've spent too long in a big city. I should have realised that this young man from the Villefranche gendarmerie, out of uniform and off duty, had probably played *boules* with Romilly on Sunday mornings, maybe even taken her out on a date.

'Perhaps you can tell me,' I said. 'Does she have any special friends, any special boyfriends in the village?'

'Boyfriends? She'll have a coffee with anyone. That's what we all like about her.' He paused. 'She's very young of course,' he said carefully. 'But like most American girls, she seems older. Does she like anyone in particular? I never heard of it.'

'No one with a motorbike?'

'I don't think a moto is Romilly's style.'

'No.'

'She's going to be alright?' the young man said.

'A day or so . . .' I looked out over the tangle of the rock and pine, bright with the new day's sunlight. The herb-scented tang of Provence when the morning sun first hits the hillsides is a powerfully optimistic drug. I smelt rosemary and thyme, pines and wild flowers I could never possibly identify. I took a step or two out onto the road, away from the jeep. I suddenly felt confidence in Romilly's recovery, confidence that all this would turn out right.

I was wrenching my mind from this strange, inappropriate euphoria when the gendarme came forward to stand next to me.

'What's up there if you continue on this road?' I asked him. I pointed to the rocks beyond us.

'Nothing much. There's the lake, Lac St Juste. You can see it through the trees here. And the château. The Château St Juste.'

The château of St Juste, of course. Where the Coultards lived. 'Is there a village to go with the château?'

'No longer. A few years ago they emptied it of people and flooded the valley to make the lake.'

'I can't imagine that was popular.'

'The people resisted of course. The old wartime Resistance Committee of Seven was reformed. There were demonstrations in St Juste and Villefranche. The two villages were always very closely linked. Same families, intermarriage. This was 1973, the riot police, the CRS, were called out and there was violence. Heads got cracked.' He shrugged. 'But it was no use. Paris was determined. A new feeder lake was needed for the reservoirs that would supply all the new tourists coming to the coast. The *toutous* we call them. Marcel Coultard and the Committee decided they were not prepared to kill Frenchmen to defend the valley from flooding. It was a bitter moment for the two villages. Inevitably, Paris won.'

'And the whole village disappeared under water.'

'Except the Château St Juste. The Coultard château. That survived. It's still there – perched on the edge of the lake.'

'The Coultard family have been bound up with this region for a long time, then?'

He shrugged. 'Like everybody else around here.' He pointed to the edge of the road almost opposite where we stood, to the Resistance monument. A headstone flanked by columns framed with carved vine leaves. A military emblem made up of crossed swords, a drum with a large crossed seven worked into the centre. The red paint picking out the number seven had been fairly recently renewed. Then a simple inscription: *Pierre Coultard. Hero of the Resistance. Killed on active service, November 2, 1942. Mort pour la France.*

'That's the Coultard memorial,' Rodinet said. 'Seventeen years old when they killed him.'

'The Germans?'

He expelled breath explosively, bubbling his lips. 'There were no Germans in southern France in the early years, Monsieur.'

I frowned, trying to recall what had happened after the French defeat in 1940.

'People don't realise,' Rodinet said. 'For two-and-a-half years this was the Unoccupied Zone. The so-called Free Zone. This part of France ran itself for most of the war. Or was run by the collaborationists in Vichy. Vichy, what a place to choose for the government of France!' he said with surging bitterness. 'One day our capital is Paris. The next, our government runs off to a collection of hotels and hot springs in a health resort over there in the mountains.' He shrugged contemptuously. 'A health resort for the capital of France.'

I could hear in his angry voice that history was not far away.

He ducked his head, readjusting his kepi 'Pardon, Monsieur Chapel. I was saying, Pierre Coultard was murdered by Frenchmen, by the Vichy police. In those times we were a divided people.'

We walked back towards the jeep. He leaned in and turned off the Dave Brubeck.

'Has anybody decided what exactly happened up here?' I asked him.

'There's not much doubt about what happened, Monsieur. She fell or was pushed from a moving vehicle. The crime scene people took scrapings of brake marks but they weren't optimistic. Too many tyre marks on a steep bend like this. But there was blood too.' He hesitated with a quick glance at me.

I nodded to him to go on.

'Blood where Romilly landed. It's marked off in chalk.'

I looked up the road. I'd missed the heavy blue chalk oval and cross hatching on the black surface. I pushed away the images of Romilly tumbling across the road. I looked past the gendarmerie jeep, uphill. 'And the driver of the car she was in . . . assuming he drove on, where was he going? Up into the hills?'

'Anywhere. Unless he was taking her to some place he has. Like the other one.'

'The other one?' I felt my blood racing. 'There was another girl? Attacked up here?'

He nodded cautiously.

'When was this?' I was bursting to press him for more details

He looked white faced with anxiety. 'Please Monsieur, I shouldn't have said that.'

'This girl, she was found dead?'

He didn't answer but I knew the answer from his expression.

In my pocket I felt the edge of Lieutenant Bisset's card. 'Okay,' I said. 'I'm not pressing you. I'll take it up with gendarmerie in Nice. Your name won't be mentioned – but thanks.'

He nodded.

For a moment, eyes prickling, I stared at him. 'Another girl!' I said. 'Christ!'

Then I walked back to my car. At four or five places in the road I saw black marks which might have been oil or rubber, or might have been blood. It didn't bear thinking about.

L ESS THAN AN hour later, I was standing one side of a wide
desk in the sunlit reception lobby of the Gendarmerie
Nationale. Behind it, three young gendarmes in short-sleeved blue
shirts answered phones and obtained clearance for visitors who
were waiting on black leather benches against the wall. Lieutenant
Bisset was called and I was given a card printed in the national
colours, blue, white and red with my name in large black letters.

A young gendarme led me along the barrel-vaulted, white plastered corridor. At one of several doors along the passage he asked
me to wait and went in. After a few moments he reappeared with
Bisset. They came out, Bisset following the gendarme and shut-
ting the door behind him in that way people have when they
don't want you to see what's inside.

He was slightly more casually dressed than last night. Dark
pants, a dark blue shirt without tie, a beige linen jacket hooked
over his shoulder on his right index finger. With the shoulder
holster he looked like any NYPD black cop.

'We have a self-service upstairs, Monsieur,' he said. 'It's not
bad.'

I nodded towards the door he had just exited. 'Your office is
fine.'

'It's not my office,' he said. 'It's an incident room.'

'Can we use it?' I was anxious to know what he had been
reluctant for me to see.

'Police enquiry rooms are some form of Sartrean hell,' he said.
'Ringing phones, chattering typewriters, cigarettes burning in
overfull ashtrays. You read Jean-Paul Sartre, Monsieur?'

'No.'

'Very wise. But for a policeman, existentialism isn't without
interest. If we could identify that defining moment when a criminal chooses crime over virtue, we could develop a preventive
police philosophy.'

He was already walking down the corridor. 'I can see you think it's all French nonsense.' He smiled. 'How can I help you, Monsieur?'

'Lieutenant,' I put a hand on his arm and we stopped in the entrance of the big lobby.

'I have a question. I should have asked at the hospital.'

The young gendarmes were still taking enquiries at the long desk. The visitors were still lining the long, black benches, and the sunlight from the atrium was bursting on the floor where *Gendarmerie Nationale* was inscribed in dark blue tiles.

Bisset was studying my face. 'You've had no sleep.'

'No.'

'Lack of sleep makes hard times harder. Put your question, Monsieur Chapel. I'll try and answer it quickly. Then go back to your hotel or wherever you're staying and get some sleep. What did you want to ask me?'

'Last night, at the hospital when we were talking about the possibility of an accident . . . What I should have asked was whether there had been any similar cases in the area. I'm talking about attacks now – attacks on young women.'

He grunted and looked down at the tiled floor. 'Perhaps you should go over to the Palais de Justice and talk to Monsieur Fabius,' he said. 'He would have the full departmental record.'

'I'd sooner talk to you. And I'm talking about attacks somehow related to what happened to Romilly. I'm asking a direct question, lieutenant.'

'Because somebody has already told you something?'

'Just talk I've heard. In the café in Villefranche. But there's something to it, isn't there?'

He was silent, his deep brown eyes on me. He was making up his mind. His chin moved abruptly with the decision he had just taken. 'A young woman was attacked earlier in the year,' he said. 'A month or so back.'

'In the Villefranche region?'

'She was left up in the hills there, not far from where your daughter was found.'

'A sexual attack . . . rape?'

'Murder.'

Cold air played on my back, between the shoulder blades, down the spine. 'And Fabius is in charge of that case?'

He raised his eyebrows.

'And the investigating officer?'

'Myself.'

'So Fabius obviously thinks they're connected, despite all his talk about an accident.'

'You don't understand French police administration, Monsieur. Once a case goes from your hands, you don't easily get it back. If Romilly *is* connected with the other young woman, this way I'm in charge of the whole investigation. If not, and it emerges as a simple but tragic accident, we hand her case back to Sergeant Duval at Villefranche.' He paused. 'You'll find Monsieur Fabius is not a fool.'

I swallowed hard. 'Okay. But did he have to hammer this accident business, when he knew, in all probability, it was no accident?

'You'd prefer Fabius told Romilly's mother she had been abducted by a serial murderer – and then found he was wrong? That there really was a boyfriend with a motorbike?' He shook his head.

'No . . . okay,' I said. 'I'm sorry. Let's start over. Do *you* believe there's a link between Romilly and the other girl?'

'I don't know. I suggest you say nothing to Madame Chapel for the moment. We have just one connection linking the fatal attack on the other woman and Romilly. The other girl was taken here in Nice.'

'Taken. Abducted. The same way Romilly was?'

'Maybe.'

'And she was also found no great distance from where Romilly was found.'

A crisp nod. 'On the side of the same ridge, but well off the road. More than a kilometre into the woods.'

'The other young woman . . . Murdered, you said.'

His head moved slowly from side to side. 'A savage attack.'

I clasped my hands behind my back to stop shaking.

'It hardly seems so at the moment, Monsieur, but it may be that Romilly has been lucky.'

I thought of her bandaged almost head to toe, breathing oxygen through a tube, linked up to ECG and SATS monitors. Alive but unable to break through to consciousness. Lucky.

The police canteen was a long room with windows facing onto an inner courtyard. There were twenty uniformed officers, men and women, drinking coffee, or if they'd just come off a relief, preparing to tackle a full-size meal. The self-service counter ran the length of the blind wall; patés, crudités, steak haché, salads, brioches and tartes aux pommes were on offer. Small thirteen centilitre bottles of wine, red and white. Beer. It didn't look a lot like film I'd seen of NYPD canteens. Where was the big tray of donuts?

We collected our coffee and sat down, Bisset apologising that there was no cognac. Colleagues came up and exchanged a few words and it was only hearing Bisset speaking French that I realised how fluent he was in English.

I asked him where he'd learnt it. 'I did a six-month *stage*,' he said. 'An investigatory course with the Illinois State Police.'

'The big hats.'

He smiled. 'I was assigned to the Major Crimes Unit. Interesting.'

He wasn't like any cop I'd ever met. Or even read about. I asked him where he came from.

'I'm French. I was born here. My folks were born here. I never think about being anything else.'

I nodded. We looked at each other for a long moment. 'What is it you have in the incident room you didn't want me to see?' I asked him.

'The usual incident room stuff,' he said. 'Pictures, diagrams.'

'Of the murdered girl?'

He inclined his head. 'More than that, there are a lot of young guys in there. Mostly trying to impress the women officers by their machismo. Incident room humour is not what a man whose daughter has just been attacked wants to hear. Stay away from it.'

I wanted to. The last thing I wanted was to go into that room and see his pictures. I braced myself and took a deep breath. 'I'd like to see anything you can show me,' I said. 'Any details you have. Anything at all.'

'Why?' The eyes hardened. That immediate suspicion cops have of the motives of our world.

'Because I'd like to see what we're up against, the three of us, Elaine, Romilly and myself.'

'I promise you, Monsieur, these are not pictures that a man should see. In police work, we can't avoid it. We're here to put a barrier between people like you and scenes like this . . .'

'So we can pretend the world isn't the way it sometimes is? I've done a lot of pretending in my life.' As a small boy I'd spent the time before sleeping pretending that my mother punished me because she loved me. That's what General John said.

Bisset stood up. 'Okay,' he said. 'Your call.' And I heard the echo of a dozen Illinois State Troopers.

We stopped outside the door to the incident room. He gave me one more chance. 'You sure?' he said.

'I'm sure.'

He pursed his wide lips, doubting the good sense of my decision. 'Okay.'

He opened the door. Narrow metal desks were backed up against the walls, each occupied by an officer, man or woman, in uniform or plainclothes, about twenty of them in all. The sudden chatter of phones ringing, of calls being taken, reminded me of entering an aviary from the silence of the corridor. Cigarettes burned in overflowing ashtrays. I looked through the rising spirals of smoke to the pictures on the walls.

There were several crimes being worked in the incident room with pictures and key details for each. I caught a glimpse of one huge and shocking enlargement of a man's head which had been battered in and I turned away.

'I warned you,' Bisset said.

'Where is she?'

He nodded to the far wall and we walked through the closely placed desks. She was Nicole Tresselli, aged 27, waitress. The information card gave her disappearance from Nice as Sunday, April 5th. In her blown-up main picture, her dark eyes stared from a white – it seemed to me – terrified face. A dead face, puffed up, discoloured. She was mostly naked, lying on her back among rocks and bushes. Her clothing seemed to have been cut away from her, rather than removed. There was the right shoulder strap of her bra still in place but the rest had gone. Her left arm still carried seven or eight inches of the ripped cuff of a white shirt. The rest trailed away out of the picture. On her left foot, ruched round her ankle, was a bloodstained stocking. All over her body there were small cuts as if the murderer had jabbed at her tormentingly, concentrating most obviously on her breasts and pubic region. In one of the smaller photographs, I saw the weals of lashes across her back.

A uniformed gendarmerie sergeant joined us, standing at the desk next to Bisset. A strongly built young woman with full breasts and heavy haunches. Her pocket tab read Sgt Lucienne Barrault. Bisset made a quick introduction and we shook hands. It was a welcome respite.

I turned back to the pictures. 'Was she born here?'

Sergeant Barrault answered. 'Born in Nice. Immigrant North African parents. She took live-in work mostly. She'd served at tables all along the coast from Monaco to St Tropez. Good-looking girl in a North African way. She did a bit of dancing from time to time. Open to the right offers when she was short of money.'

'What does that mean? Prostitution?'

Bisset took over. He shook his head. 'Not professional. Just made a little pocket money from time to time. We hoped to find a little black book, a list of old clients. Cops are always hoping for little black books. No luck, of course.'

'Where was she last seen?'

The sergeant took over again. 'A special market Sunday evening, the *marché nocturne*. Mostly clothes, discs, music equipment. A market for the young. She was seen there by several friends, probably semi-professional like Nicole. It was before the beginning of the tourist season – there wasn't a lot of custom about. She told one of her friends she had a date for that evening.'

'You never traced who with?'

'No. The witness claims Nicole winked and laughed when she asked her who the man was.' She stopped, one hand resting on an officer's desk. 'Nicole then said, according to the witness, something that might have no significance at all. Might have been a joke. Or just might mean something.'

'What did she say?'

'She said: "Who's to say it's got to be just one of them?" On Wednesay they found her body.'

'What was Nicole saying? That there were others involved?'

'Boasting perhaps. Winding up her friend. Claiming clients she didn't have.'

'Was there forensic evidence . . . you know . . .'

'Semen?' the woman sergeant said. 'Yes she'd had sex the evening she died. There was evidence of a condom's spermicide preparation. *And* semen.' She twisted her lips. 'Work that out.'

'I can't. What does it mean?'

'It either means that one man fucked her,' Lucienne Barrault said, 'first with a condom, then, for reasons unknown, without. Or that two men fucked her, one using a condom, the other, not. Or that several men fucked her, all using the same brand of condom, except for the last bastard, who decided not to use one at all.'

I winced. Women talking tough I find hard to take.

'There was also some pubic hair. Not hers,' Lucienne Barrault said. She shrugged.

We walked back along the space between the desks. 'Who found Nicole's body?' I asked Bisset.

'A hill walker with his dog. She was found quickly, before the animals got at her. Some victims . . .' he gestured round the room, '. . . are not so lucky.'

That word again. I glanced at Nicole Tresselli's hideous face and battered body. Lucky.

'No description of a man seen talking to her at the market?'

'No.' He rubbed his eyes. 'Stall-holders, of course. Friends or family members. But no strangers.'

'Usually you can tell, can't you, where they were killed?'

'Sometimes. With Nicole we don't know. Maybe in a vehicle. Maybe out on the hills where she was found.'

'But you don't think she was killed here in Nice?'

'You're too eager for certainty, Monsieur Chapel. I can understand it, but it won't help. We don't have certainty.'

'But you know when she was killed.'

'Not even. Between nine o'clock Sunday when she was last seen at the market – and dawn Wednesday morning when she was found. There were no useful body temperatures to give us the time of death. We've made a guess she died closer to Wednesday morning than Sunday night. Maybe sometime Tuesday.'

'So he took her somewhere?'

'Where she was raped. Tortured with a degree of sophistication . . .' He shrugged. 'And finally killed . . . by drowning. That we do know. A short immersion in water, the head pushed into a stream, possibly even a bath or a bucket.' He gestured to the photographs behind her. 'Then she was taken to the hillside and dumped there, way off the road.'

'Could he have reached the spot by car?'

'No. The body was carried on the killer's shoulder deep into the woods. We traced the route he took through blood splashes. No vehicle could have made it. So we can guess he's probably young. Certainly strong, and fit. You'd have to be to carry a body a kilometre or more across those hills.'

'You'd have to know the hills well, too.'

He nodded. 'So that's what we have in terms of significant connection with Romilly's case. The disappearance during a market?' He waggled his hand to indicate a faint possibility. 'Maybe. But essentially, we have the common location. Even so, I'm not satisfied with our explanation of what happened to Romilly up there, Monsieur.' He stood tugging down the points of his shirt collar. 'I think our man was taking her somewhere. Then something went wrong with the plan and he had to abandon her.'

'You think he has somewhere close by? Some sort of hiding place.'

'Not necessarily that close. We've searched all the farms and shepherd's *bergeries* and caves on three separate sweeps of the area. Those hillsides are hard to search. They're ridged and badly broken with rock outcrops. Yet he certainly has somewhere, how close we can't guess. But I still think it's a place where he kept Nicole for at least twenty-four hours before killing her and dumping her body on the hillside.'

'I see.' I was trying to remain calm but I was shaking at the thought of what might have happened to Romilly. Of what *had* happened to her.

'Come.' He took my elbow. With his free hand he gestured to the horror show on the wall. 'Forget the rest of the gallery and we'll go take a coffee-cognac at one of the cafés on the square.'

I liked Polydore Bisset. Unlike Fabius, he listened. And his manner suggested the sort of common sense that I respect more than that labyrinthine cleverness that I thought I saw in Fabius. I took one more quick look at the pictures on the wall. One showed in close-up Nicole's wrists, bound behind her with a sort of yellow raffia. Another showed four threads of jute that had been found in her hair. The caption note suggested her head might have been tied in a sack before she was drowned.

For a moment I stood, staring at the picture of the slashing marks of a whip or cane across her back and buttocks. Only a monster, I was thinking, devoid of any humanity, could have done this.

Then I yielded to Bisset's pressure on my elbow. 'The café across the street,' he said. 'Cognac.'

# 15

MARTY PEARSON LAY on his bed in the best room in Villefranche's *Hôtel* de France and read through the four bound notebooks he had already filled over the last years. His question to himself was the question he had repeated every time he flipped through the pages which were now, in the older books, beginning to crackle and yellow round the edges: was there any angle he had missed? Was there any further step he could have taken to trace this person or that?

Over ten years he had been in London a dozen times, Paris, Bonn, Rome and a number of smaller European capitals. He had searched Canadian phone books and marriage and death records. Two visits to Sydney had covered Australia.

And now he was in France. Back on the Riviera where it had all begun.

It was what he had promised himself. And now, as a retired executive of one of the world's best-known companies, he had the funds and the time to do it. He had never told his wife, when she was alive. Never told his son or daughter. But the desire to come back to this part of France had nagged at him, sometimes even raged within him, for forty years.

Some memories do that to you. Not memories of happy times. Not even memories of sad times. The times, to really qualify, have to be spiced with sex, lost opportunity, guilt, danger. A life so different from his time after the war as a senior executive at Hallmark Cards in Kansas City that the two could never stand together, could never really live together in the experience of one man.

That's why he had told nobody. Perhaps even that's why he was thought of, among his friends in Kansas City with their opulent houses out at Mission Hills, as somewhat withdrawn. He was known for the punishing exercise he favoured, the swimming and jogging sessions even under the Kansas summer sun.

He was known as an efficient, first class international company executive. But nobody at Hallmark would claim to have known him well. Perhaps they sensed he was a man who lived partly in the past. A loner.

But, in truth, he was not a loner, with all the aimlessness that often suggests. Instead, he recognised himself as a committed personality dominated by a single aim.

Marty Pearson was a searcher.

He had not come directly to the village. It had seemed to him, quite simply, that he would be best able to carry out the mission he had set himself if he weren't recognised, at least at the beginning. Later, when he'd learnt more about today's Villefranche sur Bol, he might reveal who he was.

But you could never tell, of course, how closely you resembled your younger self. If he were recognised by some of the older people, that wasn't by any means the end – but it would certainly make it more difficult for him to operate.

For this reason he had tried a couple of test runs on his arrival in one or two of the bars in small towns and villages in the area. He had stood up there at the zinc in the bar of the Café de la Paix and the Bar des Négociants in Villefranche and faces still recognisable to him after forty years had not spared him a glance. Of course he was expecting them to be there – and they were hardly expecting him.

It would be an exaggeration to say he had affected a disguise. The years had achieved a disguise of their own, of course. All the same, to be extra careful, he had, between his retirement from Hallmark and his arrival in France, experimented with his crisp, grey hair cut close to the skull. He found it made him look less than his age. True that his face was lined and the bags under his eyes were heavy, but his lifetime regime of exercise had kept him fit and he walked with the easy agility of a much younger man. In his early sixties, he looked six or seven years younger.

He had other advantages. From his years here before, he spoke fluent French with a natural Provençal accent which enabled him to blend comfortably in crowded bars or restaurants. To support the persona, he had bought clothes at the local agricultural supply shop, some rough work-blue trousers and a similar jacket, and stained them here and there with a paste made from the thick reddish dust of the area.

To discover whether he was going to pass, he had taken quite deliberate risks. In Villefranche he had stood next to Paulette Garrard, as she once was, in the *tabac* as she bought cigarettes. He had gathered from the way the patron addressed her that she must have married one of the Rodinets, probably Georges who was always chasing her.

And when she'd dropped her pack of Peter Stuyvesant, she had thanked him as he'd picked them up. But that was all. Thanked him with a broken toothed smile. Thanked an anonymous stranger.

Strange to think she was the first woman he had made love to. Made love, a ridiculous term for the quick roll on his narrow bed, but she had been the first. She was then, of course, in her early twenties, not yet betrothed, a vivacious dark-haired girl who was reputed to be easy with her favours. And it had been on the night of the St Juste Carnival in 1941 that he had discovered how easy. For three days in that July, the privations of war had been forgotten. Marty had supplied tins of butter and sausages and Hershey Bars. The men of St Juste had gone out and shot a half dozen wild boar. In the village square they had been roasted on open fires while the villagers danced to the music of accordions and poured rough wine down their throats like peasants in a Breugel painting. Meanwhile, Marty Pearson had lost his virginity in eight hot, slicing strokes into Paulette Garrard upstairs in his apartment overlooking the square.

But then in those wartime days, probably half the women in St Juste would have been ready to have taken Paulette's place. Married women too. And who would blame them? Mostly their husbands were away in Germany among the million and a half men who were prisoners of war. Food was short in this part of France, the southern unoccupied part. And where food was short, women gravitated towards the man who could find it for them.

Marty Pearson, representative in the area of the American Food Program at Nice, was a prime target. He smiled as he thought of it now. A lusty young man's dream. If he'd walked through St Juste or Villefranche or any other village or small town in the whole area, there'd always be a girl or young woman calling to him, ready to walk out of her way, sometimes not too subtly suggesting how grateful she'd be for something extra from 'the Program' as everybody called it.

Of course, those days were long ago. He'd been too young or too honourable to take advantage of his unique position, though he hadn't, of course, refused all offers. But the night with Paulette had been one of very few. And he had soon become involved in much more serious things, things he shuddered at when he thought of them today.

Even now something stirred in him at the memory of those days. Days spiced with sex and danger. Even after travelling the world for forty years as a successful company executive. Even after thirty years of marriage to a very pretty, genuinely good American woman and raising two children with her, a daughter who was an English professor at Vassar and a boy now a Communications Officer in the US Navy, he had still promised himself that, on his retirement, he would come back to France, to the Riviera, to St Juste and Villefranche.

It had been a shock to discover the village of St Juste was now submerged, or, in this year of the great drought, partly submerged, beneath the great lake. But Villefranche sur Bol was remarkably unchanged. So many of the same families lived there, and although he'd no doubt the older ones were dead and had been succeeded by their children and grandchildren, there were the same names over shop and café windows. No doubt there were great differences. There were tourists now, of course. Mostly English and German it seemed to him, chatting together with the friendly cameraderie of tourists against the host country. Of course there had been no English here in the times he was thinking about – no Germans either, come to that. It was only much later, at the end of 1942, when the war was more than half over that the German Army first came south. That was to secure the French Fleet at Toulon and prevent an allied landing on the Riviera coast.

Between the French defeat in 1940 and November 1942, this southern half of France ruled itself. Of course, the big boyfriend, as the French called German power in the north, *le grand Jules*, required food deliveries, bauxite, timber, wine and finally labour from the south. But old Marshal Pétain and his government, part ridiculous, part sinister, huddled in the cluster of tourist hotels in the spa town of Vichy, made the new laws on which a new France was to be built – laws favouring the Catholic family, the Protestant work ethic and the removal of the rights of Jews to own or work in a thousand enterprises. And finally, of the right of Jews to breathe the same air as their fellow countrymen. There was no denying these same laws had proved a great opportunity for a great many Frenchmen. He stiffened with that very special rage he had come to associate with these thoughts of the past.

Marty Pearson put aside his notebooks and took up the thin folder of houses for rent that the agency on the corner of the market square had provided. Only two appealed. Of these he could take one, a villa on the St Juste road, starting this week. It had the slightly sickening name: *Mon Espoir,* My Hope. But why not? He had come here in hope. In the hope of unravelling a forty-year-old mystery. He threw the other brochures into the trash can and swung his legs off the bed. He would go down to see the woman at the *Immobilier*, the real estate office, immediately and tell her his choice: Mon Espoir. After all, it was hope alone that had kept him at this task for forty years.

# 16

IN THE DAYS following my arrival in France, Elaine and I established a basic rota. She sat by Romilly's bed from eight in the morning until late afternoon, early evening. I took it from there till midnight and often through the night. Watching over someone in a coma is full of false fears and falser hopes. One single unfamiliar peak or trough on the monitor and your own heart rate jumps until the line evens out. Or a faint facial muscular spasm is enough to convince you she's about to open her eyes and smile or even speak. You imagine that first smile, those first words a dozen times every hour . . .

But the truth's different and harder. Long hours pass, taken up with talking, reading, even singing to her. She'd reacted very briefly to stimulus on that first day – the hope you hang on to is that she will again. But the oxygen hisses, barely audible. The blood pressure rates seem immovable. The breathing maintains its regular, anxious pattern. Only the pulse is there to comfort or alarm. Only the movements in the pulse rate suggest activity within that slim, still body. Or even more important, activity behind those closed eyes, activity within that mind.

Each night I would drive back to Villefranche, turning down the lane to Elaine's house just before the stone bridge before the Porte du Roi. She had built there a big, comfortable, beige crépi modern villa with Roman tiled roof, a columned portico, and a paved terrace with a D-end swimming pool in front. Everything about it said success as it was measured in 1980s terms. The drive back from Nice took no more than half an hour, part autoroute and part twisting third grade roads as you climbed into the foothills of the Alps. Mostly Elaine was still up when I got back. She would put out some cheese and salad, or I would make an omelette. In the kitchen, doors open to the trilling Provençal starlit night, we would drink a glass of wine or a Scotch together while I recounted the false hopes of the evening. Then she would go to bed.

We never talked about our marriage, our time together in Newton. Never talked about Margot, except for that one brief reference to her when I had first arrived at the hospital. What were we, friends? Companions in adversity? Anything more? I'm not sure.

Some afternoons while she was still at Nice, Elaine called me at her house to tell me she wanted to stay on with Romilly at the hospital. Perhaps they were the times she had some sort of intuition that Romilly was going to come through, was going to burst her way back to consciousness if only Elaine was there to give her that extra little bit of help. Mothers have these feelings. Some mothers. For me, with each day that passed I found it harder to hope. The doctors were as supportive as you could want, prepared to talk and speculate with a refreshing openness. But I felt sure that somewhere, perhaps beyond science and professionalism, they too were quietly abandoning hope.

Wednesday night, Bisset came in to see me while I was alone at the hospital. Elaine had returned home; I was reading to Romilly's pale, expressionless face, still swathed in bandages. He admitted straight away that he had no real news.

'We're doing a reconstruction at the Villefranche market on Friday morning,' he said. 'Don't shake your head like that. These things sometimes produce.'

'Sometimes,' I said.

'Not often,' he conceded. 'Did you tell Madame Chapel about the other girl? About Nicole Tresselli?'

'I felt I had to. I toned it down as much as I could.'

He nodded.

'She's got a lot of grit,' I said, 'but I don't know how long she can take all this.'

'Or you, Monsieur,' he said.


Everything was strange. I had lived in France when I was a boy and even attended a French school but I had never lived in the south. The more time I spent down here the more I realised it was a very different world from Paris and the north. I had never lived in the countryside either, and I was touched and moved by the people who came to Elaine's house with prayers or best wishes, fruit or offers of practical help. The village names, I soon got to know. The Rodinets, Bestes, Rolins, Mantels, arrived as grandparents or parents, known to Elaine, or as children or grandchildren, friends of Romilly. The mayor, Monsieur Hercule Mantel, was one of the first visitors, giving formal assurances that he and his council would not rest until Villefranche was again safe for young women to walk unharmed. In all this I was struck, above all, by the unity displayed by the people of the village in the face of a tragedy that they saw as theirs as well as ours.

Of course there were some unwanted, or rather embarrassing visits. Old Auguste Martin, who had found Romilly on the hill up to St Juste, broke down when he called. The local gendarmerie sergeant, Duval, was pompous and unconvincing as he tried to boast that he was really in charge of the case. Oddest of all was a visit late on Tuesday night.

Elaine and I were sitting on the terrace as the heat slowly drained from the air. We had had a drink together and a quick supper of local goat's cheese salad and rough bread. I was just about to leave for a night at the hospital when I saw a movement out in the lane beyond the green spill of light from the old lamp hanging from the plane tree.

We were making a few last arrangements, the time Elaine planned to arrive at the hospital next morning, that sort of thing, when I saw the movement again. 'Elly,' I said, peering into the darkness beyond the plane tree. 'There's someone out there.'

Elaine nodded equably. 'I thought I saw something a few minutes ago,' she said. 'It's probably Sanya.'

'Sanya?'

'She's very shy.'

'A cat? A dog?'

She laughed briefly. 'A woman. An American as a matter of fact.'

'What's she doing out there?'

She dropped her voice to a whisper. 'She's pretty strange. But bright enough to have learnt Provençal. She can talk to the old village ladies in the language they grew up speaking. I'd say there aren't too many of Villefranche sur Bol's dark secrets that Sanya hasn't heard.'

'Is that so?'

Elaine smiled. 'You know what a *masco* is? No? In these parts it's a sort of curse. It can effect your life for ever.'

'I've got one,' I said. 'It's called my mother.'

'Don't be so slick. Listen. Sanya's recognised by the old ladies as a *démascaire*. Somebody who can lift the curse, the *masco*.

The old ladies swear by her. And some of the younger folk too.'

'She lives in the village?'

'Up in the hills somewhere. She keeps goats. I think she moves from cave to cave.' She stopped and raised her voice. 'Sanya, are you there?'

I saw a shadow in the lane about thirty yards away. She had paused just out of range of the gate-light. A goat bleated somewhere in the darkness.

'In winter,' Elaine continued, her eyes straining into the darkness, 'she quits the cave dwelling, nobody knows where for. One year she told me she wintered in South Africa.'

'She can afford that sort of trip?'

'I think she's pretty well-off.'

'And pretty eccentric?'

'She's a long way past eccentric.' Elly dropped her voice. 'She's totally obsessed with the past. She believes she's a reincarnate.'

'A what!'

She leaned closer to me. 'She believes she's the reincarnation of a woman who lived in this area fifty years ago. When village people see Sanya walking the hills, they give her a wide berth. Those with guilty consciences, maybe.'

'They think of her as a sort of witch?'

'A white witch, perhaps. She's just too strange for some people.'

'But not for you?'

She thought for a moment, a wry smile. 'No . . . I find her very friendly. Very sad.'

'Wait a minute. Could I have seen her in the market place on Friday?'

'Keep your voice down. If you saw her you wouldn't miss her. There's a weird sort of elegance about her. Her clothes are all thirties, forties stuff. A flower print one day, a silk ball gown the next. She must trawl the local markets for the stuff. And the goat. You wouldn't miss that either. In the village, she's known as the goat lady.'

We sat for a moment watching the figure flitting back and forth beyond the light.

'How come she fetched up here?'

Elaine shrugged. 'The way I hear it she first came to the region with a group of young people during the demonstrations against the flooding of the St Juste valley in the early seventies. They found a cause, a good cause incidentally, and they dug in and made a Peace Camp. She was pregnant at the time and the baby was born up there in the hills. I can imagine Sanya was in her element. She was the Earth Mother figure of the commune. Then tragedy. And my God, it was tragedy.'

'What happened?'

'It was the night of the great confrontation, village and demonstrators against the police. Everything apparently. Petrol bombs flying over the hillside. So that she was free to take her part, Sanya had left her baby in a makeshift crib at the commune they'd established in the hills.'

I looked at Elly's face go drawn with horror even at the thought of what she was about to say.

'Animals,' she said. 'Wild boar trampled the crib. Broke it open.'

'Jesus.'

'Nothing small and human could survive out on that hillside at night. There are boar, foxes, rodents, even night birds . . . Sanya refused to identify what was left of the child. Denied it *was* a child. She's been looking for it ever since.'

There wasn't anything to add to that. I emptied my glass and poured us both another.

Elaine stood up and walked to the edge of the terrace. 'Sanya,' she lifted her voice, 'is that you?' A long pause. 'Sanya, I've got someone here I'd like you to meet.'

Very slowly, the figure edged out of the darkness. For a moment she stood under the light, a white goat silently by her side. She was younger than I had immediately imagined, in her mid thirties, her tattered pink silk dress flowing, her hair long and wild. You might have said she was beautiful, had her right eye not been placed, by an accident of birth, some quarter inch lower on her cheekbone than her left. The distortion made it impossible to see the eyes as aspects of the features in front of you. Instead I found it necessary to look at one eye, then the other, the adjustment producing a weird and unsettling face, drawing you immediately, even eerily, beyond the everyday. She came forward, very tentatively.

'This is Romilly's father,' Elly said and Sanya dipped her head. She was carrying something with infinite care.

'Come up on the terrace,' Elaine encouraged her. 'Come and sit down with us for a few minutes.'

'I brought you a gift, Elly,' Sanya said, still standing in the lane,

'What is it?'

She came up the short flight of stone steps to the terrace. She was holding a doll in her arms. 'You could look after it for a while,' she said. 'It'll help you take the pain of Romilly.'

I didn't quite know what that meant but I stayed quiet and still. I could sense, from her fearful glances towards me, that she was ready to turn and run at any moment. Very nervously, she came forward, onto the lower step of the terrace and stretched her arms, offering the doll to Elly.

Elly advanced towards the edge of the terrace and took the ancient stuffed rag doll from her. I glimpsed an old-fashioned mob cap and a face scratched and discoloured by time. Then sitting on the top step, Elaine invited Sanya to sit next to her.

Behind them, I slipped into the house and took a quick shower. I was getting dressed when I heard raised voices, or perhaps only Sanya's raised voice from below. I went to my bedroom window and opened the shutters. Sanya was standing in the lane. One hand lifted towards the sky, hair flowing in rhythm with her dress, she powerfully evoked a figure in a Greek tragedy. She was speaking in a strong, urgent voice now. 'It was murder then, Elaine, and it's murder now. Murder with no end in sight.'

Elaine was trying, vainly, to quieten her. The goat was becoming agitated, running from one side of the lane to the other.

'You understand Elaine, you understand what happened, Paris found a way.' Sanya's voice carried up to me, low but strong – excited and not by any means entirely sane. 'Paris found the perfect way to cover everything. To flood the valley where the murders happened. That's why we demonstrated in the seventies. Dave wrote me from California. He explained it all. Governments stick together – even over centuries. They don't want truth. They want a bland silence to reign. Just because something happened a long, long time ago doesn't mean it's not still with us.'

'No,' Elaine was saying placatingly, 'I guess Dave's right.'

I finished dressing and hurried downstairs and out onto the terrace. Sanya had gone. Elaine, pale-faced, was pouring herself a drink.

'What was all that about?' I asked her.

'She doesn't mean any harm. Forget it,' Elaine said shakily.

'But wait a minute, what was she saying about murder?'

'She sounds off sometimes. She can be quite frightening.'

'So what was it all about?'

'Just nonsense. Nearly four hundred years ago there was a religious massacre up there,' she waved a hand towards the dark hills behind the house. 'She says during the war there was another. Forty women murdered, she says. I don't know what she's talking about. She claims she's the reincarnation of one of the dead. It's crazy but you can see how it distresses her. Now she says it's breaking out again.' She shivered.

'Who's Dave?'

'God knows. Some California guru. He guides her life.' She paused, still holding the doll. 'She means well but she can still be pretty upsetting. Thing is, all this talk of murder isn't utterly impossible. In the last part of the war, you can't guess what went on here. People were tried by kangaroo court, taken up into the hills and murdered. Resistance killed Vichy, Vichy killed Resistance. There was a civil war going on all along the coast until the Americans arrived.'

'I was beginning to get the idea that unity against the Germans was just a myth.'

'It's one all sides want to preserve now. But you don't have to live here long to know that it's not true. There was a lot of blood shed – French blood shed by Frenchmen. In the early days the Resistance wasn't at all popular with the vast majority of Frenchmen in an area like this. Many people saw them as bandits.'

I sat there a moment, thinking. 'Forty murders,' I said. 'Who by? She doesn't claim to be psychic too?' I shook myself. 'Forget it. Best thing is not to dwell on what she says. She may not mean any harm. But she's the sort that can get under your skin. People like us, under pressure the way we are, we shouldn't listen to a woman like Sanya.'

Elaine nodded and we went back to talking about Romilly.

I'm no longer sure why I left it until Thursday evening to tell Elaine about the lawyers in New York, Roddam, Spurling, Jones. Perhaps the truth was that those first few days were a very special nightmare for both of us. I know the stress of what was happening left us both with no inclination to talk about anything but the minutiae of Romilly's condition. Peripheral things seemed unimportant. Even millions of dollars.

There was also the simple fact that an inheritance of this size meant headaches of one sort or another and I just didn't believe Elaine was in a condition to take much more. And frankly, I didn't feel comfortable. I was embarrassed. This was Elly's part of the world. She knew all the people involved. Coultard had even been her boss. The man who had headhunted her from London for the job. Yet he had left me money.

What was I doing in all this? I would run it back and forth through my mind, especially in the hours I was on auto-pilot reading to Rom, but I never even got close to any answer. But that didn't stop me feeling embarrassed and uncomfortable about the whole thing – as if, uninvited, I'd elbowed my way into Elly's world.

So in the brief hour or so we saw each other most nights when I got back to her house in Villefranche it wasn't too difficult for me to say nothing about the inheritance. It was easy to duck it. But, of course, it had to be done. And there was a chance, after all, that it might provide some sort of distraction for her to wonder why her boss was leaving Romilly a very uncool twenty-eight million.

So, on Thursday night, arriving back from the hospital a little earlier than usual, I told her about being called to see Roddam, Spurling, Jones. And I told her Romilly had received a bequest.

Elaine had cooked a risotto and we sat across the table, she with a scotch, me with a glass of the local over-sweet red wine. I didn't at first mention the size of the bequest and I see now that Elaine immediately concluded, as I had, that it was money coming from my mother or one of the Bannerman family trusts. I think the whisky I had poured her was not her first that evening. I also doubt that she'd eaten much, or even at all, that day. Certainly she hadn't touched the risotto. I saw her eyelids drooping. I shouldn't even have mentioned the subject. It could have held over for another day or so.

'I'm sorry, Elly,' I said. 'I should have left it. You have enough to think about.'

She shrugged and got to her feet. 'And in any case, what does it matter the way things are?' She stood before the old oak dresser, back to me, repositioning the doll Sanya had given her. 'Who's it from, the bequest? One of your mother's lot?'

'No.'

Something in my tone told her I was reluctant to get it out. She looked round, waiting.

'It's kind of a surprise.'

She sat down again and picked up her glass. 'Okay. Surprise me.'

'Coultard,' I said. 'Marcel Coultard. I just wondered if you had any idea why he should be leaving his money to Romilly?'

Her glass banged down on the table. 'Marcel Coultard?' She sat back, her mouth open in shock. 'Marcel left money to Romilly?'

Before I mentioned Coultard's name she had been barely listening. Suddenly, what had seemed peripheral to our concerns about Romilly took on a new quality. I knew I'd better spell it out. 'One hell of a lot of money,' I said.

'Did she know about this?' Then before I could answer. 'No, of course not. She would have told me.' She paused. 'Wait a minute, at the funeral she was funny. Talking about the will. Even suggesting he would perhaps be leaving something to me.' She frowned, thinking. 'She knew something. Maybe not all the details. But something. You'd told her?'

'How would I have done that?' I said. 'I only knew myself the day it all . . . happened to her.'

'But why?' She was totally mystified. 'Why . . . ? He barely knew her. Hadn't met her more than half a dozen times.' She got up from the table, glass in hand. 'And you said a lot of money. How much?'

'It's not just a few thousand dollars.' I felt the need to introduce the shock figure. 'He left everything, Elly. The château, the business. Romilly is more or less sole beneficiary.'

'Sole beneficiary.' She looked at me with an expression I couldn't easily interpret. 'Well, why didn't anybody tell me for Christ's sake? How is it you know what's happening to my daughter and I don't know a damned thing?' Violently, she pushed her chair back and got up, spilling my wine as the table shook.

'I know because I've been appointed trustee. With Rolin, the attorney.'

She span round. 'Marcel appointed *you*? He couldn't have. He didn't even know you. Why not me?' She was splashing Scotch into her glass.

I took a deep breath. 'I haven't seen the local lawyers yet but in New York they told me that . . . that I was to draw an annual amount from the estate.'

'What sort of annual amount?'

I hesitated. 'Seventy-five thousand dollars.'

Stated starkly like that I could see how totally bizarre all this was. Even more bizarre for Elaine who knew the man, who worked for him.

'For life? You're actually named?'

'Yuh,' I said flatly. 'I'm named.'

'What about Claire Coultard? And her brother?'

This was a lot harder than I thought it was going to be. 'The family. Uh . . . Nothing.'

'Jesus.' She stood looking out into the Provençal night, shaking her head. 'His own children . . .'

'If anything happens to Rom,' I said carefully, 'they inherit.'

'They inherit! You mean if Rom doesn't recover consciousness . . .'

I nodded. 'They inherit.'

'My God.' She turned away and stood staring at the window.

'Does any of this mean anything to you?' I asked her when she turned back to face me. 'Had he ever said anything about leaving her money?'

'Why should he for Christ's sake? I told you he hadn't met Romilly more than half a dozen times over the six years we've been here. So why? Why? I just don't begin to get it. And why make you a beneficiary and trustee?'

Her tone was so accusatory I lifted both hands. 'Can't guess, Elly. As trustee I've been asked to go up to the Coultard château tomorrow morning. Perhaps we'll know a little more then.'

'I'll go with you.'

'Better not,' I said. 'Let me handle it.'

Her face tightened angrily. 'Why?'

'In any case,' I said quickly, 'You'll be at the hospital.'

She was silent, nursing her whisky, shaking her head in bewilderment. 'Why would he do it?' she said to herself again. 'Why would he leave his whole fortune to a seventeen-year-old girl?'

'Put it to the back your mind, Elly,' I said. 'You've got enough to think about.'

She gulped down her Scotch. 'Romilly is to inherit Ciné-Coultard? Don't you realise, we're talking about a huge amount of money?'

I couldn't hold the rest back now. 'The American lawyers put the whole estate at roughly twenty-eight-million dollars,' I said.

'My God . . .' She dropped into a basket chair and sat for a moment, thinking, her chin in the palm of her hand. I left her thinking as I cleared the plates into the dishwasher.

When I sat down again she was still staring into space. 'Listen, Tom.' She refocused to train her eyes on me. 'You must have thought of this already. This isn't all just a coincidence what's happened to Romilly. These things are connected, they have to be. You must see that.'

I had to tell her now. I had to stop her running off down the wrong road. 'Hold on, Elly,' I said carefully. 'I told you Bisset is investigating another attack. He's pretty sure Romilly was a victim of this same man. A crazy, Elly. We don't have to look further than someone who's sexually unbalanced. We don't have to look for an old man's will for a motive.'

Her cheeks were flushed red. 'You really believe that?'

'Yes.'

'You believe your daughter is attacked within a week or so of being left property and a huge fortune in Ciné-Coultard, and there's no fucking connection? Believe that,' she said brutally, 'and you're soft in the head.'

'Coincidence, Elly. They happen.'

'Then you know nothing about life down here.' She jumped to her feet. 'Listen to me, Tom.' She began to walk up and down. 'People come to the South of France and see bright sunshine, beautiful sun-tanned bodies, great food and a stunning coastline.'

'They see a great place to live. So?'

She swung round. 'So then they go home to London, Hamburg, Amsterdam or Oslo without knowing a damn thing about what's under the glitz. You have to work here to find out. The mafia's more ever-present here than in Chicago. There's more violent politics than the Balkans. There's more family hatred than in *Romeo and Juliet*.' She took a deep breath. 'Okay, I'm exaggerating. But not entirely. I don't know how the pieces all fit together – but believe me it could easily be the will.'

Suddenly I felt I'd been too dismissive about any chance of a connection. In some way I didn't begin to grasp, she could easily be right. 'I'll get in touch with Bisset,' I said. 'He's going to be in the market place tomorrow asking questions. I'll see him on my way to the château tomorrow.'

# 17

On Friday morning I drove the half kilometre into Villefranche. Even before the bridge, the approach to the village was lined with cars parked up on the sidewalks, vans throbbing out diesel fumes in the heat. It had not occurred to me that on market day it would be almost impossible to park, or that the police operation in progress, seeking witnesses to Romilly's walk through the market place last Friday, would make it even harder.

Taking a side track at random I found a steep bank that hadn't yet been risked by anyone else, and parked the car. I found myself stepping out into relentless heat. Even my light linen jacket that I'd put on for my visit to the château felt like far too much clothing. I took it off and draped it round my shoulders.

The walk to the village took me in a half circle to a section of fallen rampart and straight into the medieval alleys of the village. The houses here were narrow, built in worn yellow limestone, sometimes with elaborately carved and bright painted mullion windows. I might have been in Sicily. It was cooler here, too. Small squares, just a few yards across, were in black shadow, each linked to another by arched entrances often carrying a time-ruined carving of the arms of the Knights Templar. Villefranche had once been a fief of that robust but mysterious order.

A few dogs roamed the streets but beyond one very old woman in black I saw nobody. Yet even in these narrow alleys between high walls I could hear the noise from the market place. The loud-speaker played accordion music. Trucks and vans revved their engines. Men shouted to each other amidst bursts of laughter.

I came onto the main square with a suddenness that surprised me. Less than an hour before the midday klaxon, the market was at its busiest. Women with baskets of produce drifted from stall to stall, met neighbours, haggled over beans, or beef or cheeses.

The horsemeat stall, as always in French markets, had a small group of customers backed up waiting to be served. Next to the horsemeat, live rabbits were sold from the back of a van, live that is, until the peasant selling them pulled one out, stretched front and rear legs and struck it a death blow on the back of the neck.

On either side of the Place Mistral I could see several gendarmerie vehicles and men in pressed blue shirts and kepis moving between them. The two main entrance roads to the market place had been narrowed by blue tape and vehicles and pedestrians were stopped as they entered the square. At each control point a group of gendarmes were checking registration numbers, showing a photograph and recording drivers' answers to their questions on clip-boards cradled in their forearms. I swallowed. The photograph would be of Romilly of course. The questions about whether the respondent had seen her in the *place* during the market last Friday.

In the far corner of the square canvas screens had been erected with *Gendarmerie Nationale* printed in big fading letters. I assumed there were tables and chairs within where the more promising witnesses to Romilly's movements were being interviewed.

I stopped for a moment, watching the scene in front of me. All this was a part of Romilly's world about which I knew nothing. Last Friday this market place had looked much as it did today, except for the two groups of blue gendarmerie vehicles and the screened area. Romilly had crossed it as she had hundreds of times before, coming from tennis lessons, waving to friends at one of the cafés. Standing in the shade of the big plane tree next to me, I asked myself why I had never been here to visit her. Elaine had given me the address, had told me she wouldn't stand in my way if I chose to come. But I didn't. And now I asked myself what had been so obsessively absorbing in my life in the US that the thought had never really crossed my mind? And the answer, of course, was Margot. Margot's ability to keep me, year after year, on the end of a leash. I shook my head angrily. I shouldn't be thinking of Margot now.

I pushed away from the tree and started towards the middle of the square. There were several faces I recognised, village people who had called round to see Elaine in the last few days. The American woman, Sanya, dressed today in a battered and stained narrow brimmed straw hat and a torn linen Mrs Simpson frock, was drifting from stall to stall, leading a pair of white goats. I noticed the way she stopped to talk to the old ladies with nut-brown, deeply lined faces who sat in shaded doorways all around the square. Privy to all the secrets of the village. Then, among the gendarmes, talking to Sergeant Duval, I picked out Bisset. And with him, Judge Fabius.

The judge's position of authority was evident. Gendarmes approached and saluted him before addressing their questions to Bisset or Duval. Fabius himself stood, next to the olive stall, arms folded across his chest, aloof from the police activity around him, his eyes roaming the square.

Then suddenly I was aware that the officers, though not the villagers, were all turning toward the far entrance of the market place. Weirdly, there seemed to be two strata of sound. The village market continued, as noisily as ever – and beyond that every gendarmerie officer seemed to have fallen completely silent. I stood, watching.

The girl in white appeared at the far end of the market. She was blonde, tall, young, dressed in tennis shirt and skirt. She carried a zipped racquet cover strapped to a red tennis bag.

I could never have guessed the effect on me. I couldn't stand here and watch her. I was hit by a desperate need to rush through the bargaining tradesmen, to scatter the village women with their baskets and bags and shout a warning to her. If I could stop her crossing this awful, sunlit space, I could reverse the events of last Friday, I could save her.

I knew the madness of it, but I still had to struggle to stop myself. I stumbled back into the shade of the big tree. I turned from Romilly's alter ego and rested two hands against the trunk of the plane tree, dropping my head.

Bisset was suddenly next to me. I felt his hand on my shoulder. 'Monsieur,' he said. 'Monsieur Chapel . . .'

I looked up.

'You okay?'

'It's a shock, that's all. I'll get myself some coffee.'

'Wait till she's through the square,' he said.

I turned round, leaning my back against the side of one of the vans. The blonde girl had reached the middle of the square. An officer with a hand-held video camera recorded her progress. She stopped and examined some cheap dresses, moved on and stopped where Fabius was standing by the olive stall. Without a glance at him, her hand roamed across every imaginable kind of olive. stuffed, peppered, garlic, chilli. Then she selected one, popped it in her mouth and walked on.

At one point the crowd suddenly thickened. Village women had gathered around the man selling live rabbits from the back of a van. In order to continue, the girl would have to push her way through, or duck under the awnings of a nearby stall and weave her way through the jumble of produce vans parked behind it. She chose to make her way through the vans, disappearing from my sight completely at one point. The lieutenant, I saw, was watching intently. 'I wonder,' he said mostly to himself, 'if the rabbit van was there last Friday.'

The girl reappeared in the middle of the square. Slowly she sauntered on until she reached the far end of the market and disappeared among the gendarmerie vehicles near the control point.

'What happens now?' I asked.

'We manufacture a million pieces of paper. They'll question everybody in the market and record the results. We're looking for just that extra piece of information. We're looking to jog someone's memory of last Friday.'

I stood up straight. 'Seeing that girl . . . it packed more of a punch than I expected. She really looked like Romilly.'

We began walking across the square. 'Fabius wants to see you,' Bisset said.

'I want to see him. I called him this morning at his office at the Palais de Justice.'

'You want to talk about the will.'

I nodded. 'If he'll listen.'

'He's not a bad guy,' he said. 'I've worked with him a few times. He has his own problems.'

'What are they?'

'Problems.' It was a sort of dignified reprimand. No levity. But it wasn't an invitation to ask more.

Then he seemed to change his mind. 'Fabius's father, old Professor Fabius, was on the wrong side during the war. He was a senior administrator in Nice for the Vichy government. Ran the Nice office of the Jewish Commissariat Police. They specialised in rounding up Jews, among other activities.'

'What happened to him?'

'He was put on trial after the war. Took a four or five year sentence. Came out, changed his name, went into the half life I guess.'

'What's the half life?'

'Once a collaborator, a *collabo* people called them, served his sentence, he usually disappeared into a big town, Paris, Lyon, maybe even went abroad. You can guess they weren't welcome in the areas they'd been operating during the war. I'm not talking about the women, the girls who slept with the wrong people and got their heads shaved for it. Stripped naked and made to walk through the town. Old Fabius was on a different level. After the war he would have been taken into the woods and shot if he'd shown his face in this area.'

'Never been heard of since?'

'Nobody asks. Probably dead by now, he wasn't a young man even then. But dead or alive, he can't live around here. People down here take these memories with them to their graves.'

'Would Judge Fabius have known his father?'

'Just, maybe. As a small child. He's certainly suffered enough from having a *collabo* as a father. He was working in Paris. Took a lot of guts for him to accept a promotion down here. He gets a hard time whenever he leaves his big office in the Palais de Justice in Nice and comes up to a place like Villefranche. Have you seen anybody shake his hand today?'

'Jesus, this is forty years on.'

'Even so . . .'

We reached the point where Fabius was standing alone in the shade of the olive stall. Bisset was right. Nobody was within five yards of him.

'Monsieur Chapel,' he shook my hand and I thought about what Bisset had said. 'You saw the reconstruction?'

'I hope it gets results,' I said. Bisset, I noticed, had kept going. Towards where the blonde girl was standing among the gendarmerie vehicles.

'We wanted to track your daughter's exact path through the square. We have an advantage.'

'What's that?'

'People will remember her, even if they don't know her by name. The men especially. She's a beautiful girl.' It was a flat observation, no compliment intended. He paused. 'Will you have coffee?'

'A beer maybe,' I said and followed his lead towards the Café de la Paix.

He gestured to a table in the shade of a plane tree and we sat down. 'Don't expect any answers to emerge just yet. We're getting dozens of names of people who saw her crossing the square – going to and coming from her tennis lesson. There are a lot of anomalies to work out.'

'Anomalies?'

'People make mistakes, confuse times, days or even weeks. The simple asking of the question will convince some people that they saw Romilly at times and places which we think are impossible. These anomalies have to be resolved. In the meantime,' he said, 'you want to speak to me.' His face tightened. 'You left a message for me. About the will of Monsieur Marcel Coultard.'

'I'm really speaking for Elaine. For Madame Chapel. When I told her about the will, she reacted strongly. She believes Marcel Coultard's bequest could have a bearing on what happened to Romilly.'

'She does? She has good reasons?'

'Hell . . . it's a coincidence that's worth looking into, surely.'

He nodded slowly, the dark eyes on me. What it was, I don't know, but his Frenchness suddenly seemed so remote from all things Anglo-Saxon. One of those complex and clever minds that I had always found so intimidating.

'It is not for you, Monsieur Chapel, to decide what is and what isn't a coincidence in this case.'

'Elaine knows more about life down here than I do. *She* believes it's worth looking into.' I paused. 'That means I believe it, too.'

Those dark eyes were unblinking.

'I see.' He said slowly, dismissively.

Anger exploded in my chest. It's the only time I can be forceful. 'Hey,' I said. 'Hold it there. I know you're investigating the death of another girl. I know the possibility exists that Romilly was meant to be the second victim of Nicole Tresselli's killer.'

He pursed his lips in irritation. 'Bisset had no right to pass that on to you.' Very slowly he ran his tongue round the inside of his cheek. 'Among many cases on my desk at the moment, Monsieur Chapel, I am supervising an investigation into the murder of Nicole Tresselli.'

I waited – as he intended me to.

'However . . .' he fixed me with those dark eyes . . . 'You will recognise that if your daughter was attacked, and if the attack was by the same man who attacked the other girl, then it is unlikely to involve the will of Marcel Coultard.'

This man slithered like a snake. 'It's pretty early to say,' I said lamely.

'There's no connection, no imaginable connection between Nicole Tresselli's death and a will which was written after she died. You can't have it both ways, Monsieur Chapel.'

I didn't accept that. I couldn't accept that. But right now I could think of nothing to say to refute it.

# 18

Outside one of the cafés Sanya was spinning slowly in an unfamiliar dance to the music of an old man playing the accordion. Market traders and locals who had stopped for an apéritif laughed as they watched her. The two goats, tethered to a bicycle rack foraged among the leftovers of the morning's market. I made my way back to my hired car, extracted myself from the traffic around the village and headed up the St Juste road just as the market klaxon began to sound below me.

From Villefranche the road rises steeply past the Lac St Juste and the great rock plateau and then, via another series of rocky foothills to the Alps beyond. The Château St Juste lay at 3000 feet. There were few roads up here, the plateau bleak and hot in the midday sun. To my right I could see the great artificial lake of St Juste itself, fed through the dramatic gorges of the river running down from the high Alps.

The château was a sprawling grey stone mass on the edge of a steep limestone cliff. Even from a mile away I could see it was mostly in ruins and probably had been for centuries. Closer, I saw that the arched entrance was hung with flower baskets and the keep beyond that was a towering stone block in which windows had been pierced. Under the arch, a dark green Mercedes sports car in the courtyard was being polished by an old man in a leather apron.

I drove in and pulled up next to the Mercedes. I had just got out and exchanged greetings with the old man when Claire Coultard came through the open oak doors and onto the stone perron just above me. She leaned forward, crossing her arms on the parapet, looking down at me. 'Welcome to St Juste,' she said. The white teeth against the dark skin had a brilliant effect. More than that, there was a lightness, a relaxation about her smile which I attributed to being on her home turf. Until I remembered it was just about to become somebody else's home turf. Yes, difficult times for her.

'I'm glad you could make it, Monsieur Chapel,' she said as I came up the steps. She was wearing white chinos and a dark blue Lacoste shirt. A single gold chain round her neck and a heavy bracelet on her wrist, an adapted man's antique watch chain. Make-up and nail varnish. She wasn't dressed to kill but it still wasn't a casual outfit.

'It doesn't get much hotter than this, I hope,' I said conversationally.

'I hope not,' she said. 'We've now had sixty days of official drought. The forest fires haven't reached us yet but the water level in the lake is being drawn off at a metre and a half a week. You'll be able to stay for lunch, I hope, Monsieur Chapel?'

'I'd be pleased to,' I said and followed her into the dark stone-flagged hall.

If you like this sort of thing, and I do, it was pretty breath-taking. A hall with rib vaulting arching above my head; a stone staircase curving away to the floor above. Contained in a massive gilt frame on one wall, was an enormous painting, a Napoleonic battle scene, all cannon and prancing horses, which might have been by Géricault. Opposite there were tapestries which I could no more than glance at before we passed through a low door and out onto a stone terrace with a blindingly bright view over the plateau towards the mountains.

To the left of the long terrace, lunch was set for two on a teak table shaded by a thick vine. She stood with her back to the stone parapet, making no effort to disguise her examination of me as I looked out across the plateau. I could see the basin of the lake from here, the mud sides cracked and dry where the water had receded. Old leafless trees lay, dead now, their roots exposed. There were signs of the village, which had been flooded to form the lake, in the green outlines of buildings just below the water and the church steeple, and collapsed roof of the ancient church, rising above the surface. In a strange cinematic effect a little higher up the side of the valley, a few stone village buildings seemed to be dragging themselves from the water, one end still part submerged, the other rising, dark-green with algae, above the lapping edge of the lake. I brought my eyes back to Claire Coultard.

'How would you like to approach this?' she said. The relaxed air was gone.

'I'm not entirely clear about what we're approaching,' I said.

'I'm sure you know what I mean.' She gave a quick, irritated flick of her hair. 'What we're approaching, Mr Chapel, is for us, the family, a shattering situation. Before the will was read we had no idea.'

'Ah . . .' I said, ineffectually. Roddam, Spurling, Jones had hinted at just these problems in New York but, until today I hadn't given enough thought to the people who might have been dispossessed by the news.

'Obviously there's a degree of embarrassment involved,' she said, 'on your part.'

'Embarrassment?' I wasn't going to go along with that. 'There's bafflement,' I conceded. 'A great deal of that.'

'You're not embarrassed?' Her voice hardened.

I suddenly realised I was going to have to stand my ground with this woman. I wasn't good at standing my ground, but I had the feeling that since I'd arrived in France I was learning.

'Embarrassed because your father made a bequest to my daughter? No, Madame. I'm not prepared to be embarrassed. This is something that's happened *to* me, to my daughter and myself. It's not something I can be embarrassed about. At least, not yet. Not until I know something of the background of all this. As you know, I've other preoccupations at the moment. My daughter's lying at death's door, in Nice.' I walked over and stood next to her on the terrace. The sun was hot and heavy on my back.

She was treating me to a look, smouldering heavily with anger.

'No,' I said. 'Don't expect me to feel embarrassed because your father did this. I don't know why he did it and I'll be honest with you – at this very moment, I don't very much care.' I laid my hands on the hot stone parapet. I'd surprised myself.

'You don't care?' I thought she was going to slap me.

'Not just at the moment.'

'You're telling me that you don't care that you have been left an income for life. And that your daughter has been left nearly thirty million dollars! I don't believe it.'

I lifted my hands and let them drop. I wasn't going to try to persuade her.

'What is this, Monsieur Chapel, an act of indifference?' She stopped, furious. 'More important *why* this act of indifference?'

'What I meant,' I said, probably as tight-lipped as she was, 'is that I'll start caring about all this later down the line. Not just now.'

'So we shall have to wait to see justice done until Monsieur Chapel decides he's ready to care. I see.'

Something about this woman made me stick it out. 'I'm sorry, but that's about the size of it. There's a few million dollars and there's life and death for someone I love. Between the two it isn't even a choice.'

She came away from the parapet, away from me. She walked a few steps forward and swung round to face me again. It wasn't difficult to see that she was still very angry. 'I'm trying to be as civilised as possible about this extraordinary situation, Monsieur Chapel. Of course I know your daughter is in hospital. I know she's seriously ill. You have my very sincere sympathy.' She stopped. 'I mean that. For a father . . . or a mother, of course, it must be as terrible a situation as can be.'

'It is. But . . . ?'

She threw her head back, eyes closed for a moment. The effort to change the tone was visible on her face. I wasn't even sure I wanted to stay here, to hear what she had to say. She seemed to sense this. 'A terrible thing has happened. But we do have to talk,' she said in a milder tone. 'Let me get you a drink first. A kir?'

I hesitated. Hell, I was here. I had nothing to lose. 'Okay,' I said and she gestured to a table further along the terrace. I walked with her until we reached the shade of the vine. We were silent as she took a bottle of Aligoté from an ice bucket and poured it into glasses already containing a quarter inch of cassis.

'I grew up here, Monsieur. My brother, Sébastien, and I were born here. All my memories are attached to this house . . .' she gestured. 'Not really possible to call it a house, is it? Let's say all my memories are attached to St Juste. My first nightmares were of the ghost of the murdered troubadour who is supposed to walk the ruined battlements.'

'The murdered troubadour, when was that?'

She flipped her hand dismissively. 'The troubadours, nine hundred years ago now. In the great days of Provençal poetry.'

'Lot of stories of murder in these parts.'

She looked at me. 'Yes. We are a passionate people. But my memories of St Juste are gentler. They're of a childhood spent here. They're memories of my father.'

I realised that she had effectively introduced the Coultard family concerns by the use of one or two sentences. This was their home.

The foreign intruder was about to take it away from them.

'What happened to make his will the way it was?' I said. 'Did you fall out with your father before he died? Is that the way it worked?'

She looked at me in astonishment. 'I find the suggestion offensive,' she said slowly. 'Designed, I imagine, to take you off the hook.'

How was it everybody spoke such good English down here? 'You're getting back to my supposed embarrassment again, aren't you?' I said. 'Are you saying there was no falling out with your father?'

'None at all.'

I looked at her. I'd never felt my blood up like this before. There was a throbbing sexual attraction emanating from her – and she was aware of it. This made her strong in her own right, and seemed to absolve me of any need to play it soft. 'No falling out,' I said. 'Yet, unknown to you and your brother, he cuts you out of his will. I'm sorry, I don't believe you.'

I thought she was going to slap me. 'Nobody accuses me of lying in my own house, Monsieur,' she said, her voice rasping.

I didn't go as far as to remind her that it was no longer her own house. I didn't need to. Her angry gesture said she understood.

'If there was no falling out between you,' I said, trying to bring the conversation down to the discussion we'd thought we were going to have, 'then why would he have done what he's done? Without apparently telling you he was going to disinherit you?'

She looked at me steadily, big hazel eyes forcing me to speak my own solutions. Except I had none.

'When do you claim your family first heard of my father's will?' she said.

I took it slowly. 'It's not when I *claim*, Madame. It's when I did. In a New York lawyer's office the very Friday Romilly was attacked.'

'If my father *intended* to make your daughter his heir why wouldn't he have told you, her father, before? Why wouldn't he have told me?'

'I think you're accusing me of lying,' I said as calmly as possible.

'Someone's lying,' she said. 'Have you considered the possibility that the document that purports to be my father's will was forged?'

Wow! Too easy. 'Dangerous ground, Madame Coultard,' I said. 'As I'm sure you realise. The only real candidate for a forgery is Elaine, Romilly's mother. She had access, no doubt, to your father's offices, papers, whatever. Conveniently his old friend and lawyer had just died.'

'Exactly.'

Those bright, hard eyes continued to hold me. Elaine . . . Christ! Was she capable of something like this? I realised I had just made a thumbnail sketch of a good case to someone who could probably prove a dangerous enemy. I tried to recover. 'Needless to say, I don't believe a word of it. Elaine is simply not that sort of woman.'

My defence couldn't have sounded feebler. Claire Coultard had the art of saying nothing, of letting you get yourself deeper in. She stood three, four yards away from me, dark brows knitted, eyes unwavering, arms crossed beneath a curved tan cleavage, a formidable opponent. I knew I had to change tack.

'Look,' I said. 'I have no intention of making any moves just yet. I want the situation to remain as is for the present. I'm seeing Mantel, Rolin, your father's notaries this afternoon. But, for the moment, I'm planning to do nothing. Nothing until we see Romilly out of this coma.'

Arms crossed, she walked the terrace, turning, head down. Then looked up. 'Of course I understand your and Madame Chapel's priorities. But nevertheless, the time will come when we are all forced to face this extraordinary situation my father has presented us with.'

'Sure,' I said. 'At some point. But not yet. I don't want to cause anybody unnecessary suffering – God knows there's enough of that about just now, but I'm not throwing myself into this problem just yet. I hope I make myself clear.'

She handed me a glass. 'On our side,' she said slowly, 'I should tell you that the family have not yet made a collective decision, but it's perfectly possible that my father's testament will be contested. You may know that in French law there is, broadly, an obligation on parents to leave property to their children.'

'I don't know much about the law, but I would guess that that's adequately covered by your father having consigned this house and all his property and holdings to a limited company in London.'

She took a deep breath. 'That may be the case. It would have to be tested, I imagine in both the English and French courts.

That could take years – and involve great expense, either to us or you. If it could be avoided, it should be.'

'If . . . ?'

She nodded curtly.

She was threatening me. Politely but surely. 'But beyond that,' she went on, 'there are a variety of legal grounds we might consider. Not least my father's state of mind when he made the will.'

Much as I didn't want to get into a discussion with her, I couldn't resist the question. 'Your father's state of mind? He was sick?'

'No, physically he appeared extremely healthy, active for an old man, right up to the time of his death. Sexually active, certainly. He was very much attracted to very young women.'

I took a moment with that. I needed it. What was she saying? And the stress she'd put on the phrase 'to very young women'. Did that mean Romilly? I didn't like the way this was going, the inferences she was inviting me to make. 'Let me know when the family decides,' I said shortly.

I sipped my kir. Not too much cassis, enough to allow the Aligoté to come through. This was one of Margot's favourites.

She came back to it. 'Is it really the case that you have no idea why my father left everything to your daughter?'

'It's the case.'

In the silence between us all the sounds and scents of Provence came flooding across the parapet. She took a pack of Benson & Hedges from the table, juggled it in air towards me. I shook my head.

She withdrew a cigarette from the pack and lit it with a Dunhill lighter. Emeralds glittered on her tan fingers. 'You don't smoke, Mr Chapel?'

'Rarely.' We sat down at the lunch table. 'I thought all French husbands came home for lunch,' I said.

'Not from Paris,' she said.

'Your husband works there.'

'He lives there. My husband and I live mostly separate lives, Monsieur.'

'I'm sorry,' I said automatically.

'It could be no other way,' she said enigmatically. 'It means it's more convenient for me to be known as Claire Coultard – rather than by my husband's name.'

135

'I'll remember. And your brother?'

'Sébastien lives in Nice. He prefers the atmosphere of the big town. It's easier for him to run his rather dubious nightclubs from there.'

Dubious night clubs. She got up and pressed a bell-push half concealed among the vine. Distantly through thick stone walls I heard a the bell ringing.

She turned back to me. 'Will you allow me to talk, just very broadly, about what's happened?'

'What's happened to you – or to my daughter?'

She closed her eyes for a fraction of a second. 'To all of us, Monsieur. Let me, at least, tell you who and what is involved here at St Juste.'

'Okay,' I said reluctantly, trapped by the lunch that was about to be served.

A short, very broad-beamed woman came out carrying a tray with a tureen. She put two bowls before us and waved a silver ladle. 'Vichysoisse, Monsieur?'

'Thank you.'

Claire Coultard waited until the maid had gone. 'That woman,' she said. 'Bernadette. She's lived here all her adult life. She's been with the family for forty years . . .'

'If you're trying to pull at my heartstrings, I warn you, after four days in that hospital, they don't have any elasticity left. Who and what, you were going to tell me.'

'Very well. My mother . . . perhaps thank God, is dead. My father was a rich, perhaps even a very rich, man who made his fortune after the war in film exhibition. He owns, owned, something like a hundred and fifty cinemas along the coast, from Nice, right down to Perpignan near the Spanish border.'

'I know these things, at least in outline.'

'Of course.'

'You've met Elaine?'

'Not often. Once or twice at film business receptions she organised here. My father thought very highly of her. He had her head-hunted by a specialist firm in London. She had a . . . very generous contract with Ciné-Coultard.'

What was it with this woman? I took a deep breath. 'You're not suggesting a relationship between Elaine and your father was the basis for his will?'

She thought for a long time. It wasn't the first time she'd

thought about it. 'No,' she said finally. 'I'm not. Although of course, I can't be sure.'

'You don't mind if I say that you are very outspoken.'

'How else should I be?'

'Okay. You're suggesting a relationship between your father and Elaine. Makes no sense. The bequest is to Romilly. More marginally to me, the separated husband. Elaine has no part of it.'

'No. So the question is why Romilly?'

'I'm not sitting here,' I said, 'and speculating about why Romilly.'

'Very well.' She seemed as if she were about to say something, changed her mind and said, 'But that of course, is the heart of the mystery. It's at the heart of what makes this whole thing so painful to us.'

'Who are us?'

'Ah yes. I was telling you who was involved.'

'Okay. Your parents are now both dead.'

'That leaves in the immediate family, myself and my brother.'

'And your husband. You have a husband.'

She inclined her head. Very slowly.

'He can't be without an interest in the question.'

That got me a look so intense I was unable to interpret it. Like the way cats sometimes fix on you. What they mean by the look is completely beyond understanding. But it's meant for you, you alone.

'He has no interest in the financial aspect at all.'

'An unusual man.'

'He is. He is a massive intellect in a corrupt body. A brilliant research scientist who will not survive multiple sclerosis for more than another five years.'

'I'm sorry,' I said. 'Really sorry.'

She made a gesture, short, angry. 'If you're about to ask why I'm not by his side, the answer is his work is in Paris. My work is in Nice. I go to Paris every second weekend. Voilà.'

'Your brother . . .'

'You've probably already heard of him from the local people.'

'What does he do? Nightclubs, you said.'

'You're really asking is he short of funds, is that it?'

I shrugged agreement. 'Since we're being frank.'

'Since we're being frank, I think Sébastien does very well. He is a director of Ciné-Coultard. He has clubs in Nice, Cannes, St Tropez, and I believe one in Marseilles. But more important to his financial well-being, he's in politics. In right-wing politics. Very right wing.'

'National Front?'

'Further right still. The National Party. Yes. He's a National Party councillor on the *Conseil Général* of this department, the Alpes Maritimes. He'd be a fool to have done the sort of thing you're thinking.'

Metaphorically, we sat back and summed up the clash so far. Pretty even, I would have said. It helps me to have a running undercurrent of anger, and this woman was certainly capable of engendering it. I let my eyes roam across the expanses of stone walls, bright grey in the sunlight.

'I have an apartment . . .' she pointed, '. . . up there.'

'Great view.' I didn't want to exchange chit-chat with her as if twenty-eight million dollars didn't sit between us. 'So who else is involved?'

'Perhaps a half dozen others who are dependent for a living on St Juste. One other, I suppose. We are advised by an uncle, a much younger brother of my mother's who is a deputy, a member of Parliament, in Paris.'

'Politicians in Nice. A deputy in Paris. Big guns,' I said.

We ate our soup. Spoons on china making a loud, awkward clinking. Mine especially.

'I should tell you,' she said, breaking the silence between us, 'that money is not really at the root of my determination to see justice done here. I'm not financially dependent on the estate. My father saw to that years ago for both my brother and myself. And I have my job.'

'Let me see. A professional woman. A lawyer.'

'Acute,' she said without a trace of admiration. 'I'm a lawyer by training but I've never formally practised. I'm involved in something else. More politics, I'm afraid.'

'You're a member of the National Party, too?'

'No, Mr Chapel. I'm not. You're perhaps aware that we have many tens of thousands of North Africans along this coast. Legal and illegal. Some are French, born here, some genuine asylum seekers. Some smuggled in. There is, as there would be in any country with competition for work and cheap housing, a good deal of very ugly discrimination. Beneath the fair face of the

Riviera there are people, families living in conditions of pure horror. Or working for a pittance. Twelve or fourteen hours a day is not uncommon for an illegal, man or woman. And the sexual exploitation . . . well I'm sure you can imagine it.' She paused. Perhaps she was pushing down her anger. 'I work,' she continued more evenly, 'for an organisation which helps to put the point of view of people of African and North African origin. The Congress Against Racial Discrimination. We are international in our interests so we use the English acronym C.A.R.D.'

'As you say – a problem the world over. I can see though, that you and your brother must come eyeball to eyeball sometimes.'

'Often,' she said. 'But on this one thing, we're agreed.'

'The château.'

She nodded. 'I'll be frank with you, Monsieur Chapel. I asked you here today to broach . . . no more than that . . . the idea that we might come to a compromise on St Juste.'

'A compromise?'

'Yes. This is my own proposal. It does not yet have my brother's approval, but I believe it will. If you would accept a price . . . a price favourable to us, we would buy St Juste from you and your daughter. The motion picture business you would keep.' She bit her lip. 'It might save you, and us, the cost and stress of a very unpleasant legal confrontation.' She watched me. 'There. I've put the idea on the table. That was all I'd hoped to do. I just hope you will consider it.'

'At this moment I wouldn't even know how to begin,' I said.

'That means the offer is still on the table.'

'It means what I said,' I said shortly.

'I'm sorry,' she said placatingly. 'I understand. No more about it now.'

The old woman shuffled in on battered espadrilles, cleared our soup plates and replaced the tureen with a bowl of Salade Niçoise.

I made an effort. 'Let's go back a step,' I said. 'You've told me who is involved. You were also going to tell me what.'

'What's involved? In terms of the business, Ciné-Coultard, I think that's best left to your visit to my father's notaries, Mantel, Rolin. Ciné-Coultard is obviously the most valuable part of the estate. It has considerable property assets and significant cash flow. I'm sure you know all these things from Madame Chapel.'

'Believe it or not, we haven't talked much about this situation. About the bequest to Romilly.'

She didn't believe me. She indicated that with a brief shake of her head and pressed on. 'Ciné-Coultard has assets but that's just a business. Money in the bank. What's involved centrally and most importantly is this house, this château, St Juste.'

I wasn't sure I bought that.

'You'll let me show you round after lunch.'

'I'd rather not. Not just yet, anyway,' I said. 'Tell me instead, about your family's involvement with St Juste.'

She bit on her lip. 'There have been Coultards living on this plateau for centuries,' she said. 'There used to be the village, just there, in the valley as you can see. It was flooded to make the valley into a reservoir in 1973.' She half turned and waved a brown arm, the short sleeve of her blue shirt riding up it. 'The church you can see already. An old Crusader church with a nineteenth-century spire. A month ago it was completely submerged with the rest of the village.' She looked up quickly and reddened slightly as far as it was visible on her tanned face. 'I'm sorry. The point of recounting all that was to tell you I salvaged papers from the village *mairie* before the waters rose. I have documents going back several centuries. A hundred documents showing Coultards who borrowed or lent money. Who bought or lost land. Who sailed with the army to take Algeria and whose horses and mules were confiscated by the military for the Franco-Prussian War of 1870.'

'The family owned the château all that time?'

'No. We are a village family. Over the centuries ownership of the château changed in wars, civil disturbances, bankruptcies. But after the Revolution, the French Revolution, it was usually a village family who had the château. A peasant who had grown rich, became a corn merchant or an olive oil presser . . . whatever. My father was the last in a long line of villagers who have lived here.' She paused, tears in her eyes. 'Only to give it away again to a seventeen-year-old girl!' she said quietly but explosively. Then, 'I'm sorry. You must understand I can't believe it. Can't accept it.'

I watched her face as she fought for control. 'My father loved this place. Every stone of it. He spent much of the last years of his life on vital repairs to the fabric of the building. Not refurbishing rooms to make them more comfortable, you understand. This was work that would safeguard the château for centuries. For his family. So why would he just give it all away to a seventeen-year-old stranger?' She paused. 'If she was a stranger.'

'What the hell does that mean?' Fury blew in me like a water spout. I knew I was too angry to make sense but it made no difference. 'Allegations of forgery, suggestions of an affair between your father and Elaine, allegations of a relationship between a seventeen-year-old girl and an eighty-year-old man . . . for Christ's sake!'

'I'm sorry,' she said. 'I shouldn't have said that.'

'No, dammit, you shouldn't have.'

'But, as you must appreciate, I'm completely baffled by what's happened.'

I was rigid with tension. 'Why your father chose to do what he did is not my problem, Madame Coultard,' I said. 'And just at the moment I'm going to resist all attempts to make it my problem. I think what *you're* doing is unacceptable.'

'What am I doing, Mr Chapel?'

'Hell, let's be American about this. It was a dirty trick to ask me to come here. Your idea was to catch me off balance . . .'

'No!'

'To give me a few nice smiles and a touching sob story and try to come to a deal while I'm still reeling from the news of Romilly's accident.'

'I object to that.'

'Object away,' I said.

For a moment, we sat staring furiously at each other across the table. Then I stood up. 'Thank you for the lunch, Madame Coultard,' I said. 'I'll call to make arrangements to come here again after I've seen your father's lawyers. Perhaps you'll let me know, when you decide, whether or not you are going ahead with legal action.'

# 19

I DROVE BACK to Villefranche with rags of ideas tumble-drying in my head. Was the passionate commitment of Claire Coultard to her home, her château, her belief that it was being stolen by a foreign carpet-bagger, strong enough to provoke her to violence? To organise violence, perhaps. And how about her National Party brother? Pretty much by definition he was some sort of thug. But then if it were the Coultard family behind the attack on Romilly, then what about the other girl, Nicole Tresselli? Reluctantly I had to acknowledge Fabius's reasoning: if Marcel Coultard's will was the driving motive then I had to believe that there was no connection between the murder of Nicole Tresselli and the attack on Romilly.

I passed through the town gate and came into the market place and stopped the car under the line of plane trees, waited for the hot dust to settle and got out and stood in the deep shade. Claire Coultard had a powerful feminine magnetism. I'd felt it even while we were at each other's throats. I didn't find it difficult to imagine men acting crazily about her. She was too significant a woman, too intelligent, too determined, too good-looking, to be anything but a very serious opponent. But it was too early to know how far she might go. Or too early for *me* to know how far she might go. This is where I needed some worldly advice. Margot, I guess I was talking about. She had that streak of life-saving cynicism that Elaine lacked. That I lacked.

I leaned back against the car, half ridiculing myself, half serious. I was going to need to make changes, to grow up. To take myself seriously. To put away childish things. I was on my own here. No General John, no Bannerman family prestige and fortune.

And most of all, no Margot.

For the first time in my life.

\* \* \*

Mantel, Rolin was an ancient firm of lawyers such as is found in most bigger French villages or small towns. It was placed, importantly, on the market square. The doorway was an impressive dark green *porte-cochère* let into a stone façade. A rampant passion flower arched over the door and twisted through the ornate hanging coach lamp. A smaller, human size door had been cut into the right-hand segment of the *porte-cochère* and carried a brass plate *Mantel, Rolin, Notaires*. Beside that an ivory circle enclosed a brass bell push. I rang and waited.

From an alley to the right I could hear banging and a cheerful, tuneless male voice singing. I was about to investigate the alley when I heard footsteps crossing a paved courtyard behind the *porte cochère*. A moment later the door was pulled open and a voice invited me in. I ducked inside.

I was standing opposite a woman of what the French tactfully think of as 'a certain age'. She was dressed in black and white, in the height of a fashion that had passed almost forty years before. The long black pencil skirt was Dior 1947. The ankle strap high heels were of the same era and the frothy white blouse exuded perfume. Her hair was sparse but highlighted blonde, the lines on her face sealed with powder, her lipstick thick and bright red. She introduced herself as Mademoiselle Bertin, secretary to the bureau. On clattering heels, she led me across the courtyard, complaining, as we crossed towards the bureau, about the noise made by the builders in the alley.

The main office, entered through a handsome glazed archway, was cluttered with filing cabinets and ancient roll-top desks of which there were three. A Second Empire loveseat stood in one angle of the room, the covering under heavy attack from the claws of a black and white cat. Sheaves of yellowing papers bound with green ribbon and grey files were piled on every available surface. I didn't have the impression that the fashion conscious secretary to the bureau was entirely on top of the job.

'Pay attention to the wires,' Mademoiselle Bertin advised me. She stepped with exaggerated care across the black and yellow electric cable which trailed across the floor. 'Young Monsieur Rolin insisted,' she said in a mildly disapproving tone, 'that we have a anti-burglar alarm system fitted.' She giggled. 'Slamming the stable door after the horse has bolted, if you ask me.'

I didn't have time to pursue the matter. A man of at least seventy-five, perhaps even eighty, was coming out of a door on the left. He was of medium height with broad slightly hunched shoulders and a hooked nose that gave him the air of an old vulture. 'This,' said Mademoiselle Bertin, 'is Maître Mantel.'

He seemed to know who I was. He stood for a moment in the doorway of his office and looked at me. I could make nothing of his long inspection but eventually he came forward, his expression grave, and extended his hand.

I shook hands with the lawyer. 'Marcel's testament,' he said and nodded to himself. 'Marcel's testament.'

'Young Monsieur Luc is dealing with it, Maître.'

'I know that, Yvette,' the old man said sharply. 'I've not yet lost all my wits.' Then lifting the spectacles which he was wearing on a black velvet tape around his neck, he examined me again as he might a prize bullock at a sale. Satisfied perhaps, he let the spectacles drop. 'I am exceptionally happy to meet you, young man,' he said. 'Exceptionally so. Is there any further news of your daughter?'

'It's good of you to ask, Maître. No change,' I said. 'But there's no question of giving up hope.'

He stood for a few seconds, swaying. 'No. Of course,' he said deliberately. 'No question of that.' With that he turned abruptly into his office.

Rolin's room, as I stood in the doorway, gave a quite different impression from the outer office. There were papers and files but there was also a sense of order. A modern electric fan was positioned on his desk. And Rolin himself was probably not yet thirty, slim, wavy black hair falling over his forehead, his jacket abandoned over the back of his chair, his tie loosened at the collar of a dark blue shirt.

He greeted me and gestured to a chair. 'I'm Luc Rolin, Mr Chapel,' he said in comfortable English. 'Another exceptionally hot day.' His manner, accent, appearance were more that of a big city lawyer than a partner in a provincial notary's office like *Mantel, Rolin*. 'My father died after a long illness just a week before Marcel Coultard. I'm helping out Maître Mantel until he arranges for a new partner. I offered to deal with the Coultard estate for him.'

I took a moment to take that all in. 'And where do you normally practise?' I asked him.

'Paris,' he said.

Where else? he might have added.

'I know Romilly, of course,' he said. 'Everybody in Villefranche does. Our hopes are with her.'

I noticed he didn't say prayers.

He adjusted the fan so that I got some benefit and sat back in his chair. 'I'm sure you have a hundred questions.'

'I do.'

'Where would you like to start?'

'Before we begin – does the village know about the will?'

'I don't think so. Not yet, although news travels fast in village conditions. The Coultards know, of course, but it's been in no one's interest to talk about it – village people assume that Claire and Sébastien will inherit, of course.'

'And would they be upset if they didn't?'

'Upset enough to attack Romilly? No, I don't think so.'

'Is the Coultard family popular?'

He looked at me and smiled. 'Old Marcel, yes. He had long ago assumed mythic proportions. You'd have to know something of the deep divisions in our community to say what people think of Claire and Sébastien. Many dislike her, very sincerely. As many hate her brother for the very opposite political reason.'

'He's National Party – she's opposed.'

He inclined his head slowly. 'But what they have going for them is of course that they're locals. Despite what I said a moment ago, it's true that you won't be too popular once the people here find out what's happening. You'll be seen as a . . . what's the word?'

'A carpet-bagger.'

'Yes, a carpet-bagger.' He looked up at a knock on the door. A man in overalls entered and asked where Rolin wanted the alarm sensor placed in his room.

'Can we do this later?' Rolin asked and turned to me apologetically. 'I'm sorry Mr Chapel. This is all my doing. The *bureau* had a break-in last month, kids from the next village the police think. It's taken me a month to persuade Maître Mantel and Yvette that you can't keep confidential documents in a *bureau* which kids can break into. Thus the alarm fitting ceremony.' He paused. 'So Mr Chapel . . . your hundred questions.'

'They all flow from the first one,' I said. 'Why Romilly? Why did Marcel Coultard leave his estate to my daughter?'

He looked at me for long moment. 'You're telling me you don't know?'

'No. But you do.'

He lifted his hands, palms upwards, an old man's gesture for so young a man. 'I'm sorry to disappoint you. I was hoping you'd be able to shed some light . . .'

'What about the will?' I said.

'It's no help.' He nodded towards the papers on his desk. 'No reasons are given. The testator is under no obligation.'

'Not even to the children he's disinherited? I was convinced the will was going to clarify everything.'

'It doesn't. It's a very simple, very sparse document. Perfectly legal and binding. But, remarkably, it doesn't say why he has chosen your daughter as his heir.'

I sat back, deflated. He stood up and took a single sheet of paper from the desk, walked round and handed it to me.

It was dated less than three weeks before he died. It read, in English:

*I, the undersigned, Marcel Calixte Coultard of the Château St Juste, Department of the Alpes Maritimes, renounce all former testaments. After making the attached bequest I leave all I possess to Romilly Bannerman Chapel of Les Espions, Villefranche sur Bol, France, on her attainment of the age of twenty-one. Should Romilly Chapel die on or before her twenty-first birthday, my estate will be divided equally between my children Claire and Sébastien after providing for the aforesaid attached bequest to Thomas Bannerman Chapel of Apartment G, 1829, Baldrick Street, Boston, USA. A copy of this testament is held by Lawley and Lawley, of Pump Court, Middle Temple, London, England.*

*I appoint M. Luc Rolin of Mantel, Rolin, Notaires, of Villefranche sur Bol and the aforementioned Thomas Bannerman Chapel as my executors.*

*Signed: Marcel Coultard.*

There were two witnesses: Mademoiselle Bertin and her daughter, Clara. The signed and witnessed page attached gave a list of disbursements to people I guessed who mostly worked on the château estate. My seventy-five-thousand dollars per annum headed the list.

I turned back to the will itself and read it through again. I found the stark statement of his intentions breathtaking. 'That's all?' I said. 'That's all a will to a twenty-eight-million dollar estate amounts to?'

He lifted his shoulders and let them fall. 'And as you see it tells us nothing about why Romilly was chosen. Nothing at all.'

We sat for a moment in silence. 'There's an additional point to be made,' Rolin said. 'Marcel's estate was actually the property of a company, wholly owned by Marcel of course, but registered in England. Thus the mention of the London lawyers. By this means Marcel was able to avoid any filial entitlement.'

'What does that mean?'

'Under French law, there's a requirement that the children inherit a major portion of the estate. By transferring his whole estate to a British company, he has made it simpler to leave it as he wished.' Luc Rolin got up and poured me a glass of Perrier water and set it down on the desk in front of me. 'So, how far have we worked through your hundred questions?'

'Not far.' The all important first question – *why*? – having no answer, I wasn't by any means sure where to start. In the Anglo-Saxon world you know where you are with lawyers. They are either yours, in which case you only have to worry about the money they're likely to be charging you. Or they're somebody else's in which case you worry about every last thing they do and say. In France, I knew, it wasn't quite that adversarial. In certain circumstances the two sides could use the same lawyer. I decided to begin by seeing what personal connection there was between Rolin and his client. 'You lived in Villefranche as a young man?'

'I was born here. Lived here until I went to Paris to become a lawyer. Why do you ask?'

'Did you know Marcel Coultard well?'

'As a boy knows a man generations older than himself. Marcel Coultard was a friend of my father's. A good friend. You'd always see them together at the restaurant across the road, whenever they had business to discuss. Sometimes my father brought Marcel to our home, but not often.'

'What was he like?'

'You ask strange questions in a notary's *bureau*, Mr Chapel. What was he like? He was massively energetic, a great extrovert of a man. Not big, but filling a room. You understand me.'

'I do. It's more or less as my ex-wife describes him.'

'But he was a hard businessman. He knew when he had a bargaining position – and when he had one he made ruthless use of it. On a small scale you'd say the approach of any Provençal peasant. On a large scale, it was highly successful. But I expect your ex-wife had told you this, too.'

'More or less.'

'What else has she told you? About Coultard?'

'That's about it. Is there more to be told?'

'Perhaps not for the moment.'

We sat in silence until Rolin raised his eyebrows and opened the palms of his hands, inviting me to go on.

I lifted the papers he had given me. 'There's nothing in the will to tell me why my daughter and I were chosen to be the principal beneficiaries in Coultard's estate. But he must have told somebody. For Christ's sake, he didn't choose me from a phone book.' I started forward in my chair. 'You're telling me you, his lawyer, have no idea why your client did this?'

'None.'

'I don't believe it. I'm sorry, Monsieur Rolin, I just don't believe it.'

He rocked back in his chair, relaxed, but his eyes had hardened. 'You're forgetting Monsieur Coultard was not my client. I was not even working here until two weeks ago.'

'Okay. Then what about your father's partner? Mantel must have some idea.'

'I've asked him,' Rolin said. 'I've asked him several times. After all, Coultard was not just a client. He was by far the biggest client this tiny practice has ever had, is ever likely to have. I agree with you that we should know why Coultard decided to leave his money as he did. After all, if Claire Coultard decides to contest the will, we shall be involved in one way or another. As notaries or as witnesses.'

'Let me ask you, Monsieur Rolin. Do you think your father knew the answer?'

'I would say, yes,' he said slowly. 'Monsieur Coultard and my father were old friends. A friendship that went back into their youth. After all, they came from the same village.'

'So he probably knew. And your mother? Would she have been told?'

'I've asked. She knows nothing. She knew little of my father's activities. For years he had a mistress up in the village of St Juste before it was flooded, Paulette Rodinet, an old lady now. Everybody in St Juste and Villefranche knew my father visited

Paulette on Wednesday afternoons at the Hôtel de France behind the square. My mother knew nothing.'

'Or chose to pretend she knew nothing.'

He thought for a moment. 'You may be right. But I don't think the same goes for Coultard's bequest.' He got up. 'Mademoiselle Bertin is making coffee,' he said. 'Would you like a digestif with it?'

'A cognac would be good,' I said and he went through to the outer office. Through the open door I heard him talking to Mademoiselle Bertin.

'Somehow, Monsieur,' he said, when he came back, 'I think we're going to have to look further afield for the answer to our mystery.'

'Further afield? Where?'

'I don't know yet. Let's say somewhere in the motion picture business, perhaps.'

'You're suggesting my ex-wife had a relationship with Coultard?'

'No . . . no, I'm not. It's not entirely unknown for a man to hand over his entire fortune to his mistress. Even to his mistress's daughter. But not to include her estranged husband. He doesn't deprive his son and daughter of every last franc, of the house they was born and grew up in . . . at least not down here, he doesn't. We're all peasants at heart in this region, Monsieur. Soi-disant aristos and professional bourgeoisie alike, we're all peasants. We believe in old stones and dynastic bonds. That's to say we believe our old properties should move through the generations. The law of inheritance, for the most part, supports that belief. You might leave an apartment in Nice to your mistress, Monsieur Chapel, if you have that sort of money – but you would *never* leave the family home. Without sophisticated foreign company set-ups it would even be contrary to the *code*. You understand what I'm saying?'

Mademoiselle Bertin knocked and tripped into the office. In 1947 she must have been a knock-out. She placed a silver coffee tray on Rolin's desk, handed first me, then him a demi-tasse of coffee and a glass of cognac and left the room with a septuagenarian wiggle.

I sipped the coffee in silence. An idea was forming in my mind, not a stranger because in the last few days it had visited and withdrawn, visited and withdrawn again. But this clever young man had led the idea back and forcibly sat it down in the office between us. I had no choice now. I had to face the possibility.

'Before I came here,' I said. 'Before even I heard about the Coultard will, I discovered that I was not, as I'd believed all my life, my father's child.'

Both hands tapped the desk. '*Eh bien* . . . Do you know who your real father is?'

'No.' I hesitated. It seemed so bizarre. 'My mother refused to tell me.'

He saw possibilities straight away. He turned down his mouth in that totally Gallic facial expression which can mean a hundred things but at this moment meant: So – there you are, then. 'Is there any chance your mother was in Europe forty years ago.'

'She was . . . At one point she was even in France.'

'Is it possible that she met up with Marcel Coultard, they fell in love? There was a child?'

I shrugged uneasily. 'I suppose it's possible – but there has to be more to it somehow. It's all pretty ragged.'

'Why is that?'

'Just before I left New York, I learnt more about my origins. Or less, whichever way you like to think of it. I discovered this photograph of myself as a very young child. It's dated on the back by the company that developed it, a date which makes me about two and a half years old at the time. I haven't consulted a specialist but you can see I must be closer to four.'

I took the photograph from my pocket and handed it to him. He examined the picture, turned it over and read the pale blue stamp on the back, reversed it again and studied it carefully.

'Let's see what you're saying . . . that your real birthday was sometime in 1942? And that for some reason your mother changed it? You can't guess why?'

'No . . .'

'What does your mother say?'

I laughed shortly.

'I see.' He finished the cognac in a quick gulp. 'With so much we don't know, let's turn to what we do. That's that your daughter Romilly is Marcel Coultard's chosen heir. His entire fortune passes to her with certain reversion clauses. You are trustee until she reaches the age of twenty-one. Should she fail to do so the property passes to Claire and Sébastien as the residual beneficiaries.'

Rolin took a mouthful of his coffee. 'A testament designed to cause trouble, you might say.'

'I *would* say.'

'But a testament that also points, however shakily, in the direction of the truth.'

'And that is?'

'Despite the ragged edges as you call them, I think, as a working hypothesis, we should assume you are the son of Marcel Coultard?'

# 20

I CAME AWAY with a great file of papers, a headache and serious doubts. In the file were details of the Coultard estate, the property, the land, the assets of Ciné-Coultard itself. And tucked down beside all this impressive material, the document that was about to alter Romily's life, that maybe had already, the will, its clauses and reversions.

The estate was much more complex than I'd imagined. Registered in May 1945 as the European conflict ended, Ciné-Coultard had taken full advantage of the great need of French people to take a deep breath of relief after the complex and dangerous war they had just endured. In all probability the same need felt by all European peoples. The movies filled a good part of that need. A great mass of Hollywood product, made during the war, was now available to the French. Coultard, working throughout the war first as a projectionist then as a manager of two or three cinemas, had bought a small company which owned several flea-pit cinemas along the coast. Throughout the forties he added to them, converting garages and small factories sometimes, in big cities like Nice and Marseilles but also in smaller places that were just gaining a name, like St Tropez.

A quick glance at the papers seemed to show that the business had flourished from the beginning. Since then, of course, Ciné-Coultard had built up multiplexes in every big town along the Riviera; it had become a household name. Coultard, and more recently Elaine, had kept the business in good shape. Even the Ciné-box, the tiny cinema across the square from me now, showing Robert de Niro in *Mean Streets*, had been recently repainted, the entrance refurbished and fitted with a popcorn dispensing machine. Among the papers was a record of past and present directors of the company. Elaine had never been promoted to the main board although her contribution to the company was recognised in her title of Operations Director. In recent years the executive members of the board had comprised Marcel Coultard, chairman, old Jean Rolin, deputy chairman, and Sébastien Coultard, financial director; three men, two of them now dead.

All this, plus stocks, land and château, now belonged to Romilly. Before I left his office, Luc Rolin had brought up the delicate matter of the 'handover'. There were rumours, he said, that the Coultards might take legal action to contest the will. Rumours I knew from my disastrous lunch with Claire Coultard were well founded.

'In provincial France,' Rolin had said, 'such threats are not uncommon when a large estate is involved. My suggestion is that we clear this matter up as quickly as possible. Call a meeting of interested parties here, or on neutral ground. Ask Claire and Sébastien directly whether they intend to take legal action. And if not, what arrangements they propose for the handover of the property.'

I blew air though closed lips. 'Will they come to a meeting?'

He wagged his head from side to side. 'Claire; I don't know. Sébastien, you won't be able to keep away.'

I crossed the square to the café where Marcel Coultard and old Maître Rolin had sat over lunch plotting this extraordinary change in fortune for his own children, and for a teenage American girl. I ordered a glass of rosé, squinting past the waiter into the sunlight.

For a moment I saw a man, not tall, not young, but fit looking though his hair was a grizzled grey. He was wearing working clothes, standing twenty or thirty yards along, on the corner of the Rue du Vieux Hôpital, outside Villefranche's Museum of the Resistance. He had been there before I went into the notary's. And I was sure he was looking at me. Until he dropped back into the black sun-shadow of the edge of a building and disappeared.

I shrugged. I only remembered him because he had been standing below a small brown metal plaque, a sign I'd noticed up there when I arrived for the meeting with young Luc Rolin. The plaque told of a woman, Claudette Cousin, a member of the Communist Party who had been tortured to death in the basement of the old schoolhouse, in 1942. Such plaques abound in the village squares of southern France if you look for them. But I'd found this one curious, not only for the fact itself, the murder by torture of a woman of the town, but also because there was no indication of who had done the torturing.

The waiter brought me my drink. The rosé was cool and refreshing. It's a wonderful thing about rosé, it can be *vin ordinaire* and still be enjoyable, which is fortunate because ninety-nine percent of it is very ordinary indeed.

My thoughts went back to Luc Rolin and Marcel Coultard's will. Remembering what Rolin had said about old stones and dynastic connections, things still didn't fit. If Marcel Coultard had known that I was his son, why hadn't he contacted me while he was alive?

Yet there was something here, I was sure of that. After all, Coultard had sought out Elaine in London. Headhunted her is the term she used – and if I really was his son and Romilly his grand-daughter that obviously was no coincidence. In which case, my clear first step was to speak to Elaine. I lifted my glass to drain it, squinting into the sun again. The man was still there on the corner, still staring at me. But when he saw I was aware of him he stepped back into shadow – and was gone.

# 21

I SAID NOTHING about my visit to Mantel, Rolin to Elaine when
she returned from the hospital later that afternoon. She looked
too drained, too gaunt to talk about the Coultards. I imagined,
as usual, she wanted only to talk about Romilly, the possibility
that she had moved her arm a fraction, the inflection of the
consultant's voice when he talked about the length of time a coma
might last.

But I was wrong. She told me quickly but quite briefly about
Romilly, a report that added up essentially to 'no change whatsoever', then poured herself a kir and walked onto the terrace. I
followed.

'How was it with Claire Coultard?'

'Sticky, hostile,' I said.

'Are you surprised?'

'I'm surprised that her father had said not a single word to
her about what he was doing with his money. Or so she claimed.'

'Do you believe her?'

'I just don't know, Elly. I don't want to even think about all
this at the moment.'

I went back into the kitchen to pour myself a drink. When I
returned she was standing at the same spot at the end of the
terrace, staring up into the hills towards the Château St Juste.
'I've been wondering,' she said.

We sat down at the round table in the shade of a plane tree.
To the south the hills fell away towards the coastal plain. You
couldn't see the sea from here, but somehow you felt its presence, an aroma carried perhaps on a small breeze, or just the
knowledge that it was there. 'You've been wondering,' I said.

'About Marcel. About his death. Do you know how he died?'

'No idea. He was nearly eighty. Old age got him, I thought.'

'He was found up in the hills, lying among the rocks.'

I glanced behind us. Behind the house the hill rose towards

the Château St Juste. Beyond, the limestone outcrops were even more jagged and dangerous looking. 'Rough country for an old man to be walking in. No sign of violence?'

'Not unless you count the fact that his head was crushed in.'

'What!'

'He'd fallen, slipped. A shower of big stones fell from a ledge above him. One of them broke three ribs. The other crushed his skull.'

We sat in silence for a moment.

'And you think it was murder.'

'I think it *could* have been.'

'Who are you putting up for it? The daughter? Or brother Sébastien?'

'Drop the sarcasm,' she said sharply. 'Think of it this way. Marcel Coultard was murdered less than a mile and a half from where Nicole Tresselli was found. And a few hundred yards from the section of road where they found Romilly. Okay, Marcel was a man not a woman. It wasn't sexual. But for Christ's sake, a man died within a few thousand yards of one murder and one abduction. Are we going to ignore that?'

My stomach turned. Fabius must have seen the possibility of Marcel Coultard having died an unnatural death. Why hadn't he said anything to me? Okay, to him, I was a simple American appendage to the case. He had no obligation to tell me. But then again, on the surface, he had no reason not to say something.

I looked across at Elaine. She was visibly thinking, in the way I had seen Romilly think as a young girl, eyes narrowed, brow furrowed, lip tucked under her lower teeth. But her face was grey with worry and fatigue.

She had worked for Coultard for six years. She was a trusted executive of this old man who, perhaps in his dotage, had left his fortune to her daughter. Was she really as surprised as me or, say, Claire Coultard? Or . . . I put the question to her as delicately as I could. Did she know more?

'More?' she said.

I was overwhelmed with feeling for this woman with only the remnants of attractiveness, now gaunt, shaking in most of her movements, unable to eat more than a fraction of what she needed to stay healthy, a woman I suppose on the edge of a breakdown.

'It was Claire Coultard who set me off,' I said. 'She even suggested the possibility of someone having forged old Marcel's will.' I paused. 'I think she dismissed it as a crazy idea – but you can see she's scratching around for some plausible explanation. She said there was no family falling out, and I think I believe her. But it made me wonder,' I said carefully, 'whether there was something about Marcel Coultard that you hadn't told me.'

'Such as?' Her mouth hardened.

'Anything, Elly. Anything to help me out. Anything to help us understand why he suddenly off-loaded this huge business onto our daughter.'

'You mean was I fucking him?' she said harshly.

'If you were, you were, for Christ's sake, it's not a crime. *Were* you?'

She sat down in the corner of the sofa. Collapsed really. 'You bastard!' Then surprisingly she smiled. 'You're thinking of Marcel in terms of Claire, aren't you?'

I shrugged. 'Maybe. You mean I shouldn't be?'

'It's her mother that had the looks. She was a peasant woman, spoke with a local accent. But physically, she had something. No doubt about it.'

'So? Claire takes after her mother.'

'Her father was overweight, fat, a withered arm. Not what you'd think of as handsome. A huge personality in a small ugly body. I liked him. I loved working for him. I don't know what you've heard from his daughter, but Marcel was no more French landed gentry – even the somewhat tatty Southern landed gentry – than any man you see running the bars and brasseries along the coast. At heart he was a peasant. But with voluminous energy.' She paused. 'I was not his mistress, Tom.'

'Claire Coultard says you have a pretty generous contract from Ciné-Coultard.'

'I do. But then I do a good job. In return, the company funded this house at a peppercorn mortgage – and pays for your daughter to go to the International School.'

'All this because of the job you do.'

'I know no other reason, Tom,' she said evenly.

'Okay.' I kissed her on her forehead. The skin was like an old woman's skin. She was thirty nine. Looked sixty-nine. I was struck by the horrible thought that she would not survive the worst happening to Romilly. 'You've got to look after yourself, Elly,' I said. 'You've got to eat more. You've lost pounds in the few days I've been here. It's got to stop.'

'It'll stop,' she said. 'When Romilly comes out of her coma.'

I had no answer to that. I poured her a drink, made her a chicken sandwich and some salad and left her on the sofa with a picture album of Romilly since babyhood. Taking my car I headed down towards Nice. But I planned not to go straight to the hospital. The International School at Sophia Antipolis, a mile or so outside Cannes, would be open on the weekend for foreign boarders. Anne-Marie Schiff, Romilly's best friend, would in all likelihood be there.

Sophia Antipolis, between Cannes and Nice, is the international school that serves the American, British, German families and many Russian families in France's silicon valley. An unusual mixture of standard French lycée and English language school, its glass and cement buildings include boarding accommodation for weekly boarders and the children of absentee parents, many of them Russians who live or work thousands of miles from the south coast of France. Straddling what an American would think of as High School and junior college years, Sophia Antipolis is not only a great place to be. At the same time, Elaine tells me, it carries a considerable academic cachet.

To me the setting looked distinctly Club Med. There were about a hundred adolescents moving back and forth across the square, boys and girls carrying improbable loads of sports gear or even books. They met and parted in that easy way young French people have, although they were not all native French speakers. I thought of Romilly and how much I'd missed by not seeing her at school, not seeing her play tennis at which she reportedly excelled, not hearing her speak French with her friends and German and Russian which she was doing as subsidiary subjects.

I sat in the car where I had parked by the roadside until the heat, even through the dappling chestnut leaves, became too much for me, then got out and began asking students how I could find Anne-Marie Schiff.

Being the father of Romilly Chapel got me through the main gate and to an interview, in one of the concrete blocks, with a supervising teacher. Ten minutes later I was in a café beside the school square where senior pupils were allowed to congregate on Friday and Saturday evenings.

Anne-Marie Schiff was sixteen, a little younger than Romilly, a pretty, slender girl from Padeborn in Rhine Westphalia with an impressive ability to speak English. I assumed her French was as good.

We ordered coffee and I brought her up to date on how Romilly was. The reaction was genuine. Once or twice tears started in her eyes as she asked for details about the coma. Most of the time she sat there shaking her head in disbelief or biting at her handkerchief.

Her parents, she said, who were both on a German Foreign Office posting in Washington for a year, had forbidden her to go further than this brasserie until they returned on leave in two weeks' time. She thought it possible they might take her back to Washington with them. But she supposed the police would have to give their permission: they had already questioned her twice.

I had to get it over with. 'You're close to Romilly.'

'Best friends. Have been since she came here. I phoned the hospital the moment I heard. Wanted to go and see her but I was told I couldn't. Not yet anyway.'

'You know her mother and I are separated.'

'Of course.'

'Anne-Marie, one of the gendarmerie investigators I was talking to mentioned a stalker.'

'Someone was following us around, yes.'

I nodded. 'Was it you who told Lieutenant Bisset?'

Her pony-tail bobbed. 'Yes. Wednesdays we're free for the afternoon. We're allowed to go into Nice. We have to go in pairs and aren't allowed to split up. Romilly and I always went together."

'And what did you do there?'

'Mostly just hang out. Get our hair done perhaps. Sometimes we'd meet a couple of boys, you know? But most time we were looking over the boutiques, going to the market – shopping.'

'And this man?'

'That's the funny thing. He wasn't a man, not an ordinary man.'

'I'm not with you.'

'A priest.'

I must have frowned in disbelief. 'You're not serious.'

She hesitated. 'Serious. Twice. On two different Wednesdays.'

'What did he do?'

My tone must have been disbelieving. She bridled. 'Lieutenant Bisset believed me.'

'What did you tell him?

'What happened. This priest followed us through the crowds, holding back sometimes when we looked round. We thought it was crazy. A priest! I shouldn't say it but to tell you the truth, the first week we had a good laugh.'

'What did he do? Did he try to speak to you?'

'Not the first week. The last we saw of him he was sitting in an old blue delivery van, a Citroën maybe, in a side street. He was still watching us.'

'And after that?'

'The second Wednesday Romilly saw him again. He seemed to be following us. We lost sight of him, then, later that afternoon, we were in the market and we suddenly realised he was standing next to us.'

'You're saying he spoke to you?'

'He asked us when we had last been to mass, to confession. He told us we had a duty to ourselves. Stuff like that. He said it was easy for a young person to lose her way. He was saying these things, talking as some older guys do – they don't mean it, their eyes are all over you. Pretending to be concerned for your welfare. But it was obvious.'

'What did you do?'

'We just stood and listened. We were trying to go but he'd got Romilly backed against one of the stalls.'

'What then?'

'He just ignored it when we told him we weren't Catholics. He said his church was just round the corner. He offered to hear confession from both of us. But it was Romilly he was interested in. It all sounds crazy, I know.'

She was such a calm sensible girl. It was impossible to dismiss what she was saying for teenage hysteria.

'I believe you, Anne–Marie,' I said. 'What did you do?'

'We left him. I think we ran.'

'And you didn't see him again?'

'Well, not dressed as a priest. After three or four weeks when we'd both forgotten all about it, I saw a man get out of a blue van just over there. Romilly was talking to somebody near the gate. He started walking towards her and I called to her. Very loud. Sort of screamed at her. She came running over and the man saw what happened and got into the van and drove off.'

'You're sure it was the same man?'

She went very still, locked her fingers together and nodded her head slowly. 'I'm sure.'

'Did you report all this?'

'Yes.' She gave a wry grin. 'But we're teenage girls, Mr Chapel. We're supposed to have fantasies about priests.'

'Okay. I take your point. Did you describe him to the police?'

'I tried. He was older than you. A lot older. About like my father who's sixty.' She paused. 'But very fit. The way he ran for his van the day I called to Romilly was like a much younger man.'

'Tall, short. Dark, fair.

'Shorter than you. A bit, not much. But broad. I'd say he's very strong. And he smells. Not dirty. Not at all. Of a sort of unscented soap. Medicated perhaps.'

'You're doing really well, Anne-Marie,' I said. 'Now, dark or fair?'

'Grey. Short cropped hair. A sort of square head.'

'Clean shaven?'

She hesitated. 'I think. Now that's crazy, isn't it? I've got recall on all the other details . . . but clean shaven, I'm just not that sure of.' She sat frowning. 'If he had anything of a moustache or beard it wasn't prominent. Kinda designer beard maybe. Do priests have to shave every day?'

'You speak good French. Did he have an accent?'

She nodded, on secure ground here. 'A local accent. Not too strong. Local but not peasant. And he had a manner, lecturing almost.'

'So you think he could have been a real priest?'

She paused. 'Oh, no. No, not really.'

'What about Romilly?'

'Romilly thought it was a good laugh,' she said. 'She *wanted* to believe he was a priest.'

'Did you ever see him again?'

'One last time. We were on the bus into Nice. At the back. I looked out the window and a blue van was behind us. I had blue vans on my mind – so I looked harder. The sun was on the wind-shield but I could see his face. I told Romilly and as she turned to look, the van pulled out and overtook the bus. I'd lost the chance to take his number.'

'You said it was a blue van.'

'I told Lieutenant Bissct,' she said. 'Blue, very battered. An old delivery Citroën. Not much help.'

'It could be,' I said without really knowing. 'So this last time you saw him was when?'

She thought. 'A Wednesday, obviously, because that's our after-noon off. It wasn't the Wednesday before Romilly was attacked. It was the week before that.' Her eyes filled with tears which she brushed aside with her hand. 'I should have reported it again. I should have insisted they believed me.'

She was a good girl. A good friend to Romilly. 'Don't blame yourself,' I said. 'There's only one person to blame.'

We had finished our coffee. 'When Lieutenant Bisset came to see you,' I said, 'did he ask to go up to Romilly's room?'

'Yes. She and I share together.'

'Can you take me up there now?'

'Sure. We'll have to be a bit careful about it – or the House Supervisor will think you're my *bel ami*.' She beamed.

'I'm flattered,' I said, 'however improbable the idea.'

To judge from this L-shaped room with two beds, two desks, two cupboards, a German sense of order definitely does exist. Anne-Marie's wing of the L was impeccably tidy. Books were stacked on her desk, clean clothes on the bed, nothing on the floor.

Romilly's half of the room was a mess. Jeans were strewn across the bed. Sweaters and underwear spilled out of half-closed drawers. A school bag had been dropped on the floor and books had tipped from it across the carpet.

'I would have cleared up,' Anne-Marie said apologetically, 'but I spooked myself about it. I said I wouldn't clear up Romilly's half until she came out of the coma.'

I sat down on Romilly's partly made bed. 'Did you know, Anne-Marie,' I said carefully, 'that Romilly had been left quite a lot of money? Not for now. For later, when she's twenty-one?'

'Really?' Her eyes lit up. I think she was thinking of the vast selection of clothes Romilly might acquire. Mature as she was, she still had the preoccupations of modern seventeen-year-old girls. 'She didn't say anything to me.'

'That's why I asked. I don't think she knew.'

I was looking around at the equipment on display in Romilly's part of the room. There was no shortage in the German girl's side of the room and obviously she had a generous enough allowance from her diplomat parents. But what Romilly had on display was of a different order. The Bang and Olufsen equipment. The Pentax. I opened cupboards and drawers. Mixed with market junk in her cupboard were expensive designer labelled items. The contents of the jewellery in the box on the chest of drawers looked real. I couldn't believe Elaine had supplied the money for all this. Elaine was a devoted parent but she wasn't one of your modern day push-overs. Romilly would have had an allowance, and she would have been expected to keep to it. I looked around me, letting my eyes rest on one piece of expensive equipment after another. I didn't feel good.

'Did the police take anything away with them?' I asked.

Anne-Marie watched me as I closed the jewellery box. 'They took her bank statements away with them.'

I sat down on Romilly's bed. We were sparring with the facts now, I could see that. But not in a hostile way. 'She had a lot of things,' I said.

Anne-Marie lifted her eyebrows in agreement.

'You must have asked her where they came from?'

The German girl looked uncomfortable.

'Do you know, Anne Marie? Do you know where Romilly got all these expensive items from?'

'She said she had her own money.'

'Left to her?'

She nodded. 'But she also said it laughing. In a way as if she didn't want me to believe it.'

'The things didn't come from her mother?'

'Definitely not. When Mrs Chapel was coming we had to move all Romilly's stuff over to my side of the room.'

I watched her as she flicked back a stray lock of hair, hooked her hands down the front of her jeans, looked away.

'So, no idea, Anne-Marie?'

She sat with thump on her bed. She didn't answer.

In the silence a fly buzzed at the window. She looked down, picking at threads on her Mexican bedspread.

'I think you know where the money came from,' I said. 'You're not betraying Romilly, Anne-Marie,' I said. 'You can only be helping her at this point.'

She blew her cheeks, nodded, desperate to get out of the room. 'So where?'

'There was a man,' she said. 'He used to invite her to dinner sometimes. At weekends Rom was free if she didn't go home.'

'A man.' I really didn't like this. It was responsibility churning in me. Nobody could say she'd gotten much in the way of moral guidance from me. 'A man,' I repeated. 'Not a boy of her own age?'

'It was just dinner. She was always back by eleven.'

This was hard to take. 'And this man was giving her money, you think?'

'It wasn't the way it looks. I swear to you, Mr Chapel. I know Rom well enough. She would never have done something like that for money. Never, never, never,' she said with sixteen-year-old fervour.

'But he was giving her money all the same.'

'I don't know. If he was, Rom never said so in so many words. She kept it, like a secret. She was seeing him – she had money. I connected the two, but the money may have come from America. From her grandmother.'

'I can check that,' I said. I walked around the room feeling deeply troubled, my mind, unaccustomed to working in any really methodical way, grasping thoughts from the air. 'This man,' I said. 'You don't think there's any chance it was the man who was following you, the fake priest.'

'No.' she inhaled a deep breath. 'No.'

'Okay. And you really don't have any idea who it could have been, where she might have met him?'

She stayed silent.

'Listen Anne-Marie, I know the score. You don't rat on your friends. But it's not like that. This man . . . did she meet him here? At school? He's one of the teachers, is that it?'

'No.' She closed her eyes and opened them wide on me. China blue. 'Not one of the teachers. It was her mother's boss. Monsieur Coultard.'

'Jesus . . .' I said. 'Jesus Christ.'

I left Anne-Marie Schiff at the gate. She wanted me to make an arrangement for her to see Romilly and I promised her I'd fix it as soon as the doctors agreed. I was turning my car towards the Nice road when an idea occurred to me. I braked, reversed and pulled up at the school gate with a double blast on the horn. She came running back.

'The time the fake priest asked you and Romilly to come for confession . . .' I said. 'Where were you exactly?'

'Just behind the American Quay, as we call it. The Quai des États-Unis. There's a Wednesday market there.'

'And talking about his church, he gestured over his shoulder?'

She made the gesture. 'Like that,' she said.

'In which direction?'

'Towards the Place St Firmin. Why d'you want to know that?'

'I was just thinking . . .'

'What?'

'Think for a moment, Anne-Marie – could he really have been a priest?'

Her eyes widened. 'A *real* priest, you mean.' She blew her cheeks in horror. 'Cool,' she said.

# 22

THE EGLISE ST Firmin was a nineteenth century church of no
great beauty, its nave lined with garish paintings and chipped,
plaster saints. But it had the right name and was more or less
where Anne-Marie had indicated. When I arrived there on
Saturday, its oak doors were wide open. The woman who
scrubbed the diamond-pattern red and black tiles in the wide
porch told me that Father Patrick was with the rat catcher.

'Taking confession?'

'In the last few weeks rats have been seen in the church,
Monsieur,' she said severely.

'That's bad,' I said.

'Worse is that they are believed to be nesting under the altar.'

'That's very bad,' I said.

I stepped over her bucket and went into the welcome cool,
perhaps slightly dank, air. The priest was certainly not the man I
was looking for. He stood alone, very tall, thin, not much more
than forty. As final proof that he was not the man who had followed
the two girls, he had a great, uncontrollable coxcomb of red hair.

His accent was Parisian when he greeted me. The despair that
I had no doubt observed in his expression was not for the human
condition, he explained. 'It is more at the ability of rodents to
nest anywhere. My problem is as theologically exquisite as any
head count of the numbers of angels who might dance on a pin
head. It is this: am I justified in poisoning God's creatures who
are claiming sanctuary under the altar? How can I help you,
Monsieur?'

I told him who I was and, as briefly as I could, what had
happened to Romilly.

'I suspect you would not be here unless you thought it was an
abduction that failed.'

'I'm here,' I said, 'because I believe my daughter's friend. I
don't think she's a teenage fantasist.'

I recounted the story of the afternoon in the market when the girls were approached by a priest. He was immediately interested. There was an alertness in his eyes.

'It sounds an unusual approach to you, Father?'

'Of course. Yes, very unusual.'

'Are there other priests here at St Firmin?'

'Sadly no. I am alone to deal with both the lost souls and the rats. What are you really asking me, Monsieur? Whether I have heard of any similar behaviour, perhaps?'

'Have you?'

'Walk with me,' he said.

We crossed the nave to a small door that took us into an enclosed garden. A few irises and cheap pine-scented shrubs were growing among nineteenth-century statuary of saints and virgin and child, of Romans in togas or centurions in helmet and armour.

'Appalling, isn't it?' the priest said. 'But at least it's in the open air, at least, it doesn't smell of dead rats.'

'You've heard something,' I said. 'A priest . . .'

'Claiming to be a priest.'

I conceded that.

'At the beginning of the summer a priest, a man claiming to be a priest on holiday from a parish in the North, Father Damien, came here to St Firmin and asked if he could park his van here. We have a courtyard at the back . . . parking space is impossible to find in Nice . . . a fellow priest . . . Of course, I said yes.'

'What happened?'

'As he said. He parked the van. He drove out most days to visit Roman sites, medieval churches . . . When he was here I heard his confession. One priest staying with another.'

'Roman sites? He's an educated man?'

He hesitated. 'Yes . . . On quite a direct, simple level.'

'And do you know where he stayed?'

'He lived, I believe, at a small hotel nearby although I offered him the rather sparse accommodation of our visitor's room. He declined the offer. The rats perhaps.'

We followed an overgrown path until we reached a wall and the shade of a mulberry tree. Fruit squished underfoot. Wasps and hornets buzzed around our ankles. There was a Roman statue and a few stone plaques set into the wall. He stopped and gestured to me to sit on the shaded bench. I guessed it was a place he came to be away from parishioners. He sat beside me, leaning forward, sucking in his cheeks. I knew he was having difficulty about something he was about to say.

'This man,' he said, after a few moments, 'had had his van here about three days when one of the local girls came to see me. She was very embarrassed. She told me that Father Damien had cornered her in the courtyard the night before. He had, she said, used sexually suggestive language. He had touched her, fondled her body before she was able to break away from him.'

I felt breathless, chilled at the thought of this man, excited at having come so close to him. 'What did you do?'

He closed his eyes for a second. 'I'm afraid I did what the Church has done so often with accusations against its priests. I told myself the girl had probably exaggerated, although I reluctantly admitted to myself that there was probably cause for *some* complaint. I went to see the *soi-disant* Father Damien who was doing something to his van's engine in the courtyard, and I asked him to leave immediately.'

'Did he protest?'

'He made some remarks. Offensive remarks. Suggesting I had an unnatural affection for boys. We priests, he said, are either one thing or the other. He smirked a great deal, slammed the engine closed and drove away.'

'You never told anyone about this?'

'The cleaner, Jeannette, had heard some of the shouting. But I said nothing to anyone in authority until a police officer came asking questions yesterday.'

'Lieutenant Bisset from the Nice gendarmerie?'

He inclined his head.

'Was there anything else to tell him?'

'During the week one or two strange stories began to reach me. Through Jeannette.'

'What sort of stories?'

'Of women being followed by a priest, usually at night. In quiet alleys he would make obscene comments or sexual suggestions. I've no doubt it was the same man, the so-called Father Damien.'

'You described him to the police.'

'Not really tall, but strongly built. Grey, grizzled, you might say.'

'Grizzled?'

'That was the effect. Unshaven each time I saw him.'

'What age?'

'Not young. Late fifties. A few years more even. Perhaps sixty.'

'You weren't able to give Lieutenant Bisset a registration number for the van.'

'Only that it was an 83 registration, that's the department of the Var, next to us here. I remember wondering why he had a local registration if he came from the north.'

'And what colour was the van?'

'Blue. A Citroën. An old model, with corrugated panels.'

'It's the man,' I said. A rage was rising in me that I'd never felt before. I stood up.

'The man who attacked your daughter, you think?'

'I'm sure of it.'

I stood still for a moment in the white sunlight. At the base of the statue in front of me, the young Roman centurion. I expected some religious text. Instead it read: *To our son, François Thierry, aged 19 years, lieutenant, 357th Infantry, Second Army. Killed at Verdun, March 13th, 1916.*

'One of a million men, French and German, killed and maimed,' the priest said, 'in one single battle.'

My rage drained slowly away. Romilly at least, my child, was still alive.

# 23

I DROVE PAST gently waving palm trees along the Promenade des Anglais. The Beach Regency Hotel had some photo shoot going on with two American actresses I thought I recognised, understandably pleased they had made it to the Riviera. Black and stainless steel equipment and cheerful American voices raised everywhere. At reception I asked to use the hotel office suite. I ordered a bottle of St Veran and sat in comfort to make my calls.

I began with Margot. This was our new relationship. I found myself feeling totally differently about her as I waited for the call to be answered. No dryness in the throat; no heat rising in the loins. An asexual friendship between equals. I could do it. I knew I could.

She was quick. I could hear from her tone that she knew I meant what I said when I called her from London Airport. She listened calmly while I filled her in on all the detail, first of Romilly's condition and the priest, then the weird story of Marcel Coultard's will.

For a few seconds she was silent, thoughtful. 'I see what you're wrestling with, Sonny.' A pause. 'Sorry. Old life. New life: Tom.'

'What am I wrestling with?' Knowing what she meant.

'Marcel Coultard obviously liked Romilly. You're asking yourself how much she liked him. Or how much she was prepared to pretend she liked him.'

'Say it,' I said. 'How far she was prepared to go to make him grateful? Isn't that what you mean?'

'Don't thrash yourself, Tom,' she said. 'There could be a dozen explanations.'

'Do they all end with girl, seventeen, being left twenty-eight million dollars?'

'No,' she said thoughtfully. 'Frankly, they don't. But one might.'

'Go ahead.'

'You're not going to like this, Tom.'

'There's not much I like about any of this at the moment. What are you saying?'

'I'm saying there's one normal, straightforward circumstance in which Marcel might leave his whole fortune to Romilly.'

'And that is?'

'If she's his daughter.'

I nearly threw up. It was as if a stomach pump had been suddenly activated in my gut.

'Sorry, Tom,' she said. 'But it's something you've got to face.'

'Wait a minute. That would mean Coultard had known Elaine way back. It would mean she and Coultard were sleeping together when Elly and I were going together back in Cambridge, for Christ's sake.'

'That's what it'd mean, darling,' she said. 'So much for bloom of youth time. Not nice, uh?'

I called my mother. She answered the call herself. I planned to brush aside our last few minutes together in Boston with the dutiful son's account of what had happened to her granddaughter. I was just beginning to reassure her that Romilly was going to be okay when she hung up on me.

I found myself gasping in astonishment. I sat for maybe ten minutes drinking my St Veran. The discoveries I seemed to be making about her personality were a good deal more shocking to me than the discovery that I was not General John's son. Surely she couldn't feel completely indifferent to her granddaughter . . . Romilly had made efforts, no doubt under Elaine's promptings, but efforts all the same. She'd sent birthday cards and Christmas presents. She'd come over to Boston for General John's funeral. She didn't deserve this shit.

Nor did I. I called the number again and again my mother answered. I was steaming. I had to stop her in her tracks before she could hang up.

'I have a simple question to ask,' I said quickly. 'If you hang up on me I put a quarter page ad in the *Globe* tomorrow asking for anyone who knows the name of my father.'

'They'll never take it.'

'Someone in Boston will.'

Silence. Then, as cold as a sliver of ice: 'What do you want to know?'

'I have one thing to ask you about Romilly,' I said. 'That's all.'

'And that is?'

'Are you giving her any kind of allowance?'

'Allowance? Do you think the Bannerman money is inexhaustible, Sonny? If I had money to spare for a granddaughter that I haven't seen since my husband's funeral . . .'

I stopped her. 'I'm not *expecting* you to give Romilly an allowance. I'm just asking if you are already giving her one.'

'Why?'

'Are you?'

'I am most certainly not.'

I hung up, mouth dry, hands slightly trembling. So there was nothing coming from the Bannerman family. Which meant, almost certainly, that it was Coultard who had been giving Romilly money. There was no one else. And on his death he had left her his whole estate. I hadn't felt this bad about things for a long time. Was my seventeen-year-old daughter sleeping with him? Sleeping with her mother's eighty-year-old boss? Crazy. Or was Margot's idea closer the truth – that Romilly was not my daughter at all? I sat there. It was Margot's idea, that had the real power of pain.

Jesus, life can be a bitch.

I swung away from the beach, took the big Boulevard Jean Jaurès, jumped to the Boulevard Risso and headed for the Acropolis. I was late back for my watch at the *Centre médical*. I hurried through the lobby to the elevator. Took the fourth floor and strode fast along the now familiar I.C. corridor. The nurses at the desk smiled and waved me through. On the way here, I had been building a fantasy that Romilly had taken a turn, miraculously, for the better. The reception nurse's smile seemed to confirm it. But as I reached the door the house doctor was emerging. One glance at his face and I didn't have to ask.

'I'm sorry, Monsieur Chapel,' he said. 'No change.' He offered one of those peculiarly Gallic shrugs. 'But that, at least, means no change for the worse.'

I stood back to let him pass. Through the almost opaque glass of the senior nurse's office I could see the blue uniform of a gendarme. He was a young man, standing, sipping coffee. I could see the outline of a second gendarme sitting at a desk.

When the man with the cup saw me, he hurriedly put it down and came out into the corridor. His uniform cap was on a chair beside Romilly's door. I hadn't noticed it before.

'You're stationed here?' I asked him.

He hesitated and I called over the senior nurse. 'I'm Thomas Chapel,' I said. 'Romilly Chapel's father.'

The nurse confirmed with a nod.

'My apologies, Monsieur,' the gendarme said. 'Yes, I'm here until I'm relieved in two hours' time. Your daughter has been assigned twenty-four-hour surveillance.'

'Who by?'

'By Lieutenant Bisset, the investigating gendarmerie officer. On Judge Fabius's order.'

'Usually it means someone's thought to be in danger, is that right?'

'I'm here just to make sure nobody unauthorised goes in. That's all I know.'

I thanked him and turned towards Romilly's room. Would Romilly's assailant follow up his victims in hospitals? God knows. Or was it press intrusion Fabius was worried about? But then journalists in France were a lot more disciplined than British or American reporters. So, at least, I'd heard. Swallowing hard, as I always did, I let myself into Romilly's room and sat on the plain wooden chair next to her. Her face, bandaged like a nun's, was beautiful and serene. I felt confused, uncertain about what Romilly had been doing with Coultard, queasily uncertain about Margot's suggestion, uncertain if there was any connection between Coultard's huge bequest and what had happened to Romilly. Weary with feelings.

I took a book from the shelf beside me, any book. I opened it at the beginning and began reading out loud. '*Call me Ishmael . . .*'

## 24

DAYLIGHT SLOWLY FILLED the small white painted room. Monitors flashed their messages in peaks and troughs; a green dial showed a comforting 99 on the blood-oxygen control. Outside there were the sounds of brisk hospital activity. I got out of my chair and put *Moby Dick* on the bookshelf. I stretched a few times. Not a muscle moved in Romilly's face. I could feel her breath on my hand but for every other sign of life I was dependent on the machines. I bent down and kissed her forehead. 'Be back tonight,' I said. 'Your mother'll be here in a couple of minutes.' It was a new day; Saturday, eight days into the coma.

I looked down at her again and thought of the blonde girl strolling with tennis racquet and bag through the market place yesterday. Full of life, full of a beautiful lazy, feline energy. That was Romilly the week before. Now her skin was white as candle-wax, her brow domed where she had been shaved like a fashionable Renaissance lady. I touched her hand goodbye and left.

The nurses' station was busy with the changeover. Phones were ringing and being answered. I waved to Colette, one of the duty nurses and headed for the corridor.

'Monsieur Chapel,' Colette's voice called me back. 'Call for you. Inspector Bisset.'

I took the call at the desk.

'No news on Romilly?' Bisset asked.

'Everything's the same. I talked to the priest at St Firmin yesterday.'

'Did you? A smart piece of detective work, Mr Chapel. He told you about Father Damien?'

'He did. What are you doing about it?'

'We still don't have enough information to establish whether or not he's a real priest. But I've got officers touring churches throughout the city to see if he's known to any other parish priest.

And I'm having a photo-fit built up. If it's good enough we'll broadcast it on the local news.'

'Good. You wanted to speak to me.'

'Listen, I just got in. The desk sergeant gave me a minor incident report to read. Complaint from a hooker named Justine Bombard about one of her protégés being beaten up. Badly beaten, you know what I mean. Really badly.'

'Like Nicole Tresselli?'

'Could be. I've got a meeting here that'll take fifteen, twenty minutes, then I'm going over to her place to see her. You want to come along?'

'I want to come,' I said, 'if what you're saying is that it might have something to do with Romilly.'

'It might have something to do with this case. Good enough? You said you want to know who you're up against. This could show you a few things. I called Justine Bombard a few minutes ago. A name came up.'

I waited.

'Sébastien Coultard.'

'Jesus. Yes, I'm coming. What about Fabius? He won't like me being there.'

'He's in charge but he's not my boss. You understand?'

'Very French. No, I don't understand at all. But I'll profit from my ignorance.'

'Okay. We'll deal with Fabius when we know if we've got anything to deal with.'

'Listen, I really appreciate this.'

'A chance to see the lowlife side of the Riviera,' he said, cutting off my attempt at thanks. 'Most American visitors don't think there is one. Most French visitors, come to that. You'll change your mind when you meet Justine.'

It was only a few minutes drive down through Nice to the gendarmerie at Bas Cimiez, but enough to get the brain moving again after a night of reading and dozing beside Romilly's bed. Enough to make me ask myself why a police lieutenant would call in the early morning and invite the father of the victim to accompany him on the investigation. Okay, things were different in France – but not that different. Cops the world over wanted to get on with their job without interference. They would all tell you that interference from the bereaved or aggrieved was something they could do without. So why was Bisset inviting me in? And at the risk of irritating Judge Fabius, his boss who was not quite his boss.

Bisset was waiting for me in the lobby of the Gendarmerie Nationale building with a brown paper bag of croissants and coffee in styrofoam beakers. He looked cool and relaxed as ever in well-cut gray pants, a pale shirt and linen jacket. Not like a cop. With a quick handshake, he led me through swinging fire doors and past the kitchens to the rear parking lot. As we crossed the gravel lot towards a line of vehicles, I asked him straight why he was taking me along this morning. 'You're not going to persuade me you do this with all your cases.'

'No,' he said. We stopped by the blue cars. He handed me a cup of coffee, took one himself and put the bag of croissants on the roof of the car while he thumbed off the lid of his cup. 'Fabius is angling to get me sent back to Paris,' he said slowly. 'I don't know why yet. The given reason is that I've finished running repairs to the homicide table here in Nice.'

'That was why you were originally sent down south?'

'Parts of the murder brigade here in the city were thought to be too tied in to local politicians. The minister in Paris sent me down to do a quick repair job. What do you say – kick a few asses?'

'Was Fabius involved in this in some way?'

'No. At least not that I know of. He's just part of the local establishment that gets unhappy when the status quo is disturbed.' He paused. 'He's trying his best to get me posted back to Paris. But then I don't need anonymous letters to tell me I'm not popular with the powers that be down here.'

'I still don't see how I fit in with this. I don't see why you're taking me with you.'

He sipped thoughtfully on his coffee, reached out and broke off a piece of croissant in the bag. 'Fabius wants to see this case a certain way. He hung on as long as he could to a hit and run solution for what happened to Romilly – elbowing Nicole Tresselli out. Now we have some path lab work that points to a connection. He doesn't like that. He may be right. I might be straight off the rails. But either way he doesn't like the way I'm seeing it.'

'What made the connection?'

'Bruise marks. Finger distancing. Our man has big hands, a concert pianist's span. He left marks on Nicole and they look like the same marks on Romilly's upper arm.'

I flipped the lid off my coffee. Too shaky, too hard. The lid frisbeed away across the lot.

'Don't ask me why Fabius is dragging his feet on this. I don't know. I know that if I suddenly disappear back to Paris on the next Air Inter flight, I want someone to have enough information to make trouble if this is settled as a simple hit and run by an unknown driver.'

'Me?'

'At headquarters, the moment I'm gone all my guys here will have to keep their heads below the parapet. You can imagine.'

I nodded.

'So I'm relying on you. You don't seem the type to take a whitewash.'

It was the first time in my life anybody had said anything like that to me. I'd spent my childhood being told by my mother that I had to be cured of a wimpish cowardice. I'd come to believe it. And now I was being told I wasn't that sort of guy at all. I don't know if I entirely believed it, but I sure as hell appreciated it. 'Thanks,' I said. 'Thanks for the vote of confidence.'

Within minutes we were driving across Nice in a blue gendarmerie Renault Nevada, drinking coffee from the styrofoam cups and breaking off pieces of croissant from the greaseproof paper bag. Bisset kept the windows buzzed down as we drove through narrow alleys down to the harbour. The smell of boats and ship's chandlers and the welcome bite of the early morning sea air for the moment dispelled the tiredness.

'Justine is a girl known to the police, as they say.' Bisset drove with one hand, holding his coffee in the other. 'She's not a kid. Thirty-six, seven, eight. Maybe forty. She got badly beaten up by a client eight or nine years ago. She no longer has the face for the job. So she looked to exploit her skills in another direction. She's now Madame La Présidente of the *Working Girls of Nice*. She keeps an eye on girls new to the city. Dancers, club-girls, streetwalkers, outcall specialists, porno queens . . . She knows her rights and doesn't cringe from the law.'

'You mean she runs a union for hookers?'

'Why not? They need a union more than most. I give her as much support as I can. She gives me the sort of information I could never get otherwise.'

'Such as?'

'The names of the sort of men who get their kicks from beating up women like Nicole Tresselli.'

I looked at him with astonishment. 'Are you saying Sébastien Coultard is one of them?'

'Could be. But Coultard has a clean sheet. He's had his clashes with the law but none of them have ever come to a charge.'

'Political clout.'

'Who knows? But let's see what Justine has to tell us this time. Let's stay with the evidence. It's easier to read than guesswork. That was one of the favourite lines of my boss in Illinois.'

We came off the quayside and turned into the alleys beyond. Half way along he pulled the Nevada onto the sidewalk and parked. A squad car pulled in behind us and a uniformed gendarme got out. He was carrying a black nylon camera bag.

'Since the body of Nicole Tresselli was discovered,' Bisset said. 'I've had Justine looking out for the sort of hard sex that interests our *mec*.'

'*Mec*?'

'Our guy. The killer. Her idea is that Nice is getting a reputation with sado-perverts. Summer visitors. Foreigners mostly who come down to Nice for the sport. So far none of the incidents has come to anything. The girls get beaten up but are usually paid off or scared off before they can lodge a complaint. According to Justine, Sébastien's name lurks in the background of too many of these incidents. Often enough the girl has been employed as a "dancer" in one of his clubs. She gets propositioned by a couple of the customers. Obviously she doesn't know just how far they want to go. Three or four hours later, they return her beaten, whipped, punched, whatever takes their fancy, to the streets of Nice. Typically, she'll also have a purse stuffed full of francs. The girl refuses to lodge a complaint. Case closed.'

'But this morning's incident looks more promising?'

He nodded. 'Girl beaten up and paid off. Often enough the girls are willing to tell Justine in private they started off in a Coultard club. There they'd meet two or three "important" customers. Sometimes even Coultard himself encouraged them to go off with them.'

'Where are the girls taken?'

'Somewhere outside the city. We don't know where. There are some rooms, a mock-up torture chamber. That's where the beatings take place. Maybe this time we'll hear the details.'

'So wasn't this what happened in Nicole Tresselli's case?' I was suddenly as excited as I'd ever been. 'Isn't this it? Isn't this the answer? Sébastien Coultard and maybe some "important customers" are responsible for Nicole Tresselli's death. Then the whole question of his father's will blows up in his face and he loses it and snatches Romilly . . .'

'Sébastien has an alibi for the Tresselli time of death. I haven't chased him on it, but it looks to me he also has an alibi for the abduction of Romilly. Put Sébastien Coultard in the frame and that makes the priest no more than a coincidental stalker.' He paused. 'My money's still on the priest.'

The heat drained from me. 'Sure. My first attempt to play detective – not that successful, huh?'

'Who knows in the long run?'

'"Back to the evidence" as your old Illinois boss would say. You think Justine's going to have something for us?'

'Let's go see.'

We got out of the car. The street was a mix of houses, work-shops and North African cafés. The few houses were different shades of peeling orange and yellow ochre, high and narrow with at least a half dozen bells beside each door.

We walked down the alley and stopped at a chipped black door beside a shoemaker's workshop. All the original brass door furniture was missing leaving letter slots and key holes crudely drilled in the wood. But on a wooden plate screwed onto the wall there were bells that looked as if they might work. Bisset rang. The gendarme with a camera bag stood to the side.

We waited. Bisset finished his coffee in a last gulp and tossed the beaker into a dented bucket placed under a broken down-pipe in the forlorn hope of rain. He rang again and we waited for another full two minutes before I heard heels on a bare staircase and a broken nosed sallow-faced woman opened the door. 'You're too late,' she said. 'I warned you. The bitch is having second thoughts.'

Justine Bombard was not a good-looking woman. She had a thin-lipped face and a nose and jaw-bone out of shape – but I saw, as she walked up the stairs in front of us, that she had a spectacular figure.

Her apartment was on the top floor. The door opened onto a kitchen with a jumble of unwashed plates in the sink and two cat dishes with a spray of cat food on the floor beside them. Yesterday's cat food at least.

The living room was a large attic with a big TV set in one corner and a double bed with a faded purple satin eiderdown pushed against the wall. On a sofa a younger woman sat smoking. I had a first impression of dark, curly hair and rounded Arab features. Plump, be-ringed hands, much darker at the knuckles. And jeans that bulged at the thighs. Justine introduced her as Lara. From Egypt.

Bisset took a cigarette from the pack on the table in front of the girl, sniffed it and lit it with her lighter. Sitting on the arm of the sofa, he looked toward the older woman. 'So, Justine . . . A simple fracas in a nightclub? Or what?'

Justine gestured to the girl on the sofa. 'She'll tell you.'

Bisset turned towards Lara. 'Who hired you?'

The girl looked down. 'I don't know his name. He was French.'

'So are most of the people in this town!' Bisset said.

Justine was on her feet. 'You stupid bitch!' She turned on the girl. 'He and his friends nearly kill you and you still don't want to name names. What about next time? What about the next girl? We've got one dead already and probably another three or four nobody knows about. Tell them what you told me.'

Lara shrank back into the sofa, shaking her head. 'I don't remember what I told you,' she mumbled.

Bisset turned back to Justine. 'What did she tell you, before she lost her memory?'

'She told me it was a club owned by Sébastien Coultard. The *Odalisque*, it's called.' She looked towards me. 'Your friend's a foreigner, does he know what that means?'

It rang bells somewhere. *Odalisque*. Dancing girl in the Turkish Empire. Slaves kept as whores by the caliphs and sultans. 'I know,' I said.

'For Sébastien Coultard,' Bisset said, 'it's a porn theme. Slavery, perfumed sex, sadism, drugs.'

'Coultard uses a lot of your girls in his clubs?' I asked Justine.

'Basically he's a pimp for the visiting rich. They watch the show. If they like what they see, somebody approaches the girl. She says yes. And they're taken off into the hills somewhere. Mostly they get a lot more than they bargained for. But they come away with a stack of francs or dollars or pounds and a few whiplashes on their back. With Lara it went further.'

'Tell us what happened last night, Lara,' Bisset turned towards her.

The girl looked up from the sofa at the three of us staring down at her. Her eyes turned down.

'You'll be safe,' Justine coaxed her. 'Coultard's not going to hear about this.'

'Maybe.' Lara exhaled a long plume of smoke.

'Crying her heart out last night,' Justine said. 'Underneath she's scared for her life. Just playing it cool now for the cops. Show them, Lara.'

The gendarme, kneeling in the corner, had unpacked his bag and was screwing lenses into the camera. He stood up as Lara got to her feet. 'I do private dancing,' she said. 'I'm a top class dancer. Belly dancing, you call it. It's traditional dancing. No cheap shows.' She shook her midriff and winced with pain . . . 'Men like it. They like me.'

'No time for the commercial,' Justine said. 'Just show them.'

The Egyptian girl turned down her heavy lips. '*Voilà*,' she said. Her two hands had crossed to grip the waist-band of her tee-shirt. She pulled it half way over her head and turned her back on us at the same time. 'Two broken ribs,' her muffled voice said through her tee-shirt. The camera flashed and twice again.

I found myself drawing breath through my teeth. The brown flesh undulated across her ribs. There were seven or eight separate white plasters, some of them ten inches long, at all angles from her shoulders to her waist. Parts of her back had been covered with a dried white ointment, now tinged pink with blood. Where the cream had rubbed off, the long lines of whiplashes were visible. The deep yellow-black of bruises covered her shoulder blades and her upper arms.

Lara turned round. 'You see my hips,' she said. She was unzipping her jeans. 'I've lost work for a month. It's too bad I don't know the name of the club.'

'Tell us what you remember,' Bisset said. He meant tell us what you're prepared to tell.

'One of the guests approached me after my act.' Lara said sullenly. 'It's not unusual.'

'French?'

'An Englishman, I think. He said he was from London.'

'He asked you to go with him?'

'He offered to pay me well. A private dance for him and a few friends, he said. I wasn't allowed to know where we were going.'

'And you agreed? You must be mad.'

'She's young,' Justine said.

'Was he alone?'

'There were other men in the car. Friends with him at the club.'

'All English?'

'The driver was French. The men ask to cover my eyes. They're very polite. They give me cigarettes. They pinch me and tickle me. When we got there, it was a stone room, very old. That's all,' she said. She was on the point of tears.

'Tell them,' Justine said.

The girl dabbed the tears away with a Kleenex.

'Finish the story,' Justine said.

'There was music for me to dance to. Then they put on strange clothes. Cloaks. Devil's masks. When the dance was finished, they chained me to the wall and beat me with whips. The leader began to cut me. He cut me many times on the hips until someone stopped him.'

'Were you sexually assaulted?' I asked. 'I mean apart from the beating . . . Forced to do anything . . .' My voice trailed off as she laughed, quick, contemptuous, and looked towards Justine.

'That part of the evening was what they were paying for, Monsieur New York,' Justine said heavily.

Of course.

Bisset turned to the gendarme who had finished packing his bag. 'You get ahead, Georges,' he said. 'See you back at headquarters.' He turned back to Lara. 'And in the end?' Bisset asked. 'What happened in the end?'

'They brought me back to Nice. They gave me good money. Ten thousand francs. But I was sick. Losing blood. I was beginning to faint. Perhaps I did faint because I realised suddenly I was in a different car, like a truck with comfortable seats.'

'A Range Rover?' I said. 'Jeep?'

Bisset nodded. 'Maybe.'

'The driver took me to hospital. To St Roche. At the entrance he pushed me inside.' She lit another cigarette. 'At the hospital, I think they gave me blood. But I refused to stay till morning. I discharged myself and was looking for a taxi when Justine passed on her way home.'

'Looking for a taxi!' Justine said. 'I found her collapsed on the street corner. Not even strength enough to crawl into a doorway.'

'You brought her straight here?'

'Put her to bed with a big cognac. As soon as I could get her to sleep, I took a taxi over to the gendarmerie. If you leave a complaint till daybreak the *flics* tell you you couldn't have been seriously hurt.' She had turned her head to address me. 'Same in New York, uh?'

'Same the world over,' I said and received an emphatic nod of agreement.

Bisset took another cigarette from the pack on the table and turned back to Lara. 'How long was the car journey from the club to the place they took you?'

'I wasn't paying attention. I had the blindfold on but we were all laughing. They were making jokes with me, I told you. Touching me up, but nice, uh?'

'And the journey back? Did you think it just might be important enough for you to make a guess?'

'I was half dead. How could I be making guesses about how many kilometres we'd covered? A long way. They sat me on a plastic sheet for the blood. All I know, I was hurting and bleeding for a long time before we got back to Nice.'

'What time was it? When you got back to Nice?'

She shrugged. 'Four o'clock. Five maybe.'

'Okay. Describe the man. The man who first offered you money to dance?'

'I don't look at men, Monsieur,' she said defiantly. 'Clients are clients. I don't even like men. He was a man, that's all. Not very big, not very small. "Casual but well dressed." She turned to me. 'Like a New York cop.'

Bisset smiled. 'Hair colour?'

'Don't remember.'

'But definitely English?'

'German or American, maybe.'

'Could you recognise him again?'

She shook her head. 'Anyway,' she said, 'Sometimes this is dangerous for a girl. I've heard that.'

There was a screech of fury from Justine. As she lunged forward, Bisset grabbed her wrists to stop her pummelling the girl. 'I save your fat ass,' she was screaming. 'I bring you here for the night – and you won't even co-operate. Think of the next girl, you fat bitch . . .'

'Justine, chérie, I think you've been wasting your time,' Bisset said. Still holding her wrists he bent to her ear and whispered something. She stopped struggling, whispered back and he nodded.

Whatever he'd said had the desired effect on Justine. She shook her wrists free. To my surprise, as she turned her back to the Egyptian girl, she winked at Bisset.

Justine led us both downstairs. At the bottom, we stood in the narrow passage. 'The hospital . . . ?' Justine said. She was continuing their whispered conversation upstairs. 'You really think it'll work?'

'Every chance.'

She tapped Bisset's cheek with the palm of her hand. 'You're not only beautiful, you're a clever boy – for a black.' She waved her hips and smiled her ugly-face smile.

We stood in the gendarmerie headquarters video room looking through the newly developed pictures of Lara which had been pinned to a green baize-board. Bisset's sergeant, Lucienne Barrault, pointed to a head and shoulders of the Egyptian girl. 'I'll get someone to show this one to the staff at the Odalisque.'

'You really think they're going to cooperate?'

'No. But we should try, *d'accord*? We need a firm connection between Lara and the club before you start on Sébastien Coultard. Okay?'

Bisset nodded, hands in pockets. 'Let's see what young Marc has for us.'

They turned towards a young officer who was feeding a VCR with a cartridge marked *Hôpital – Entrée Principale – Urgence*.

'What are they?' Bisset asked. 'Twenty-four-hour tapes?'

'Twelve,' the officer said. 'This one covers from seventeen hundred hours last night until five this morning.'

'Have you seen it yet?'

'Not yet, Chief.'

'Let's take a look them. Start it an hour and a half from the end of the tape. Then fast forward.' He turned to me. 'Don't fall asleep just yet.'

I shook my head wearily. We sat while the gendarme fast forwarded. Images leapt and danced in front of my eyes. I don't think I dozed off. My eyes were open but I was mesmerised by the movement on the screen. Then a change to real time brought my head up and I was watching a small TV picture of a strip of sidewalk, the camera angle from above the emergency entrance to the hospital. The CCTV was motorised to do a slow, limited seven-second pan across the entrance to the St Roche Hospital. Time was recorded on the right hand bottom corner as 03.32. 51. hours. Bisset nodded and the operator fast forwarded again for a few minutes.

The second stop showed 04.15 hours. Bisset nodded and the operator fast forwarded through another ten minutes in which no one passed the entrance. At the next stop the time showed as 04.25. 06. Two young men, quite sharply defined walked into shot. One wore tennis shoes, jeans, a tee-shirt with *Dites-le avec un pavé*: say it with a paving stone. They had mindless anarchists in France too. The camera followed them for a pace or two before losing them as they walked on out of shot. In a series of seven faint jerks the camera swept the empty street in front of the hospital and regained its start position.

For three minutes nobody passed. The camera swung slowly from A to B, from B to A. There was nothing more to see than an empty dawn street, a dawn shadow fingering the wall, a delivery truck passing every few minutes. Then, a car pulled up and a man and girl rushed to open the back door. They helped out a middle-aged man whose hands seemed to be covered in blood as if he'd caught his fingers in the blades of a vicious food processor. They rushed him under the camera. Our last shot of them was as they hurried the injured man through the swing doors. I saw a foot-smear of blood on the tiles just inside.

Then again, nothing. A few people trailed past, mostly drunks, arms waving.

'Nice usually produces plenty of night trade,' Bisset said.

In confirmation three men came into shot. They were still arguing, pushing at each other. One of them, presumably the cause of their visit, had his hand clamped over his mouth. At the swing doors, the two escorts became solicitous, helping the injured man through, patting his back.

A long minute of practically no activity – then suddenly a car's headlight appeared and stopped in the middle of the frame. Behind the flare of the headlight I could see movement. The black shadow of a man getting out. No detail. Standing by the open door, he turned and looked along the sidewalk.

Beside me, Bisset leaned forward in his seat. 'Here we are,' he said.

I felt a tremor of excitement in the room as the man moved

quickly to the back of the vehicle. But the camera was moving slowly back to its rest position. For four seconds I saw only empty street. 'Go, go . . .' The gendarme next to me was punching the air.

The camera moved back. The headlight flared. The man had the back of the car open, the curve of his bent back a black shadow as he leaned in. And then it hit me. The doors of the vehicle had opened outwards. 'It's a van,' I said. 'Christ, it could be the same van.'

I heard Bisset grunt acknowledgement. I could almost feel the strain as the man took the weight and stumbled backwards, his arms round the waist of the barely conscious girl, her hair across his face. One, two seconds and the camera began its return journey. I was off the edge of my seat kneeling in front of the screen, trying to will out of the camera that last half second of vision. The outline of the man's head behind the girl's hair remained just that, an outline.

I was holding my breath. Perhaps we all were. Certainly, I heard around me the long exhalation of disappointment as, a moment later, the camera swung away from the van, resuming the familiar deserted length of street. The gendarme was counting off the seconds . . . one, two, three . . . as the camera moved past the flaring headlight to the open door at the back of the van. A woman, in torn short skirt and blouse was standing, almost collapsing in the middle of the sidewalk. From behind the white-out effect of the headlight, she was pushed violently towards the hospital doors. She struck them and sank slowly down onto her knees. There, her head hanging, her dark hair brushing the paving, there was no difficulty in recognising her as Lara.

A man appeared beside her, a dark blur. He pushed the door open. Taking the Egyptian girl by the back of her hair, he lifted her head and at the same time kneed her violently forward. For a moment I saw her falling face down toward the tiled floor. Then, with one click of the panning movement, the camera left her – and gave us a high angle close-up of a man of about forty, dark eyed, the face savage with anger.

Bisset was smiling.

'Who the hell's that?' I asked him.

'That,' he said softly, 'is Sébastien Coultard.'

I left the gendarmerie before they brought Coultard in for questioning. Bisset had warned me that, short of a breakthrough, they would be unlikely to be able to hold him for more than a few hours. His political position in the *département* would preclude any longer questioning. And, if Lara continued to refuse to identify him as one of the men who had beaten her, all they had was a man who had delivered a girl to the St Roche ER entrance. Brutally perhaps, but delivered her all the same.

A breakthrough, though, would make things very different. As I drove, I tried to think, tried to work out what sort of a breakthrough would be possible. Two crimes, the murder of Nicole Tresselli (with evidence of a sadism not dissimilar to that vented on the Egyptian girl) – and the attack on Romilly. The two crimes linked, unless it was an astonishing coincidence, by the location of Nicole's body within a kilometre or so of where Romilly was found.

Two crimes, and two men. A priest or false priest in late middle age – and a young, successful Nationalist politician and club owner. Both with the strong possibility of connection to the crimes, but no known connection to each other.

Coultard and the priest. I could feel my heart beating as I drove, feel the blood rising. I was shaking with a vengeful fury so intense that the road before me seemed to fade until it was Sébastien Coultard that I saw filling the windshield, and just a few feet behind him the priest, obscured, but not hidden, by a muslin curtain.

I braked hard. The image fled. I pulled over and switched off the engine. I leaned forward on the wheel, breathing hard. Fatigue and fury are dangerous companions on a drive through those mountain roads.

I sat back, wide awake now. The single issue was: were Bisset and I wrong in trying to connect the murder of Nicole and the attack on Romilly? Was there perhaps no connection? And did that mean that Marcel's will did *not* figure in the attack on Romilly at all?

That, in other words, Judge Fabius was right all along?

# 25

OVERLOOKED BY THE Coultard château, out on the edge of the rocky plateau that tipped towards the Alps, Lac St Juste lay flat and leaden below a starlit sky. There was no moon. Among the scattered olive trees and umbrella pines on its banks the very faintest breeze caused a rustle of leaves. But mostly, in a temperature that had not dropped much below thirty degrees Celsius at midnight for six weeks, the trees, the lake, the whole bare landscape, seemed to lie immobile in the dark heat.

Paulette Rodinet was afraid. As she walked along the path by the rim of the lake, a basket in one hand and a long handled shovel in the other, she thought of all the stories she had heard about the lake over the years. A drowned village, a village deliberately flooded against the will of the villagers, soon gets a reputation. Madame Rodinet did not entirely believe that the lost village of St Juste had really become the home of all the devil-spirits in the region. But she and others had heard so many stories of strange sounds at night from hunters, lovers and truffle-poachers. Stories about the screams of women, the howls of what could be wolves and could be the unspeakable creature, the wolf-man who was supposed to haunt the area. Of course she knew that other parts had similar stories made up by silly women and malicious boys, and she was quick enough to dismiss them – sitting in the square in daylight. Now, walking the edge of the lake at night, alone, she didn't feel so sure.

But despite all her fears, tonight's task was something that just had to be done, something that no one else but Paulette Rodinet should do while the drought gave the opportunity. Whatever it involved, she was convinced she was still strong enough to do it. It's true that seventy years old is not thirty-five. But she was a woman who had worked every day of her life. Or at least twenty-thousand days of her 25305. On a rainy afternoon, she had once worked out the numbers to entertain her daughter, Lysette.

The path she was walking that night ran along what two months ago had been the side of the lake. At that time you could have kicked a stone from where she walked and heard it plop into the water a metre or so below.

It was different now. The water level had receded towards the bottom of the valley. By starlight the steep hillside was revealed, cracked and runneled like a moonscape and in the centre of the lake the forlorn ruins of the drowned village of St Juste were visible. The dam at the far end of the lake, with waves surging to its brim in spring, now held back no more than ten metres of still water. It was still a substantial lake, filling the bottom of the whole valley. But the demands of this year's tourist industry had been exceptionally high. Water had been drawn off in unprecedented quantities; an official drought gave no hope of replenishment. Over the summer months the lake had begun, almost mysteriously most locals still thought, to disappear into the air.

The church steeple rose commanding in the starlight. Madame Rodinet stopped for a moment, looking down on it. How many times had she polished the candlesticks, dusted the pews in the church there? How many village *curés* had she known – seven, she thought, altogether. The young one, Père Edouard, stuck in her mind, naturally. She had only been twenty-eight herself then, when he had kissed her briefly, guiltily, in the vestry that day. She had come back for more the next day, but the poor man had been to confession and shuddered at the sight of her. Then, after Edouard, two or even three quite ordinary ones. Good men who did their work with faith and charity. Then, of course, the old fat one, with the big innocent eyes. There was no doubt in any villager's mind that he had bad habits. Some of the young boys as good as said as much. Though Madame Rodinet was one of those who supported him, believed him as innocent as his eyes.

But the village mayor of those days had collected a petition to the bishop for his removal. In the end, for the sake of sticking together, the whole village had signed it, even Madame Rodinet, to her shame.

Some of the village men had made the reasons clear. Sodomy, they said. And the man with the innocent blue eyes had drowned himself the night the bishop announced his removal. Drowned himself in the village well.

There were stories about him, too. For years afterwards women coming back late from Villefranche market on a dark winter afternoon would claim to have seen him, walking above the village that had been drowned, as he himself had been drowned by its malicious accusations.

Madame Rodinet pushed these thoughts from her head, entering the little pine forest which had once been high above the village. Among these pine-scented rocks how many of the villagers of St Juste had been conceived! The old lady chuckled. She had had good times up here once or twice herself.

Coming through the pines, the starlight shone down into the valley with an almost unnatural brightness, its sheen steely on the water. Next to the church, on the sloping side of the valley, many of the houses, dark rectangular shadows, broke the surface of the water. Their roofs had collapsed, of course, marking out the shapes that made her heart beat faster. She could recognise Mayor Calmet's old *mairie*, the main street running from the drowned square up to what had been the entrance to the village and, at the far end, the *sabot* maker's shop where she had grown up. And then, beyond that, on the far slope of the hill, well above today's water level, her destination, the village graveyard, surrounded by a high stone wall.

It had always puzzled her that so many village graveyards were separated from their churches, from the village that supplied them. When her husband Georges was buried she had worried about the loneliness he might suffer up here away from the village. But within a few years of his burial on the hillside, the waters had come and it was more than loneliness that threatened his chances of resting in peace.

The graveyard had been one of the centres of village protest when, in 1973, Paris had announced the flooding. But Paris had had its way, as usual. Churchmen had been sent to persuade them that no spiritual disturbance was involved in moving the bodies. A bishop had blessed the operation. An under-prefect from Nice in a blue, white and red sash had supervised. The graves had been opened on one mist-laden afternoon in November. It was a hurried operation. There were workmen with shovels, it's true. But they were also using a JCB digger, a *pèle mécanique*. Coffins split, bones tumbled out. Porcelain roses shattered. The headstones in purple granite, angled away from the graves, had all been left behind. When the graves yawned, the gravestones had shied away in shame.

And Paulette had not been there. She had been in hospital in Nice, having a hernia sutured. When she returned a week later, the water was rising. The way to the village was barred by gendarmes and men in civilian clothes with clip boards and lists and yellow plastic hats. It reminded her of some of the things that had happened during the war. She had felt sickened.

And felt even worse when Lysette had taken her aside, and told her that she was not sure that the removal of the remains had been properly carried out. Lysette's story was that it had begun to rain heavily as the diggers reached the part of the grave-yard where Georges was buried, the seminary corner as it was known for reasons now forgotten. The sous-prefect was shel-tering under an umbrella held by one of his staff. The bishop had braved the rain but the sous-prefect had become angry at the time the diggers were taking. The point Lysette was making was that she was far from sure that the *whole* of Georges had been lifted into the new coffin. The villagers were supposed to have been allowed to inspect the remains – but the officials blocked her way. And the way of several others from the semi-nary corner. The officials were in a hurry. Promises made were quickly broken. With Paris, it was always the same.

The walled graveyard looked the same in the starlight, unchanged by nearly twenty years submersion. But she knew this couldn't be the case. The iron gates were still more or less in place, part open, heavily rusted but apparently intact. As she drew closer she saw that they were draped with water grass, brittle-dry after days of exposure to the sun, that the cemetery walls were sagging, washed free of mortar between the stones, and in places completely collapsed.

She put down her basket just inside the gates and took out an old bicycle lamp, testing it by shining it into the graveyard. It was a sight that reminded her of the Rising from the Dead depicted above the altar of the church of Villefranche. Pressure of water had smoothed but not filled in the holes left by the *pèle mécanique* on that last day when the prefect was there. Gravestones lay at careless angles, or flat on their inscriptions, family vaults were cracked open.

By the light of the lamp she made her way up to the far corner of the graveyard where her husband's grave had once been. She recognised the headstone, the deep pink marble with the zinc flower holder which had once glowed like polished silver. The inscription: To my husband, Georges, and underneath it, Georges Rodinet, 1897-1971. For a moment she played the lamp-beam on the stone, like many of the others cracked by vandals in the days before the rising waters made it safe.

Then she took the long handled shovel and began to dig.

Jean-Claude Fabius stood at the stone parapet of the château terrace, pretending to look out across the lake. But it was Claire Coultard he was watching as she poured two glasses of brandy and began to walk towards the far end of the stone terrace where he stood in deep shadow.

'Every evening the lake seems to have gone down another half metre,' she was saying. 'This is a record year for tourists. Nice and Cannes are thirsty. The devastation caused up here by drawing off water is of no importance to the préfecture. Even less to the ministry in Paris.'

He watched her move under the terrace lights, casual in jeans and sleeveless shirt and open sandals. Mesmerised by the extraordinary darkness of her complexion against her teeth, the sheen of bare arms and shoulders, he found he hadn't answered her. 'Paris . . .' he said hurriedly. 'No, Paris doesn't concern itself with our problems.'

She handed him the cognac. 'What was it you wanted to see me about so urgently?'

Fabius stood stiffly in his dark open-necked shirt, dark trousers. They had met professionally in Nice but she had never before seen him without a suit and tie. The absence of a tie was a message of course. A message that this was not simply a professional visit. He was, she acknowledged to herself, an attractive man. But she still couldn't detach from this man in front of her, the fact that his father was Professor Fabius, the sworn enemy of everything her own father stood for; a man wanted, when the war ended, as a vicious bounty hunter of Jews.

And yet this man, his son, who would have barely known his father, had suffered ever since from the pointing fingers of those who called him the professor's son, as if he shared his father's views. The world was unjust, Claire thought. And she, with her distaste for this man, was part of that injustice. 'On the phone, you mentioned a delicate matter,' she said.

'Indeed.' He sipped the strong spirit and savoured it, used to choosing his own moment. 'Has word reached you yet about your brother, Sébastien? He was brought into the Nice gendarmerie for questioning this afternoon.'

She frowned. 'Questioning? About what?'

'The immediate issue involves an assault on a dancer who probably worked at the *Odalisque*. There's no real evidence to suggest he committed the assault. What we know for certain is that he took her to hospital afterwards . . .'

'Not in itself a crime.'

'No. But more seriously, some of the background to the events seem to parallel the case of Nicole Tresselli.'

'The murdered girl.'

He nodded.

'I'm prepared to accept,' she said slowly 'that my brother consorts with political thugs, is perhaps even a political thug himself. But he is not a murderer. Nor did he attack Romilly Chapel, if that's what you're about to suggest.'

Fabius held up his hands. 'Please. This is not an official visit. I simply thought you should know that Sébastien was brought in and that he will undoubtedly be released within hours.' He looked at his watch. 'He has probably already left the gendarmerie.'

Claire Coultard put her glass on the parapet. 'Why are you telling me this?'

'I am hoping to be helpful to you. One of my colleagues, the chief investigator for the gendarmerie, is persuaded we should take a certain course in the Romilly Chapel case. He wishes to invoke your father's will as the motive for the attack on the American girl.'

'And you don't?'

'I think the case is much simpler. I think we have a man who has murdered one woman, Nicole Tresselli and attacked another, Romilly Chapel; both attacks being sexual in motivation.'

She watched him in silence. 'You have something more to tell me,' she said after a moment.

'It's not in breach of my role as magistrate to disclose certain facts . . . but it might be construed as lacking impartiality.'

'Go on.'

'I have curious information from the Chapel girl's school,' he said. 'She shares a room with a German girl. Quite obviously, Romilly Chapel was not short of pocket money.'

Her hands came down from her hair. 'Teenage girls today expect . . .'

'There were expensive clothes in the girl's room, Madame. Designer labels, CDs, music equipment, jewellery. We confiscated her bank books,' he said in a rushed addendum.

'You're saying someone, other than her mother, was giving her money.'

'Of course it might have been her mother's money.'

'But it wasn't.'

'No.' He paused, anxious about how she would accept what he had to say. 'The money came from your father.'

She said nothing. But her frown brought her brows down. She crossed her bare arms across her chest.

'Not exactly an allowance,' Fabius said. 'A gift. For a girl of her age, a considerable sum. Five thousand dollars.'

She shook her head. 'I can't believe it,' she said.

'There's no doubt, I'm afraid. The money came from one of his personal accounts in the Banque Cardeau in Toulon. I've been to the bank myself. No company secretary or accountant's name on the order. It's his signature. Your father's.'

She took up her glass and sipped slowly from it, seemingly oblivious to the burn of the powerful *digestif*. 'I'm not sure why you're telling me this, Monsieur.'

'I assume you and your brother are considering the possibility of contesting your father's will.'

'At some point. It obviously isn't something we're going to do now with the girl lying in hospital. But yes, I'm seriously considering it. Very seriously.'

'Then my information about her bank account is obviously significant. You'll allow me to speak freely . . .'

She looked at him steadily. 'Of course.'

'And confidentially.'

She dipped her head in agreement.

'This is the situation. An old man, a man in his late seventies, has been meeting, clandestinely, a young, very young girl.'

'You know that to be the case?'

'I've had investigators show photographs of each of them to restaurants in Nice. We have at least two positive identifications of them both.'

She closed her eyes before opening them wide. It was these strangely hazel eyes that had first caught his attention.

'And afterwards?' she said.

'So far, we just don't know. Perhaps they went to a hotel . . .'

'He had an apartment in Cannes. Another in Nice.'

'His chauffeur took them to the Nice apartment on one occasion. I'm afraid this must be upsetting for you, Madame Coultard.'

She hesitated, then smiled. 'Strangely no. In one sense not at all. I'm rather pleased to see my septuagenarian father was enjoying himself to the end.' The smile faded. 'The consequences of his enjoyment are something else.'

'They didn't stay long at the apartment. We've no evidence yet that there were actual sexual relations.'

'I understand that.'

'But if so your case in law is bound to be strengthened.'

'Rich old man seduced by seventeen year old gold-digger? His head was turned.'

'Just so. It makes a strong case.'

She shook her head. 'It may well be the case that she seduced my father into giving her an allowance, a car or jewellery, even a substantial sum. But not everything. Certainly not *everything*. Not St Juste. No, there's something missing here . . .'

He was disappointed at the impact of his news. 'Perhaps you're right,' he said. 'The mystery is not solved.'

She looked at him for a long moment. 'I appreciate your visit, Monsieur.'

'I know I can rely on your discretion. But your brother should be warned that this is a time to keep a low profile. Even the public suggestion that Sébastien was involved in the attack on Romilly Chapel would destroy any sympathy that might be developed for you if you decide to contest the will in court.'

She walked to the parapet and looked down into the courtyard. Turning, she leaned her back against the stone. 'I haven't seen Sébastien for nearly six months,' she said.

'You should see him, Madame. Your chance of retaining this house is at stake.'

She took a cigarette, lit it and blew a plume of smoke into the moon-shadow striking from the jutting stone. 'When all this is over,' she said, 'I intend to make a public severance with my brother. It's sad, because as children we were close. He was the elder brother, protective. Now we're too far apart.'

He wasn't listening. In silence, he watched her, mesmerised by her totally unconscious pose, the silhouette of breast and hip. Aware of it, she looked at her watch. An unmistakable gesture.

He stepped back. 'Yes, I must be going.' He paused. 'Your father and mine were on different sides.'

She inclined her head.

'They were political enemies but I recall my mother saying before she died that *au fond* they respected one another.'

Again she didn't answer.

'My hope is that the past can be put behind us now.'

'I doubt if it can ever be put behind us until it's faced.'

He hesitated. 'Yes . . . true,' he said at last. 'But I would like to believe, even so, that our friendship will not be affected by it.'

They walked together towards the end of the terrace. He was conscious that she had not answered him. He had not intended to play his last card, at least not yet. What he now knew about Thomas Chapel was a legal bombshell of the first importance for Claire. He had planned to keep it back a week, but his need for her to recognise him as a friend, more than a friend, was too strong. 'I have one further piece of information concerning Thomas Bannerman Chapel,' Fabius said. 'It's about his past. He's not quite the upright East Coast American gentleman that he likes to project. I think you, and Sébastien, will find it useful.'

Paulette Rodinet's spade rang out in the night as she dug her husband's bones. More bones certainly than could have been left over from one old man. Bones perhaps from other villagers, shamefully dug in again by the Paris gravediggers. She would have to tell the Beste family, and the Loirets and the Borellis. They'd all had family buried up here when the village was first flooded. The truth is, of course, everyone in the village had.

She looked down. She had bones piled beside the grave and there were still more left. Perhaps there were others unearthed. She shuddered, deeply fearful. She was just kicking the crumbling earth back into the grave when she saw a light, like a single huge eye, moving along the path towards the graveyard. Without a moment's thought she dropped to her knees, her head down, and began to pray as fast as she had ever prayed: '*Sainte Vierge* . . . Hail Mary, full of Grace . . .'

After perhaps a minute she looked up, the tension in her neck shooting pains through her shoulders. Ah . . . not an eye, but a lantern, with a fat oil wick, throwing moving shadows from side to side, slow and sinister. She stayed still, kneeling, her back bent among the few angled gravestones. The lantern was carried by a woman. She could see her long hair, the flow of an old fashioned skirt. She watched her enter the graveyard, swinging the lantern low now, searching. An animal, a goat trailed behind her.

When the light fell on her, Paulette froze. The woman straightened, unalarmed.

'*Bonsoir Madame*,' she said. 'I didn't mean to frighten you.' Her French carried a strong foreign accent.

'No . . .' Paulette said, shaking. She leaned forward and brushed dried mud from the front of her skirt. She recognised the woman now. An American often seen in Villefranche throughout the summer months.

'I'm looking for my child,' Sanya said.

'Your child?' Paulette was stricken. 'A girl or boy?'

'A boy.'

'Ah.' Paulette had no idea there were foreigners buried up here. In fact, she doubted it. She was no longer terrified, but the strangeness of the foreign woman left her timid and respectful. 'How old would the child be, Madame?'

'My son? Let me see now. Perhaps one, even two by now. No, older. He was a baby when I lost him.' She swung the lantern and the wick smoked. 'If you see him . . .'

Paulette bobbed her head. She understood now. She had heard this story in the village. The American woman was talking about nearly twelve years ago. At the time of the demonstrations against the flooding of St Juste.

'If you see him . . .'

'*Sûrement*, Madame,' she said and bobbed again, almost curtsied, bending at the knee, resting on her long handled spade, as Sanya drifted away between the headstones, casting long fluid shadows with her hair and flowing skirts.

For a few moments Paulette watched her go. The woman was singing a song. She didn't recognise the language but the tune was one she had liked in the seventies. That American film star, Marlene Dietrich, had sung it.

She waited until the voice faded, then Paulette Rodinet took her shovel and her straw hat and her precious bag of bones and crept away.

# 26

S UNDAY WAS A bad day. I awoke hot and cranky. I was alone at the house, Elaine having left early for the hospital. I needed to talk to her but I was scared of what I'd hear. My worst fear was not that my seventeen-year-old daughter had been sleeping with old Coultard – it was that *Elaine* had. At the time we were conducting our dreamy, undergraduate romance at Cambridge she was slipping off to screw a man more than twice her age at the Ritz or Claridges or wherever the ex-peasant stayed when he had business in London.

Jesus, I felt bad about it. The idea that Marcel Coultard was Romilly's father was intolerable to me. Something like that, a discovery to parallel my own unestablished paternity, would somehow cap my fucked-up life.

I called Bisset half a dozen times before I finally got his sergeant, Lucienne Barrault.

'Is Lieutenant Bisset in today?'

'He's in but he's busy,' she said.

'I've been calling him all morning.'

'He's been busy all morning,' she said coolly. 'Now what is it you want?'

The change of tone was so complete, that I hesitated. 'I wanted to know what happened when you picked up Sébastien Coultard.'

'I'm not authorised to give you details of an investigation.'

'Look, put me through to Bisset.'

'I told you, Monsieur. Things haven't changed in the last two minutes.'

'Is Coultard behind bars, that's all I want to know.'

'He was released last night.'

'Jesus, just like that.'

She gave me that flat intoning voice that I was familiar with in my brushes with the law in the US. 'Monsieur Coultard took one of his dancers for medical treatment early Saturday morning.

When he phoned the hospital an hour or so later, she had discharged herself. There was no basis for a charge against him.'

'So, the way he tells it he was no more than an angel of mercy.'

'He claims he probably saved her life.'

'Case against him closed.'

'Correct.'

I put the phone down at my end. Bisset was mad about something, that came over via the morning's runabout and his sergeant's tone of voice. Mad about what? I couldn't guess. It was unsettling. Without Bisset's support I felt immediately alone here.

I pushed that thought out of my mind. I was good at that. I'd spent half my life relegating disagreeable thoughts to some dark corner. Instead I concentrated on what Bisset's sergeant had just said: case against Sébastien Coultard closed. Okay – but only for the moment. We knew Lara had been heavily bribed. Probably threatened as well. The question now was, what if Lara was lying? What if Coultard *had* been with the party that took Lara up into the hills? When they brought her back her body was covered in many of the same marks as Nicole Tresselli's. Did it mean Coultard was responsible for *her* death? Did it mean it was Sébastien Coultard who had abducted Romilly from Villefranche market?

But nobody had seen him at the market that day. He didn't figure on any of the record lists painstakingly constructed by Bisset on the day of the reconstruction. So were the murder of Nicole Tresselli and the attack on Romilly connected after all? Was Sébastien Coultard anything more than a gross Nationalist Party thug? My head spun.

The sun blazed down with that bleak relentlessness that makes you long for cloud. Early afternoon, I tried to catch Bisset at the incident room again but I got the busy routine. I put down the phone and wandered about Elaine's house, glass of white wine in my hand. I felt acutely the lack of someone to discuss it with. Margot, of course, is who I'm talking about and I was on the point of calling her several times throughout that long, joylessly sunny afternoon.

Then, at just after five, I got a call from a woman describing herself as the assistant to the *juge d'instruction*. She was speaking, she told me, from the Palais de Justice at Nice. She left a short pause for me to be impressed.

'Monsieur Fabius's office?'

'Precisely. He invites you to attend his office here in the Palais de Justice at six o'clock this evening.'

'Six o'clock Sunday evening. It's something important?'

'I'm only able to tell you,' she said stiffly, making it clear from her tone how I was to take what she was saying, 'that it would be very much in your interest to attend.'

Americans don't take kindly to a peremptory summons by authorities. But then neither do the Brits, Australians or Canadians. 'Maybe I can't make it.' I said.

She was shocked. 'Monsieur Fabius made it clear that this was a matter of great importance.'

'Just kidding. I'll be there if I'm back from the beach in time,' I said and put down the phone to her gasp of irritation.

The Palais de Justice is just yards from the sea. I came off the Quai des États-Unis and parked, since it was Sunday, in the Rue de la Préfecture. Through gaps in the buildings I could catch a glimpse of white sails out at sea and even the smudge of smoke from an old tramp heading for Marseilles. Within a few moments I had negotiated the armed police guarding the portals and was crossing the echoing marble hall of the Palais de Justice. I was met by a young woman in a black suit and gold-rimmed eyeglasses. They were secured when not in use, I saw, by a black ribbon round her neck. I knew beyond reasonable doubt that she was the judge's assistant.

I was conducted up tiled stairways with thick stone balustrade rails. The huge, round-head windows were shuttered on the outside so that the light was indirect, flowing upwards towards the high ceiling. When a car passed outside, reflected sunlight fanned across the plasterwork. It was cool, even slightly chilled in here. I was surprised, at the end of a long corridor, to see young Luc Rolin sitting on a black, oak bench.

'What's going on?'

'Monsieur Fabius is waiting,' the woman said.

'Monsieur Fabius can wait a little longer.' I turned to Rolin. 'What's happening?'

'I think Fabius plans a confrontation.'

'What?'

'The system likes this sort of thing. Us facing them.'

'To what end?'

'We need certain assurances from them – the estate is still in their hands. We require arrangements to be made to transfer it to the hands of the trustees.'

'And they're refusing?'

'I don't know yet. They initiated the meeting.'

'What's all this got to do with Fabius?'

'He mentioned certain accusations.'

'Accusations?'

'He claims the possibility that they might relate to the crime under investigation.'

'Bullshit.' I stood looking towards the closed door. But did all this mean Fabius had changed his mind? Did it mean he now thought the will *was* relevant to the attack on Romilly?

Rolin was speaking. I picked up the thread. 'We're not entirely defenceless,' he was saying. 'I hope to unsettle them with some initial questions.' He grasped my arm. 'I'll do my best.'

The woman assistant rapped on the door, leaned her head forward to listen and turned the heavy brass handle. I was too caught up with Fabius's volte-face to say anything.

As the door swung open I saw a high-ceilinged, carpeted room. Fabius sat behind the big mahogany desk. Bisset stood against a book case set between two windows. He nodded. No more than that.

Seated in a half circle of Belle Epoque imitation Louis XV armchairs were Claire Coultard and the man I recognised from the video, her brother, Sébastien. He was wearing a black double-breasted blazer, light pants, a broad, pink-striped open necked shirt. He lifted his balding head and turned his dark eyes on me, but said nothing. I looked at him and then at Claire Coultard's set face and decided to forgo the handshake process.

'I might have been more prepared for this if I'd been told who I was meeting,' I said to Fabius.

'An oversight by my assistant,' Fabius said, rising in greeting before gesturing Rolin and myself to the two vacant chairs. 'This, of course is your first meeting with Monsieur Coultard.'

I looked past Claire, businesslike in a pale beige suit, legs crossed, briefcase on her lap, to her brother. He was a short, but impressively blocky, Little Italy character, dark-browed and menacing. The brooding air (and maybe that broad pink striped shirt) had him down as a stage womaniser. A womaniser but not a man who liked women. This time he didn't even bother to turn his eyes on me.

The judge leaned forward. 'We're here this evening to clear up certain matters in the most economical manner,' he said. 'The formal confrontation is often a valuable asset in an investigation.' He sat back.

I looked across at Rolin. What the hell was going on?

'Please begin, Monsieur Rolin,' Fabius said, steepling his fingers as he leaned forward.

'We, of course, did not initiate this meeting,' Rolin began. 'But I'm prepared to take advantage of Monsieur Sébastien and Madame Claire Coultard's presence here to clarify their acceptance of the terms of their father's will . . .'

'Forget it,' Sébastien said. 'There *is* no acceptance.'

'Let me finish, Monsieur Coultard. Naturally the beneficiaries are anxious to know your intentions in terms of a date for the handover of the property.'

'I thought the principal beneficiary was lying unconscious in a Nice hospital. How can she be anxious to know our intentions?'

I could have thrown a glass paperweight at his head.

For the first time, Rolin was flustered. 'I meant to say, Monsieur, that the beneficiaries have the *right* to know your intentions.'

'We're not leaving St Juste. We're not signing over the accounts of the business. Those are our intentions.'

'The law requires, Monsieur . . .'

'Fuck the law. We're not moving. My sister stays in the château.'

Through the corner of my eye I saw Fabius flinch. Bisset watched, his face blank.

'The law requires her to vacate the property,' Rolin said, desperation in his voice.

'If we decide to contest the will . . .' Claire said, pale-faced.

'It will not automatically extend your right to live in the château, Madame,' Rolin said quietly.

'My sister's right to live in the château is absolute. No trumped up will changes that,' Sébastien said.

Rolin stood. 'Trumped up will? I'll ask you to explain yourself, Monsieur Coultard. Are you accusing me or my father of having distorted your father's intentions?'

I'd had enough. 'Say you just tell me what we're really doing here,' I said to Fabius.

'Monsieur Coultard has information to present to us. You will have an opportunity to answer his charges.'

'That still doesn't tell me what we're doing in *your* office.'

'The case surrounding your daughter's injuries is taking on another dimension. That's all I'm prepared to say at this moment. You are, of course, free to leave if you choose.'

I looked towards Bisset for some sort of help but his face retained that impassive expression.

Sébastien Coultard straightened his jacket. He turned to Rolin. 'I want to lay out some facts for you, Maître. I want you to consider these facts and think what you might do in my situation – or my sister's.'

Rolin watched him, white faced.

'The first fact is that my father is supposed never in his life to have met this American.' He glared at me. 'Agreed?'

'Agreed,' I said.

'And yet we are asked to believe my father has *voluntarily* handed his whole fortune, including the home my sister and I grew up in, to the seventeen-year-old daughter of this man.' He slammed the desk in front of him. 'Give me one convincing reason why my father should do that? Give me one *half*-convincing reason.'

'Monsieur Chapel is not required to account for your father's decision, Sébastien. Or your father's state of mind,' Rolin said.

'Would you agree that *somebody* must?'

'In law . . .'

'I'm not talking about law. I'm talking about *justice*. I want to know what Monsieur Chapel thought, how he reacted when he heard a complete stranger was leaving him 500,000 francs a year for life. And was leaving his daughter a queen's ransom.'

I glanced at Claire Coultard. I think she was embarrassed by her brother. If I hadn't thought it, I don't think I would have answered him.

'Well?' Her brother glared at me.

'I think I was even more surprised than you were.'

Sébastien Coultard sat silent for a moment or two, then turned to Rolin. 'He's lying,' he said. 'I think this whole thing was faked, put up. A carefully premeditated confidence trick.'

'What?' I rose out of my chair.

'Sit down, Chapel,' he said. 'I haven't finished.'

We talk about black, glittering eyes as a cliché of menace. This man had it all. I dropped back in my chair.

'It was the idea of a confidence trick, was it, that upset you?'

I was silent. I'd suddenly, horrifyingly, understood what he was talking about.

'Are you going to tell us then, Monsieur Chapel, that you're a stranger to the concept of a confidence trick? A scam.'

I stared at him. 'I don't know what you're talking about,' I said. But it was obvious to everybody in the room that I did.

'You have never in your life, as a Bostonian gentleman, taken part in a confidence trick?'

I swallowed. 'Of course not.'

Claire was staring at me. 'My brother's information is that you've been to prison for it. Is that true?'

I stood up. But Sébastien Coultard was quick. He had blocked the door before I could reach it. 'You're going to stay – and listen,' he said, his hand out to my chest.

I looked towards Rolin. 'I'm being detained here,' I said. 'I'm not having this.'

Fabius came forward. 'Let's clear the air, Monsieur Chapel. Let's hear what Monsieur Coultard has to tell us. It might well be germane to the case we're investigating.'

I didn't yield ground. But I didn't bust out of the room either. 'What are you after?' I said to Coultard. 'What are you looking for?'

'I'm looking for an admission that you first heard of this rich old man from your ex-wife, his employee. An admission that you set up your daughter to . . . let's say entertain him and . . .'

I took a swing at him. It was ineffective and I don't really think it was meant to be anything else. He blocked it easily and could have floored me with his free hand. But he held back, turning contemptuously away.

'Just tell me this, Monsieur,' Claire Coultard said in a steely voice. 'Do you have any explanation that fits the facts better?'

I think I sagged. I think I just stood there and sagged. Certainly I reached out and leaned on the back of one of the Louis Philippe chairs as Coultard and his sister walked out of the room.

The heavy door slammed behind them and Fabius looked at the pattern on the tiled floor, then up at me. 'Maître Rolin will tell you,' he said, 'that you are not obliged to account for why your daughter and yourself are the beneficiaries of Marcel Coultard's will. But I think he'll also tell you that until you can, the Coultard family, Claire and Sébastien, are unlikely to put aside the idea of a legal challenge. Indeed, Lieutenant Bisset may well have further questions to ask you regarding your relationship to Marcel Coultard.'

'I've made that clear, there never was one. I never knew him.'

He brought his hand up and I shook it automatically, unthinkingly. As we left the room Luc Rolin looked at me and raised his eyebrows and turned down his mouth. Picture of an unhappy lawyer.

Bisset was standing beside my car. 'Just tell me,' I said. 'What is it with Fabius? He's after doing Claire Coultard a few favours, is that it?'

'Maybe,' Bisset said coolly. 'It's also that the Coultards are local, important local. We're strangers down here. I'm a Paris cop posted down here for six months before I'm moved on somewhere. You're a flakey foreigner with a deception record.'

'Thanks.' I reached for the door to get in.

'Wait,' he said.

I picked up the cold tone in that one word.

'The information came from the FBI during the night,' he said. 'I passed it on to Fabius.'

'You asked for a rundown on me from the FBI?'

'Standard practice. They carry a very full dossier on you.'

I took a deep breath. 'It was a long time ago. I got drawn into it in jail.' I shook my head. 'No, not exactly true. The prospect of the money drew me in. I was a front man. A WASP, a clean-cut preppie appearance. I swear I just sat there nodding, put in my prepared lines when called on. I knew it was a scam. I didn't know a thing about the scam itself.'

'I read the report. The court accepted that.' He paused, looked along the Rue de la Préfecture to where Claire and Sébastien were getting into his Range Rover. Then he turned back to me. 'Let's take a walk,' he said.

'To anywhere special?'

'Nowhere special.'

'Okay.'

I wanted to get to the hospital, but I didn't think Bisset's invitation to walk offered me a choice. We headed down to the broadwalk that bands the Nice sea-front.

'I've background on you I didn't show Fabius,' he said. 'Spoilt rich-kid, son of a general. Educated in France and England. All the advantages . . . and you end up working for a man like Strummer.'

I took a deep breath. 'The advantages carry a lot of demands with them. I told myself the white powder helped me through. The white powder and my sister, you could say.'

He looked at me and raised his eyebrows. 'The dossier says you might well be involved with her.'

I nodded glumly. 'At one time,' I said. 'Altogether, not a very edifying story.'

We stopped and leaned on the rail and watched the tourists on the beach. There were only a few left. They were packing their canvas bags of sunglasses, sun lotions, sun hats . . . By now the fiercest heat had gone out of the sun. It was time for showers and aperitifs on terraces and dinner at a small restaurant somewhere in the Old Town. Not for me.

'What about Strummer. You still see him?'

'Not for years. He's out of my life. I swear it.'

He nodded to himself. 'He's back in jail. If there's any fraud involved in Marcel Coultard's will, it's not his.'

'You mean it's mine.'

'And maybe your ex-wife. Or maybe even your sister.'

I was angry suddenly. 'You think I'd set up something that's put my daughter in hospital in a coma?'

'How could you have known where it was going to lead?'

'Fuck you, Bisset,' I said.

He nodded.

I held eye contact for a moment. 'What?'

'It would have helped if you'd given me advance notice of all this. Strummer. Your time in prison . . . In this business, you need a friend.'

'Do I still have one?'

'Only just,' he said as he walked off towards his gendarmerie car that had trailed us along the *quai*.

## 27

I HAD NO time to eat. By seven-thirty that evening, when I pulled into the lot of the *Centre médical*, Elaine's car was no longer there. Perhaps she was doing what we'd agreed and was pacing herself. We'd give each other our situation report tonight when I got back to Villefranche. So far it had been like tightrope walking. Every minute was progress in the sense that Romilly's vital systems had not collapsed, but every next step could bring with it the deadly tumble into the abyss.

This was now the evening of the tenth day she had been in the coma and, although no one had actually said it, I was getting the feeling that if she didn't come out of it very soon, she . . . well, she wouldn't ever. I stood in the blast of sunlight trying to take that idea in. Had I ever really thought of that before? It's strange how we shield ourselves in crises. Push pain away, forbear to use emotive words, try to limit a human being's illimitable imagination.

I passed through the revolving doors into the lobby. By now everything was familiar – the convex main reception desk, the middle-aged blonde woman and the small dark girl with the fine wrist bones who worked the early evening shift there, the coffee and food smells of the canteen as I headed for the elevators, the nurses and doctors who worked the fourth floor Intensive Care. I stood before the glass-encased elevators moving up from the basement or sliding down their chromium steel poles from the upper floors and thought thank God the French have one of the best hospital systems in the world. Romilly, if she has a chance, has a chance here.

At the fourth, I headed along the corridor for Intensive Care. A nurse whose face I knew was coming out of one of the rooms on the left. Normally she would have given me a half smile and a muted, almost apologetic, '*Bonjour Monsieur.*' Today was her manner slightly different? The '*Bonjour Monsieur*' more positive somehow? I turned quickly into the nurses' station. An *infirmière* in crisp white stood there, a nurse I didn't know. Nor the gendarme she had been talking to. He came forward.

'I'm here to see Romilly Chapel,' I said. 'I'm her father.' I pushed my hospital ID I'd been issued with across the desk to him.

The girl was looking at me, smiling. 'You've heard,' she said. 'Heard what?'

'Your daughter opened her eyes a half hour ago.'

'Jesus Christ . . .' I almost fell back against the wall. 'Opened her eyes? Did she speak?'

'One or two words.'

The excitement was unbelievable. Like the first words your child utters. 'What did she say?'

'That,' she said, 'I can't tell you. I couldn't understand. The woman with her will tell you.'

'The woman with her? Her mother?' Even as I said it I was aware I hadn't seen Elaine's car in the lot. 'Which woman?'

'Me, darling,' a voice came from behind me.

I spun round. My sense of triumph slid away. 'Margot,' I said. 'What the fuck are you doing here?'

She looked magnificent in a white suit and a necklace of perfectly matched amber. But I was blazing angry.

'I brought you luck, Tommy. Don't be mad. More importantly I brought Romilly luck.'

'You knew I didn't want you here,' I said. 'For Christ's sake, you knew that. And yet you still came.'

Margot lifted her hands, palms up, apologetically. 'No harm done,' she said. 'I've friends down here, all along the coast. I won't be hanging round your neck.'

'Okay, okay. What did she say? Tell me what Romilly said.'

'She just looked up and smiled and recognised me.'

'But she said something.'

'She said my name. *Margot*. She said: *I'm fine, Margot.*'

'That's what she said?'

'She said it over . . . once or twice, I'm not sure. She was just pleased to see me.' A self-deprecating shrug. 'Well, not specially me. Just someone she recognised, someone she knew.'

'She doesn't even like you.'

'Don't wrangle, darling. It's great news, isn't it?'

The two doctors in charge of Romilly's case came out of her

room. Both were beaming as they shook hands. 'It's good news, Monsieur Chapel,' the elder said. 'Go in and see her. Don't question her or put any pressure on her at all. Just be with her. Five minutes – no longer, uh? We've given her a gentle sedative. She'll sleep through. It would be advisable if you left her to sleep. Five minutes only.'

'No longer,' I said. I caught the part open door and went in, closing it behind me. Romilly was lying in bed and with a sharp pang of disappointment I realised she looked no different from yesterday. She was pale, her eyes shut. And then I moved across the room. As I reached out my hand for her unbandaged wrist, her eyes opened.

It was an extraordinary experience. I'd seen her breathing every time I came to the hospital but breathing, vital as it is, does not ultimately signal life. The eyes open, the moment of recognition that for a fraction of a second shapes the mouth. The minutest movement of the eyebrows – all this is life. Cognition.

For five minutes, I sat with her and held her hand. When I squeezed, she responded with an answering squeeze. Most of the time, her eyes were closed. But the three or four times she opened them, I could feel she was there, unimpaired, fully conscious.

When I left the room I was choking. There was no sign of Margot.

'Madame is downstairs,' the nurse said. 'She asked me to tell you she would wait for you in the restaurant.'

I thanked her and asked to use the phone. Discreetly she found something to do at the computer as I called Elaine.

'At the hospital,' I said in answer to her first question. 'I've got great news, Elly. Romilly opened her eyes half an hour ago.'

Something crashed over at the other end of the line. The sound of glass or bottle or ashtray smashing to the floor.

'Elly, you okay?'

I could hear she was crying. 'Okay?' There was a long pause as she gulped back tears. 'I doubt I've ever been better in my life,' she said.

'She recognised me,' I said. 'No words but a sort of smile. She's going to be okay, Elly.'

'Do the doctors say that?'

'They have tests and all the rest to do, I'm sure. But they're looking optimistic. They're talking optimistic. She's going to pull through.'

'I'll be there in half an hour.'

'No Elly. She has to sleep. To rest. The doctors are asking for no visits till first thing tomorrow morning.'

'And what now?'

'She's going to sleep through the night. I'm not staying, I'm coming back.'

'Yes,' she said. 'Come back, Tom.'

I hesitated. 'There's one thing.'

'Yes?' The immediate note of worry.

'I have Margot here with me.'

I was furious with Margot. What was important, of course, was that Romilly had come out of her coma. But it was just very bad luck that Margot had been the one to see it. I'm sure it was going to seem to Elly as if Margot once again had snatched something from her.

The arrangement was for me to drive Margot to the villa of some friends of hers at Cannes and then get back to Villefranche to celebrate with Elaine. I should have remembered that moving Margot from one place to another, however short the intervening distance, was never quickly achieved. She insisted on thanking the nurses for looking after Romilly as they had. She charmed the doctors with her thanks and even had a flirtatious word for the gendarme. It was way past nine by the time we had trans-ferred her luggage from the taxi she had kept waiting in the parking lot at the hospital and were on the road out of Nice.

In the car the atmosphere was grim with few words exchanged. We had pushed our way through Cannes before Margot really broke the silence. 'I think you're blaming me,' she said. 'You're blaming me in some sense for what happened to Romilly.'

It was near enough to the truth but I denied it.

'It's childish, Tom, but we all do it when something really terrible happens. Whether we're believers or not we look at our lives and ask ourselves what have we done to deserve something dreadful like this. And in your case the answer just popped up like the tab on a cash register: screwing your sister.' She lit a cigarette, taking her time, drawing deeply. 'Except it turns out I'm not your sister. Not your full sister – and all that's put behind us anyway. Right?'

We drove for a few kilometres more, Margot drawing thought-fully on her cigarette. 'Are you going back to Elaine now that

Romilly's pulling through?' she asked, buzzing the window and tossing out the cigarette.

'You mean tonight? You know I am.'

'Too bad. I've missed you, Tommy, you know that? At Werter's place they're a great crowd.'

'Werter?'

'Old boyfriend. Lovely man. He has a villa with superb views over the Mediterranean. He'd happily put us both up.'

She was, I realised, trying to claim me back.

'I'm staying with Elaine tonight,' I said.

'*With* Elaine?' She arched her eyebrows.

'At Elaine's place. I have a separate bedroom, if you need to know . . .'

That hit hard. She exploded. '*Need* to know? Need to know? Why should I need to know whether or not you're fucking your former wife?'

There was a gravel layby on our right. I pulled over and stopped the car. I took one of her cigarettes and lit it with the dashboard lighter. 'Listen Margot,' I said, 'things have been very tough in the last few days. Romilly's condition hangs over everything, of course. There's also a police investigation going on. The man who did this to her probably lives within a couple of dozen kilometres of the village. He has to be smoked out, caught.'

'Hanging's too good for him,' she said.

I nodded. 'You're right. So it's been a weird time.'

'Of course it has.'

'On top of it all is this bequest. Millions of dollars involved.'

'Millions?'

'Twenty-eight-million at the last count.'

She looked at me astonished. 'Twenty-eight million!'

'There's a château, stocks and this motion picture business. And we don't understand why – why the old guy left it the way he did. Haven't even had time yet to get together the basic facts.'

She was silent. 'But it's all brought you and Elaine closer together,' she said after a moment.

'We're talking.'

'Every night,' she said.

'Of course.'

She opened her door and got out. 'Well. I hope we get some time to talk,' she said reasonably.

I got out too, into the hot, scented night air. Antilles lay a sparkle of lights, just below us. The dark hillside of rock and pine and rosemary and a hundred wild flowers rose up on our right.

She stood on a flat rock, white-suited against the darkness behind her, flicking back her hair with a quick movement of her head. An Athene, a Diana, a Persephone. 'So what are you really planning, Tommy? Do you think you'll get together again, you and Elaine?' she asked.

I walked over to where she was standing. 'I don't know. Maybe some things point that way.'

'You're not just carried away by events?'

'I don't think so.' I paused. 'Look, none of this has come up between us, between Elly and myself. If it's anywhere, it's all in my own head at the moment.'

'And what about us, Tommy?' Again the words were delivered in a quiet reasonable tone, purged of the play-acting she so often escaped to. Standing on the rock, she was a good foot above me. She reached down and put her hands on my shoulders. 'We're not brother and sister any longer – though I'll never stop myself thinking about you that way.'

I knew what *that way* meant. Suddenly the saliva was drying up in my mouth. I was looking directly into her heavily scored cleavage. 'You know I meant what I said when I called you from London,' I said. 'It's over.'

She smiled. Her arms closed round my neck. She stepped down from the rock, sliding her body down mine. 'Don't forget you also said you wanted to say goodbye . . .'

I made a feeble, half-meant effort to push her away.

'But we were three thousand miles from each other.' She squirmed her body into mine. 'Let's say goodbye here, Tommy. Then after, if you want, we can start a new life as good chums. The past behind us.'

I didn't believe a word of it but by then it didn't matter. With one hand she wriggled her skirt up her thighs. The removal of underwear was quick and skilful. Then she brought me down on top of her on the flat rock, one hand round my neck, the other unzipping me. Cars were flashing past ten feet from us as I pulled open her shirt and began to kiss her breasts. When I penetrated her, her always extravagant screams and gurgles were lost in the hum of passing traffic, our bucking bodies shielded by the roadside darkness.

Then, suddenly, a blaze of light illuminated the rocks around us. I turned my head, half blinded by headlights from a truck that had pulled into the layby, the driver hitting his horn and bawling encouragement as he leaned from his window.

I moved to withdraw from her but with that recklessness that was always part of her love-making, and most other things in her life, she locked her arms round my neck, screaming unspeakable words in my ear, thrusting her body at me to the rhythmic blasts of the truck's horn.

I was totally absorbed in the ferocity of the act, aware of the truck but desperately needing that final moment. I ejaculated. When I arched my back away from her she rolled from under me, laughing, breathless. 'Not my first public performance,' she gasped. 'But one of my best, I hope.'

Within moments, she was sitting on the rock, her hair mussed, a breast casually exposed to the nipple, her skirt still up to her hips, drawing deep on a cigarette. As she blew smoke through the halo of light I could only think of a low budget film set.

Casually, she waved the truck driver on. The show was over. With a salutatory double blast on its horn the big truck pulled away. I stood miserably in the darkness beside her. I felt I had betrayed Romilly and Elaine and, perhaps most of all, myself.

'Okay, Tommy?' Margot smiled across at me as I zipped up my pants and tucked in my torn shirt. She had succeeded in getting what she came to France to get. She had reduced me to a quick fuck by the roadside. She had gotten back on top.

# 28

I TURNED INTO Elaine's drive much later than I had promised. She probably didn't need the skills of a hot-shot California detective to guess what I'd been doing. I had no buttons left on my shirt and an exhibitionist's bite on my neck. I started trying to tell Elaine the good news details about Romilly, but she stopped me.

'I couldn't wait for you,' she said. 'I've called the hospital. I've talked to the doctors. You didn't tell me you let Margot into the room with her. You didn't tell me it was Margot who got her first words in nearly ten days. Jesus, what a prick you are!'

'Nothing I could do about it, Elly. She was there when I arrived. I meant to tell you myself. I didn't realise you were going to call the hospital.'

'I wasn't going to sit around here waiting for news of my daughter while you dawdled with your sister on the way back. What were you doing – fucking by the roadside?'

A likely story.

'She's not my sister,' was all I could think of to say. 'No more than a half-sister,' I added feebly.

'And that makes it different?'

I shrugged. Trying to defend myself, I realised all I'd done was admit more than I wanted to. To me it didn't feel *quite* the same. But I didn't want to argue with her, even reason with her. These things weren't a matter of reason. They were the stuff of taboo.

'I thought you told me it was long over.'

'It was.' I had lied a little about Margot when I first arrived in France. I'd told Elly that I'd ended my relationship with Margot a long time back. And I felt there was a sort of truth in what I'd said. I'd ended our relationship with that phone call to her from London Airport. I really meant it. I felt sick at the way Margot could call me back at the beck of her index finger.

Elaine gulped down the Scotch she was drinking, spent half

an hour on household chores and went to bed a few minutes later. I hoped there might be a chance for a return to the warmth and companionship Elly and I had shared in the last few days, but it wasn't working like that. As she said goodnight, she was flatly polite, even quite friendly. But something had gone. In ten days I had gained – then lost – her trust.

I made some coffee and took a cup up to my room. I planned to read something light and not too demanding selected from the bookshelf under the window. But the book that attracted me most was a gift to Elaine from Marcel Coultard: Paxton's *Vichy France 1940–1944*. I settled to the sad and moving story of a great nation in utter, and finally bitter confusion, and read on into the small hours.

Big men don't cry. But as I walked into the hospital room the next morning and saw Romilly smile and stretch out her hands to Elly, the lump in my throat nearly choked me. Life hadn't prepared me for anything like this. I hoped everybody thought I was discreetly leaving Romilly and her mother a few minutes alone as I backed out. But women know our wiles. A nurse gave me a tissue and smiled a teary-eyed smile herself and said: '*C'est normal*.'

I suppose it was – but not for me. For the next two minutes I fought back what would have been distinctly unmanly sobs. Old General John would have been proud of me.

I went back into the room and it was clear that Elaine and Romilly had both cried their hearts out. The doctors, looking on, found Romilly's reaction an immensely cheering sign. '*Bon. C'est normal*,' one of them said. '*Oui, c'est normal*,' someone else echoed. There were a lot of smiles about the place.

Elly herself was overwhelmed with happiness. For a while, at least, she forgot all about Margot. We stayed with Romilly less than half an hour. She was weak, there was no doubt about that, but she had responded intelligibly to all our questions about pains and discomfort and when Elaine asked her what she could bring in, 'Diet coke,' was her clear and prompt answer. The only question she initiated was to ask when Anne-Marie could come to see her and we left the room promising that the German girl would be allowed there the following day. 'Soon, soon,' Romilly whispered. Another good sign, the doctors thought.

Jean-Claude Fabius was in the waiting room with an assistant, a young woman in her twenties. Somehow you could tell she was a technician. She wore her hair in a short King John cut, framed spectacles and a dark trouser suit. On a shoulder strap she carried what I guessed was recording equipment. Fabius introduced us so briefly I never got her name.

'First, congratulations on the excellent news,' he said with a bow to Elaine. 'I drank half a bottle of champagne last night when the hospital called me.'

I wondered if Claire Coultard had drunk the other half. I wondered if the champagne was for Romilly's recovery or the sudden increase in the his chances of solving the mystery of who attacked her. I felt I was going to be wondering about Monsieur Fabius for some time.

'I've checked with the medical authorities here,' Fabius was saying, 'and they are not prepared for your daughter to make any kind of statement yet. Nevertheless she could, inadvertently, utter some words in the next few hours which could be of very great significance in the investigation. I want to ask your permission to allow us to install a twenty-four-hour tape in the room just for today and tonight.'

I looked at Elaine.

'Of course,' she said.

'Monsieur Chapel?' Fabius cocked his head slightly in my direction.

'Sure. It's worth a shot.'

'And tomorrow, I'll come back and see if we can take a full statement from her. I'd like one or both of you to be present, since she's a minor. How would eleven tomorrow morning suit you? That seems the best hour for the hospital staff.'

We agreed.

He made a crisp bow to Elaine and ignored me as he turned away and began to give instructions to his assistant. He had made no reference to yesterday, no reference to the discovery of my chequered past. I had cause to be grateful to him for that at least. Elaine knew I had been to jail for doing cocaine – but she knew nothing of the second visit for association with Walter Strummer. I was content that it should stay that way.

# 29

I DROVE BACK to Villefranche leaving Elaine at the hospital. It was just before midday and I parked the car and sat at the Café de la Paix and ordered a kir from Madame Beste.

Romilly was pulling through. Margot was in France and very likely to cause trouble but she knew the good and bad about me and I still found her easier to talk to than any woman I knew. I suppose she was the only woman I knew from whom I had nothing to hide. In the next few days something told me I was going to need her.

I was sitting back in the deep shade watching the village women shopping for fruit and vegetables from the open boxes outside the small Casino *supermarché* next door, watching how carefully they bought, how they'd pick up peaches, sniff them for the right aroma, weigh them in their hands, unselfconsciously apply a thumb to test for ripeness. I was so absorbed in this moment of southern French life, the kir, the vegetable marketing, the deep, almost viscous shade, that I didn't notice the woman stop next to me.

'Would it offend you, if I joined you?' Claire Coultard said.

I jerked my head up. Then got to my feet. 'No . . .' I said. 'It wouldn't offend me. But I would have thought it might offend you.'

She was carrying a string bag of wrapped provisions from the Casino and a briefcase. She put them both on a spare chair and sat down. She wore jeans and dark blue espadrilles. Her shirt was brilliant white against her dark skin, the material fine enough to see the shape of the bra beneath it. Madame Beste appeared almost immediately and Claire nodded to my kir and ordered the same.

We sat in silence. But I'm not good at silences. I broke first. 'Do you believe I organised your father's will in some Machiavellian way? Never having met him, three thousand miles distant?'

'It's possible you met him.'

'How?'

'Through Walter Strummer.'

I formed a whistle. 'Fabius doesn't keep you short of information, does he?'

'No.'

'Why is that?'

She shrugged.

'Is he your lover?'

'Perhaps he'd like to be.'

'So this information is a little down-payment.'

'You're offensive, but probably right. I would think he might well see it that way.'

This cool acceptance wasn't something I'd ever encountered before. Unless it was from Margot. Yes, Margot might play it this way.

Madame Beste brought a kir and exchanged a few words about the continuing drought. She made it clear with fluttering hands on the apron that she regarded Claire's presence at the café as an occasion.

French people play with their drinks. They don't quaff them with the vigour of Anglo-Saxons. My glass was empty. I ordered another before Madame Beste left us.

'No, I don't believe you somehow tricked my father into making Romilly and yourself his beneficiaries.'

'You did yesterday.'

'I was shocked by what Jean-Claude Fabius had to tell me. When I got an opportunity to put it against what I myself know about you, I decided it was highly unlikely.'

'I'm flattered.'

'Don't be. It's simply that I'm not sure you're clever enough.'

I couldn't help smiling. 'Okay, if not flattered, at least relieved.'

She sipped her drink, then pushed it away. 'I still have no answer to why my father behaved as he did. Equally, you have no answer to what happened to your daughter.'

'You believe the two things must be connected.'

She was very slow answering. 'They must be,' she said, finally.

'Then we have *something* in common.'

My eyes were on the long brown neck above the white shirt. I watched the movements in her throat as she swallowed. 'We'll have to spend a good deal of time in discussions of one sort or another. It'll be easier if we are at least on formally neutral terms.'

'Is that why you decided to sit down here? You could have walked past.'

'It's why I sat down.'

I nodded. 'Okay. I have a question I'd like to put to you, Madame Coultard,' I said carefully. 'I'd like to ask you this question without explaining why I ask it. Is that acceptable to you?'

She laughed. No humour. Not really contemptuous. Just a laugh. 'I think you must know that that depends entirely on the question. Why not just ask your question, Monsieur? I will then choose whether or not to answer.'

'To hell with it,' I said. 'It's no big deal . . . I just wanted to ask you whether your father ever spent any time in England?'

'Yes . . .' she said slowly. 'Mostly of course he was in America. The film business is an American fief . . . but there was a certain amount of home film production in Pinewood and Shepperton. He also visited England to meet up with US studio heads who were in London. Once or twice a year at least. Why is this important?'

'Okay,' I wanted to take this carefully. 'And might he have been there in, say, the mid sixties.'

This time there was a long silence. Then, 'Yes. As I said, quite often. Back and forth. He was an energetic man then, still comparatively young. He certainly spent a lot of time abroad in the sixties. But mostly in the US. At one time he stayed for a period of six months. He took my brother and me with him. We were just teenagers, of course. But what better way to learn English? Does that answer your question?'

I was struggling here. 'It's not his time in America that really interests me. Do you have any reason to believe he knew Romilly's mother in England? I mean did he know her that far back. Of course she would have been a very young woman then. An undergraduate at Cambridge University.'

'Which you were yourself, I understand.'

'Yes.'

Those eyes were unavoidable. 'You mean did my father know Elaine when your daughter Romilly was born? Or more precisely when your daughter was conceived?'

What a bitch! She was enjoying this. '*Did* they know each other then?'

'I suppose it's possible.'

'Did he mention Elaine?'

'He mentioned a lot of women. To him it was the one great benefit of working in the film business.' She looked at me, exasperated. 'Listen, only one person today can tell you what you want to know, Mr Chapel.'

'Ask Elaine, you're saying.'

'I am.' There was an impatient note in her voice. 'Just ask her outright if Marcel Coultard is the real father of Romilly. Isn't that what you want to know? Isn't that what we all want to know?'

It's what I wanted to know but the words felt like a blow in the stomach. Claire Coultard was my opponent, or at least had signalled that she might well be. I knew I shouldn't be asking her these questions, but I preferred asking her to asking Elaine. 'Did your father ever hint that you had a sister? A younger sister?'

'If I had reason to believe my father had another child, I wouldn't welcome it, Mr Chapel, but I would tell you. You can believe that or not – as you choose.' She got up. She picked up her bags and stared down at me before she gave a brief shake of her head.

Did I believe her? Somehow, with a reluctance I didn't understand, I was inclined to.

'I shouldn't have asked,' I said. 'I'll speak to Elaine.'

'And perhaps when your ex-wife gives you an answer, you'll consider passing it on. It will make many things which are embittering my life a lot clearer. A lot more bearable.'

'It's a deal,' I said. What else was I to say?

I stood in Elaine's garden feeling lousy. She had come back from the hospital in better spirits than I had seen her since my arrival in France. Romilly was making rapid progress, the sort of progress only young bodies are capable of making.

It was early evening and the *breep, breep* of cigales and the scent of lavender and wild herbs was heavy in the air. Elaine's garden sloped to a stream, all but dried up this summer to a pebble-filled scar. Rock outcrops rose around the house; in the laziest breeze, lights winked and peeped from among the bushes. But Elaine wasn't feeling good any longer. Not after I had put my question – carefully phrased, but still sounding blunt and clumsy, asking her if there was any possibility that Marcel Coultard thought of Romilly as *his* daughter.

Normally Elaine has a pleasant, rather than a markedly beautiful face, but just now her expression changed into something not far from a snarl. 'Let's get this straight,' she said incredulously. 'You are accusing me of screwing around with a fifty-year-old man while we were at Cambridge.'

'All I am trying to do is to make sense of what's going on around us.'

'You're accusing me of sleeping with Marcel in the 1960s, at a time when I hadn't even met him. And given that he was thirty years older than me, you must be saying I was doing it for the money or for a job which I later, very much later, got with Ciné-Coultard. Am I hearing you right?'

I should have thought more before I asked her. I tried to say something but a gesture with her free hand silenced me. She was white with fury, her hand clenched round the glass she was holding. I thought for a moment she was going to throw it at me.

'Please Elly . . .' I began.

'God in Heaven,' she exploded. 'I know you haven't got an ounce of fidelity in your make-up but don't you realise what you're doing? Accusing me of sleeping with someone else virtually from the night we met. Accusing me of lying to you all these years, making you believe you're Romilly's father when all the time it was Marcel.' She collapsed in a garden chair. 'You really think I'm capable of that. Jesus, what a rotten thing to say!'

There was no talking to Elaine that evening. There was nothing further to say. I believed her. She had been so genuinely affronted at the idea that I thought her capable of conducting a hot romance with one man, me, while still sleeping with another, Marcel Coultard, that I had to believe her. Romilly was my daughter. The dynastic connection I was looking for, the only link that Rolin thought worthwhile considering, had to be between Coultard and me. To begin to understand this inheritance, I needed to know where I came from. Who I came from.

I sat on the terrace, thinking about making a quick flight back to Boston to talk to my mother. But would I get anything from her? Could I force some information from her? I kept it in mind as a last resort.

Elaine had gone to bed. Or at least to her room. I locked up the house and went into the courtyard, got into my car and drove,

It was ten minutes before I really paid any attention to where I was. I was driving west through a valley with great dark mountainsides rising around me. Cannes was marked somewhere ahead. I drove slowly to facilitate thinking. Was I getting towards the answer? Was the attack on Romilly linked to her inheritance? Was Sébastien behind it? He had motive enough. But then how did Nicole Tresselli fit into this? And the 'priest' who had been following Romilly in Cannes? If I could only make a connection between the priest and Sébastien, the mystery would be half-way solved.

I was driving along the coast. I don't handle being alone well. I wanted company. At an *auberge* en route I stopped for a coffee and brandy and I called Margot.

Margot's voice came over the line mixed with music and the chatter of dozens of people in the background. 'Lovely one,' she said. 'I'm so glad you called. I was just screaming the praises of my ex-brother to some Swedish baroness here. She's a-quiver to meet you.'

'What's going on there?'

'Werter and Kisha are having a *méchoui*, you know? A whole sheep roasted in a pit in the garden, North African style. Gallons of wine and dozens of beautiful people.'

She was drunk. Not very drunk. Maybe a little stoned, too. But I didn't want Margot drunk. I wanted her quiet and sober – just someone to talk to about Romilly and her recovery and what part inheriting twenty-eight million dollars might have played in what happened to her. 'Will you meet me?' I said. 'We could have a drink in Cannes. Grilled sardines overlooking the Mediterranean.' And when she didn't answer I pressed her harder. 'Margot, I really need to talk to someone.'

'What about Elaine?' she asked, that special sexy-sly note in her voice.

'To you. I need to talk to you.'

She weighed it. She liked that. 'Okay,' she said. 'Come and pick me up. Be prepared. You'll have to weed me out of this party. It's getting out of hand.'

# 30

I COULD HEAR the party long before I pulled up in the lane in front of the house. Iron gates stood open between stone pillars. A short gravel drive led up to a newly built, sprawling white Provençal villa with green shutters and a red Roman tiled roof. In the front garden couples moved about among flambeaux burning among the terracotta pots of cacti and flowering tobacco plants. At the many windows figures were dancing or maybe just locked in an embrace. From the far side of the house the music was deafening.

I left the car and walked into the front gardens. Couples waved in a friendly fashion. Somebody volunteered that the real action was by the pool.

Like the gates, the front door stood open. My first impression was that I could have loaded my car with a few thousand dollars worth of rugs and china and small furniture and walked on by. Or burnt the place down with the click of a zippo. There was a lot of flammable material. Books, magazines on low tables, pure wool drapes, Japanese paper screens. But I was wrong. Three heavily muscled young men stopped me one foot inside the door. Two wore pants, but were bare chested. The leader wore a light suit and black tee-shirt. I did some quick explaining, Tom Chapel, brother of a house-guest of Werter's . . . Margot.

Margot's name did it. Or maybe Werter had told them to expect me. The menace slipped away, muscles relaxed. 'Go right on through, Monsieur. Werter's over by the *méchoui*.'

I passed slowly, curiously, through the ground floor of the big house. In dark corners there was some manual sex, but not much. More white powder than anything else. A few needles, not really furtive. It was a scene I'd known only too well in my New York days.

I came out through a big wooden-floored music room onto a more vigorously bacchanalian scene. On the long terrace overlooking the sea there were two L-shaped pools. Barbecues smoked and sputtered between them, fireworks crackled and flared beyond them. A couple of dozen people were dancing. Most of the guests were close to naked, a lot of the girls wearing thongs and high-heeled sandals and going topless. Everybody dark brown with days of sleeping, drinking, smoking in the hot sun. There were also a lot of dark glasses worn against the bright light of the moon.

I accepted a drink from someone and responded to an American girl who told me I was the most overdressed man at the party. I told her, whatever happened, I was going to hang on to my jacket.

'Okay,' she said. 'Hang on to your jacket. But lose the pants. Could that be a deal?'

'For later, maybe,' I said. 'Right now, I'm looking for Werter and Kisha.'

She took my arm.

Who said men like thin girls? This one was wearing a flame red bikini but was so thin you could have drunk champagne from her collar bones. Not at all my type. 'I really have to see Werter,' I said. 'It's business.'

'National Party business?'

I made eye contact, nodded and made for the pools. Something was happening at the bigger pool, green spotlights and Arab music. A single woman, visible only in outline, edged from the shadow, slowly swirling, twisting sinuously. Within moments she was joined by others. I had only ever seen a belly dance as we in the West disparagingly call it, in Las Vegas or Chicago, or once, I remember, at a private party organised by English under-graduates when I was in my final term at Cambridge. We'd gone down to London to a brothel in Battersea run by a woman called Ma Bash. It was a cheap, tawdry evening. The dancers were from the east end of London rather than the eastern Mediterranean. They were thin, unaccomplished, English whores. They gave us a crude dance with veils and plangent music and afterwards, included in the price, we could take a girl upstairs for half an hour. As young men in our twenties, we barely remembered the rest of the evening.

But this performance was different. The girls weren't slender cockneys. They were full-bodied Turkish or Egyptian girls. They moved beautifully, the rotundity of the bejewelled belly seemingly counter-clockwise to the hips. It was sexy in a way but it was also mesmerising. I was almost forced to shake my head clear of the music and scent of sandalwood and swirling half-veiled bodies in the pale green light. 'Gets to you, does it?' Margot said in my ear.

I looked round. Margot wore a shimmering green dress, long but split at the sides. At any other time it would have been a dress to make my groin ache but not tonight. Tonight, I needed to talk. She put her arms round my neck and began moving approximately to the music but I unfixed her wrists and stepped back. 'Let's go,' I said. 'Grilled sardines, overlooking the Mediterranean, remember?'

'Come and say hallo to Werter first. He's a very important man in the area.'

'National Party,' I said.

'Departmental chairman.' We began walking out onto the terrace, lit by blazing flambeaux. Couples, people alone sometimes, sat in the warm darkness, grinning to themselves like decorative satyrs.

'They're a great lot of people here tonight, but watch what you say,' Margot told me. 'None of your East Coast liberal chatter here.' She leaned over and kissed my neck. 'They're *all* National Party, honeystick. Some nights here, it's like a beer hall meeting of the Nazi Party – but great fun.'

'I'm not up for beer hall meetings, Margot. Tonight or any night. I need to talk,' I said desperately. 'I need to have you on your own.'

She rolled her eyes. 'Of course you do, darling.'

'For Christ's sake,' I said.

'You should take a dip first,' she insisted. 'Then try some of this grilled lobster and Bâtard-Montrachet, I love that name, don't you? If I met a man named Olivier de Bâtard-Montrachet, I'd marry him on the spot.'

'Cut the fucking performance,' I said. And at that moment we passed through a screen of oleander and I found myself staring at what might have been an Edwardian photographic grouping, except they were mostly wearing shorts and bikinis in the twenty-eight-degree night-time temperature.

Werter, the Regional Councillor, was a big man in shorts and rubber sandals. He was well into his fifties, his skin mahogany colour, his hair blond and thinning, his blue eyes devoid of warmth. Kisha, his Norwegian girlfriend, was one of those extraordinarily perfect Nordic girls, with I suppose, a symbolic role to play for Werter, among any other roles she might have played. Werter crushed my hand in a handshake which I think was purely malicious and told me how long he'd known Margot and how she was one of his favourite human beings. It wasn't long before he lost interest.

'Henri,' he said to a hanger-on. 'Take Margot's brother over and introduce him to a few people.' He was smiling.

I was led towards a whole group of people who, I now realised, were standing round a huge barbecue pit in which a whole lamb was turning on a spit. Names were named and hands shaken. A stocky gym-fit man in shorts had his back to me. As he turned I saw it was Sébastien Coultard.

'Sébastien Coultard,' Henri said, with a knowing smile. 'You two have a lot in common.'

'You're wrong there. We've met,' I said. 'We didn't have a lot in common.'

Sébastien nodded agreement. I noticed for the first time, a strange wolfish quality to the eyes. We stood staring eyeball to eyeball for what was probably only a matter of a second or so. The only movement in his face was the odd flinch of his eyes. The silence spread rapidly to the people around the pit where the lamb was roasting.

'You're not welcome here,' Sébastien said in slow deliberate tones. 'I'm sure you understand why.'

I was thinking of the Egyptian girl. 'Oh sure,' I said. 'I understand why.'

'You've got five minutes. Make yourself scarce.' He came straight at me. I tried to step aside but our shoulders thudded hard against each other as he walked on past.

I stood, the breath momentarily knocked out of me. The group of guests were smiling, not understanding, but amused at what had clearly been some sort of clash of antlers. I was turning to look for Margot when I saw Claire Coultard, pushing her way through the crowd round the *méchoui*.

She wore one of those plain cream classy dresses that proclaim you were born and bred in Provence, you take your sun tan year round and don't need to prance around half naked like a ten-day tourist. She took my upper arm, her nails digging in. 'You shouldn't have come here,' she said angrily.

'You mean it's off-limits because you and your brother are here?'

'No, I don't mean that.'

'Why then?'

'Common sense, for God's sake. These people are friends of Sébastien's. What in the name of God are you doing here?'

'My sister's staying with Werter and Kisha for a few days.'

'Margot?' She stopped. 'Margot's your sister?' She raised her eyebrows.

'You know her? You've met her before?'

'Only this evening. I don't spend a lot of time at Werter's parties, Mr Chapel, fabled as they are,' she said. She had calmed down a little. 'Tonight I had some things I just had to discuss with Sébastien. Nothing else would bring me here' She looked across at him. He was standing next to the sizzling *méchoui*.

'I don't want you talking about me, Claire,' he shouted from where he was collecting a plate of lamb. He came forward. 'Not to him. In fact I see no reason for you to be talking to him at all.'

'I'll make my own choices about that,' she said.

'Carpet-bagger,' he snarled at me. 'Isn't that what Americans call someone like you?'

I looked at Sébastien for a moment and thought of the Egyptian girl, Lara. I had a great desire to hit him. But I suddenly realised I was facing an even greater desire to hit me. I turned to Claire. 'I think I should be going,' I said. 'I think my welcome's running out.'

Margot was hugging Werter and with one trailing hand caressing the lower ribcage of a slender well-built boy. I didn't think she was planning to leave in the sort of hurry that seemed necessary. I turned away. As I began to walk through the allée of oleanders, Claire Coultard was beside me. Behind us, I heard her brother call but she ignored him.

'You're leaving without saying goodnight to your sister?' she said.

'I doubt she'll notice.'

'I talked to Margot for a few minutes earlier,' she said. 'An unusual woman.'

'You didn't like her.'

'I did, as a matter of fact. I think I was just surprised at how open she is in her sexual ambitions.'

227

I looked at her. 'In whose direction?' I asked cautiously. All I needed now was for Margot to start making a pass at Claire.

'In this case, Sébastien's direction,' she said. 'But then I don't imagine its an exclusive interest.' She smiled to soften the insult.

'Seldom,' I said, truthfully.

She nodded. 'I was pleased to hear that Romilly has regained consciousness.'

I didn't ask her how she'd heard. I was already accepting that news travels faster than the speed of light down here.

'Her mother must be ecstatic,' she said. She looked as if she meant it.

'She was ecstatic until I started asking her the questions about Romilly's birth.'

'Ah . . . It did not go well.'

'It was a disaster.'

'She was angry.'

'Very. She didn't even know your father at the time Romilly was born.'

'You believe that.'

'Absolutely.'

She nodded, deep in thought now. We walked on in silence and climbed the terrace steps and stopped, turning towards the garden. 'I suppose now you feel no pressing need to solve this mystery,' she said slowly. 'Elaine has assured you that you are Romilly's father. And the whole Coultard estate is coming to your family. *Why*, I can imagine, is an irrelevant question.'

'Wait a minute. Whatever your brother says, I'm not a carpet-bagger,' I said hotly. 'This inheritance is none of my doing – and I'm as baffled, confused and downright anxious to know what it's all about as you – or your brother.'

We walked on.

After a moment she touched my arm. 'I'm sorry,' she said. 'What I said was stupid. Every now and again something wells up in me. Just bare facts: St Juste is my home. A stranger has come to take it from me.' She held up her hand. 'I know the stranger has problems too. But sometimes you don't want to think of what's going on the other side of the fence.'

For a moment we both stood in silence. It was a much bigger garden than I had realised. We could see the shadows of a lot of activity beyond the garden lights. From the poolside there was a roll of drums. The spotlights in the plane trees shone down on a group of topless girls in long shimmering, spangled skirts. They were less graceful, less practised than the earlier dancers. Showgirls. Then whips cracked and men shouted at the dancers, words I couldn't hear but meanings that were plain enough. The dance changed, became more crudely erotic, a pastiche of what we'd seen before.

I could see the group around the fire from here. Margot had transferred her attentions wholly to the young man. Werter was feeding wine to Kisha. There was no sign of Sébastien. 'Listen,' I said to Claire. 'Thanks for escorting me out of the danger zone. I have a feeling you saved me from the sort of trouble I don't relish.'

She nodded slowly. 'Watch out for Sébastien. He's clever, devious and ruthless.'

'That's a hell of a thing to say about your brother.'

'I'm frightened of him, too – or I wouldn't say it.'

I was out of my depth here. What do you say to a confession like that?

'I've embarrassed you,' she said. 'Not frightened for myself, you understand. For others.' She held out her hand. 'Goodnight, Mr Chapel.'

I took her hand. The hazel eyes, the sheen of moonlight on her bare arm had an almost hypnotic effect. I think she knew. I'm damned sure she did. She smiled.

'Goodnight, Madame,' I said formally.

'Claire?' she corrected me hesitantly. 'Or not?'

I hesitated for a moment. 'Maybe not, uh? In the circumstances.'

She gave a barley perceptible nod.


I crunched gravel as I walked down the lane to where I had left my car. My thoughts were on Claire Coultard. Somehow I preferred to think of her that way rather than as her married name, Claire du Roc. I had left the Renault under a spreading, low-boughed lime tree and as I looked up now I saw the outline of a man leaning back against the driver's door. I took him for one of the guests. Only when I drew closer did I see with a jolt of alarm that he was wearing no shirt, that he was one of the young men who had checked me over when I arrived at the door.

I walked forward under the thick low branches and stopped

a dozen paces from the car. 'I'm leaving,' I said, rattling the keys in the air. He nodded.

To my left, in my peripheral vision something moved. I turned and saw the second bare-chested doorman.

I'm no street fighter. I'm reasonably well built but I can't recall ever taking a punch in my life. Or ever delivering one. General John had once taught me what he called the rudiments of unarmed combat but I remembered nothing of it. Nothing that would do me any good now. Now I'd have to talk.

'I'm leaving,' I said again. 'I won't be coming back.'

The man by the car nodded again. In the half second my eyes were on him, I lost awareness of his friend. The first blow, coming from the left was an ill-aimed punch, the knuckles slashing across my cheek and down the jawbone rather than connecting full-square.

I reeled back, turning to run, but a hand – whose hand I wasn't sure – caught me by the hair and dragged me backwards while punches, three, four, five thudded against my ribs.

It felt as if I was surrounded by a half dozen assailants. Blows fell, missed, then struck as I was held up by one and pummelled by others. Beaten like this, I discovered, you lose the power to feel pain; your vision bursts into kaleidoscopes of colour, then a thick green mist bobs at eye level and you begin to slide into the depths. Like drowning.

Did I hear Claire's screams? Not the first or second time perhaps. But gradually the screams of a woman penetrated my consciousness. And by then I'd recovered just enough to look up to where she was being held by one arm, screaming, pouring an incredibly rapid stream of abuse at the men around me.

You lose seconds at a time like this so that the sequence holds but the narrative is like a badly cut film, jumping forward, missing moments. I saw the men rear back from Claire's vituperation. But I didn't see them go. They melted away. I didn't see who was holding Claire – he too seemed to slink away. Then conscious-ness was a jump cut to sitting on the path in front of my car, one arm braced supporting my weight, the palm flat on the sharp gravel. My other hand, almost disembodied, was exploring my bloodied face. Pushing myself forward, I got onto my knees, and with Claire's help, to my feet.

'Quickly,' she said. 'Your keys.'

I fumbled in my pocket and found nothing. The men were

shadows, poised like guard dogs. As they moved forward, Clare screamed again at them and they stopped, flexed but uncertain, momentarily arrested by her incredible show of fury.

I held onto Claire's shoulder for balance, noticed the red mark I left on her pale dress, focused my interest on it, wrenched my attention free and peered down at the ground. My knees were going. I could hear noises coming from the house. Not music.

'Quickly,' she said.

Unable to speak, I pointed at the ground. The men in the shadows came forward.

She moved rapidly, retrieving the keys from among the gravel, unlocking the door and bundling me into the car. I could hear voices now, shouts behind me as she started the engine and we took off, fishtailing along the lane.

I lay back on the headrest. Trees and bushes flashed past me. I suppose I passed out.

## 31

WE WERE WELL away from the villa before I felt able to do more than grunt. But she had said very little herself, instead driving quickly but confidently along the narrow, night roads. At one point, less than a kilometre from Werter's house, she had pulled into a lane and we sat there, lights out, watching for any cars that might be following. But there were none. After that we drove more slowly for a few kilometres until she turned into the forecourt of a small bar.

'You can get cleaned up here,' she said. 'And we can have a café-cognac to steady our nerves. How are you feeling?'

'Pretty strange,' I said.

'Strange?'

'If I told you the truth I think I'd say elated.'

She smiled. 'Which is an odd thing to say for a man with a possible broken nose.'

I took my nose between finger and thumb. It was painfully but, I think, firmly in place. 'I think it's survived,' I said.

We went into the bar and Claire had a word with the owner whom she seemed to know. He was, I noted, a young Arab. He nodded a few times and indicated I should follow him. The few customers, mostly old retired men in thick shirts and plaid caps, stared unblinkingly at me as I passed.

The cloakroom I was shown into had hot water, soap and paper towels. I washed blood from my face. I didn't need a medical degree to know I was going to be badly bruised tomorrow, my face less badly than my chest. Holding open my shirt, I could see dark red marks down both sides of the ribs. Probably similar marks down my back too. I did up my shirt, winced as I swung my jacket onto my shoulder, ran my fingers through my hair and went out into the bar.

Claire was sitting with two black coffees and two glasses of cognac. 'You *look* better,' she said.

I rolled my eyes. 'Who told the heavies on the gate I was *persona non grata*?'

She poured cognac into her coffee and stirred. I followed suit.

'Werter?' I said. I didn't want to suggest it was her brother.

She knew what I wasn't saying. She shook her head. 'The name you're looking for is Sébastien. I saw him follow you to the door and say something to the thugs. I had gone back to the pool when I heard you shout.'

'Did I shout?'

She smiled. 'Loud.'

'I was pretty scared,' I said.

'I don't blame you.'

'Thanks for coming to my rescue.'

'I don't think I stopped more than the last few kicks. They weren't planning to kill you.'

'Reassuring. What were they planning?'

'Sébastien is angry,' she said. 'About the will. He's a bully. This is how he reacts. Your sister should never have asked you to come there. Did she know Sébastien would be there?'

Did Margot know Sébastien would be there? Not impossible.

Clare sipped her café-cognac, watching me over the gold rim of the green Apilco cup. 'Your sister told me she's only just flown in. No reason to know anything.' She was offering me a chance to make excuses.

I shook my head. *That* hurt. 'Just as likely she knew who Sébastien is,' I said. 'Margot likes to add a little spice to life.'

She raised her eyebrows. 'A little spice to life? Dangerous,' she said. 'Down here in the south we're a different type of French. Paris and the north are psychologically a long way away. Airplanes, phones and faxes haven't made any real difference to that.' She looked up at me, marking the point. 'Remember that, Mr Chapel.'

'I've changed my mind.' I said. 'Call me Tom. In America it's traditional when you've just saved someone's life.'

She looked at me for a long moment, then shook her head. 'We shouldn't get too familiar, Mr Chapel. That really would be wrong. In the circumstances, as you said.' She looked at me evenly. Somehow there was no invitation in her tone for me to pursue her meaning.

We stood and left the bar. Again she drove. I wasn't really feeling up to it, a little queasy, a little lightheaded, with some pretty heavy aches building up. As we drove back to Villefranche I wanted to ask her about Sébastien but I couldn't think of a way to phrase it. Why did she go to the same parties if she disapproved of his way of life. Well, she'd explained. She needed to talk to him about her father's will. Maybe that was all there was to it.

In the end, as we passed under the arch and into the market square, she glanced across at me. 'You're not thinking of getting your own back on Sébastien, are you? Not thinking of talking to the police about this? I hear you get on well with Lieutenant Bisset.'

'I may mention it to him for the record. But I won't be taking it further. I'd already thought this was one to put down to experience. Even so, I'd still be interested to know why.'

'Why I'm suggesting you don't talk to the police, to your friend Lieutenant Bisset?'

I nodded. More shooting pain in the head.

'Sébastien and Werter are powerful figures in this area, Mr Chapel. Werter is already a regional councillor – real power.'

And Sébastien?'

'At the next mayoral election Sébastien will be the Nationalist candidate for Cannes. Okay, he may not get elected. But if he does that's more real power. And your Lieutenant Bisset is dark-skinned.'

We were silent for a moment.

'You're very outspoken about your brother,' I said.

'Which makes you wonder why I don't just break away from him. For good and all.'

'I was thinking about it, I admit.'

'His capacity for violence is not limited to urging two gatemen to beat up one of Werter's guests. He knows a lot of the hard types down at the Toulon docks. His drinking friends, he calls them.'

'What does he use them for?'

'I'm not sure.' She paused. 'So far, we've had no fire bombs hurled at refugee hostels. But someone turns the thugs out when they're needed. Intimidation happens all along the coast. At the office, we're building a dossier on him.'

'Does he know that's what you're doing?'

She gestured with one hand off the wheel. 'Probably.'

I said nothing.

'I know it has to be done,' she said.

She swung the car to a stop outside Elaine's house. Her tone changed, became brisk. 'If you allow me to take the car up to St Juste, I promise to get someone to drive it back to you first thing in the morning.'

'Sure.' I didn't move.

'Shouldn't you get out,' she said, eyebrows raised.

Somehow I found I didn't want to. 'Not just yet.'

She smiled. I wasn't sure what it meant.

'Can we talk about the will?'

She glanced up at the dark house. 'What do you want to say?'

'I have a question or two.'

She shrugged a sort of Gallic acquiescence.

'There are a lot of things here that don't tie up. But more than anything, I don't understand why your father told you nothing about the will before he died.'

'I'm sure he intended to,' she said slowly. 'But I believe he died before he had the opportunity.'

I was thinking of what Elaine had said. 'Died.'

'Or was killed.'

'Fabius thinks that? Thinks your father was murdered?'

'Fabius's moves are difficult to follow. But I think that's what he believes.'

'So who by?'

'By someone who had discovered that my father intended to write a will in favour of your daughter.'

'It would still have to be someone who had expected directly or indirectly to benefit from your father's death.'

She remained silent, her eyes on the twisting, narrow road ahead.

'Sébastien?' I said.

'If I thought that he would be dead by now.'

That shocked me. I knew she meant it. I tried to imagine the cold fury of my mother. But this was different. Hot. Lethal, no doubt about it. More human? I wasn't sure.

'So who?' I said.

'Anybody. Anybody who owed Sébastien a favour and in the political world there are plenty of them. Down here, it's not a world that flinches from the occasional "accident". You'd better make sure your sister knows that before she tries again to entertain herself at your expense.'

She set her lips tight and stared at the road ahead.

'You're saying,' I said carefully 'that one of Sébastien's cronies might have been responsible for your father's death, and for what happened to Romilly, without Sébastien knowing.'

'That's what I'm saying.'

I let myself slump down in the seat. 'There's one thing we haven't thought about. Whoever killed your father, if he was killed, did it because of the provisions in the will. Yet not even *you* knew what they were. Sébastien couldn't have told some trigger happy comrade because he didn't know himself at that point.'

She nodded slowly. 'Only old Jean Rolin, the *notaire*, knew. And he died in his bed a few days before my father. The question is, did old Rolin tell anybody before he died?'

'Or did someone break into the Mantel, Rolin office. When I was there they were fixing an alarm. Luc Rolin said something about it being too late. They'd just had a break-in.'

She thought about that for a moment, nodding to herself.

'What do you do now?' I asked her.

'What are you asking?' I looked at the pride in the set of her features. The pain, too. 'Whether I'm going to contest the will?'

'No. I'm not asking that.'

'Thank you,' she said. 'But I'll tell you. I've told Sébastien I refuse to come to a decision until I find the answer to what my father would have told me if he'd lived. I need to know why he left everything to Romilly. If I understand, I can accept it. I'm sure I can. But until then . . . I don't know, I can't accept what's happened. I spend nights with awful shadows, suspicions of everybody, even my father. Then morning comes and I know, for certain, that this man I was closer to than anybody would never have turned my life on its head for nothing. He had a reason. A big, compelling reason. I need to find it. I need to find it as much as you do.'

'Is Fabius helping you?'

'He has no help to offer in what I want to know: why my father did what he did.'

We sat without speaking for a moment. 'Why did you ask if Jean-Claude was helping me?' she said.

'I guess because I'm trying to see what side he's on. Sure as hell doesn't seem like mine.'

'No.' She had a slightly teasing smile on her lips. 'he's no friend of yours, Monsieur Chapel.'

236

'Why not?'

'Why not?' She smiled. 'Who knows? Perhaps because he thinks you too, have ambitions to be my lover.' She looked at me, raised her eyebrows in mock astonishment and laughed. 'Perhaps he thinks of you as a too attractive rival. Although if he saw you at the moment . . .'

'Okay, okay . . .' Despite the pain in my face and ribs, I laughed. I liked this brief moment of relaxation.

Very slowly the smile faded from her face. 'Jean-Claude Fabius' story is a long one.' she said. 'His father was a prominent figure in Nice. A graduate of one of the Paris *Grandes Ecoles*, a senior legal lecturer at the university here when the war began.' She paused.

'I heard he made the wrong choice.'

She assented. 'He was not a man of honour.'

'What does that mean?'

'Some men worked for Vichy as a cover for their Resistance activities. While the war was on, of course, they had bad reputations. But they were given papers at the end of the war, more precisely a little red booklet signed by the local resistance leader, attesting to the fact that such and such was, in fact, a man of honour. This book could mean the difference between life and death for someone like Professor Fabius.'

'From what Bisset said the professor wasn't about to get one.'

'No. He had commanded an action unit of the Vichy special police, the SEC. By 1942, the name of Professor Fabius spelt terror for Jewish people throughout the Nice region. They paid him money – and he still arrested them and sent them to their deaths. His prison sentence saved him from much worse.'

'What happened to his family?'

'Madame Fabius and her small son were left without support, ostracised by neighbours. They were bitter times in France as the war was ending. We didn't have, perhaps we didn't deserve, the triumph of pure victory like the Anglo-Saxons.'

'And the professor?'

'If he *is* still alive in Uruguay or somewhere, he'd be almost a hundred by now.' She paused. 'It hasn't been an easy life for young Fabius. No doubt it's made him what he is.'

In the house a light went on in an upstairs window. Elaine's bedroom. For a moment her shape appeared at the window, then she pulled back and the light went out. I didn't want to go into the house just yet. 'Before I go in . . .' I hesitated, 'I should tell you that your father was giving Romilly an allowance a few months before he died. He was also taking her out to restaurants. Just the two of them.'

'I know. Fabius told me.'

'Fabius told you? Jesus.' I shook my head. 'What did it mean, your father taking Romilly to dinner? I know what it seems to mean. But I can't believe it.'

'Listen,' she said. 'My father was not that sort of man. Oh, he was quite capable of being interested in a beautiful young woman. That goes without saying. But he would never leave everything to her. He was a peasant at heart. With peasant values.'

'That's more or less what Rolin the notary said.'

'*Voilà.*' For a moment we sat in silence. 'Your mother was in France during the war.'

'More information from Fabius?'

'I'm asking. Is it so?'

'True enough,' I said. 'My mother was in the American military. Welfare services behind the advancing US armies. But my understanding was that she was in north-west Europe. She arrived in France behind the Normandy landings.'

'But it's not impossible you only know part of the story. The Americans and French landed here on the Riviera after the main Normandy invasion. The landings were not thirty kilometres from where we're sitting. She could have been here.'

'That's possible. Yes.'

She cocked her head. 'A wartime liaison with my father?'

'It still doesn't quite fit. That would have been in 1944. I believe I was nearly two years old by then.'

'However it fits,' she said, 'I still think you're the son of Marcel Coultard. I think my father was simply having dinner with his granddaughter.'

'I wonder.'

After a moment, she said: 'If it's true you realise it means you and I are related. A very strange thought.'

I looked at her, shaking my head. 'It still doesn't fit,' I said. 'If it's true, why didn't he divide the estate three ways – between you, Sébastien and myself. Or maybe four ways – you, Sébastien, me and Romilly?

'God knows,' she said. She sat for a moment, rubbing at the blood on her dark-tanned shoulder with a Kleenex. 'We're getting close – but not there yet.'

We sat for some time without speaking, pursuing our own lines of thought. Over to the west of us a forest fire glowed like a dark red abscess on the outlined hills. She broke the silence first. '*Eh bien!*' She slapped both hands, palm down, on the top of her thighs.

I waited.

'That's all,' she said.

I felt we were engaged in a conversation without words, a process of getting to know each other beyond the normal conventions. She turned to me, a wry smile at herself. That half smile which I was beginning to think of as characteristic. She looked towards the house as the upstairs light flicked on again. 'I think you should go in.'

'I wanted to thank you. Or something. Just thank you for what you did this evening anyway.' I looked up. Elaine was standing at her bedroom window. I moved to open the door of the car. 'You're right – I should go.'

'Madame Chapel is up at her bedroom window wondering who this strange woman is at the wheel of your car. I don't think she could recognise me from here.'

'She's not worrying about me. We split up years ago.'

She raised her eyebrows. 'You're still married.'

'A real split,' I said. It was strange how, sitting next to this woman, I knew I meant it when I said that.

She glanced up at the window. 'You should still go in.'

'You're right,' I said. 'But Elaine wouldn't think it was a strange woman I'd picked up at a party somewhere. She'd assume it was Margot.'

'I see.' Claire turned on the ignition. I had one foot already out of the car when she asked: 'What happened? Why did your marriage to Elaine break up?'

'The usual reasons,' I said.

She turned in her seat, one hand on the wheel. 'Another man? Or another woman?'

I didn't think twice about it. She had told me so much – why shouldn't I tell her? 'Another woman,' I said. 'I was having an affair with my sister.'

## 32

WE WERE WRANGLING like a married couple. As if we were
still a married couple. As Elaine moved about the house,
slamming bathroom doors, I was trying to explain what
happened last night. But she wasn't interested in my face. She
was interested in the woman in the car. 'The woman with me
last night was *not* Margot,' I shouted through the door into her
bedroom, but I could almost see her spin the knob in fury as
the radio poured out the civilised tones of a BBC Radio 4 discussion. She listened to it every morning, but not normally at this
volume.

I stood half way up the stairs in just a pair of khakis. 'I'll put
some coffee on and we can talk,' I called through the bedroom
door. Whether she heard me or not I don't know. There was no
answer. I went back into the kitchen to make my peace offering.
Then suddenly upstairs the BBC snapped off. As I came out into
the hall, she sailed past me, fully dressed for the hospital.

'Coffee,' I said.

'None left,' she flung over her shoulder as she headed out into
the courtyard for her car.

I ran out after her. The terracotta tiles were already hot on
my bare feet. I could see by the way she moved that this was
not anger that was going to wear off in a few hours. I needed
to be away, apart from her for a couple of days. I made the decision in a split second. 'There are things I have to know from my
mother,' I shouted above the exaggerated roar of her engine. 'I'm
going back to Boston for a few days. I'll make the meeting at
the hospital first."

'Boston?' Her window zipped down. 'Great. Take that trollop
sister with you,' she said as she pulled away on a screech of tyres.

Elaine was right. There was no coffee in the kitchen. I got dressed
and went down to the village and ordered coffee under the yellow

umbrellas of the Café de la Paix in the market place. My face had looked and felt better. One eye was puffed up dark yellow. There was a cut across my forehead that John Wayne could have made something of, but I don't have the face for a Band Aid.

Yet, despite all, I felt pretty good. Romilly was on the mend. I didn't have any illusions about the psychological trauma she might have suffered, along with the more apparent physical injuries, but I had a lot of faith in Elaine to give her the kind of love and care I thought she'd need most. And what would my role be? Whatever Romilly allowed it to be, I guess. But for a start, I'd no doubt it ought to be to try to make some sense of the Coultard will. I had a role there. I was, after all, the trustee.

The waiter put down the big green cup of *café au lait* on the table. As he turned away another shadow fell and an American voice said: 'D'you mind if I join you in one of those?'

I looked up. It was the man who had been hanging around outside Rolin's office a couple of days ago, the man looking at the plaque to the woman whose death had been recorded but whose killers were not mentioned. 'Sure,' I said. 'Sit down.'

'You look like you might be hurting.'

I touched my face. 'Wounded pride more than anything.'

I didn't add anything and he nodded comfortably enough and took a chair. I didn't really want to talk tourist talk, but he was a fellow American and, I thought, looked a little lost. At least I thought that until I heard him call the waiter and order his coffee in fluent, Provençal-accented, French.

'This isn't the first time you've been down here in the south,' I said.

He shook his head. 'It's a long time, but it's not the first time, no.' He stretched his hand across the table. 'Marty Pearson,' he said.

'Tom Chapel. I saw you the other day. Are you touring the area?'

'Just visiting. And you, you're the man whose daughter was attacked. I was truly sorry to hear.'

'Where did you hear about it?'

'Spend an evening in one of the bars, sit for an hour here in the Café de la Paix . . . and the *patronne*, Claudine Beste, will soon bring you up to speed. Hereabouts, people talk. They don't always tell you the truth, but they talk a lot. It's a way of life.'

'You seem to know these people really well.'

'I was down here in 1942,' he said. 'American Food Aid Program. We worked out of Nice with the Quakers and YMCA but my patch was up here – Villefranche, St Juste. All the little hill towns and villages in this part of the *département*.'

I frowned. Was this man giving me a line? 'I'm not sure I understand that,' I said. 'You were here in 1942? But the US had been in the war since Pearl Harbor. Since December '41. What was an American doing in a country on Hitler's side?'

'Okay, Hitler was in Paris but he left the south unoccupied for two-and-a-half years. Collaborating with Hitler, sure. But at the same time trying to hang on to a sort of neutrality. There was a US Ambassador, Admiral Leahy, up there in Vichy, the spa capital of France. And US agencies had an arrangement with the Royal Navy to pass through the British blockade to get food aid to the people here. I was just one of the young men and women handing out packages.'

The waiter brought his coffee.

'Yeah,' he said, tasting his coffee. 'It was a France suspended between the German blitzkrieg victory and the Allied liberation.'

I took a moment to take it all in. 'Must have been a weird time down here then,' I said.

'The Vichy government was pretty weird altogether. Hated the Germans for occupying half their country; hated the Brits for fighting on. The Resistance had a dozen fathers. One of them, at least, was certainly a deep sense of shame. A need to drag France back into the action.'

'How did most people feel down here?'

'Most people still put their trust in the Vichy leader, old Marshal Pétain. Pictures everywhere. Schoolkids singing his praises. But come 1942 resistance was growing. There were big groups, of course, political movements. But the small groups like Marcel Coultard's Committee of Seven here were often as not inspired by the appalling sight of the first big Jewish round-ups in summer 1942. French policemen leading screaming three year olds away from their parents. The stinking rail-cars that people saw waiting in the sidings in the August heat. Faces behind bars begging for a cup of water. This was what France was doing to *France*. A good man like Marcel Coultard could take it no longer. He went out *looking* for Jewish families and arranged for them to get to safety in Spain and Italy.'

'Italy too?'

'Just across the mountains there. And the Italian people had no truck with anti-Semitism.'

'So for the Resistance, 1942 was the key year?'

'Yes sir. The independent groups began to come together. But in 1942 there weren't that many. You had to wait until the Germans came down here before the big switch took place. That's when Vichy turned against itself. That's when guys like the present President of France made the sideways jump.'

'President Mitterand was in the Vichy government.?'

'Minor league. But he did receive the *Francisque*, a medal presented by the Marshal for loyal and distinguished service. Not widely known.' He paused. 'Lot of people hate him for his smooth late switch. These old hatreds live on in France. Lot of people in this village, the old real Resistance, won't forget the bitter struggle between the SEC, the Vichy secret police, and the Committee of Seven.'

'The SEC was Professor Fabius's outfit.'

'You know your stuff. *Service d'enquête et de contrôle*. Tight-knit and murderous. With the later *Milice*, a good match for their friends the Gestapo. These were hard times for the French, Mr Chapel. You can't understand French attitudes today without scratching around those roots.' He laughed. 'Like a truffle pig.'

'Did you ever come across Professor Fabius?'

'I was invited to meet him once or twice for questioning. He believed individual Americans in the Aid Program were supplying the Resistance groups with food. Which, as a matter of fact, most of us were. Tried to scare the pants off me.' He laughed. 'Succeeded too. Tall, thin, a greedy academic. A poor boy who'd made good – and planned to make better. He had a hard reputation.' Pearson shook his head. 'I can't tell you how many people, men and women and children, French Jews and immigrant Jews he sent to their deaths. But we're talking big numbers. Strange times, hard times,' he mused.

'Hard times but they don't go un-commemorated.' I gestured over towards the museum on the other side of the market place. 'Ever been in?'

'No.'

'Got ten minutes?'

'I'm flying back to Boston this afternoon. I have to call in to the hospital to see my daughter on the way.'

'Sure . . . Some other time.'

'But . . .' What drew me? Something in his manner as much as his story. I checked my watch. It was early, not yet ten o'clock. 'If you're going across there . . .'

'Pleasure.' He dropped some francs on the table, enough to cover both our coffees.

The *Musée de la Resistance* was the old schoolhouse fronting onto the market square, converted just after the war to one of the first Resistance museums in Provence.

'See those gates,' Marty Pearson said. 'I had those fitted January 1, 1942 to form a secure warehouse.' I followed his pointing finger and saw that a building by the side of the school was secured by a massively ugly pair of iron gates. 'In 1942 you couldn't store Hershey bars and cans of jam and Spam and Armour's sausage just anywhere.' He laughed. 'And just there's where I parked my brand new shining Dodge truck. I used to keep it like that, sparkling in the sun, the sides inscribed *American Food Program*, the Stars and Stripes painted underneath. Pretty brash I suppose. But Americans didn't have to apologise for doing good in those days. I was proud of my job, Mr Chapel. Every time that truck passed it represented America's wealth and good-will among the hungry people here. And something even more solid – a meal to put on the table for your kids that night.'

'Why were they hungry?' I said. 'I thought France fed itself. Always had.'

'One and a half million French prisoners of war in Germany,' he said. 'More than half of them peasants. Women did what they could, but they couldn't do everything, work the farms, look after the kids, the old folk. French women were the heroes of those days.'

Marty Pearson and I paid our thirty francs in the glazed porch where the children of Villefranche had passed back and forth day after day between 1909 and 1923. The inscription still read *Ecole*. A plaque to the side gave the details: the murderous cost in young men's lives France had paid in World War I had reduced Villefranche to a place of too many young widows and too few children. Five years after World War I ended, the school was closed and the building stood empty – until the mayor offered it as a Resistance museum at the end of World War II.

The main salon, the school hall, was a combined rest room and photographic display. Six or seven old men from the village were sitting round on the dark green banquettes under the photographs, talking the morning away.

'They don't recognise you?' I said.

'Why should they? It's over forty years ago. Somebody will in the next couple of days, but the way things are at the moment is okay with me.'

He was a strangely, maybe impressively, self-contained man. Something of a loner perhaps, certainly someone who didn't need recognition.

Leading off the hall were two rooms – one with a sign inscribed simply 1940–1942: the other carrying a more confident sign reading: Victory: 1943–1944. Pearson moved towards the first room. 'This is it,' he said. 'These are my years.'

We walked slowly into the room. It was empty of people. Pearson looked at me and grimaced. 'These years don't stir a lot of interest,' he said. 'I guess young people don't come to such places. These times are too tangled for them. At school, Vichy hardly gets a mention. They stick to Joan of Arc, Molière, Napoléon, Cézanne, the Battle of Verdun, great, safe landmarks of French life. I don't blame them. Who wants to scratch and scramble in a war without a name – 1940, '41 and '42 when Frenchmen fought Frenchmen. It was a time of France's heroic suffering, Mr Chapel. But also of its greatest shame.'

'Shame?'

'There were seventy-five thousand Jews transported from France to Auschwitz. Too many of them in the Vichy years.'

'By the Gestapo and SS.'

'Not by any means all of them. How could the SS have transported Jews from this part of France in 1942, when they weren't even here? No, I'm sorry to say that in those days our enemies were the SEC, Professor Fabius and his like, supported by ordinary French gendarmes under his orders.'

'It's a long time ago,' I said.

'Sure.'

'But it's not hard to see you still feel it like yesterday.'

His grey eyes rested on me and he nodded. 'Among the thousands of Jews desperately trying to find safety, were forty Jewish women, brought here to a secret transit camp in the hills by Marcel Coultard and his Resistance group. From the transit camp they were to be smuggled, over a period of months, along the coast to make the crossing into Spain.' He pushed his hands deep in the pockets of his light slacks. 'I knew them all, Georgie Helbronner, the Weinberg sisters, Isobel Berne. I supplied them

245

with food while they were hiding up here, food from the Program. After the war I was curious to know how they'd made it – or which of them had made it.'

'And . . . ?'

'I was an executive for Hallmark Cards, the international division,' Pearson said. 'I travelled for the company – and on any free afternoon in New York, London or Paris. Or Amsterdam, Rome or Stockholm. I checked records. Sometimes I enlisted the help of survivors' associations.'

'And you found them, most of them?'

'No . . .' He drew it out. 'In no major city in the US, in none of ten major cities in Europe, did I ever find a single one of those forty Jewish women, Mr Chapel.' He pursed his lips. 'Funny story, uh?'

Forty missing women. The hairs on the back of my neck were rising as he spoke. The words of Sanya, the self-styled reincarnate were inescapable now. *Forty women murdered in these hills.*

'Do you know Sanya?' I asked him.

'The American woman? Heard of her. Saw her at the market the other day buying a goat. The village people say she claims to be reincarnated.'

'So I hear.'

'In the café they say she roams the hills looking for her baby. Seems she lost a child during the demonstrations against flooding St Juste in 1973. Never got over it, poor woman. Why d'you ask about her?'

'She says forty women were murdered up in the hills.'

'She says that?' he said tonelessly. I couldn't tell if he were interested or not. It seemed to me he must be. But his face remained expressionless. His eyes roamed round the room.

'So that's what you're doing here,' I pressed him. 'Looking for those forty Jewish women.'

'You could say I promised myself. I promised myself that when I retired I'd come back. Start at the beginning. See if I could find where the trail petered out.'

'The trail of one woman in particular?' I asked.

'Yes, of course,' he said slowly, with a wry, almost sheepish smile. 'I was young. I'd fallen in love. I believed Isobel Berne was one in a million, but I was wrong, of course.' He paused. 'She was one in *six million*, wasn't she?'

\*   \*   \*

We stood in silence. Then his features moved as he worked the muscles around his mouth. The moment was over. He walked forward, his footsteps echoing on the old classroom polished floor, towards a wall of black and white photographs of bread queues, of SEC arrests, one in the main square here in Villefranche. Five or six men in trenchcoats and trilby hats were dragging a woman from the house next to the Café de la Paix where we had just been sitting. The caption identified her as Claudette Cousin, the woman whose death at the hands of unidentified killers is commemorated by the plaque outside in the market place.

I bent forward, examining the photograph for a few moments. I saw that two faces of the SEC men had been airbrushed out.

As I straightened up, Pearson tapped me on the shoulder. 'They were brushed out at the request of their children when they grew up. Why should the kids suffer for the sins of the fathers? One used to be the local undertaker. Making work the villagers used to say. The other tall one on the right there, is his boss, your Professor Fabius.'

I couldn't help wondering if Professor Fabius's son had ever been here. Couldn't help feeling how much guts it had taken to appear out there in the market place for Friday's reconstruction. 'Did many of these SEC men get clean away?' I asked Pearson.

'A lot of Fabius's subordinates got what they deserved. In France, there were maybe thirty thousand murders the year the war ended. Guys dragged off their tractors, thousands shot in the woods, some in their own beds. Old scores.'

A school group had come in behind us, chattering like starlings. 'You know, Mr Chapel,' Pearson said. 'Getting to the bottom of what happened here at this time . . .' he gestured to the photographs '. . . can be near impossible. Can be dangerous too.'

'Even now, all these years on?'

'All these years on,' he said.

We stood looking up at a huge photograph, of a man about thirty, life size, which occupied the centre position on the long wall. He was not tall. He wore a suit that might have fitted better. Buttoned shirt. No tie. His left arm hung at a slightly odd angle. But Marcel Coultard's face radiated a strength and confidence that was unusually direct. He carried the staff of the French tricolour in his right hand and the inscription below the photograph read:

Colonel Marcel. March past before General de Gaulle of the Resistance Battalion of the Committee of Seven at Nice, August 1945.

'I've kept you long enough,' Marty Pearson said. 'Old men talk on, Mr Chapel. Never know when to call it a day.'

I made a gesture of denial but he laughed it off.

'You have a plane to catch. And a dozen other things to do, I've no doubt.'

'I'll be back in a few days.'

He nodded, smiling to himself. 'I'm renting a house here for a few weeks,' he said. 'See you around, I hope.'

# 33

I GOT TO the hospital shortly before eleven o'clock. A small knot of people were standing outside Romilly's room. Lieutenant Bisset was talking casually to one of the doctors. The gendarme on guard was talking to the girl who'd been had introduced yesterday as the police technician. Fabius stood alone, to one side. Elaine, I guessed, was in with Romilly.

I said an American good morning to all of them without going from one to the other to shake hands. 'How is she this morning?' I asked the doctor.

He nodded cheerfully. 'Everything we could wish for, Monsieur Chapel.' He took me by the elbow, moving me aside. 'Examination of a patient still requires her response – are you feeling pain, nausea etc . . . We've had our first chance to examine her thoroughly this morning and she's in much better shape than we feared. Most importantly we've done new brain scans. We are very, very pleased with the results.'

On occasions like this the gratitude you feel is not disproportionate but extraordinary all the same. I gulped and shook his hand. If it had been a woman doctor I would have kissed her.

I went into the room where I had sat through some of the loneliest hours of my life. Romilly was partly propped up on her pillows, her head bandages removed, a thin adhesive band across the top of her forehead. From the front I couldn't even see the shaven patch on the top of her head. She gave me a slow smile that said reams about how she felt, about the past in New York, about promises for a future.

I bent down and kissed her, unable to speak. Elaine was at my side. You would have thought this morning hadn't happened as she rested an arm on my shoulder. I knew of course who she was doing it for. She was a trooper, all right.

I looked down at Romilly. Her lips glistened with some cream they used to stop them drying. 'The doctor says you're doing brilliantly.'

'The young guy?' The voice was weak but interested. 'I bet he says that to all the girls.'

Elaine was smiling.

'What happened to your face?' Romilly asked and guiltily I watched alarm flash across her features.

'I fell into a ditch,' I said. 'Your mother didn't tell you? I was celebrating.'

She liked that. Elaine liked it less.

'I'm going back to Boston,' I said. 'I have some business there but I'll be back in a few days.'

'Promise,' she said.

That one word was heart-lifting. 'You couldn't keep me away. Your mother's told you the police are here to ask you a few questions.'

She gave a faint nod.

'How do you feel about that?'

'Good,' she said. 'Sooner they pick him up the better.'

'Sure.' I found I could barely breathe. That single line was the first real confirmation we'd had that Fabius, from the beginning, had been hopelessly wrong, as he tried to convert this whole thing to his version of an 'accident'.

'The moment it gets too much,' Elaine said. 'You'll let us know, right? We'll be in here with you the whole time.'

Romilly took a breath through pursed lips. A schoolgirl gearing up her courage. 'Okay,' she said.

I stood there, undecided. There was something I needed to know. Something only she could tell me. I glanced at Elaine and I think she realised I was about to ask about Marcel Coultard, about the cheques and Romilly's secret dinners with the old man. Elaine's face hardened. You couldn't miss the prohibition.

I was frozen with indecision. One simple answer from Romilly could have cleared it up. Why had she met Marcel? But what if she really had been servicing an eighty-year-old man for a monthly cheque? Christ!

Don't do it – that's what Elaine was saying with that forbidding look on her face. I nodded surrender to Elaine's will.

*　*　*

We had been asked by the doctor to leave the room for a few moments. We stood in a group, Fabius not disguising his impatience. Even less so when a second doctor insisted he needed to go in for another few moments before the questioning began. Elaine was talking to a woman doctor about counselling. The British aren't so keen on it as us Americans. I think they see it as a sign of weakness. My guess was that, at some stage, Romilly could use some counselling. My fear was that, in the wrong hands, and probably most of the hands are pretty maladroit, it could do more harm than good.

I signalled to Bisset and we walked along the corridor. 'Your boss is not a man who likes to be kept waiting,' I said.

He smiled that slow, African enigmatic smile. 'Fabius is the magistrate in charge of the prosecution of this case. I told you – that doesn't make him my boss.'

'Very subtle. I have something to tell you. Just for the record. Not for action, okay?'

'Okay.'

'I was beaten up last night by a couple of thugs paid by Sébastien Coultard.'

Eyebrows. He was looking at my face. 'I wondered.'

'I got mixed up with the wrong party. I was pulled out of trouble by Claire Coultard.'

More eyebrows, wrinkling the normally smooth brown forehead.

'Sébastien's very, *very* pissed about the Coultard fortune going to Romilly. Thus the beating.' I paused. 'Just something for you and your notebook.'

'Where it'll stay until needed.'

'Good.'

On a signal from the doctors, we all trooped in. With the exception of the technician and Fabius, who drew up chairs to the bed, the doctors, Bisset, Elaine and myself all found pieces of wall uncluttered by medical equipment, to lean against.

Fabius began by asking questions about the priest and Romilly answered slowly, and sometimes haltingly, but with a description of what had happened in the market at Nice and when they were on the bus, all of which corresponded very closely with the account of Anne-Marie. Clearly, Romilly's memory was not impaired.

Fabius looked towards the technician to see if she had all that, and then back to Romilly. 'What I want, Mademoiselle,' he said, 'is for you to give as detailed account as you can of what happened when you left your tennis lesson at Villefranche.'

For a few moments Romilly said nothing. She looked down at her hands and smoothed the sheet pulled up to just above waist height. There was complete silence in the room, everybody's eyes on the pale figure in the bed.

'I was at the tennis courts,' she said. 'I wanted to leave early. I'd promised to be back. My mother,' she glanced up at Elaine, 'had an important meeting in the afternoon and wanted us to have lunch early.'

'This we know,' Fabius said impatiently.

Romilly blinked at him. Anger seethed in me. 'For God's sake,' I said, 'she's been unconscious for ten days. She has no idea what you do and don't know.'

Romilly looked down at the sheet. Elaine took her hand and squeezed it encouragingly.

'I had finished my tennis lesson with Jacqueline. I was crossing the market place. The stallholders were packing up. It must have been minutes before the klaxon. I was weaving my way through the vans . . . One of them, an old blue Citroën, had its back doors open.'

'If they were packing up, Mademoiselle, surely a number of them had their back doors open,' Fabius said. 'You're telling us most of the vans in the square . . .'

'Judge Fabius . . .' Elaine hit him with a look that silenced him, but she kept her voice low. 'She's telling you what she remembers of that moment. Not what was happening in another parts of the square.'

I'd give a lot to be able to handle a situation like that.

'There was lots of noise,' Romilly said. 'The loudspeakers were playing, people were shouting to each other . . . I was walking past a blue van, level with the back doors,' Romilly said, 'when I was aware of someone coming toward me. I was, like, at an angle, but I could see him.'

'Enough to recognise him?'

'Not at first.'

'And then?'

'He hit me. Hit me in the back, I think.' She stopped. 'This part is difficult. He hit me. I'm not sure if it was with something or just with his shoulder. It was hard and heavy. I tumbled into the back of the van. The doors slammed. It was over in seconds.'

'You had a chance to see the man.'

'As I rolled into the back of the van, yes. It was him, the priest.'

'But not dressed in priest's garments?'

'Dressed in jeans and a tee-shirt.'

'You're quite sure you were pushed,' Fabius said.

'I think so. It's hard be absolutely sure . . .'

'You didn't trip, fall . . .'

I can't explain it. I felt enormously protective. I felt I could have strangled anybody who even questioned her word. 'For Christ's sake,' I said. Perhaps I was close to shouting. 'She told you she wasn't sure exactly how it happened. But it's clear enough, isn't it? You're crossing a market place, you don't just fall into the back of a goddam van.'

I wasn't certain about the next few seconds. Elaine was next to me. 'Go outside, Tom,' she said in a vehement whisper. 'You're making a fool of yourself. You're upsetting Romilly.'

I allowed myself to be moved towards the door. Bisset had taken over. I could feel the gentle strength of the man. Before he eased me outside, I heard Romilly saying there was some sort of wire grille, a divider like some people have between the driver and the back to keep dogs from distracting the driver. 'I tried screaming at him. I was clawing at the wire, screaming at him. And when he didn't look round, didn't even speak, I threw myself against the back doors. Two or three times perhaps. I could feel them giving. The man was shouting – and suddenly the doors burst open and I was flying through the air.'

The door closed and I was alone in the corridor, the duty nurse about ten yards away, head down writing at her desk.

Deeply ashamed at my own performance, I didn't wait. I took the elevator down to the ground floor and picked up my car and drove the twenty minutes along the Mediterranean to the airport.

I'm a wimp. I know it. Apart from college banter I've been called a wimp maybe ten or a dozen times in my life but each time the context has been seriously real. Elaine called me a wimp when she found out about Margot. So did Romilly.

I don't know if you're born with it, or if you grow into it. We all know how to stop being an alcoholic – just stop drinking. But how does a guy stop being a wimp? Wimp, the dictionary says, weak-kneed, cowardly, one who displays moral cowardice or is incapable of taking pressure. A son of Margaret Flee-from-Adultery Bannerman, it could add.

As I boarded the aircraft and stumbled towards my seat, a stewardess thought I suffered from fear of flying.

# 34

LOGAN AIRPORT. THE streaming lights of the runway visible as we bank. The low approach across the ocean. The thud and bump of landing. The sudden different mindset you get as you're back in the United States.

I took a cab to my apartment near Quincy Market. It's not a smart apartment, far from it. It has four rooms above an all-night convenience store. Big, high-ceilinged rooms but shabby from lack of paint, from lack of floor wax, from lack of decent furniture. Often the nights erupt in shouting. Too often there's the clatter of broken glass and the sound of running feet. Margot said I lived in a slum. But it was a slum with one advantage. My mother had never yet paid me a visit.

I showered, poured myself a glass of Bordeaux, and slumped on the sofa. It was too late to call my mother, too late to do anything but think about how alone I felt here in my own apartment. What was it that I was missing? Or who? Romilly? Not exactly. Margot? Not at all. Elaine? Strangely, given her hostility, that seemed a possibility. Or maybe all of them. Maybe I'd taken to the Riviera like home. It was, after all, a home or temporary home to the people I was most concerned with.

It was also home, I felt sure of this, to the deepest and most disturbing mysteries of my life. And home, of course to Claire Coultard.

Had I let my defences down too far last night when she drove me back? I was going to have to remember, and keep remembering, that she was intelligent enough to be devious, if she wanted to be. And long experience with my mother and sister has told me that I don't deal well with wilful and devious women.

Still, I went to bed thinking about Claire.

It was not a confrontation even the most feisty of battlers would welcome. The woman in her late sixties, but upright in her chair, her face looking more ravaged than ever from the stroke. But not pleading for consideration, not begging for mercy. Hard as she'd ever been, hard as Plymouth Rock.

I could see it all as a replay of my last interview with her, the wrangle over the Cape Cod photograph when she had flattened me, sent me off to command Maria, the nurse, to prepare her lunch. But I wasn't going to let it happen this time. I hadn't flown from Europe for a patrician brush-off. I wanted to know who had fathered me. I needed to know. If I had to be direct, brutal, I would be.

Wouldn't I?

I wandered around my apartment, again feeling that sense of what it was I had felt last night. That sort of hole-in-your-life loneliness . . . With an effort, I called myself back to the issue in front of me. I poured myself the last glass from the bottle of Bordeaux I had been drinking last night and paced and thought.

And my first thought was devastating. Something I should have thought more rigorously about before. In the South of France, with a huge legacy directed towards Romilly, it had been easy to believe that everything that had happened, even the attack on Romilly, flowed somehow from my being the son of Marcel Coultard. It seemed to fit so many of the known facts. But the one fact it didn't fit was the essential fact I had brushed aside. If, as I believed, I was born in 1942, up to two years earlier than the date recorded on my birth certificate issued by US Army Field Hospital 389, then Marcel Coultard could not be my father. I had allowed my imagination to gallop ahead, allowed it to persuade myself that Marcel Coultard must somehow have met up with my mother in early 1942. But there was, of course, absolutely no evidence for believing that. Indeed, very little possibility. To the best of my knowledge, throughout 1942 my mother had been in London. I had even met old friends of hers, the Goffs, the Barretts, the Van Scholters, who still talked about the old days in 1942 London. When they reminisced, nobody even mentioned my mother being flown out and dropped by parachute over moonlit southern France. Even less did they talk of her returning a minimum nine months later having been forced to leave her love child on the Riviera. Love child! True enough they did talk about her doing a course in Scotland in the later part of 1942. That would cover the birth. But it wouldn't have helped to put my mother in Marcel's arms sometime in March 1942.

I felt nauseous at the thought. I opened a bottle of Burgundy. I'm a fault-finder when it comes to anything but Bordeaux. I poured a glass but it tasted corked, bitter. Or was the bitterness just disappointment that there were no easy solutions.

And then as I poured away the bottle of wine and watched the red liquid swirl down the sink, the answer hit me. And the answer had come from Marty Pearson. *He* was American. And *he* was in the South of France in 1942. The Vichy government were happy enough to allow aid workers in through Marseilles right up till November 1942 when the German army advanced down to the coast. And wasn't that just what my mother was involved in? Civilian aid was my mother's role. Of course, she could easily have been sent to Provence in say early 1942 . . . as an army-trained expert to evaluate the supply situation. And perhaps her orders were to carry out a short fact finding stopover, maybe via Gibraltar on her way over from the United States. And once there in France she could have met with Marcel, a young man of exuberant personality. Fallen in love. Or maybe just enjoyed a good hillside humping among the sharp scents of pine and lavender. Before returning pregnant to a chilly, damp embattled London. Omigod, had I got it? I certainly might have.

I open a bottle of claret. Bordeaux is incomparable fuel for thought. So she returns pregnant. The child, me, is born in secret. Probably in Scotland. And fostered there. When exactly she tells General John (Colonel John as he was then) the grim truth we can't guess. Probably she waits until he too arrives in London to start preparations for the landings in France.

God knows when she told him, but he accepted it. The General was basically a good man, I'd always known that. More, the general had guts. So General John, recovering from the blow to his *amour propre*, agrees to tear up my Scottish birth certificate. More than that, since they were on different sides of the Atlantic in 1942, he agrees that my age has to be adjusted. He can't obtain a 1944 fake British birth certificate, so he has my birth registered in November 1944 by some old friend at 389 US Army Field Hospital in mid-campaign in France. So there it was – *Ecce homo*! Tom Chapel, aged two years, makes his official first, half-assed appearance on the stage of life.

I grabbed my coat. I drank another glass of the Bordeaux

savouring its pleasing depth. I was ready to face her. Was Marcel Coultard my father, or what?

We were in the drawing room. A long, narrow salon furnished with English eighteenth-century pieces, dark mahogany gleaming under the tender care of ages in a way I always found slightly sinister. As a child I imagined they had slaves polishing this furniture and in my imagination they were always singing (of course) until the lady of the house came in, looking remarkably like my mother, her house-whip meant to encourage rather than maim, and lashed them into silence. Well, I'm sure that things were never like that in old abolitionist Boston but all these surreal imaginings had left me with a marked sense of intimidation whenever I walked into this room. I carried it with me now.

My mother sat in her upright Queen Anne chair, her hands smoothing back and forth along the worn carving of the arms. She wore a peach silk afternoon dress, face powder and a discreet glaze of rouge and lipstick, her hair coiffed by the woman who assisted Maria to get her dressed every morning.

She heard me out. Sometimes she nodded. Sometimes she folded one palsied lip over the other in a gesture of thoughtfulness. 'You *have* been thinking hard, Sonny,' she said, as I sat back in my chair. 'Of course, it never was your forte.'

Her very coolness and control left me in no doubt that I was right. Why else wasn't she blazing with fury? I had, after all, accused her of adultery (although I have to admit that, by telling me I wasn't General John's son, she had admitted to it anyway – unless she was laying claim to an immaculate conception). I had accused her of deceit and falsifying vital documents. But none of these things seemed to faze her. She sat there, fully in command. I sat opposite, still convinced, no . . . still pretty sure I was right. Still mostly sure I was right. But nevertheless shrivelling beneath her amused contempt.

'Get up, Sonny,' she said. 'Go to the bureau.'

I got up. 'What am I going to find there?' I tried to put a sceptical note into my voice but I knew it didn't work.

'My service record,' she said. 'Third file in the top drawer.'

I went to the bureau, opened the drawer and took out the file: Capt. (honorary) M. Bannerman Chapel, 1941–1944. US Army attachment.

'Look through it,' she said.

I opened the file and flicked through it. The speckled, browning paper. The crests of various commands and posts. The old uneven face of the typewriter. *Recruitment*, it said. *Posting to the European Theatre / England*, it recorded. *'Supply in Aid of the Civil Power' US Army training course, Windsor Castle, Berkshire, August, 1942*. London and the London area postings throughout 1942, the last part of the year, a mere two weeks, in Scotland. In 1942, no mention of France.

There were many more items. Things I didn't know about. A British medal for bravery in a bombing raid on the World's End, Chelsea, February 23, 1944. Then, of course, posting to the North-West European theatre, civilian attachment to Third Army, Patton's army in August, 1944. Then an honourable discharge following the birth of a son, Thomas Bannerman Chapel, in US Military Hospital 389 at Claviers, France, on November 2, 1944.

'Well?'

'Just as you say,' I said shakily. 'But it still doesn't explain the dates. It still doesn't explain the fact that in that picture I was definitely not a two-year-old.'

'You *threatened* to take your problem to a paediatrician. I *did* it,' she said. She leaned forward and took a thin wad of letters from the low table in front of her, shuffled through them and handed me an envelope. 'Read it,' she said. Then continued as I opened the envelope. 'You'll see it confirms that the growth rate of children varies so greatly that most professional estimates would be no more than guesswork.'

I tried to be quiet, controlled. 'It was you who told me I was not General John's child, remember.'

'I remember. It was untrue. I was trying to hurt you. No more than simple spite.'

I was really trying hard now in a final attempt to bring her to an understanding of what was happening in France. 'I've explained to you why I need this information,' I said. 'I've explained to you that I have reason to believe it has something to do with the attack on Romilly. This is something the French police believe too. It was an attack that nearly killed her. Even, conceivably an attack that might be repeated.'

She gave the faintest of shrugs.

I flipped. 'But still you sit there and smirk. Haven't you had enough victories over me? Hasn't that been what our life's been like together?' I stood and turned towards the door. 'All I can say is that I know, somewhere, you're lying.'

Not exactly strong stuff. Not what I had come all the way from the Mediterranean to say. Jesus, surely I could do better than this?

I got to the door and turned as she called to me. An automatic, little boy reflex of my part.

'I know no Marcel Coultard,' she said. 'I have neither met, nor heard of him. I've been to Provence once in my life, as I believe you know. I was with my husband during our tour of the landing beaches in 1958. We spent two days at Cannes and Toulon where General Patch's 7th Army landed with the French in August, 1944. As a staff Colonel my husband served with General Patch and wished to revisit the beaches. We then went on to visit the Anglo-American battlefields in Italy.'

I reached for the door handle. 'OK,' I said, 'But God save you, you're still lying.'

She smiled, well content.


Maria, my mother's nurse, was in the hall as I left the drawing room. She gave me her spectacular smile, then keyed it down to a grimace of sympathy. My guess is that she had heard almost everything that had gone on between my mother and myself.

A guess quickly confirmed.

'Mr Chapel,' Maria tugged me by the arm, drawing me away from the door. 'You remember the last time you were here? The same day Jack asked me to marry him?'

'I remember.'

'You had an argument with your mother about photographs of you when you were a small boy.'

'You heard us.'

She nodded. 'That day Mrs Chapel burnt many photographs. In the fireplace, hundreds of old pictures. She took them from a box in her bedroom.'

'Did she? Pictures of the family?'

'I think. Some I saw were only pictures of you. When you were very small. Pictures of Miss Margot, she kept.'

'I see. Thanks for telling me this Maria.'

'And something else,' she said. She drew out an envelope from the bosom of her uniform.

It was one of those continental envelopes with a pale green lining. Along one side it was badly charred. She handed it carefully to me. Inside was a photograph of a child between one and two years old, standing unsteadily, one hand stretched towards a chair left for support. The child's hair was cropped short, its clothes a pair of overlarge trousers and a sweater with the sleeves rolled in a thick bunch round each thin forearm.

I turned it over and read the inscription.

I didn't go back into the drawing room straight away. I felt in too much turmoil for that. Instead I went into what had once been General John's study, poured myself a Scotch and sat just there in the shaft of sunlight, from time to time glancing at the picture. I felt, and I couldn't possibly say why, immensely sorry for this little boy in the ragged reach-me-down outfit, standing upright for what was probably only one of the first few times in his life, his hand out to steady himself against the turned, ornate chair leg. In the half-an-hour or so since I had first seen him, the power of his image to move me had become already part of my being.

I realise, of course, the foolishness of all this. The little boy is me. It says so on the back of the photograph. But because I've been brought up to believe that I was not a little boy like that, that I was a general's son, with a mother who was a New England Bannerman, I can feel both apart and joined to this sepia image in the photograph.

I went back into the drawing room. My mother's eyes went directly to the picture I held in my hand. 'Yes,' I said. 'Another photograph. One you didn't burn.' I held it in front of her. 'Of me,' I said.

'Let me see.'

I turned it slowly round so that she could read the writing on the back. She scrabbled for her spectacles.

'In General John's handwriting,' I said. 'It reads, *My very first sight of Sonny at the convent. Cable answer by return – yes or no.*' I paused for breath. 'For Christ's sake, we both know what that means.'

She was silent.

'It means what it says. The child's yours for the asking. Just say yes or no. The lousy truth is that I'm not your child either.'

I stood there, aware that my heart was racing. Throughout my childhood I'd been haunted by this sense that I didn't really belong. Hadn't really earned the right to belong. No intimations of adoption, you understand. Not at all. But just this sense that I was outside the magic family ring. Looking at it now, I suppose the existence of this feeling in adopted children in not particularly unusual, whether they were aware of adoption or not. But what most people miss is that it's a feeling that doesn't stop at childhood; in later years, it can grow to suffocating proportions.

I looked down at my mother, holding the reverse of it to her. She stared, breathing heavily, but said nothing.

'Can't mean anything else, can it?' I said. 'I was adopted. So what's so shameful about that? Like many couples you found you couldn't have children. You adopted me – and within a year or so, Margot's on the way. It happens all the time.'

Her breath made a hissing sound as it came from her nostrils. I almost expected accompanying flames. Pure fury.

'Except for one thing. You couldn't admit to it.'

She was silent, breathing hard.

'Things were loose in Europe then. Hundreds of thousands of small children needing care. Yet still adoption takes time. Questions of religion snarl things up. The French, particularly, don't plan to lose their children to passing Americans. But hand over a few dollars. Guarantee the kid a good home and drive off with him in the back of the jeep. Easy. Except upright, straight and narrow American officers should not be found to be engaged in a little post-battle looting. Especially the looting of children.'

'You're disgusting,' she said with a fervour I suspect she'd long felt.

'But I'm right, aren't I?' I said. 'What was his name, for Christ's sake? '

'What?'

A lump was forming in my throat. 'Before he became American Sonny,' I said. 'Was he Belgian, Dutch, French, German?'

She shook her head. A lack of interest, even distaste for the plight of those children so long ago.

I tried to keep my tone neutral, though I was far from feeling it. 'Tell me something about him. Anything. I have a right to know. You must see that.'

She looked away, towards the window. 'We never asked,' she said. 'Why should we? America had lifted Europe from the gutter. What did we want to know of existence there? We were taking you to a much better life.'

I closed my eyes, opening them slowly. 'Where was it?' I asked her. 'Where was this orphanage? Obviously you weren't around. So just after the South of France landings when the general was able to take an hour or two off to check out a few orphanages.'

She didn't answer but her breathing was becoming so strange I thought I'd best call the nurse. A lightning strike of panic passed through me. Caught up in my own past I hadn't thought how all this might be affecting her condition. 'Are you all right?' I asked her. 'Let me get the nurse.'

She shook her head. For a moment she continued staring with her yellowy eyes, then she jerked her head. 'Closer.'

I was leaning forward, bent over her, expecting some sort of Protestant benediction when her hand flicked, the hard knuckles striking me across the face. My head snapped back in shock.

'Get out,' she said. 'You are no son of mine – you never were.'

With my hand I pressed the stinging side of my face. I could see she felt she had won the last round. But in fact she'd just lost it. She had aroused some determination in me I never realised I had. 'Where was the picture taken? In France, somewhere? In Germany . . . ?'

She scowled silently. There was a world of contempt there. A lifetime, I suppose. 'Just go,' she said. 'Don't come back, ever.'

It was the boundless contempt that released that flicker of ruthlessness in me, ruthlessness she didn't believe for a moment I was capable of. And perhaps without her I wasn't. 'You tell me,' I said slowly, you tell me where that picture was taken or every Bannerman in New England will receive a letter from me tomorrow morning. Plus the Office of Veterans in Washington.'

Her face changed. Muscles tightened. 'Never. You'd never do that.'

I paused, gearing myself up again. 'Difficult for you to grasp, I know. And late for you to start learning. But watch my lips: Other people have rights that can't be trampled on. I want . . . no, I intend to have, the name of that orphanage.'

'What use would it be to you to discover you were the child of some German soldier and French farm girl? You're too late, Sonny. It was forty years ago. The convent's long gone by now,' she said. 'Dismantled, the nuns dispersed to other orphanages.'

'That's your answer?'

Her lips rubbed together in a sort of smile. 'That's my answer,' she said. 'That's all the answer you're getting.' Not a hair in her grey-blue rinse had been ruffled. Not a pleat in her peach dress

I turned and walked for the door. As I opened it, I looked back 'The name of the orphange,' I said. 'Or a letter to every Bannerman. And a letter to the Office of Veterans revealing the child looting activities of the much decorated Colonel John Dwight Chapel in 1944.'

For a moment she stared at me. But in the end she was a realist. 'It's a town called Pézenas, not far from the Spanish border,' she said. 'The Convent of the Pauvres Soeurs.'

# 35

THE WEEKEND WAS approaching when I flew back to France, this time Boston-Paris, Paris-Nice. At the airport I picked up my hired Renault, all costs covered from the per diem Luc Rolin had arranged for me to have from the Coultard estate. Did I feel entitled to take the money? Not entirely. But certainly since talking to my erstwhile mother, I was more sure about one thing. I was Marcel Coultard's son. No other solution made sense. Did it?

It was mid-morning as I drove along the now familiar Promenade des Anglais, the city rising to my left, the flat, sunlit Mediterranean on my right. A large white yacht with a pale blue sail moved in towards its mooring at one of the marinas between Nice and Cannes. A few people dawdled along the broad side-walk overlooking the pebble beach and watched the yacht or a Delta jet making its descent across the Bay of Angels and onto Nice-Côte d'Azur. Turning up the Avenue de Verdun, confidently following the line of the gardens and the River Paillon, I felt like an old Riviera hand, my spirits lifted by the success, as I saw it, that I'd scored with my mother – or Mrs Margaret Chapel as I was now determined to think of her. Spirits lifted, too, by the prospect of seeing Romilly again.

I had called the hospital each day I was away in the US and the reports on Romilly had grown in optimism. I turned into the *Centre médical* now, bought a twenty-franc ticket from an attendant and left my car in the lot.

As I crossed the lobby with its restrained decoration and silently moving glass elevators I saw Elaine coming from the canteen entrance. I had called her twice from Boston to check Romilly's progress and she had been muted but not too unfriendly on the phone. I expected to pick up on our former arrangements. She didn't.

The warning was in her expression as she came towards me. She stopped a yard or so away. 'You're back,' she said shortly

'I'm back with some amazing news.'

She shrugged it off. '*My* amazing news is that your girlfriend is up there with Romilly. And has been up there with Romilly at least twice a day since you left.'

'You're talking about Margot.'

'Okay, your sister if you prefer to keep the kinks in your relationship.'

'Margot's not my sister. That's what I found out. I was adopted.'

'Margot's not your sister. That's the amazing news?' she said dryly. 'Now you can do what you've always wanted to do and live openly with her.'

I had to get her off the subject of Margot and on to Romilly. 'I talked to the doctors,' I said. 'It's looking good.'

'It would be looking better if Margot wasn't worming her way back in.'

'Just tell her no.'

She made an exasperated gesture. 'Rom's happy enough that she's there. I guess that's what's important.'

'Look, Elly. I need to ask you. Did Rom remember anything more about the whole thing?'

Elaine shook her head. 'No . . . no, you heard it all.'

I knew it had to surface. 'There was nothing. Nothing going on?'

'No,' she said angrily, 'of course not. Is your mind just saturated with sex? I don't know what Marcel was up to. Just getting to know her, maybe. There were only three meetings. At each one he made her swear not to tell to anybody they were meeting. He told Romilly that a member of our family was going to be the beneficiary of his will. Rom, as a seventeen-year-old romantic, believed he must mean me. Secret love for me over the years, that sort of thing. He said if she spoke to *anyone* about this before he informed everybody concerned, there were the possibilities of massive law suits, and hinted at worse. Violence.'

'Violence? Who by?'

'That he didn't say.'

'She didn't ask?'

'For God's sake he was her mother's boss. She was in awe of him. She wasn't in any position to quiz him.'

'No, of course, ' I said placatingly.

'So, convinced her mother was going to inherit a fortune,

Romilly kept quiet. Even to me. Except for a few probings at the funeral.'

I stood next to the lift doors, preoccupied, moving aside as they slid open and people streamed past me. 'This still doesn't tell us why he left the estate to Romilly,' I said carefully. 'But it's like a finger, pointing in one direction.'

'What are you talking about?'

'I'm talking about that fucking son of his,' I said. 'I'm talking about Sébastien Coultard.'

'Sébastien? You can't think he had anything to do with what happened to Romilly?'

'I can,' I said. 'And I do.'

'For God's sake, you have not a scrap of proof.' She looked at me with the old contempt. 'You're just play-acting the suffering father, aren't you? Play-acting your suspicions of Sébastien. Christ, you're a worthless individual. If Sébastien Coultard walked through that door now, you'd shake hands and make some polite remark about the weather.'

'You're wrong about that, Elly,' I said. But her lip curled at my protestations.

I hurt more than I dared show. Was it all true? Had I snatched up this opportunity to inject some purpose, some drama into my life? Was I play-acting?

'For God's sake Elly.' I blocked her way as she tried to move past me. 'We have to try to be friends. I've had a long flight. Not a hell of a lot of sleep and I want to see Romilly.'

'Stand in line,' she said. 'I'm next. You can see Romilly when I'm through.'

'Just cool down enough to tell me – the doctors are still very positive?'

'She's being discharged tomorrow. She'll have a nurse visiting twice a day and has to take it very easy. But she's coming home.'

'I'll drive,' I said. 'You can sit in the back with her.'

'There'll be an ambulance,' she said coldly. 'And let me tell you here and now – I don't want Margot anywhere near that ambulance or near the house. She's dripping sentiment like hot molasses all over Romilly.' She shuddered. 'It's sickening.'

'Okay,' I said. 'That's Margot. What about me?'

'You can see her whenever you like. But I don't want you staying at the house, Tom. I'm not playing happy families with you and Rom.'

I looked at her. The last few days had clearly been no less stressful than the week before that. 'I'll go up,' I said. 'I'll tell Margot you want to see Romilly alone.'

'Don't you think I haven't told her that? But she hangs on. I can't risk open warfare in front of Romilly. Minimum emotional excitement, the doctors insist for the next week or two. That damn woman plays on it.' One of the elevators slid silently down. The doors opened. 'Speak of the devil,' Elaine said.

Margot looked stunning. South of France stunning. Dressed in a yellow shirt, blue skirt, her face tan, her blonde hair caught up behind, a pale jacket on her arm. Next to her Elly looked drab and motherly.

'Tommy, darling.' Margot pulled no stops as she came towards me, barely seeming to notice Elaine moving past her to stand in the lift.

'Tell her,' Elly said, as the lift doors began to close, 'to stay away from my daughter.'

'I'll go up with you,' I said.

'You can see her this afternoon,' she said harshly. 'I want to see my daughter alone.'

Margot watched Elaine slide upwards with a wry expression on her face. 'Astonishing,' she said. 'Anybody would think I was . . .' she rolled her eyes . . . 'fucking her husband. Let's get ourselves a cup of coffee. Or perhaps even something for lunch. My treat,' she added.

We had lunch. Not at the hospital canteen but on the Boulevard des Anglais, of course. At the Chantecier Restaurant in the Hôtel Negresco, of course. We sat facing Aubusson wall hangings and surrounded by the political and business elite of Nice and a sprinkling of the wealthier German, Italian and American tourists. Margot looked the part perfectly. Myself, a good deal less so.

She told me she'd heard about my bar brawl with a couple of the men at the party. 'Not like you, Tommy.'

'Not like me because it wasn't me.'

'Wasn't you?' She reached out and traced my cheekbone with her index finger. 'You've got the marks to prove it. Makes you look rather handsome. Sort of lived in.'

'For Christ's sake, listen to me, Margot. I was attacked by three of Sébastien Coultard's nationalist thugs. I was lucky to get away without broken legs.'

She pursed her lips. 'Tommy . . . I *talked* to Sébastien. He says it was a miracle you weren't really hurt. Apparently you were pretty provocative to the men on the gate. Wouldn't identify yourself. They took you for a reporter or something. People in the Nationalist camp have to be very careful.'

I pushed back my chair. 'I don't have to listen to this stuff,' I said. 'Do you realise, you stupid bitch, that that man could well have been the one who attacked Romilly?'

I hadn't seen the waiter approach. I only saw him bend over Margot, a white visiting card with a couple of lines scrawled across it, and heard the murmur of his voice. 'Waiting in the lobby,' is what I think he said.

Margot slipped the card into her purse. 'I'll ignore the remark about being a stupid bitch, probably because it's richly deserved.' She flashed a smile. 'Won't be a second,' she said, getting up.

'Who is it?' I stood too.

'No great friend of yours, Tommy. Now just sit tight. I'll be back.'

Her long stride was already taking her across the dining room as I sat back in my chair. *No great friend of yours*. That could only mean one thing. Sébastien Coultard.

I got up and dropped my napkin on the table. A wimp, Elaine had called me. Not in so many words maybe, but that's what she'd meant. I was not more than half a dozen or so steps behind Margot, but neither she nor Coultard saw me coming.

I could see Margot's smile broaden. She stopped before him and they embraced. While he was kissing her, both cheeks and a touch on the lips, I had a chance to see that on top his hair was thinning, revealing a half circle of scalp. When he stopped smiling he looked far from amiable.

I heard scraps only. 'The Prince . . . chartering a plane . . . A guest . . . asked me to bring you . . .'

Margot's lips formed an exaggerated Oh!

'We leave in two hours.' He turned her deftly by the elbow at that point and they spoke several sentences together that I couldn't hear. But I could see Margot's reaction. She was impressed.

As his head moved he saw me. 'Ah, Monsieur Chapel himself . . .' He produced a parody of a bow. 'Yes. Two of my security men apparently mistook you for a sneak-thief on the night of Werter's party. You're going to have to be more careful, you know. It was fortunate for you that my sister was there to intervene.'

269

I didn't answer. Forget words, I should do something. Wimp, I was thinking. The sort of man who'd shake his hand and chat about the weather, Elaine had said. Was that me?

The whole weight of the Negresco seemed to bear down on me, the soft splendour of the place, the well-dressed guests . . . But I had to do something. I could feel my face flushing. My fists clenched. I stepped forward.

'No harm done, was there?' he said casually. And his hand came up, placed flat on my chest, exercising a gently but unmistakable pressure. The same movement he'd employed in Fabius's office. 'You'll be more careful next time, I'm sure,' he said full into my face.

I could still hit him. I could bring my knee up into his crotch and . . . The concierge was already coming forward. I allowed myself to rock backwards slightly; Sébastien let his hand drop.

'Can I help, gentlemen?' the concierge asked. He was already clicking his fingers behind him to bring two assistants forward.

'Not at all,' Sébastien said airily. 'A bientôt, then,' he said to Margot and left to rejoin some people at the bar.

I walked back to our table. Within a moment or two Margot was sitting opposite me. 'Whatever happened at Werter's, it wasn't Sébastien's fault you know.'

'It wasn't?'

'Promise.'

I drank my kir.

'You don't mind if I go, do you, Tommy? Private jet to Senegal. The prince's elder brother has a huge place there . . . Not bad uh?'

'You do what you like.'

She looked up at me. Perhaps for the first time in my life I detected a faint alarm in her eyes.

'Tell me about Boston,' she said. 'What made you go jetting off home without a word.'

I told her what happened.

She sat back. 'Hell,' she said. 'Really? You belong to neither of them. Well . . . Hell!'

I didn't feel like talking about it now. I had wanted to tell her more. I was planning to ask her to come on a visit to the orphanage in Pézenas. But that clearly couldn't compete with a flight down to Senegal on the prince's jet. Which prince? Did I care?

'Adopted . . .' Her eyebrows lifted speculatively. 'So you really could be . . .'

'Could be what?'

'Marcel Coultard's son. Listen, darling,' she leaned across the table, covering my hand with hers, 'there's only one reason you and Romilly were left the Coultard money. You *must* be old Coultard's son. Thomas Bannerman Coultard. How intriguing! And of course, you'll be frightfully rich when you get that shrieking French harridan evicted from the château.'

'It's Romilly's money,' I reminded her. 'Old Marcel left everything to Romilly, his granddaughter.'

'But you control it for the next few years.'

'Are you suggesting I rob my own daughter?'

'No,' she said coolly. 'Only that you make sure you exact the benefits you're clearly entitled to. You're too soft about these things, Tommy. You have to keep an eye on Elaine. After all, the money comes through you. You're the son of Marcel.'

'I don't know that for sure, yet.' I looked at her. 'And what's Elaine got to do with this?'

'Don't be naïve, Tommy. Elaine will try to edge you out. Of course she will. Within a year you'll just be the guy who countersigns the company accounts. She's a businesswoman. She'll run circles round you if you let her.'

'You two will never get on, will you?'

She sat back, thinking for a long moment. 'No. I don't like her any more than she likes me. But then, no two women can, Tommy, if they're after the same man.'

Something lurched in me as she said that. Was it because of Elly – or of Margot herself? I didn't know. It just felt good – the idea that I was being pursued. Even if it was for Romilly's money.

'Let's finish lunch and take a room,' she said, stretching. She fluttered her eyelids like a Zeigfeld girl. Strangely enough it had always worked before.

'That quick wham, bam, thank you ma'am on the highway,' she said lazily, 'it didn't do a lot for me. Dr Johnson said we should keep our friendships in good repair. He must have meant more than a few minutes in a truck's headlights. What do you think?'

I shook my head. 'You'd better hurry,' I said. 'Don't want you to miss your plane. Private jets, Senegal, Balkan princes or whatever. Enough to give a girl a real rush.'

Her eyes narrowed. 'That's very cool,' she said. 'But I was offering not to go. Screw Senegal, I'd sooner stay here on the Riviera.'

'You told Coultard you were going.'

'I did, didn't I? I was teasing you. Weren't you disappointed I said yes? Be honest, Tommy.'

All my old promptings would have been to say yes, of course I was. I was missing a companion to Pézenas – and an afternoon with her in a suite in the Negresco. But now it would have been a lie. I was suddenly glad she was going. I shrugged.

Very slowly she said: 'Should I get this straight? You're not saying you don't care if I go?'

I didn't answer.

'You heard me, Tommy.'

'You go,' I said. 'It'll get you out of Elaine's hair.'

'It's not a lot to do with getting in or out of Elly's hair, is it?' She was sitting up straight, beautiful, the rejected woman. A certain thespian nobility. By thespian I mean phoney. Is that fair? Was I really causing her pain?

The architectural structures of our lives are often pathetically evident to other people, although *we* see them as subtle, concealed, uncertain, ambiguous. But this time I knew what had happened. For the first time in my life I'd turned her down. I don't mean just sex. I mean every minor suggestion she'd ever put to me, I'd said yes to, if I possibly could. That's something to suddenly realise.

And now I was saying no. And we *both* knew how big a no it was.

She looked at me. Those big blue eyes. The first faint crow's feet hit women just before forty. 'You know, Tommy,' she said, 'you've grown hard in these last few weeks. So much harder than you used to be.'

I waited it out, fighting to get my voice right. 'I just hope to Christ you're right,' I said in a whisper.

I thought of the scene with Sébastien a moment ago. So much harder than I used to be? Maybe. But still not hard enough, Sonny.

# 36

I DROVE SLOWLY along the Promenade des Anglais, continued on to the Quai des États-Unis and turned off the coast road to make my way up to the *Centre médical*. At the nurses' station they told me Elaine was taking a late lunch in the canteen. I took the opportunity to spend a few moments alone with Romilly.

She was sleepy but not to the point of exhaustion. Very slowly, as easily as I could, I brought her up to date on what had happened, the will, Fabius, Bisset, my trip back to the US and the discovery that I was adopted.

She was intrigued. She asked searching questions. I guessed the doctors maybe and Elaine certainly, would not have approved of me giving Romilly all this background in one solid lump. But she could handle it, I felt sure of that. I didn't mention Nicole Tresselli, that's true, but I kept back nothing else.

'Are we in trouble, Dad?' she said at the end of my story.

'Twenty-eight million bucks is the sort of trouble most people would welcome.'

'She nodded. 'Except I just don't feel it's mine. When he was asking me out, I thought he was planning to leave something to Mom. That's what he seemed to be hinting. So suddenly, why me?'

'I don't know honey,' I said, standing, 'but I need to find out as much as you. Until we know why the old guy left the money to you and not one or other of his recognised children, you're not going to feel any different about this.'

I went out to pick up the Renault. It stood in the sun, glistening dark green in the sort of heat that made you wonder what sort of paint they used on cars to stop them blistering. I got in and gave it the full air-con for a minute or two while I thought about what next. I already knew *where* next – but I didn't really want to go alone.

I drove out of the hospital lot and began to work my way

down to the old town. Pulling up on the sidewalk, I asked three passers-by before a young man said yes he knew the offices I was asking about. His cousin had done a *stage* there, helping out in a university vacation.

I parked illegally at the back of the nineteenth-century red tile building and walked the stairway to the third floor. It was like a campaign office in a US election. There were young kids all over-excited, feeling they were in the middle of things. They spoke on phones to ministries in Paris or hit keyboards in open-door offices. In some rooms Arab workmen sat leaning forward with a rolled cigarette smoking between their fingers, waiting for news of a job, or an all important *carte de séjour,* waiting with that resigned patience that can be so touching among the truly desperate. There were a lot of posters on the walls. Anti-racist posters, advice and help posters for refugees. And piles of pamphlets on tables with invitations to take one or even a pack if you could distribute them somewhere useful.

Claire Coultard had an office to herself at the end of a long corridor. The door was open and I could see her, as I approached, her head down at her desk, her dark hair lustrous in a shaft of afternoon sunlight. When she looked up at the sound of foot-steps, I've seldom seen anyone so genuinely surprised. 'Monsieur Chapel,' she said.

I looked around the tiny office. 'We're alone,' I said in a stage voice. 'So it's Tom. Okay?'

She didn't answer. Instead, she stood up, smoothing her skirt, her eyes on me. Her expression was sombre, her mouth in a faint interrogative pout. She wore a dark blue shirt and some gold at her throat. She touched the gold, a watch or locket and I realised she was not nervous but maybe slightly thrown by my visit. 'Well . . .' she said, 'this really is a surprise.' She waved towards the single chair. 'Sit down. I don't suppose this is a social visit.'

'No.'

'You just got back from America?'

'This morning.'

'And you've learnt something in the United States. You have something more to tell me about our extraordinary situation. Is that it?'

'That's it,' I said.

*   *   *

274

I don't think I really expected her to say she'd come, although that must seem pretty unconvincing when I had driven across Nice asking strangers to help me locate her office. I told myself I had really sought her out because I wanted to tell her what I had learnt in Boston. But before I could ask her, she'd immediately said she'd go with me and in moments she was moving back and forth about the office sweeping papers from her desk and locking files.

We took my car. With a quick stop at St Juste for her to pack an overnight bag and change into jeans, we were on the road again by late afternoon. From Nice to Pézenas is pretty well the length of the French Mediterranean coast. We stayed with the autoroute most of the way and raced past Aix, Arles, Nîmes and Montpellier, all of which, Claire told me, had Coultard cinemas, some small, some new multiplexes. It was nearly ten that night before we booked two rooms in a hotel near the east gates of the extraordinary city of Pézenas.

In the restaurant we sat opposite each other at a window table, looking out on the seventeenth-century streets, bizarrely roamed by men in D'Artagnan costumes, on each arm a doxy with puffed up bosoms. In Pézenas, the summer is one long season of fêtes and tourist shows, Claire told me. I could have done without the Musketeers but the view across the lamplit corners of streets and alleys took me by the throat.

I had been reluctant to mention my lunch with Margot at the Negresco because that would inevitably have exposed the fact that I'd met up with Sébastien and done little more than what Elaine had predicted – shaken him by the hand. But tiredness, or the familiarity which a few hours together in a car induces, relaxed my scruples. I told her I'd seen Sébastien today in the Negresco.

She nodded. 'He called me,' she said. 'He told me the prince asked for Margot to come along. I don't believe it, of course. Sébastien invited her for himself. He thinks a quick affair with your sister will uncover all he needs to know about you.'

'The only thing left to uncover is about Margot and me. And you know that already.'

'Yes. I know that already,' she repeated. Something descended between us. I poured her some wine and we both stared out at the floodlit battlements.

'You had no objection when he asked your sister to go with him?' she asked after a moment.

'Why should I?'

'After what you told me.'

I regretted telling her now. I'd been prompted by some obligation of reciprocity. Usually a mistake. 'The thing with Margot is over,' I said. 'It was over a long time ago. It was most certainly over this afternoon.'

She stared at me.

Fool or not, I don't know. But I told her exactly what had happened, what Margot had proposed, what I had turned down.

She nodded, stared at me again, still nodding slowly, then pushed her unfinished glass of wine away. 'I'll book us both an early call for tomorrow,' she said, standing. 'No way of knowing how the day will develop.'

I watched her go. Somehow, by a simple mention of Margot, I had blown the trust I had been building up with her; I knew that. Tomorrow morning we were going to be back to the position of reluctant allies.

At the hotel reception next morning we found someone who assured us the Convent of the Pauvres Soeurs was still to be found in the city. Following his directions we came upon a nineteenth century Gothic building constructed round a square, cobbled courtyard. The main door was contained in a massive Norman arch carved with a Latin inscription I couldn't translate beyond the words faith, hope and charity. A chain pull bell hung to one side of an oak door.

I pulled it, heard it jangle somewhere inside, and waited a long minute or more for the door to be opened. A small, very young-looking nun stood there in a grey habit.

We had agreed that Claire should make the pitch. Patiently, she explained to the nun that we would like to see the Mother Superior about children orphaned or, for whatever reason, given shelter during the war.

We were asked to wait. The young nun came back five minutes later with the message that the Mother Superior was unable to see us. She could, however, offer an appointment at six o'clock that evening.

With a whole day to kill we became tourists, driving over to Carcassonne, having lunch overlooking the medieval walls, then visiting the incredible Disney restoration by which the nineteenth-century architect, Viollet-le-Duc had recreated the city. It seemed to me that we spent the afternoon in separate capsules, thinking our own thoughts, talking only perhaps to admire a restored tower or turret or the view from the genuinely medieval, or some-times even Roman walls. Each, at different moments, caught the other stealing a glance when we imagined it was safe. I would watch her move towards the window of a shop selling antiques, bend forward to examine some item, make a gesture of rejection at the price or quality and turn back towards me – and in each movement or expression there was some gesture, movement of her body that bestowed on her a unique quality I found physi-cally disturbing.

There was nothing easy in this. We behaved in an arm's length way that allowed neither of us to forget we were on different sides. We didn't laugh together, or flirt. When our eyes met we both quickly looked away or perhaps self-consciously checked our watches.

I think as we got closer to the time of our appointment we were both suffering an attack of nerves, exacerbated by having spent so long together. I couldn't really guess what outcome she was hoping for. Presumably she had nothing to gain if the convent were able to confirm that I was Marcel's son. Indeed, everything to lose.

For myself, I was sure this evening's meeting would tell me that Marcel Coultard was my father. Would it also tell me why he had placed me with the Poor Sisters of Pézenas?

We left Carcassonne a little before four and arrived back in Pézenas just after five, time to freshen up at the hotel. At six we again presented ourselves at the convent.

# 37

MOTHER FRANCESCA WAS a tall, heavily built woman of perhaps seventy-five. Her face, deeply lined, hung in folds like coarse linen. The hands were the size of a man's hands but her voice had a softness which was firm and direct. I had feared an old nun, her memories hazy and unreliable. But Mother Francesca was far from that.

We introduced ourselves and she asked us to sit. She remained standing behind her magnificent desk while we took the upright oak armchairs arranged to face her. In a few sentences, Claire explained why we were there: essentially, that I was seeking to discover more about my origins; that, at present, I knew only that I had been adopted as a very small child from this convent during the war. Even my original name was lost.

Mother Francesca arranged the sleeves of her grey habit. 'In the past we had many enquiries,' she said. 'They've stopped now, of course. The war was a very long time ago. How close can you get to the date of this adoption?'

'My father,' I said, 'the man I thought of as my father, was a soldier, a colonel at the time. He was with the American and French forces that landed down here after the main Normandy landings. So the date is going to be in the second half of 1944.' I spread my hands. 'Perhaps not very helpful.'

She nodded thoughtfully. 'During the war, we kept no records of children who were brought here. It was a necessary protection from the SEC, and later the *milice,* for both the children and for ourselves. By the autumn of 1944 we had been liberated, we were not afraid to keep records. If you were adopted from this convent we'll have some sort of record of it. Though not necessarily complete.' She turned and took from the shelves behind her a thick, leather bound cash ledger 'What were your adoptive parents' names?'

'Colonel John Dwight Chapel and Margaret Bannerman Chapel.'

Still standing she opened the ledger on her desk. 'She ran her index finger down the page. 'November, 1944? Might that be it?'

'It could be. The colonel would have been alone, of course.'

'There's an entry here that reads simply J.D.C. Someone has added US Army.'

'J.D.C. – John Dwight Chapel. Why not enter it in full?'

'Secrecy.'

'Did people often disguise their names?'

She smiled. 'What we were doing was illegal, of course. Or, at least, outside the law. Everybody accepted that. Colonel Chapel must have asked us to enter no more than his initials.'

'You mean the adoptions were not sanctioned by French law?'

'There was very little French law in existence at this time, Monsieur. The whole region was desperately short of food. The children were undernourished. Most were already a year or two behind in their physical development. If the right sort of people came along, able and anxious to adopt, to offer one of our children a new life, we certainly didn't put difficulties in their way. In this case . . . an American, a senior officer . . .' She looked down at the ledger.

'You wouldn't have hesitated.'

She smiled. 'An American senior officer. We would have given him the whole orphanage if he'd taken it. No we didn't hesitate, illegal as it undoubtedly was. Food alone becomes of extraordinary importance when you have sixty children to find for every day. Were we wrong, Monsieur?'

I hesitated. But I wasn't here to run my life before an old woman who once saved it. 'No,' I said. 'You were not wrong. I'm deeply in your debt.'

Relief showed on her face as she pursed her lips together. 'Today's world doesn't understand the makeshift world of 1944. Today it would be unthinkable to hand a child over to a single unknown soldier, even a senior officer. Then we did what we could. We trusted in God.'

'You were not wrong,' I repeated. 'General Chapel, as he became, was a good father.' I don't think she noticed that I'd no similar handy commendation for his wife.

She leaned over the ledger. 'The child our colonel adopted was approximately two years old,' she said. 'There is an entry here showing that the child arrived as a baby without a name on November 2nd, 1942, no age recorded. Probably a few weeks old only. While he was here we called him Pascal. We chose November 2nd as his birthday.'

She looked at me. A question.

'My birthday, yes.'

She nodded to herself. Claire, I saw, tightened her locked fingers in her lap. The Mother Superior closed her book, her broad hands resting on it, smoothing the frayed leather.

'What we're now hoping to establish,' Claire said, 'is where the child, Pascal – the child we believe to be Mr Chapel – came from. Whose child he was.'

'Very much more difficult, Madame, I am sad to tell you. We had children from all sources, all races. Lost and orphaned French children. And of course, many, many Jewish children, French or foreign.'

'At the time, was there one nun here in charge of receiving children?'

'Myself. I dealt with all receptions from 1941 onwards when the Vichy government's first laws against the Jews were promulgated. Our Archbishop in Toulouse made ringing denunciations of the shameful happenings of those years. The rounding up and internment of innocent people; the inhuman transport to the East of Jewish men, women . . . and finally even children. Privately he called on all religious houses to give what sanctuary they could. Here, at Pézenas, we were happy to obey.'

I wondered what she thought of the notorious silence of Pope Pius XII in this huge tragedy but this was not the time to discuss it.

'Obviously,' I said, 'you don't remember individual children?'

'Some,' she said. 'Not many.' She looked down at her big hands flattened on the desk. 'But I remember something of this little boy during the two years he spent with us. He was, for his age, touchingly self-reliant. He would try to make up his own cot or wash the tin plates we used. Sometimes you come across very small children like that. You are amazed at this drive to be self-reliant. I was very fond of Pascal.' She looked up. 'Are you Jewish, Monsieur?'

I was totally baffled. 'I just don't know,' I said. 'I'm not . . . I'm not circumcised. I'm not even sure what being Jewish means. I was brought up an Episcopalian. Why do you ask me?'

'From the very beginning we had small numbers of Jewish children whose parents had been interned in the camp not far from here at Gurs. But by mid 1942 most of the children we were receiving were Jewish. Perhaps as high as four out of five.'

'Which makes you think the child you called Pascal might have been Jewish?' Claire said.

'That I'm in no position to say, Madame. But I can tell you that a child was at risk from these modern Herods if just one of their parents were Jewish. Under the Vichy laws that was enough, with appropriate grandparents, to make you legally Jewish.' She grimaced. 'And your life legally vulnerable, whatever your age.' She nodded heavily to herself.

We sat silently for a moment. It was clear she intended to continue. She had that quiet force of personality that made an interruption unthinkable.

'Let me explain to you how it was in those days.' She clasped her hands in front of her and began to pace the area behind her desk. 'In late 1941 Marshal Pétain's government's Statute of Jews began the repression in this part of France. Jews were first reduced to poverty and then sent to internment camps. There they suffered malnutrition, sometimes starvation. There was one of these evil places at Gurs, as I said, not far from here. By 1942 Jews began to be transported, usually terrifyingly crammed into cattle-trucks, to Paris and then on to what we now know was mass murder in the East. In August of that year, the great *rafle*, the round-up of Jewish families, shocked the honest people of southern France. They saw it happening in every town square. They saw police being sent to search for children in convents like this one. They began to realise that their trusted, white-haired, old Marshal was the devil behind all this suffering.'

I glanced at Claire. She knew all this of course, but the reminder that it was a French government that had committed these atrocities had drained the colour from her face. Tears, I saw, had filled her eyes.

'There was very little French people who opposed this barbarity could do,' Mother Francesca continued. 'It's true there were innumerable instances of individual help. Thousands of families hid Jewish neighbours. Police officers warned Jewish families when a new *rafle* was about to occur. Some very senior policemen resigned in protest. But the crucial fact for French people, what's lived with them ever since, is that it was their *own* government giving the orders. Not the Germans – there were no Germans here until the very end of 1942.'

'There was also the Resistance,' Claire said. 'Resisting those orders.'

'True. The Resistance was growing rapidly. And, thank God, there was part of the church, not so many Archbishops like Monsignor Salière of Toulouse if one is to be honest, but many thousands of simple parish priests prepared to disobey the law to help. It was men like these who brought the children to us.'

'You remember them?' Claire asked. 'You remember the names of these men?'

'It would have done little good if I had. The names were false. Or simply forenames. They were all sorts, priests, builders, teachers, even gendarmes who had taken part in the *rafles* and had hidden the children, then gone back for them.'

'We think it's possible the child, that's to say I, was delivered here by a man named Marcel Coultard,' I said.

'People never used family names.'

I felt the disappointment in my stomach.

She stopped a moment. 'But Marcel.' She smiled recognition. 'A man named Marcel came often. He had business here every month or so in Pézenas.'

What did he look like?' Claire asked her.

'Young, always laughing. With an arm damaged at birth?'

I looked at Claire.

It took her a moment to speak. 'Marcel was my father,' she said. 'Marcel Coultard.' The colour had jumped back into her face. 'You remember him?'

I felt the excitement racing through me, urging Mother Francesca on, urging her to expose her memories.

'Marcel, the film man, we called him. I never knew where he came from, but he used to deliver new films and posters to the cinemas in towns along the coast. Nîmes, Montpellier, Narbonne, Perpignan. He also delivered children to us. Possibly as many as twenty or thirty in those years.' She paused.

'And you believe Pascal was among them?'

'Marcel would turn up, late at night, in an old rattling truck sometimes with one or two, sometimes with five or six children in the back. He would pull up and open the door and the children would get down, dazed, sleepy from the long ride. Then, as they trailed through the courtyard door downstairs, the same door you came through, he would hand each one a bar of American chocolate.'

'In wartime?' Claire said.

'Indeed. It was a mystery to us where that man could find American chocolate, here in France in the middle of the war.'

I knew. I sat there with a tingle of electricity passing up and down my spine. Marty Pearson was the supplier of those Hershey bars, I had not too much doubt about that.

The Mother Superior was speaking. 'Did Marcel bring Pascal to us? I'm sure he did.' She paused. 'A father to be proud of, Madame. And for you, Monsieur, the man who saved your life.'

She closed her ledger and put it back on the shelf. She stood for a moment, her back to us. Then she turned slowly. 'But I have to tell you that the story had no happy ending for him. For Marcel.'

We waited. In the room the darkness of the panelled wood was emphasised by the two narrow shafts of late sunlight that angled through the high windows.

'Marcel took great interest in the children he had brought us. Pascal was obviously a special child to him. Why, who knows? Perhaps the risks taken to save him from the SEC had been greater than usual . . . I don't know. But I know that Marcel promised to come back for the child,' Mother Francesca said slowly. 'He forbade us to arrange Pascal's adoption.'

A strange wave passed through me, something I could only recognise from childhood. For a moment, it was as if I actually were a child again. 'Marcel was coming back . . . ?' I said 'You mean when the danger had passed.'

She nodded. 'I was very sick that winter. Undernourished, I had succumbed to pneumonia. While I was in the hospital here, unable to think, remember, barely able to talk, the American officer came. I never saw him. He chose a child.'

'And he chose,' Claire said, hardly above a whisper. 'He chose Marcel's child.'

'My deputy in the orphanage handled the adoption. I can't blame her. She had no reason to know that Pascal was the one child who should not have been presented.'

'And Marcel?' Claire said.

'I remember the morning he arrived here to take the boy away. He had chocolate bars for the other children in a big brown paper bag. And, in a box, an American toy for Pascal. A model jeep. I had gone out to meet him. To explain. It was the first time I had seen him in daylight and he stood beside the van that had delivered so many children from the ovens. A scratched and battered children's ark.' She walked from her desk and looked down from the window into the courtyard below.

'You told him what had happened.'

Mother Francesca kept her back turned towards us. 'Yes, I told him.' She turned. 'Marcel was devastated. Angry too, I admit. With me especially. I called for my deputy, Sister Scholastica . . .' Mother Francesca crossed herself. 'I remember we went, the three of us, into the small visitors' room off the hall. Marcel asked a hundred questions, but we had no answers for him. Sister Scholastica knew nothing of American Army insignia on the jeep.'

'Why should she? Why should any of you?' I said to relieve the guilt I could feel coming from this woman even after forty years.

She turned to face us. 'And of course, Sister Scholastica knew nothing of army ranks either. American officers, we now know, wear very much the same clothes as private soldiers when they ride in jeeps. Isn't that so? The American was in uniform. I think she was able to tell him he was an officer, but that's all. It was not enough. He left.'

'And never came back.'

'Never.'


It was growing dark as we left the convent and walked slowly through the lamp-lit courtyards of the city. I was trying to see myself as a Jewish child, as a Jewish adult. Then again, almost simultaneously, I was asking myself if there was something wrong, illegitimate, in even the process of re-envisioning myself. I'd so long accepted that I was a Wasp, a white Anglo-Saxon Protestant . . . I'd so long bitterly (though silently) ranted against the dicta of General John and the Boston Bannermans, that this new discovery threw me completely. But did being born a Jewish child involve a necessary change of loyalties? Or would I be untrue to or uncaring of all the millions who hadn't been carried off to safety during that terrible time, if I didn't start now the process of becoming fully Jewish? But wasn't that racist in itself, to believe that to be born a Jew meant I had to *become* one. I stopped in confusion.

Claire broke through my thoughts. 'What do you think?' she asked.

I walked on for a moment. 'I think, step one,' I said, 'that my mother was certainly Jewish. What happened to her, I'll probably never know. Transported most probably to Treblinka or Auschwitz or Sobibor.'

We walked on, perhaps both of us trying to absorb that idea. I'd read accounts of daily life, such as it was, at Treblinka and the name seemed to bring my mother into some form of life. What was she, twenty-five perhaps? A refugee who had scrambled with her child through barbed wire from Germany into what she thought was safety in France. Or a Polish girl, a Hungarian, Romanian?

We had walked back by another route. It was only as we passed under the stone archway into a narrow medieval lane that I saw the plaque recording that we were entering the fourteenth-century Jewish ghetto. A chill passed down my back. I glanced at Claire and saw that she too had seen where we were. 'Even then,' she said.

I wanted to put my arm round her shoulder. I stretched out and she came in closer. For a moment we walked down the middle of the narrow, cobbled lane, between the silent over-arching buildings, then she reached up and took my arm away. I half turned but she swayed away, leaving a clear gap between us. Like this we walked under the exit arch, back into Christian Pézenas.

There were lights and cafés all around us now, old buildings but with the trappings of modernity. Music, and friends shouting across the street.

'I guess I'll never know who my mother was,' I said. 'But for the moment it's step two that's the important step for us. Was I just another child Marcel had delivered to the orphanage? Or . . .'

She finished the idea for me: 'Or were you *his* child?'

'No proof,' I said. 'Except that he was coming back for me. He wasn't planning to come back for the twenty or thirty others.'

For a long time she was silent, looking at me, a look that wasn't expressionless but carried an expression beyond my understanding. 'Even if we wanted to,' she said, 'I don't think we can escape the conclusion that you are Marcel's son.'

I wasn't at all sure what she meant by escaping, even if *we* wanted to, the conclusion that I was Marcel's son. 'Perhaps,' I said. 'But it doesn't give us the answer to Marcel's will. Why he left everything to Romilly. But assume the people he had working on tracking me down also added a few salient facts about my past.' I stopped. 'Bisset had no difficulty filling in the details. Your father must have been presented with the same facts about my going to jail. Maybe even they discovered what was going on between me and Margot, there were times I wasn't too discreet about it. The whole picture didn't do a lot to leave him feeling proud of his new-found, felonious, incestuous son.'

She shrugged agreement.

'Okay, so he decided, instead of making me his heir, to make Romilly. So far that works.'

'You're not easy on yourself,' she said.

'I didn't mention I was a wimp. I was going easy.'

'You really believe all that?'

I thought about it a moment. 'I guess I believe that pride is the only reason to hide what I am, what I've been. And it's pride that's been beaten out of me.' I didn't want to say any more. I changed tone. Got brisk. 'So his main bequest went to Romilly, his granddaughter, rather than to me, his reprobate son. That sounds all okay to me.' I paused. 'But it doesn't answer the other question. Why at the same time disinherit his much loved daughter.'

'Not to mention Sébastien.'

'Okay. Why didn't he share it between Romilly, you and Sébastien?'

'In the last few years,' she said, 'my father and Sébastien were deeply, openly divided.' She made one of these French explosive movements of the lips. 'Divided suggests politics, I suppose. They were certainly divided there. But it went much deeper than right and left. He just couldn't get on with Sébastien. He found him . . .' She stopped. 'People talk about the Ugly American. There are Ugly Frenchmen, too. Narrow violent, arrogant . . . We're proud of being French, but we're not unaware that there has been, from time to time, a darker side to the glories of France. I think my father saw in Sébastien some of these darker aspects of the French past – the intolerance, the chauvinism . . .'

'You're saying that he cut you out of his will because he was determined Sébastien was not going to share in his estate? That doesn't make a lot of sense.'

'No . . .' Her hands flew in the air. '*Mon Dieu*, I don't know. I'm sure he planned to tell me why. I can't believe he wanted to leave me like this. Not knowing, is for me some sort of hell.'

'You think he meant to tell you?'

'Yes.'

'But he died first.'

She looked at me, a flat accusatory look. 'Or was killed.'

'Hey,' I said angrily . . . 'You're not saying I was somehow involved?'

She stopped,. looking down at the pavement, her arms folded across her breast as women do. 'No, of course I don't believe that,' she said. 'Forgive me.'

We stopped at a brasserie and ordered an omelette and wine, eating and drinking in silence. We were enemies. Or at best, rivals. Nothing that had been learnt this evening had lessened that. But we were also something else. I think we both felt these electric tensions passing between us. The discovery, the *almost* certain discovery that we were half brother and sister, charged the atmosphere between us. We would start a sentence, pull back . . . look at each other, take a gulp of wine and return to our omelettes. I believe we were both thinking of my confession about my relationship with Margot. I think for both of us, it was generating an intense physical awareness of the other.

We ordered another carafe of red wine and lit cigarettes and sat back in our bentwood brasserie seats, trying not to catch each other's eye, but looking away at a group of soldiers and their girls drifting past outside the window. We watched as one of the young soldiers caught his girl round the waist and swung her round until she was tight against his body. Her light summer skirt lifted at the back. The others guffawed and pointed at her exposed thighs. The girl laughed and took the soldier's face between her hands and kissed him, a long, serious kiss, her body hard against him, there on the sidewalk in front of twenty people at the brasserie tables.

Claire looked down at her glass. The soldiers and the girls moved on. I wanted to talk more about what we had just learnt at the convent, but not what she thought of it all, what she *felt*.

'I don't know what I feel,' she said. 'Except, of course, exclusion.' She laughed bitterly. 'And bewilderment. Why was my father planning to exclude me?' She shook her head. 'If he had good reason, could he not have told me? He wrote the will weeks before he died. I saw him every day. There was all the time in the world to tell me. Was he forced in some way?' She looked up at me. 'Was he *compelled* by someone to leave his whole estate to Romilly?' She paused meaningfully. 'The answer has to be yes.'

I said nothing. I paid the bill and we got up and walked down the street towards the hotel. It was hot and cooking smells floated from open windows, along with the clatter of plates and cutlery and the sound of families arguing.

We turned into the hotel lobby to collect our room keys. As we stood at the concierge's desk she astonished me. She reached down and twined her fingers in mine. 'I don't mean these things I say,' she said. 'Or perhaps I mean them and don't mean them at the very same time.' For a moment she tightened her grip, then pulled her hand free again.

In the small elevator we stood close. I put my arm round her waist and she drew back a fraction then moved closer until our bodies touched. Within a moment she was straining against me, as the girl had against the soldier.

Then, as if ashamed of herself, she turned her face away, a signal for me to release her. 'It's just sex,' she said. 'You know that.'

'Does it matter what it is?'

'It matters to us.'

I bent my head before she could say more and she came up towards me, opening her mouth to mine. Our lips and tongues had barely touched when the elevator bumped to a stop and she pulled back as an old couple entered with polite nods and embarrassed murmurs.

At our floor we walked towards her room. When she stopped, she turned to face me.

'Open the door,' I said.

She unlocked the door but her hand remained on the handle. 'We came close this evening,' she said in a way that underlined that the evening was finished, over. 'As man and woman or as half brother and sister, I'm not sure. We mustn't let it happen again.'

I reached past her for the door handle, but she was already shaking her head.

I went back to my room and sat there dazed by all that had happened. Dazed by the heaviness of the night heat. In this modest hotel there was no air conditioning. At one point I got up and took ice from the minibar and wrapped it in a towel and held it to my head. I'm not sure how long I sat like that on the edge of the bed. The windows were wide open to the airless night and I could hear the street life below me. It wasn't that late, the cafés were all open. A truck with water sprays and whirling brushes was cleaning the gutters. I could smell the mix of dust and water.

I sat there neither happy nor sad at what I had learnt about my own past but somehow churned up by what it could mean to Claire – to Claire and me. Okay, I'm a little crazy. There is no Claire and me. She sees me as intense competition, a threat to all she most prizes among the material things in her life. And a dubious figure at the centre of this mystery that has engulfed her. But she also feels something else. What did she say in the elevator? It's just sex. But I don't feel that coming from her. Christ I don't know what I feel. But if she wants to say it's just sex . . . Okay. So be it.

I got up and left my room, walked a few paces down the corridor. At her room I stopped and, for a moment, leaned against the door-jamb, resting my head, my nose no more than an inch or two from the brass number 15 on the door.

I knew what I was doing. I knew I was about to immensely recomplicate my life. I knew I was about to open my defences to a woman who was my rival, perhaps even my sworn enemy. But of course, it went deeper. A matter of hours ago only, I had brought to an end a relationship with a woman I'd believed all my life was my sister. And now I was on the point of urging a sexual relationship on a woman who was, in all probability, related to me through a common father. Was there necessity in all this? Was I really so dependent a creature, so desperate for family that I was willing to forge a bond of any sort to acquire it?

Or was she right with her brisk, matter-of-fact assessment: it's just sex? Either way, it's what I chose to believe at that moment. I brought up my hand, made a fist and knocked softly.

She must have been awake because she opened the door quite quickly. She was wearing a black tee-shirt – and what years of living with an Englishwoman had taught me to call black knickers, briefs if you like, but never the American 'panties' which now rings a queasy, almost paedophile note to my reformed ear. Under the tee-shirt I could see the crescent shape of her unsupported breasts. Even barefoot, half-dressed, she was still imposing. There were tiny beads of sweat on her upper lip accentuating the curve of her mouth. She looked at me without speaking. I was convinced she was about to close the door in my face.

'For Christ's sake,' I said.

She hesitated, then stepped back and pulled open the door, her face still sombre, no smile of welcome.

'As long as . . .' she said, 'as long as it means nothing more than what it means now. As long as it changes nothing between us.'

'Just sex,' I lied, as I pressed the door closed with my back.

But I knew that was bullshit even before I lay above her, even before the moment I pressed myself between her thighs.

# 38

WE STOPPED FOR lunch in Nîmes next day to break the long drive back to Villefranche. We had played music on the way – discovering a more or less parallel interest in jazz – but we had talked little. I was tortured by desire for her, not just a physical desire, a desire to touch her arm, to look at her with the recognition of last night. And I wanted to feel it coming back from her. I wanted to feel she needed all these reassurances as much as I did.

I think she knew. Just conceivably she was thinking the same thing. But I knew I wasn't going to find out. She was tougher than me, able to hold back, to avoid any talk about what had happened between us.

Now sitting outside, under the towering stone walls of the amphitheatre at Nîmes, the sun glinting through the stretched joints of the red restaurant awning, I cracked. I asked her what she felt about last night.

She smiled, not happily, I thought. 'Our trip to Pézenas was a truce,' she said. 'We both know that. At heart we have no reason to trust each other. You think I might somehow be implicated, perhaps with Sébastien, in the attack on Romilly.'

'No . . .'

'You will. At some point you will.'

'And you? What do you think?'

'I think you might, by some means, have forced my father to make a will in favour of your family.'

'And these suspicions, meaningless and untrue, will determine everything between us.'

'No . . . What determines everything between *us* is the fact we have the same father.'

'So when we get back to Villefranche the truce will be over.'

She nodded decisively. 'It must be,' she said. She looked at me. 'You're an attractive man, Tom. But I'm not going to sacrifice St Juste for a passing attraction.'

I had started off by asking her what she felt about last night. About me. And now I knew. She felt as you would feel about a travelling circus, a rodeo show.

A passing attraction.

Before we left the restaurant I called the hospital in Nice. To my surprise, I was told that Elaine had already taken Romilly home. I asked to speak to one of the doctors and got the young surgeon who had been most connected with Romilly's case throughout. He was clearly pleased with the way things had gone. In the six days since she had recovered consciousness, he told me, her body had made the sort of recovery that seventeen-year-old bodies can. It was of course, far from a complete. Some neurological areas still required overseeing – but that could be done as an outpatient. She still had need of lengthy periods of physio on her right knee which had taken the primary impact when she jumped from the van. But, in very real terms, she was on the way back. Quiet and rest was what she needed – and she would best get plenty at home.

It was late evening when we arrived back at Villefranche. I stood on the perron of the Château St Juste and handed Claire her duffel bag through the half open door. Behind me, cicadas trilled; down by the lake an animal shrieked. How did she look so cool in this heat? One or two strands of dark hair had fallen across her face, but no beads of sweat, no dry lips, rimmed with dust. Do you have to be born here? Or born cold?

'No point in asking you in,' she said.

'No . . .'

She stood, leaning against the edge of the door. 'We're one step forward. The trip was worth it.' She spoke it as a sort of announcement.

'You mean we have the same father. That still leaves quite a way to go.'

'But this is where our paths divide.'

I nodded and stepped back. The great oak door closed with much creaking and a dull thud. I turned and came slowly down the perron steps. Around the old wall lights hundreds of white moths circled frantically. My car was parked in the corner of the ivy-covered courtyard, beyond Claire's Mercedes. Only now, another vehicle, a green Range Rover, was pulling in beside it.

I stopped on the last step of the perron, looking down into the courtyard, wondering what I should do. I was too confused, too rattled to know how I was going to react to Sébastien.

He was getting out of the Range Rover and, maybe, hadn't yet seen me. I hesitated no longer. I went down the perron steps, got into my car and started the engine. Behind me, I heard him shout.

I turned my head and saw that he was running towards me. I saw too, couldn't miss seeing, the short wooden baton in his hand, and the fury on his face as he headed for me.

I had no time to put the car in Drive. Time only to slam the door before the first blow struck the roof. He was bawling like a madman, words I could only intermittently understand, but the basic French insults leapt out of the mass of verbiage hurled at me. The baton thundered on the roof of the Renault. Then with one powerful blow he shattered the window on my side, showering me with shards of glass.

His face filled the gap. 'Stay away. You understand me?'

'What the hell's it got to do with you?' I said.

'Claire's telling me some trash about a visit to an orphanage at Pézenas,' he bawled into my face.

She must have called him from the hotel before we left this morning. 'We went to Pézenas, that's right.'

He brought the baton down on the dented roof above my head. 'You're no son of my father's. You understand that. Try to claim that you are . . .' He poked the baton hard into my chest, held it there, pressing hard on it. 'Try to claim that and I'll drag you out and beat the life out of you. Now get going. Don't even think about coming back.'

As I started the engine, blows rained on the roof and trunk of the car.

I was shaking so much I could hardly keep the Renault on the narrow road out of the château. I had left the drive and was two or three minutes down the steep road to Villefranche when I saw the headlights behind me. Suddenly they seemed to swoop closer as the other vehicle picked up speed. Eight kilometres down a narrow twisting road with a heavy car inches away from the trunk, eight kilometres where the roadsides fall away from you into gullies of raw rock and enough depth to crush any car . . . this is the stuff of filmic nightmares. Perhaps he actually hit me no more than two or three times, but the effect was shocking, jerking the Renault forward towards the white posts that lined the road, whip-lashing my neck, forcing me to fight the wheels sliding under me on the edge of the drop.

A kilometre or so from Villefranche he dropped back. As I came up to the lights of the first houses round the last tight bend in the road, he had gone.

My mind was racing in that wild, scared way they call panic. But I was still thinking. What had made Claire call him from the hotel this morning? To update him with the latest news of my paternity, I guess. Which had proved important enough to him to put him on the next plane back from Senegal for a family conference. Claire had said maybe I should have understood more clearly: the truce was over. Now I knew what she meant.

I drove into the market place and pulled myself out of the driving seat. The trembling in my legs was pathetic. I stood for a moment, my hand on the badly dented roof of the car, looking down at the shattered window. The cafes that edged the square were crowded with customers; where I had parked was in the dark centre of the market place. Sébastien Coultard was the man, I had told myself, that I was going to ram against a wall and force out of him all he knew about the attack on Romilly. And I hadn't as much as lifted an arm to defend myself. Hadn't got out of the car. Hadn't demanded the answer to a single question.

I stood with one hand on the roof of the Renault, one palm braced against a tree. I was retching. Not vomiting, just dry retching but with the same exhausting effect. The voice behind me was a shock.

'Something a friend can do for you, Mr Chapel?'

I looked up. It was Marty Pearson. I nodded heavily. 'Yes,' I said. 'A friend could find me a gun.'

# 39

WE SAT IN Marty Pearson's rented house, a modern holiday villa with pale wood furnishing and beige curtains. I'd spilled everything, talking without thinking, partly from shock but mostly from a desperate need for a neutral listener. And that's what he'd been, interpolating nothing more than a few vital questions about the will when I'd stumbled off into a digression. I told him about my sit-ins for Walter Strummer, I told him about my time in jail, I told him about my mother and about Margot. I told him I'd fallen in love with a Frenchwoman who would not look at me – even if she wanted to. Hunched forward, grave faced, he'd listened, nodding, sometimes shaking his head. He was a good listener. He poured a good measure of Scotch, too.

When I'd finished he thought for a moment. 'You're not serious about that gun?' he said.

'Never been more serious.'

'You should know that, in amateur hands, guns hurt people. Usually the amateur who's doing the firing.'

'I'm not an amateur. My father was a gun-toting general. I was firing '22s as soon as I could get my hand round the grip. Just help me out, will you?'

He stood for a moment deep in thought, then he seemed to come to a decision. He crossed to a cupboard and took a compact Mauser from under a stack of sheets. He handed me the pistol. '*Sois sage*,' he said with a wry smile. 'Handle with care.'

'I will.'

'And if you need somewhere to stay . . .'

'Thanks.' I stood, not too steadily. 'I'm okay for tonight.'

I looked at my watch. Fifteen minutes before midnight. We shook hands. 'Thanks for listening.'

'Next time,' he said, 'I'll tell you *my* story.'

'About the forty Jewish women?'

'About one of them.'

'Tell me now.'

His grey eyes settled on my face. 'When I'm ready,' he said. 'When I'm sure.'

I raised my eyebrows.

'Why not now?'

He hesitated for a moment, then crossed to the table and picked up the half-full bottle of Scotch. 'Okay,' he said. He slipped the bottle into his pocket. 'Why not?'

We left the house and I followed him as he drove up the château road. My first thought was that we were heading for the château itself but he branched off early and we ran along the side of the huge crater which contained the lake, now maybe thirty or forty feet below. He stopped the car among bushes that once overhung the water. I pulled up behind him and got out of the car into a thick, dank smell rising from the drying earth around the rim of the disappearing lake. Below us, houses with collapsed roofs formed a double line as the old village main street angled into the water. Stone walls, mostly crumbled, ran in all directions. The church rose in the middle of the village, the spire covered in green vegetation, the nave roof collapsed.

Touched by moonlight as it was, I thought it among the strangest, most moving sights I had ever seen.

He led me up to a pair of tall, bent iron gates set in a wall of cut stone and we stood for a moment peering into the village graveyard, scarred and cratered by digging, the headstones and mausoleum blocks flung aside by earth movers but looking like the work of an angry God.

Marty handed me the Scotch and I unscrewed the cap and took a mouthful. As I handed the bottle back I let the spirit burn its way slowly down. We walked forward into the graveyard. I saw now in the beam of Marty's flashlight that the small-mouthed craters had once been individual graves and the larger pits were the gaping holes left when a family vault had been torn aside.

'You've heard of the demonstrations,' Marty said, 'when the village of St Juste stood its ground up here for the last time. Marcel Coultard, old as he was by then, once again led the resistance. He chose the graveyard as their front line.' The American spoke in his slow, rumbling voice, a voice that seemed to complement the story he was telling. 'The village insisted there could be no flooding of the valley before the graves were properly exhumed. The Prefect and the bishop were forced to agree, even when the villagers prevented the Prefect's men from exhuming the graves. The village held out for over a week. It was winter and there was snow on the ground. They lit fires and pitched tents. Outsiders came in to help them. When the officials tore down the tents, people made makeshift bivouacs. Then, when it looked as if the scent of victory was in the air, the CRS, the riot police, were called in from Nice. It became violent. At dawn the earth-movers were up here tearing open the graves while fighting between village and CRS was still going on. Women threw themselves into their dead husbands' graves; men fought the CRS with spades and pitchforks. By mid-morning, it was all over; the commune area of St Juste was banned to villagers. The Prefect's officials had removed all the remains.' He paused, waved the whisky bottle. 'Or so they claimed.'

I sat on a porphyry stone crazily angled at the head of a wide pit. 'Claimed? Were there doubts?'

'The villagers thought, probably rightly, that the exhumation was a botched job, hurried, disrespectful. They claimed bones were left.' He flashed his beam into the hole below me, on the remains of a rotting coffin lid, broken in two or three pieces. Slivers of small bones stuck out of the earth sides of the pit.

Pearson found a headstone firmly enough embedded to sit on and reached forward to give me the bottle. 'When the water level began to drop last month, members of the families of people who had been buried up here tried to stir the Prefecture into action. They wanted the graveyard inspected. They wanted any unre-covered remains returned to them for burial in the new Villefranche cemetery . . .' He gestured down the hillside to where the lights of Villefranche sparkled in the blackness.

'I'll make a guess,' I said. 'They didn't get far.'

'Good guess. But more than that the bishop sent a Monsignor down to warn the people of Villefranche that the St Juste grave-yard, deconsecrated though it was, still carried what he called a residual sanctity. It would be the work of the devil to come up here and rake over the graveyard for remains that, if any exist, should rest in peace until the waters returned to cover them,'

'Did the village swallow that?'

Marty Pearson shook his head. 'We think of France as solidly Catholic, but a lot of the people in these small hillside villages are Protestant at heart. Have been since the Wars of Religion nearly four hundred years ago. They have a long tradition of rebellion. They weren't inclined to listen to a Monsignor preaching the Prefect's prohibitions.'

I looked around. 'So they began to come up here? To dig?'

'Mostly at night. They dug on the site of their husband's or wife's grave and they not infrequently unearthed remains. Since the water level in the lake began to fall there's been many a secret ceremony at Villefranche. Caskets have been buried in the transferred graves. The church has got itself worked up about unauthorised ceremonies.'

'And the village people?'

'Don't give a fuck what the Monsignors think. They see the Church as on the side of Paris and the Prefect.'

'So what does this have to do with the forty Jewish women?'

Pearson shifted his position on the garish prophyry stone. 'A week ago, a village woman named Paulette Rodinet was up here digging for any further remains of her husband, Georges. He'd been buried up here long before they flooded the village.'

I watched him as he directed his flashlight beam back towards one of the green-edged graves behind him between piles of broken monumental stone. 'There have been Rodinets buried there since before World War I.

'That's why you brought me here? Do you know Georges Rodinet's wife?'

He smiled. 'Used to when she was a shapely young thing. She might not have recognised me when I first arrived here. I was checking out the ground. People don't always welcome ghosts from the past. But we're old friends again now, Paulette and me. She wanted to know if there was any way she could be sure these were Georges's bones she had in her back kitchen. There were, she said, so many bones left up here.'

'How could you help?'

'I took the bones to a doctor in Toulon for her. An orthopaedic surgeon. He had no problem about identifying them as parts of a pelvis.' He paused. 'But a woman's pelvis. And the collar bone of a young woman, probably the same young woman . . .' He drank a swig of Scotch straight from the bottle. 'Not much more than a girl.'

Our eyes met. 'We're not talking about remains of the forty Jewish women who disappeared in 1942?'

'About one of them, anyway. There were no women from the

Rodinet family buried in that small area of the graveyard between a Jeannette Rodinet in 1932 and a Lucienne in 1972. Both women were in their eighties.'

'What Paulette gave you was not *their* bones?'

'Definitely not.'

'Did the Toulon orthopaedic guy give you any sort of date?'

'He estimated the bones I showed him were buried around a half century ago. I've spent half a dozen nights up here since. There's no doubt the Prefect's men did a lousy job. There are bits of bone shattered by earth movers all over the graveyard. Maybe all remains of villagers.'

'But you think not?'

'Maybe it was just the one Jewish woman – maybe all forty of them. They weren't trying to, of course, but in 1973 the Prefect's men effectively covered a wartime killer's tracks.'

'Killer or killers?'

'It's the question we're left with.' He got up and we walked together through the mud-dust up the side of the valley. 'I think it was one. One killer, I'd say.'

He wasn't going to say any more. We reached the ridge and the clump of rosemary bushes where we had left the cars. I stopped by the Renault. 'I don't understand you Marty, you think he's still alive?'

I looked into those hard grey eyes. 'Way I see it, that's for me to find out, Tom.' he said.

## 40

I OPENED THE door of my battered Renault and brushed from the seat chips of glass from the shattered window. Marty Pearson, in his old vehicle, had pulled round me and with a wave of the hand had headed through the pine trees back toward the road to Villefranche. I stood by my car as his headlights disappeared down the road below me.

For a moment I stood there, leaning on the open door. In this part of France, Elaine had told me, traditional lore holds such stillness of the night air a presage of violent storms. By the lake nothing stirred, or seemed not to. No rodents in the grass, no night-birds, not even a shimmer of the moon's reflection, flat as a sword blade on the surface of the water. Then, beyond the ridge of the lake, a goat bell sounded its flat, empty note. And a woman's voice joined it, cajoling. I stood within my clump of pine trees and, in a minute or two, Sanya appeared, leading the goat along the ridge. I was not more than fifty yards away when she stopped by a clump of rosemary bushes and waited while the animal cropped a few dry leaves. *Forty women, murdered in these hills.*

I moved through the trees not wishing to alarm her, but before I could move out into the moonlight, she had tugged on the cord and led the goat, more sure-footed than herself in the gullies of dried mud, down towards the water's edge.

A wooden fishing punt was hidden near the edge of the lake in the arch formed by the branches of a dead willow, drowned when the valley was flooded. Tying up the goat, Sanya uncovered the flat bottomed fishing punt and began to haul it the twenty yards to the water's edge. I came forward.

It was the goat that gave the warning. A sharp frightened bleat, its head turned, its hindquarters backing away. 'Hi,' I called down from the ridge, 'let me help you with that. You remember me?'

She looked up as I slid down the slope towards her, the dried mud erupting in dust plumes behind me.

Sanya had been raised in a Philadelphia politeness to strangers. Polite, but firm in declining their offers of help. She straightened her back and shushed at the bleating goat. 'Please don't worry,' she called. But it was all she said before she was engulfed in a cloud of grey dust.

We stood together, bent forward, coughing out the fine dust. 'Sorry,' I said as the dust subsided. 'Lost my balance there. Came down faster than I expected. Let me do that.' I took the rope from her and began to haul on it. The wooden boat slid smoothly on its flat bottom towards the water's edge.

'You remember me?'

'I remember,' she said. 'You live with Elaine.'

I let that go. 'And you live where?'

'I live . . .' she waved an arm at the lake and the hills around, 'up here.'

'In the village,' I said carefully, 'they tell me you've been here a long time. That you even speak the old language, Provençal.' I waited to see how she reacted to that.

'That's so,' she said simply.

'They told me you bought a new goat. A fine billy goat you got yourself.'

'It's not a billy goat,' she said shortly. 'It's for milk.'

'Of course.' I wasn't doing too well here. 'And cheese?'

She frowned as if I was an idiot. 'That too.'

For a few minutes we stopped talking as we busied ourselves getting the goat on board, tying its lead to the seat. Panicked by the movement of the boat, the animal tugged and bleated until Sanya was sitting beside it.

'I think this is a two person job,' I said, standing at the water's edge. 'One to row and one to hold onto the goat.'

She ducked her head in reluctant acknowledgement. 'She's young,' she said. 'She's frightened.'

'Sure.' As if dealing with nervous goats had been my life's work, I stepped into the shallows and climbed into the boat. Short oars were strapped along the shallow gunwale. Fixing them in the crude wooden rowlocks, I gave her what I hoped was a reassuring grin. 'You like to tell me where to, Ma'am?'

She hesitated, then pointed. I screwed my head round to look. The old chapel and its later spire caught the moonlight as it rose from the water.

'I've made a place in the church,' she said. 'I'll be okay there until the water level rises again.'

I dipped the oars into the water. 'That could be soon, according to the locals. Drought's ending this weekend, they say.'

'Then I'll just have to move, Mr Chapel.'

I felt I was playing the Bogart part in *African Queen*. I pulled on the oars and we began moving across the flat surface of the lake. Out there in the total calm, the only sound the dipping of the oars and the occasional bleat of the goat, Sanya began to relax. To relax and, when I prompted her, to talk.

'It's something that's always interested me,' I said.

She nodded as if to say any reasonable man would be interested. 'Theological reincarnation goes back to the third century AD. Origen of Alexandria. It was declared heresy in 553 – but belief doesn't just dissolve.'

'I guess not,' I said ingratiatingly.

'In fact, in this century more and more people have succeeded in identifying their reincarnate selves.'

It was time to take the plunge. 'How does it happen?' I asked as I pulled on the oars. 'How do you become aware that you're really two people . . .'

'It's not a simple process,' Sanya said.

'I wouldn't believe it was.'

She leaned back flicking long hair from her face. 'We think of it as a journey.'

'A journey backwards in time?'

'No,' she said. 'Most categorically not. It's nothing as simple, as glib as that, Mr Chapel. The journey is through various layers of awareness.'

'I see.'

'I wonder. You're probably imagining that this awareness just descends on you. Not at all, Mr Chapel. It's a hard journey. Complete awareness of your reincarnate self is only acquired at journey's end. It's something you very much have to work for.' She leaned forward earnestly, her movement startling the goat. For a few moments she held the neck-band tight and stroked the animal's head, then cautiously turned her attention back to me. 'I lived for several years in California.' she said. 'I was a young woman then and commune life seemed to suit me well. Some people would say it was by chance that I was drawn to join the Stop Mountain

Community . . . You've heard of it, the Community?'

'Ah, no. I'm an Easterner. I've never spent much time out on the west coast.'

'Yes.' She was disappointed, I could see. She continued without explaining what Stop Mountain was about. 'I personally think it was more than chance that took me to Stop Mountain.'

'What was it?'

'Like fate disguised as chance? It has to be more than just driving along one day and seeing Dave on the roadside hitching a ride.'

'I guess,' I said. 'Who's Dave?'

'Dave Gibson? He was one of the elders of the Commune. There he was all dust-covered by the side of the road. I picked him up. I don't know how it happened but we talked up a storm all the way to Stop Mountain. By the end of it I was beginning to understand. Every one of us has a concealed life, he said.' There was an affecting earnestness in her voice. 'To the extent that that life lies comfortable with your own surface life, you're happy or miserable. Calm or violent. But you have to *know* that concealed life, you have to be in touch with it, it's incumbent upon you as a human being.'

'And you achieved that? With Dave Gibson. You got in touch?'

'Not straight away but I began the journey?' She was using interrogatives like a teenager. 'That's what's important?'

'I see . . .' I rested the blades flat on the water. From here, the encircling ridge was sixty or seventy feet above us. It was like travelling across the bottom of an extinct volcano, the sides grey as lava, the drowned, leafless trees roped with algae and twisted strangely. In the middle of the lake, the moonlight touched the collapsed roofs of village houses and the church spire rose like a living thing, straining for the light.

'I owe everything to Dave,' Sanya said. 'In the six months I was at Stop Mountain he taught me how far I was from my hearth feelings . . .'

'Your *hearth* feelings. Like the hearth in a house?'

'Right.' She stroked the goat's back. 'Just like the hearth in a house. It means those feelings closest to the core of your being? The Romans represented those feelings by their Lares and Penates, the gods of the hearth.'

'But you didn't stay there. You didn't stay at Stop Mountain?'

'No. When the time came for me to move on, to begin the

journey, it was Dave who insisted I leave the commune. Hard as it was for both of us, he insisted for my sake it was time for me to move on.'

I took up the oars again. The goat began to bleat in alarm as the boat rocked and Sanya quietened the animal, stroking its back and murmuring to it.

'I began travelling,' Sanya said. 'I did Nepal, India, Afghanistan . . . I was learning all the time, but I knew I wasn't on the right track yet. I wrote Dave and he wrote me right back. Check out Europe, he said. The Mediterranean. Italy, Spain, South of France.'

'So you came here.'

'That first time was back twelve years ago. Paris had just issued its edict to flood the valley here. More water for more tourists. Paris decreed that Nice, Cannes, St Tropez be put before the simple villages of the hinterland. You can imagine . . . The whole of St Juste and Villefranche were out demonstrating every night, small children, grandmothers . . . everybody. I was there too, of course. For me personally, the demos linked me to the tragedy the villagers were enduring. It was the beginning of a metaphysical bond. It was exactly as Dave had predicted would one day happen.' She trailed her hand in the water and I was reminded for just a second of punting at night at Cambridge on the River Cam.

'The more I learnt about the valley,' she went on, 'about St Juste and Villefranche, the more I came to realise that this was where I was from. That's how it happens Mr Chapel. Not as a thunderbolt, but as a slow awareness falling around your shoulders like soft rain.'

'This is how you learn you're someone else?'

'Another woman, but not someone else. I have no sense of two identities. Simply of two time-worlds I occupy. Hers and this present world, much more unreal to me in many ways, than the earlier time.'

'Do you know the name of the other woman . . . the woman from this other time?'

'Of course. How could I not. I *am* that woman. I know all there is to know about her.'

'Will you tell me?'

She put her head back and closed her eyes for a moment. When she spoke her voice was flat, matter of fact. 'My name is Isobel

Berne. My father and I lived here, up in the château of St Juste there.'

Hot as the night was, a chill settled somewhere at the base of my spine. I glanced over my shoulder at the great high château on the side of the valley.

'You lived there with Marcel Coultard and his wife? You rented rooms from them?'

She remained silent as we approached the wall of the church. The building was on slightly higher ground than the rest of the village. We moved along the wall. The water was only a foot or so here, lapping the stone foundations. I didn't know why I was asking questions of a woman who claimed to be a reincarnate but there was a certainty in her manner, not that persuaded me that what she was saying was true, but that demanded I ask more. 'Is that how it was? ' I asked her. 'You rented rooms from the Coultards?'

A strange look settled on her face. Distant, slightly haughty even, an expression quite unlike her easy hippie manner. It was as if I could see the shadowed outline of a younger woman there, not unbalanced but tough and determined to face life. 'Thank you for rowing me across,' she said. Her accent too, had changed. There wasn't much Philadelphia in it now. It was a foreigner speaking English.

The boat bumped high against the side of a stone buttress. Directed by Sanya, I used the paddle to guide us to a side doorway. The door itself had long gone. Low arched windows on either side, deep set, held broken stained glass hanging on its twisted leadwork. The flat bottom of the boat grazed a stone step as we floated through the opening into the vast stone nave open to the moonlit sky.

There was a silence here more profound than that outside. There were no chairs, no pews. The water was no more than a few inches deep here. I could see the paving of the floor of the nave where thin shafts of moonlight struck the surface. Sanya stood up and urging the goat forward, woman and animal leapt into the water.

She turned, holding the goat on a tight leash, ignoring the splash of water up to her thighs. 'Thank you, Mr Chapel,' she said. 'This is where I live. Take the boat back. Tie it up, if you will, under the tree where we found it.'

'Wait,' I said. 'If I take the boat you won't be able to get back,'

She stood above me, the goat splashing in the water beside her. 'I keep two boats,' she said. 'One in case I have to convoy extra goats.' She gestured towards a shadowed place beside a buttress. A second flat-bottomed rowboat was tied up there. 'At one time every family in St Juste owned a boat like this. Now St Juste no longer has families, a boat can be bought for a few francs.'

'You didn't answer my question,' I said. 'You were saying you lived in the château – with the Coultards?'

She flicked her hair aside in an impatient gesture. 'The Coultard family worked for my father,' she said. 'Marcel drove the delivery van. He took the new films to the cinemas. Madame Coultard was my father's cook.'

What she was saying, strange though it was, it carried the ring of truth. I stood up in the boat, but she lifted her hand imperiously. The boat rocked as I shifted position. I held onto a rusted light-bracket.

She paused until she was satisfied I was not going to leave the boat. 'But the new Vichy anti-Jewish laws meant we were forced to move with the times,' she said. 'Vichy law forbad a Jew to own a business. Anything to do with publishing or films got priority treatment. That's to say it was stolen earlier. So by arrangement with my father, Marcel took over the château and the company. My father secretly raised the money for Marcel to buy the property from the *Administrateur Provisoire* in charge of seized Jewish property. It was dirt cheap, of course. Corruption was rife. But Ciné-Berne now safely became Ciné-Coultard. It was the only way of saving the business for its rightful owners.'

'And your family continued to live with the Coultards at the château?'

'By trading places. Marcel became the *patron*. My father became his van driver. They were good friends. Everybody in the village knew. But my father had been a popular employer. The system worked well – until my father was denounced and arrested in 1942.'

'But you escaped?'

She bridled as if I had asked an illegitimate question. For a moment she stood, her sandalled feet up to the ankles in three inches of water, the hem of her dress trailing, floating. 'I had left France earlier, in the spring of 1942.' She stood straight. 'In those days, pregnant peasant girls got to keep their babies here in the village. Young bourgeois girls like me, Jewish or not, were always sent away if they had the misfortune to become pregnant. Usually we went to Switzerland. There we attended a boarding institution while we awaited the birth. After that our children were fostered into rural Swiss families. It was a well-established system. We accepted it as the only way.'

'And that's what happened to Isobel?'

'To me,' she said firmly.

'When did she come back? After the war?'

'Would a daughter do that?' she said. 'Would a daughter abandon her father to these monsters? Rumours were spreading from France to Switzerland that in the internment camps starving men and women were forced to perform heavy labour. Thousands were dying. Just before Christmas, I discovered from French friends, that my father was interned at a camp called Milles, outside Nice. I heard for the first time too, that the next stage would be a train to Drancy, the horror camp in the suburbs of Paris. There tens of thousands of Jews awaited deportation to the East.'

'You came back to France. You brought the baby with you?' It took me a moment to realise that I had moved into her territory.

'I was his daughter, his only hope. How could I stay in Switzerland?'

I was completely sucked into her world, her imagery, her *truth*. 'Go on,' I said. 'Tell me.'

'I was shocked at the change. France, I thought, stood, as it always had, and would again, for justice and mercy. But not *this* France. This France stood for racism and injustice – and finally for mass murder. I travelled to Grenoble under papers I had bought in Geneva. From there I contacted a Resistance organisation that was helping Jews to reach safety in Spain and Italy.'

'In Italy?'

'Yes, even Mussolini's Italy, Fascist Italy, was a safe haven compared with Vichy France.'

'From Grenoble you came back here, back home.'

'My destination was Nice. But movement was a matter of links in a chain. I was handed from one Resistance group to another. One guide passing me on to the next, they brought me through the mountains. Along the way we picked up a dozen or so Jewish women, two no longer young. Most of them had been turned

307

away at the Swiss border. At last we made contact with the final guide. Imagine my astonishment when I saw it was Marcel Coultard. His astonishment, too. He tried to persuade me to return to Geneva but I would not abandon my father. The journey on the back of a truck brought us to within twenty-five kilometres of St Juste. From there it was all on foot with the help of other men in Marcel's Resistance group, all men I knew well, of course. Hercule Mantel, Georges Rodinet, Marcel's brother, Pierre.'

'So Marcel brought Isobel back to St Juste. To the château. And did Isobel save her father?'

'Marcel came with me to the internment camp at Milles. We were ready to bribe guards. But we were too late. A few hours only. My father's transport to Drancy had left during the night.'

'Is there any record of what happened to him?'

'He was never seen again. There are no records of him in any of the Death Books from the main concentration camps.'

I was silenced by her story, completely accepting it. Then my rational self exerted itself. 'What makes you believe all this, Sanya?'

'What makes you believe the story of your own life, Mr Chapel?'

She had a point. But I pressed on. 'Did someone in the village tell you? One of those old ladies you talk to in Provençal? Do they tell you all these things . . . ? And how d'you know what's true and what's rumour, what's old wives' tales?'

She laughed. 'Most people, when I tell them about Isobel, don't believe me.' Beside her the goat lapped water. Through great gaps in the roof fell shafts of moonlight. 'But you do, Mr Chapel. You're fighting it, but I know you believe me.' Her voice rang off the stone walls. 'I can feel it. I can see it in the way you look at me.'

I was torn. I believed the facts she was giving me because they seemed to be just that – straightforward, verifiable facts. What I didn't believe was how she got them. 'I look at you this way,' I said, 'because I wonder how you know all this. None of these details came to you in a dream, Sanya. You found something up here in the hills, maybe when you found the doll you gave Elaine. Some letters . . .'

She frowned angrily. 'I've talked too much. People tell me I do that. Forgive me, Monsieur.'

I had to ask her before she turned away. 'Marcel and Isobel . . . are you saying they had been lovers? Had they been lovers earlier when Isobel became pregnant? Was Marcel the father of her child? Is that what I'm to understand?'

Her head came up. 'Don't try to understand, Mr Chapel. In the end there's no real possibility. Why does a cat jump out of the path of a speeding car? You think you understand that, yes? But you don't ask what vast procession of events brought cat and car there in the first place? No, don't try to rationalise. Answers are in any case only partial. You want to know everything about an event. You can never achieve that.' She frowned again, shaking her head angrily. 'In our superficial lives we see or hear or feel things. But our concealed lives come to us as if in a dream. Dave says that's where Freud went wrong. He never saw the real significance of the subconscious.'

I shook my head. If there was any truth in what she was telling me, it didn't come from Dave – or from Freud. 'Tell me this at least,' I said. 'Did Isobel's child survive?'

'I'm still looking for him,' she said. 'Why else would I live in these hills? Or here, making my bed beneath the dripping slime of the church walls?'

Of course I knew that she had lost a child herself so I guessed some sort of transference of her grief was quite possible.

'That old doll,' I said. 'Did it belong to Isobel's baby?'

She stared at me, then she turned her back and began to splash away through the water. It was going to be one last question. 'Sanya,' I called. She turned back. 'What happened to Isobel? Did she get to England, to America?'

She stared down at me, the strangely placed eye sharper and brighter than the other. 'You must take care, Mr Chapel. It's not safe for you to be up here in the hills alone. You especially.'

Even in the heat, she achieved a sliver of ice down my back, but I wasn't going to be diverted. 'Do you know what happened to Isobel? Do you know if she escaped from France?'

'I told you, she would never have left her child. Isobel was murdered here in St Juste,' she said.

She was murdered here?'

'In these hills,' she said. 'She was killed by Pierre Coultard.'

## 41

*SHE WAS KILLED by Pierre Coultard.* Could that possibly be true? Could Sanya possibly know that? I stared after her as she ran splashing through the shallow waters of the nave, the goat bucking and kicking as it followed, its high bleat echoing strangely among the toppling columns and archways of the flooded church.

Was I really accepting this crazy woman's story? Where did it come from? Not her reincarnated self, that's for sure. I paused. Pretty much for sure, anyway. Or had it come as some garbled snippet from the old ladies in the village whose Provençal dialect Sanya had learnt in order to talk to them.

Either way, it had, of course, a jigsaw fit with the other part of my parentage, the story of Marcel bringing a child to the Pézenas orphanage, a child he intended to return for. But to accept what Sanya had told me was to accept an account of my life from a woman claiming to be a reincarnate. *Yet her story made sense of mine.* If I were the child of Isobel Berne, then an honest man, Marcel Coultard, would want the château and business to pass back to my line. But was I that child? And was Marcel the father? And his brother, Pierre, the hero with his own monument of the road to St Juste, had he really killed his brother's lover? The questions didn't stop coming.

I sat in the boat wondering what to do. I could go after Sanya and try to find out more. I wanted to slap myself at the thought. Find out more? This woman was claiming to be a reincarnate. The Coultards working for her family? Claire's mother, the cook? No . . . I sat back in the boat. Very slowly I began to row. Out through the deep-set church door, steering my way through the crumbling gables of village houses and the reaching fingers of drowned trees.

I tied up the boat under the trailing willow branches and regained the car. The path straight ahead brought me out on the

Villefranche road, left to the village, right to the château. I recognised it without difficulty. It was where Romilly had hurled herself from the van. It was also where Pierre Coultard's monument stood among the pines.

I unlocked the glove compartment, took out the Mauser pistol Marty had given me and pushed it under my waistband. I felt good about the idea of Sébastien Coultard staring down the barrel. Slowly I walked across to the monument. In the oppressive night heat, my mind was buzzing hopelessly, mixing fact and fantasy. I stood before the florid monument, the headstone and the flanking stone columns decked with carved vine leaves, the cross swords and drum and the freshly painted number seven.

I stared in something approaching a trance. Why had I never noticed the date of his death before before? It was clear enough. November 2, 1942. The date of my supposed birthday.

And beneath it, the inscription: *Mort pour la France.* Died for France.

Or died for the murder of Isobel Berne? Died for the murder of my natural mother?

I took the road down to Villefranche, my eye on the mirror all the way. Slowing through the village, I examined the cafés in the square for any sign of Sébastien Coultard at any of the busy outdoor tables – but there was none. What I might have done if he had been sipping a pastis at the Café de la Paix or Colette's, I don't know. But the feel of a 7.65 Mauser in the waistband alters a man's view of the enemy. Sad to say, alters a man's view of himself.

As I approached I saw that Elaine's house was dark except for the terrace lights. Romilly, I guessed, would be in bed by now; Elaine in all probability, was relaxing with a glass of Scotch after a day charged with emotion.

As the road dipped towards the turn-off to the house, I saw Bisset had been as good as his word. A police car sat, lights out, in the most heavily shadowed part of the lane. I had hardly begun the turn when a gendarme rose out of the darkness and waved me down.

I identified myself as he reached out and curiously fingered the dents in the roof of the car.

'Vandals,' I said. 'I stopped off at Marseille this morning.' I added before he could begin asking questions.

He grunted without interest.

I was impressed to see that he carried a clipboard with a list of expected visitors' names. 'Monsieur Chapel,' he put his hand out to open my car door. 'Inspector Bisset has been trying to contact you. Urgently.' He opened the Renault door. 'You're welcome to use our car radio.'

I could also see that I had very little choice. I got out and crossed with him to the police car. It took a few minutes to summon up Bisset. 'You wanted to speak to me,' I said.

'I thought you'd like to know. I think we've got him. Picked up by a Municipal Police patrol in Nice earlier this evening. He was carrying a bag with a priest's soutane.

'Christ! Who is he?'

'So far he's not giving a lot away. His name's Burgos, Antonio Burgos. Claims he's an itinerant labourer. You want to come down and take a look?'

'Wait a minute . . . He's admitted it? He's admitted the attack on Romilly?'

'Not yet.'

Disappointment flooded me. 'So it's just the cassock? That's all we have.'

'There's blood on it.'

My daughter's blood. Something strange swept over me. A savage sense of triumph. I don't know.

'I'll be there,' I said. 'I'm leaving now.'

# 42

ALL THE WAY down to the coast from Villefranche I watched flickers of lightning out at sea, pale but just visible in the strengthening dawn light. Below me the thunder of a dry Mediterranean summer storm rumbled over Nice. On the car radio, Monte Carlo One was telling me in English that this was now the sixty-third day of official drought and there were still no signs of a change. But this was background. Sanya's strange story lay writhing in the forefront of my thoughts, the problem unresolved of how much I was to believe it. Unresolved, at least until I really knew where the story came from.

But despite this turmoil, every few moments it was the intense memory of Bisset's voice on the phone took precedence, the few words that had hit home to the hunter in me. *I think we've got him. Claims to be an itinerant labourer. His name's Antonio Burgos.*

I crossed the River Var at the Pont Napoléon III, drove into the city through streets almost empty of traffic and pulled into the big gendarmerie parking lot. In the tiled lobby, I was met by one of Bisset's team, taken up to the second floor and shown into a windowless room at the end of a long passage.

Inside, one single low wattage red light gave the room a misty glow. A blind covered a good part of one wall; not a window blind, the framed sort that might be used to cover important operational maps. Facing it were three swing chairs, black Rexine, all carrying cigarette burns along the arms. Ashtrays on the floor, used cans of beer along a shelf in front of the chairs. A smell not unlike the Paris Metro. My guide indicated I should sit and I chose the middle chair.

'Don't worry about speaking,' he said. 'You can't be overheard.'

'Overheard?'

On a dimmer, the gendarme switched the red light even lower,

Pressing a button he buzzed up the blind. As it moved, bright light from the next room flooded in. I saw Bisset's sergeant, Lucienne Barrault, her arms folded, her back against the wall opposite me. I saw Bisset, in shirt sleeves, leaning forward on his knuckles across a desk. And seated on the far side, three quarter facing me, a man in his late fifties, strongly built though probably of less than medium height, a dark but clean-shaved complexion, short grey hair and brown, alert, perhaps frightened eyes. What first struck me, perhaps because he was sitting without moving, perhaps because his eyes stared unblinkingly, was that the face was from a composite picture. Every facet of his features was distinctly marked, the heavy brow, the two deep creases from cheekbone to mouth, the wide thin slit of the unsmiling mouth.

He was wearing a horizontally striped tee-shirt, an ill-fitting canvas blue workman's jacket. His hands, resting loosely on the table in front of him, were big, callused by a life of manual work, the nails bitten down so that ugly pads of skin rose at the fingertips.

Why doubt passed over me in a wave of disappointment, I don't know. I sat staring at him, in apparently full eye contact. He seemed to stare back – but of course he had no idea I was behind the mirror that faced him.

'We're going to start from the beginning,' Bisset was saying.

'Again?'

'Again.'

When the sergeant came forward, punched the record button on a tape recorder on the table and spoke the date and location, Burgos raised his eyes towards the ceiling. No, those weren't frightened eyes.

'For the recording, you are Antonio Burgos . . .'

'Correct.' A dead tone.

Bisset straightened up and stretched his back. 'This is Lieutenant Polydore Bisset from the Nice Central gendarmerie Special Investigation,' he intoned. 'With me in the room is Sergeant Lucienne Barrault, one of the investigating team.'

Antonio Burgos glanced at her.

'You were stopped on suspicion by the Police Municipale on the Boulevard de l'Armée des Alpes, Nice, at 20.42 hours last night.'

'Correct.'

'You were carrying a heavy canvas bag stamped with French Navy insignia.'

'From the military surplus shop, I expect.'

'Inside the bag was a priest's soutane.'

'My luck. I thought it might be something worthwhile.'

'And you're claiming you didn't know the contents of the canvas bag?'

'Of course I didn't – or I wouldn't have lifted a priest's robes would I? I told you. I've admitted theft. I stole it.' The flat answers had given way to an underlying tone of aggression.

'Tell us how it happened.'

'Again?' He shrugged. 'The bag was in the back of the van as I walked past. Back door open. Driver fiddling with the engine. Asking for trouble. I leaned in and hooked the bag out. It could have had anything in it – a video, decent clothes, money . . . I was unlucky. I get a priest's soutane and a stop and search before I'd even had a chance to look in the bag.'

'And you expect us to believe your story.'

Antonio Burgos shifted his eyes from the mirror to Bisset's face. 'That's what you said last time. Why shouldn't you? Because you're trying to pin something else on me.' His voice rose angrily. 'It's the truth. I'm admitting I stole the bag. *Ça va?*'

Bisset paused, looked across the top of the man's head at the woman sergeant and decided on another tack. 'You're not French, you say.'

Burgos smiled, genuinely amused. 'As French as you are, I'd say, Chief.'

'Where were you born?'

He shrugged. 'Ceuta, so my mother said. Spanish Morocco. But we travelled. The truth is I don't really know where I was born.'

'You're Spanish?'

'Madrid wouldn't say so. They say I'm Moroccan. The Moroccans say I'm Spanish. Who wants someone like me? I don't have a hundred thousand pesetas in the bank.'

'You speak Arabic?'

'The sort they speak in the Souk. I don't read it.'

'Spanish?'

'It's my language, Chief.'

'But you've lived in France a long time.'

'Longer than you, I'd say at a guess.'

'You have papers?'

'In my room. I've been legal since last year when they finally

315

gave me a *Carte de Séjour*. In a few years, I'll be French.'

'Do you work?'

'When I can. Casual. Any job that comes along.'

'Before last year, what were you classed as?'

'Take your pick. Unwanted, refugee-alien, a nothing, a piece of shit? I picked up jobs with the ferias because I know bulls.'

'Bulls?' Bisset said, frowning.

'You don't know the feria? I thought you had a Paris accent. The travelling bullfights come over the Pyrenees? Three days of celebration in a place like Fréjus or Nîmes. I looked after the animals. I wasn't Spanish and I wasn't French. So I was the sort the feria masters like to take on. No questions asked if there's an accident. It's dangerous working those big animals. But if you're with the feria, at least the police aren't after you all the time for your papers.'

'Let's talk about the bag.'

Burgos shrugged. 'What's there to say?'

'Quite a lot according to your dossier. Eight arrests for petty theft. Five convictions. Three custodial sentences. You were lucky to get yourself a *Carte de Séjour*.'

'Simple answer to that. It was time I had some luck.'

'Where was the van? The van you claim you stole the bag from.'

'One of those roads off the big boulevard there. Armée des Alpes.'

'I've had men covering all the sidestreets there. No sign of a blue van.'

Burgos shrugged. 'He was a mechanic, then, as well as a priest. Good for him, he got it going.'

'You saw the man. The driver.'

'His back, bent over the motor.'

'Nothing else?'

Burgos shook his head.

Bisset slowly pulled out a chair and sat down. 'You've been in trouble before. You're a man who knows the way the law works . . . yet you don't seem surprised to find the Police Municipale have handed you over to the gendarmerie.'

'Should I be?'

'You didn't wonder why you're not being questioned by the *agents* who picked you up?

Burgos shrugged. 'Should I?'

'You're in trouble, Burgos.'

'I've been in worse trouble.'

'I doubt it,' Bisset said evenly.

'Trouble for stealing a priest's outfit? I won't lose my papers for that.'

Bisset held a long silence, long enough to let the mood change in the room. I could see it was affecting Burgos. He looked round the room, down at his hands, then up again at the lieutenant's impassive brown face. 'When you were first searched here,' Bisset said finally, 'you had a book on you.'

'Is that a crime?'

'Bisset shook his head. 'It's interesting though. An old book of poetry. By François Villon. You like medieval poetry?'

'I picked it up at a market somewhere. Fifteen francs. That's what it is, poetry? If I'd known I wouldn't have wasted my time. What interest is it to you?'

'Villon – he was a great poet. A priest.'

'A priest. So?'

'And a murderer, too.'

Bisset paused. Burgos stared at him, his mouth slightly open. In surprise? Or unable to think of one single syllable that wouldn't convict him of knowing the significance Bisset was giving to a priest-murderer?

'*La ballade des pendus*,' Bisset said slowly. 'is a poem about a group of murderers about to be hanged. In it Villon confesses his crime on the scaffold and asks for mercy.'

'He asks God for mercy?'

'No . . . that's what's so modern about Villon. He asks his fellow human beings for mercy. *Don't harden your hearts against thieves and murderers like us*, he says. Because, he knew the score, Burgos, he knew that he was finished.'

'You're making something of this,' Burgos said. 'I don't know where you're going. But you're making something of it that isn't there.'

'Not when I tell you the priest's outfit had blood stains on it?'

The brown eyes flickered with something I would swear was alarm. 'Why should that worry me?' he said deliberately. 'Why should I care?'

'The stains on the soutane could link you to a violent attack on a young American woman.'

'Oh no . . .' His big hands, big for a short, compact man,

317

came up as if protecting himself. The palms were dark-lined by years of manual work. 'An attack on a woman . . . no.'

'Maybe even link you to the murder of another woman earlier this year.'

The confidence seemed to flow from Burgos. His shoulders slumped.

'You see what I mean by trouble, Antonio? We're looking for a priest-murderer.'

'You're trying to clear up two murders.'

'One murder, one serious assault.'

'One murder, two . . . what difference? You catch me with a bag and you stuff some bloodstained priest's soutane in because it fits your case. I see what you mean by trouble, lieutenant,' he said bitterly. 'I read the papers. It's nothing to do with a stolen soutane or a book of poems by a priest-murderer. If there's a crime committed, it's got to be an Algerian, a Moroccan, a foreigner with a darker skin. Because the rules say Frenchmen don't commit murders if some foreigner can be framed for it. Though God forbid that a German or an Englishman or American might be set up. No, I've been in France long enough to know, Monsieur, that a light-skin crime needs a dark-skinned criminal Only when the police have found one can justice be *seen* to be done. It has to be one of *us*.' He glared at Bisset, including him.

Behind the glass screen, I was sitting forward. I was trying to analyse his accent, his appearance, his manner. His appearance was more or less what he claimed to be. Dark, of mixed parentage probably. A Spanish father and a Moroccan mother fitted well enough. His accent was southern French with a Spanish or Catalan intonation. It also fitted his story. And his manner, his reaction – well, to see racism everywhere in an area of France where Nationalist and National Front candidates won hundreds of thousands of votes, who could blame him? I sat back. So what was I asking myself? What could this man have to do with Marcel's will? He behaved like the quick-minded petty thief he admitted he was. He had a dossier – but there was nothing violent on it. So could Antonio Burgos have been hired by someone to abduct and perhaps murder Romilly? Someone who stood to gain from her death. Was this small, quick, confident man hired by Sébastien Coultard as soon as he learned the contents of his father's will? But then when had Coultard learned about the will?

Before Claire? And who from? From Marcel himself? Before he died – or was murdered?

Bisset turned to the sergeant and nodded. She stepped forward, bending to speak into the microphone. 'The interview of Antonio Burgos at Gendarmerie Headquarters, Nice, is concluded,' she said. She switched off the tape.

'So what happens now?' Burgos said.

'We're taking you downstairs for a line-up,' Bisset said.

I watched Burgos carefully. 'You've got a witness?' he said. If he was guilty he did it well. No blinking eyes, no tongue flicking along his lips.

'We've got the best of possible witnesses,' Bisset said, watching Burgos. 'The victim.'

'The priest . . . good enough,' Burgos said without hesitation. 'I don't mind serving ten days in the Nice *Maison de Correction* for theft – as long as your priest does the thirty years for a murder.'

I think we were all thrown by that immediate reaction. If Burgos was guilty of the attack on Romilly, his first thought would have been that *she* was the witness. But to Burgos, the victim seemed to be the priest whose soutane he had stolen. He'd spoken without a trace of hesitation.

I saw Bisset and his sergeant exchange a quick glance. It was that moment that all cops must fear, the moment in an investigation when the possibility first comes home that you've got the wrong man.

'We'll send someone to escort you down,' the sergeant said. She reached in her shirt pocket and took out cigarettes and lighter. Flicking a cigarette to Burgos, she waited while he examined the brand and placed it carefully in his mouth, then she leaned forward and lit it.

'In my experience,' Burgos said, 'Women police officers can be even tougher on a suspect than men.' He drew on the cigarette. 'You're an exception, Senora.'

When Sergeant Barrault had left the room and locked the door behind her, Burgos sat back and smoked his cigarette in long careful inhalations. At a point about half way down he very gently extinguished it in the tin ashtray on the desk, tamped it out, blew on the tip to make sure it was completely out and dropped it into his side pocket.

What he *didn't* do next surprised me. I'd seen it in the penitentiary a thousand times. Prisoners were masters of the art of passing time. I expected his feet to go up on the table, the chair to rock back, the eyes to close.

But instead he slipped forward off the edge of the chair and onto his knees, his hands clasped in front of him in prayer.

I was on my feet, my head just an inch away from the glass, watching the silent mumbling of his lips. An idea was burning into my brain. An impossible idea, on the edge of madness even. An idea that came to me the first moment I saw Antonio Burgos sitting at the interview room desk.

Now the eyes stared up at me as he prayed and I knew they were eyes I had seen before . . . For a moment a panic of doubt seized me. Had Sanya got to me? Was I beginning to believe in wild ideas like Dan of Stop Mountain's concealed lives beneath the surface of our selves?

And then I realised where I'd seen those eyes before. And not so long ago.

'A prayer doesn't make him a priest,' Sergeant Barrault said. The red light was up full. Antonio Burgos had long been taken from the interview room. Lucienne Barrault was sitting in one of the black rexine swing chairs, smoking. I sat opposite her.

It was late afternoon. We were waiting for Bisset to return from the address Antonio Burgos had given. I think the sergeant had said her line about prayers not making priests before but I wasn't entirely sure. I knew that several times in the last hours I had slipped into sleep.

When Bisset returned I pulled myself up in my chair and looked at him expectantly. He didn't have the air of a man who had gained vital information. He leaned one shoulder against the wall and waited while a gendarme handed round three cans of beer.

'How did it go?' Lucienne Barrault asked.

Bisset tipped his beer and swallowed. 'The room's nothing special,' he said. 'Above a shop in the old town. Burgos has been there for nearly a year the landlady says. Good tenant. Pays regularly. Keeps the room clean. He's got the papers he claims. Under the carpet where he told us he'd hidden them.'

'Forensic?' the sergeant said.

'Doesn't look hopeful.'

'He was still picked up with a priest's soutane with blood on it,' I said stubbornly. 'I think the blood group's going to be the same as Romilly's.'

'Group O. The most common,' the policewoman said. 'Doesn't mean that much.'

I came to my feet. 'Doesn't mean that much? For Christ's sake,' I exploded. 'Because it's the most common group, it doesn't mean the blood on that soutane *isn't* Romilly's. That guy's a priest. A priest or a wannabe. Did you see him down on his knees? I think the soutane belongs to him. I think there never was a man bending over an engine. I think that van is parked somewhere in the town with Burgos' fingerprints all over. I think Antonio Burgos is guilty as fucking sin.' I collapsed into the end chair, my head in my hands.

When I looked up they were both looking at me with the silent sympathy we reserve for those who are slipping over the edge. Somebody who has good cause maybe, but has gone over the line all the same. It was impossible now to add to what I had just said. Above all, I couldn't articulate the shattering thought that had been torturing me. Sanya's last words to me were in my head. And now I knew where I'd seen those eyes, the eyes of Antonio Burgos turned up towards the mirror in prayer.

I felt my reason lurch like a ship's deck under me. Bisset leaned over and put his hand on my shoulder. 'You need some sleep, Tom,' he said. 'There's a night room here you can use.'

He was right. And maybe even just in time. One more shake of the kaleidoscope and I felt I really would go crazy.

# 43

I HAD DINNER with Bisset and Barrault in the canteen, listening to them as they analysed the case. I said nothing. I was in no position to say anything. Everything I suspected about Antonio Burgos was based on the sad ramblings of a disturbed woman who roamed the hills looking for her dead child.

I felt I couldn't tell anybody. Margot would laugh out loud if I told her my idea was the fruit of a reincarnate; Elaine would shake her head at further confirmation that I was what the English called *simple,* meaning seriously deficient in a capacity to think straight. I wanted to tell Claire but I wasn't by any means sure how far she could be trusted. She'd given me enough warning that we were on different sides. I couldn't risk ignoring it.

But had I just fallen under the influence of Sanya's weird take on life? Had Pierre really murdered Isobel? What in God's name did happen up in those hills in 1942 as winter approached?

I needed sleep. I was emotionally drained, no longer so sure of my terrifying *aperçu.* I accepted Bisset's offer of a small iron cot in a rest room at the top of the gendarmerie and caught six or seven hours' sleep before the traffic below in the Place de la Gendarmerie made anything more than a light doze impossible.

I got up to another brilliant day, showered, dressed and drank coffee in the canteen before Bisset was back in his office.

At just after nine Elaine drove her car into the rear parking lot of the city gendarmerie and an officer closed the gate after her. I stood waiting on the back steps while she manoeuvred into a parking bay, then hurried across to the car. Opening the passenger door I helped Romilly out and held her in my arms. 'I'm sorry, Rom,' I said. 'I'm sorry you have to do this.'

Her head came up. '*I'm* not,' she said. 'I want to do it.'

I looked at her a moment, lost in admiration for her beauty, her guts. 'That's fine,' I said. Couldn't have gotten another two words out.

Nobody would believe she was just out of hospital. Brownish lipstick. Eyeshadow. The beginning of a tan returning. Her cheeks had a trace of youthful bloom set off by her Formula One pink tee-shirt. Although a thin line of bandage was visible under her Nike peaked cap and I guessed she was probably ten pounds lighter than before the attack, she looked wonderful. It was the first time I had seen her out of the hospital bed.

Elaine came round from the driver's side and I released Rom. 'We'll talk later,' I said to her. 'Let's pin this bastard first.'

Romilly smiled and I began to think that the world was running my way at last.

The claustrophobic atmosphere of the small room seemed increased by the low red lighting. A wall thermometer showed 36 degrees Celsius which I took to be close enough to a hundred Fahrenheit. There were six or seven of us crowded in. Fabius, Bisset and Sergeant Barrault, Elaine, myself and two women from Fabius's team from the Palais de Justice.

I held Elaine's arm. 'She'll be okay.' I said. 'She's got her mother's Dunkirk spirit.'

'We *lost* at Dunkirk,' she hissed at me. I could feel, through her light jacket, that she was shaking.

'*Très bien*,' Fabius said. 'Let's begin.'

Buttons were pressed, passing signals to the world outside. Cigarettes were lit. One of Fabius assistants glared at each smoker in turn but stayed silent.

'I'd like you to take the middle seat, Romilly,' Bisset said. 'It's very simple. There will be five men in the next room. You will be looking at them through a one way mirror. They can neither see nor hear you. Take as long as you like. Stage two is when we take you in the room . . .'

I saw Elaine's head turn sharply. 'In the same room as the man who attacked her?'

'It's okay, Mom,' Romilly said. She smiled. 'If he makes a move, this time I'll be ready for him.'

'There'll be two of my officers there,' Bisset said reassuringly. 'And each man in the parade is handcuffed.'

Romilly leaned forward and put her hand on Elaine's shoulder. 'Let's get it over with.'

'If you see the man who attacked you,' Bisset sat on the arm of one of the Rexine chairs, talking directly to Romilly, 'if you're sure of him, stop in front of him, point clearly at him and give his number which will be on a card hanging round his neck. Clear so far?'

'Yuh, clear. Okay,' she said, glancing round, for the first time I thought, looking nervously at the people ranged behind her.

Fabius moved forward. 'You must remember a man's liberty depends on this, Mademoiselle.'

'I know,' Romilly said. 'I know it's important.'

'An innocent man, if you make a mistake.'

I wanted to tell him to stop pressing her, but I had to accept this was his show. I was here simply as a parent. I could be ejected in seconds.

'Very well then,' Fabius said. 'Let us begin.'

Someone released the blind and it slid upwards. We all screwed up our eyes at the bright lights from the other room.

There were five men in the line-up, all of the low-medium height of Burgos. All were in different degrees dark complexioned from southern French to distinctly North African. And all wore blue gendarmerie overalls. They didn't, of course, look alike. But one looked pretty much like Burgos, and two others were close enough, although they lacked his powerful shoulders and big calloused hands. I learnt later they were civilian clerks from the gendarmerie top-floor offices.

Antonio Burgos himself stood with a number four card around his neck. Like the others, he looked every inch a criminal. Under bright lights, standing in line with a card round the neck, what else would he be? Innocent or guilty, he must have felt entirely vulnerable with only the four others to protect him.

'Don't say anything yet,' Bisset said. 'Don't make up your mind even at this stage. Just tell me when you're ready to go in there.'

Romilly nodded silently, glanced once more at the five men on the other side of the glass and stood. The attention of everybody in the room was concentrated upon her. I felt an intense wave of pride in this tall young woman in the peak cap, a ponytail of blonde hair flaring from the backstrap. Her cheekbone was still speckled with gravel cuts and I knew, so recently discharged from hospital, that she must have felt weak as hell. But that wasn't how she stood, how she moved.

She left the room with a woman from Fabius's department and on the other side of the glass a gendarme removed their numbered cards, exchanged them at random and directed them to take new places in the line-up. There was no speaking. Burgos was now number two. When the gendarme sergeant in charge had checked over each man, he opened the door to admit Romilly.

She came in with amazing confidence. Then slowed and began to walk along the line of men. Did she pause longer at number two than the others? I don't know.

'That's the one. That's the *salopard*,' Bisset's sergeant was muttering behind me. 'Point to him.'

Beginning at number five this time, Romilly came back down the line. I knew now there was something wrong. Her movement was less confident. She turned for a moment and looked towards the mirror, looked towards her mother, I suspect. Then she reached Burgos. Stood for a moment chewing on her bottom lip and – to a cry of desperate disappointment from the sergeant behind me – she moved on, glanced at number one and walked quickly for the door, already shaking her head, dabbing at her eyes with a Kleenex.

# 44

WE STOOD IN the big tiled lobby, light streaming down from the glazed cupola above out heads. Romilly looked pale now, drawn, smaller even. 'I'm sorry, Dad,' she said. 'I blew it. But I couldn't do it.'

Elaine put her arm round her. 'Honey,' she said. 'You did what you could. You came, you checked them out. Nobody blames you if they didn't have the right man standing there.'

'That's just it,' she said. 'I think they did. I think it was number two. Number four when I was looking through the two way mirror.' She looked from Elaine to me. 'Is that right, Dad? Number two in the line-up. Was that the man?'

My mouth opened but I couldn't get an answer into words. I tried again. 'What stopped you?' I said as gently as I could.

'I don't know,' she said, tears in her eyes. 'It's like Monsieur Fabius said, you have to be really sure.'

I nodded, two or three times. I had to consciously stop myself.

'I'm going to get you back home,' Elaine said. 'You need rest.' She shot a hard glance at me. I don't think she was inviting me to come too.

I couldn't let it be cut off like that. They were probably going through the release formalities for Burgos even while we stood there.

'Just one more minute,' I said to Elaine. 'Rom . . . are you saying you thought you recognised him – or was the number you just gave me, was that a guess? A hunch?'

'No . . . not a hunch. It was him wasn't it?'

'So why didn't you finger him?' I was fighting back my frustration.

'Tom, leave it,' Elaine said. She was turning Romilly away.

'It was because of what Monsieur Fabius said, wasn't it?' I asked over Elaine's shoulder. 'Wasn't that it?'

Romilly stopped at the big door. Two gendarmes came in in motorcycle gear, white helmets under their arms.

'I'm sorry, Dad,' Romilly said. 'The way Monsieur Fabius looked at me. Like the way he asked me questions at the hospital. I thought better say nothing than make a mistake.'

'Sure.' I lifted a hand to her and she made an effort to smile, then she and her mother stepped out into the afternoon sunshine.

I waited over an hour before the sound of voices on the broad staircase above me preceded Fabius and his two young female assistants.

I timed the moment and stepped forward as they reached the bottom of the stone stairs.

'Monsieur Chapel?' Fabius stopped and the two women moved on and waited for him at the main doors. 'Can I help you?'

'I want to know what's happening up there.'

He was wearing a dark green blazer, a lemon yellow shirt and English club tie. 'Up there?' he said. 'With Burgos?'

'With Burgos.'

'I think Bisset's just going through the paperwork.'

'To release him?'

'We're investigating murder and attempted murder, Monsieur. We're not investigating street theft.'

'She recognised him,' I said. 'She knew he was number two in line.'

'She didn't say so.'

'Because you put weight on her. *An innocent man could go to prison* . . . What the fuck were you doing? You knew she was just out of hospital. You knew she'd be shaky and uncertain. And if there's a prick of a magistrate whispering in her ear at the same time . . .'

'That's enough, Monsieur.' His face was flushed. He looked quickly to his left, first at the gendarmes behind the desk and then on to the two women by the door.

'Not yet, it isn't,' I said.

He stepped back. He thought I was going to hit him. 'You should know it's well within my power to have you arrested and deported for obstruction of justice.'

I pulled myself up. I couldn't afford that. I couldn't allow that to happen. I took a careful step backward. He nodded, satisfied, and buttoned his blazer, narrowed eyes on me. 'Monsieur,' he said, maintaining that gravity that irritated me so much. 'I've talked to Bisset. We are agreed.'

'Agreed?'

'We think Burgos could well be our man.'

I stepped back in astonishment.

'But in the last ten minutes he has retracted his confession of the theft of the bag. He now claims he found it in a doorway.'

'No man bending over the engine of a van?'

'No. A civil rights legal group is representing him. He's with a lawyer now. We have no grounds on which to hold him on a major charge. Our problem, Monsieur Chapel, is that we have nothing connecting Burgos to the *van*. If we can make that connection we have more than a simple act of theft. I've therefore agreed with Bisset that Antonio Burgos should be released. But under twenty-four-hour surveillance. My belief, and Lieutenant Bisset's, is that he will, within a matter of hours, lead us to the blue van. There'll be enough forensic evidence on the vehicle to re-arrest and charge him.'

Things were moving forward. Fabius had not dismissed the chances of Burgos being our man. I had to be content with that at the moment.

'Accept my apology,' I said, grinding out the words. 'I over-reached myself.'

He hesitated deliberately. 'Accepted,' he said. 'Apology accepted. Now there is another vital factor to be considered, Monsieur. And that is the danger to which we are conceivably exposing your daughter by releasing a man we all believe could be her attacker.'

'You mean he might slip the surveillance and make another attempt on her life.'

He nodded his head. 'If we're right about Burgos he represents a clear danger to your daughter.'

'She's got a police escort?'

'Of course. But I think we should go further. I've already taken the liberty of suggesting to Madame Chapel that she should take your daughter away, perhaps to England, for a week or two.'

The change in Fabius, in his manner, was complete. I thought of his bearing, his body language the first time I had met him at the hospital. This was a chastened man.

I wasn't trying to rub his nose in it, but I wanted to know if his reformation had gone all the way. 'And you now agree,' I said carefully, 'that Marcel Coultard's will is a vital element in all that's happened?'

He looked at me gravely. 'One step at a time, Monsieur Chapel.

So far, nothing but timing connects the will and the attack on your daughter. But it is a highly coincidental timing. I may well have been unwise to dismiss the idea of the will.' His nostrils flaring, he took a deep breath. 'It's possible I allowed personal considerations to intrude. I was wrong.'

Personal considerations? Claire? Friendship with Sébastien? Or something else I couldn't yet guess about? He clearly wasn't going to tell me anything further. And this wasn't the time to ask him.

I left the gendarmerie moments after Fabius and his colleagues. I knew enough, by now, to take myself round to the side entrance giving onto the gendarmerie parking lot. I chose not to sit in my own car but found a place in the deep shadow of a doorway where I could just see the shallow steps to the side entrance. He would have to walk past me, not more than ten, a dozen paces away.

When you carry a gun, they say, you want to use it. In my waistband was the compact Mauser 7.65 that Marty Pearson had given me. I took it out and turned it over in my hand. Very deliberately I put a bullet into the breech. The necessary hand movements, the oiled click of metal on metal, made the blood run faster. Tom Chapel, wimp, was lusting after the chance to kill a man.

Romilly had recognised him, I was sure of that. But she hadn't pointed to him in the line-up. Did that mean that somewhere, in some recess of her mind or memory she had real doubts? Did it mean that Fabius and, more significant, Bisset was wrong?

No. I didn't believe that. I believed Antonio Burgos was the man. I believed that to kill him would be a gift to Romilly, to Elaine – not to mention myself.

But I was far from sure I could do it. I imagined the feelings of all the assassins of the past, the assassin of Alexander II of Russia, of Jean Jaurès here in France, of the Archduke Franz Ferdinand whose death had precipitated the bloodshed of World War I . . . Had any good ever come from any of them? Although if Adolf Hitler had been murdered, or Joseph Stalin, perhaps then . . .

I was losing it. Losing that burn without which I wasn't going to shoot. I had a minute to decide. To decide whether I meant to kill him. Or decide that what I was really doing was playing to the gallery, worse, to myself sitting alone in the gallery. In this anger of indecision and self-doubt, the safety catch stayed on the

Mauser as the squat figure of Antonio Burgos came down the stone steps, casually waving a heavy hand at the gendarme who had escorted him to the door.

He walked slowly across the parking lot, lighting a cigarette, his eyes moving from side to side. Somewhere out on the street among the bustle of people, cars and light trucks was the first surveillance team. I knew that – and his eyes told me he knew it too.

He passed behind a parked car, my car. He stopped casually to examine the smashed side window. If he walked on two paces he would be in bright sunlight, ten feet from the muzzle of the Mauser. One squeeze of the trigger would cause the top of his head to lift away as in the famous Robert Capa Spanish Civil War photograph.

I could shoot him dead.

# 45

I LET HIM live. I let him live partly because I was plain scared of the consequences of killing him – and partly because we had no single piece of convincing evidence. He had unusually large hands, a wide, pianist's span. Romilly's bruises had shown fingers set far apart. Like his. But so did a million others.

No, I'd like to believe that I didn't kill him mostly because I wasn't finally certain. Certain enough to hate, certain enough to rage against him. But certain enough to kill? I shook my head.

On a summer afternoon the main boulevards of the city of Nice are full of people. On balance, I think the crowds make following a man easier. All right, I wasn't going to kill him. At least not until I was a good deal more sure of my case. And how to become more sure? By staying with Burgos, trailing him, letting him reveal his guilt. Above all letting him lead us to the blue van.

That's what they did in the movies, didn't they?

I'm being serious here. The moment our lives move out of the ordinary we look to the movies to tell us what to do next. I saw this in prison. I'd seen it a dozen times since Romilly was attacked. Hollywood, for good or ill, becomes our guide and reference. So, on this afternoon of blasting Riviera heat, I was following Antonio Burgos.

Others were too, Bisset's people, although I couldn't identify them. In the heat Burgos was taking it easy as Mediterranean people have learnt to do. Leaving the gendarmerie, he strolled round the Ruelle de l'Eau fraîche, Freshwater Lane, which took him round the walls of the prison which lay next to the gendarmerie. From there he moved unhurriedly down towards the beach. He gave no appearance of a man anxiously looking for a tail. He drifted down to the sea front at the Quai des Etats-Unis, then back up the Avenue de Verdun, peering into hotel lobbies or stopping to examine the vastly expensive clothes in

331

the boutique windows. Any passing girl with a tight or translucent skirt would attract his attention and once or twice he seemed to change direction to follow a woman for a few dozen yards. But then again, drifting aimlessly as he was, killing time as it seemed to me, it wasn't really possible to say what took him in one direction, rather than another.

Then his whole demeanour changed. I was, I realised, too far back, perhaps forty yards away when he suddenly accelerated, not running but walking at that pace, elbows up to the chest, like a competition walker. In moments he had disappeared down a side alley. Before I reached it I saw a man, whom I would have taken for a tourist, and a woman in a well-cut peach suit, duck into the alley in pursuit. A gendarmerie car slid to the kerb and three plain clothes officers jumped out and took different narrow streets off the Avenue de Verdun.

I saw, in that moment, what an amateur I was. I stood back watching the streets where the gendarme officers had disappeared. Their back-up vehicle cruised slowly on. I was about to turn away when a man emerged from a street not five yards away from where I was standing. He no longer wore a blue denim work jacket. A tee-shirt and dark glasses gave him another form of inconspicuousness. He stopped, stared in a shop window or two, then turned and crossed the Place Massena with a group of twenty or thirty people waiting for the walk light, and entered the Jardin Albert 1st on the far side. There was no sign of his surveillance team. Antonio Burgos had shaken himself free.

The garden is not more than a mostly green patch between the busy Avenue de Verdun and the Boulevard des Phocéens, a patch that narrows as it leaves the *quais* and cuts north on the line of the submerged River Paillon. I could see a double row of cream-coloured pavilions, like medieval war tents, pitched on the grass but it was only when Burgos passed under the banners of a dozen nations at the Massena entrance, that I realised Nice was holding this year's Annual International Book Fair here.

It was truly international in name only. The pavilions, open-fronted, had been created on each side of the wide and dusty grass avenue. A few countries shared space so that their flags flew in clusters. Above the rest of the tents, and these the vast majority, the tricolour fluttered in the faint breeze coming off the sea less than a hundred yards away.

Visitors crowded into the open-fronted pavilions which housed the best-known French writers and piled displays of their books. Marguérite Duras, old but still reminiscing energetically, and Françoise Sagan attracted wide horseshoe-shaped crowds, anxious to buy signed copies of their books. Among the foreigners only Graham Greene, smiling enigmatically, attracted real attention, mostly as an inhabitant of Nice and publicly sworn enemy of the mayor and local corruption.

I knew I had to get to a pay phone to call Bisset. It was possible, of course, that his team had picked up the trail again. I didn't think so. My last view of the back-up car had been as it turned into an alley on the far side of Avenue de Verdun.

I positioned myself to watch for the peach-suited woman to enter the garden and at the same time watch Burgos while he moved from pavilion to pavilion, squirming his way through the crowds in front of the most popular authors.

There was a café set up in the centre of the gardens where an open air studio broadcast writerly discussions which sometimes reached surprising levels of passionate disagreement. Burgos had been at the book fair for almost half an hour when he crossed to a table at the back of the café area. It was a well chosen position. Behind him the trees and bushes screened him from the Boulevard. In front of him, to his right, the café narrowed the field. To the left was the discussion platform surrounded by a dozen or so earnest listeners.

Sitting down, he signalled the waitress and gave his order. I took a seat well to one side of him, among the audience for the literary discussion on my right.

I ran through my known inventory of facts about Burgos. I knew he had very little money, eighteen francs, less than three dollars, on him. The police inventory had also listed two keys, house keys, and the sort of single-bladed Opinel knife that many of France's older peasants still carry, not as a weapon, but as an eating knife. I knew too that he had a room in the old town. But curiously, although I still had no doubt that he was killing time, he had chosen not to go back there. Because he had suspected surveillance from the moment of his release. I took a step back to the idea that he was killing time. Until what or when?

The young sailor and the girl at the table beside me opened a gap of an inch or two between their foreheads, I could see clearly Burgos's big hands lying on the green metal top of the café table. When the waitress came and put down his coffee and the check, he didn't even glance at her. Irritated, she rattled the canvas money bag she carried round her waist. He took out his handful of change, counted out five or six francs and pushed it across the table. All still without looking up at her. When a man at the table next to him left a copy of *L'Equipe*, France's premier sporting paper, Burgos reached across and snatched it up.

To call Bisset I would have to cross in front of Burgos to reach the café. Antonio Burgos was busy with his copy of *L'Equipe*. Beyond the Kronenbourg umbrellas, the sun lay flat and heavy on pavilions and people alike. I walked past him, with three or four visitors to the book fair shielding me as they headed for the exit.

I pressed the phone to my ear. 'You lost him,' I told Bisset.

'How do you know?'

'He's here in the Albert Premier Garden. Can you get someone down here right away?'

He covered the phone. When he got back to me, he said: 'I've got another team on the way.'

'Something I need to ask you,' I said. 'Why did you let him go before you'd put him in front of the other witnesses?'

'What other witnesses? The German girl, Anne-Marie? Her parents flew her out to be with them in Rio a couple of days ago.'

'Okay. What about the priest? The one at St Firmin. He spoke to the guy, for Christ's sake.'

'I know.'

'He couldn't miss identifying him.'

'You'd think.'

'I met him. He was a level-headed guy. He'd make a terrific witness.'

'It's out of the question. Remember, the first day they met the St Firmin priest heard our man's confession.'

'We're asking for an identification – not to reveal the secrets of the confessional.'

'It's too close, Tom. The bishop's old. The distinctions are too fine. He sniffs scandal. We've lost our witness.'

\*   \*   \*

I put down the phone and turned to glance at Burgos' place. With a sense of shock I realised that his chair was empty. A carefully folded copy of *L'Equipe* lay on the table next to an empty coffee cup.

This was a time to panic. Bisset's men were not here yet. It was getting dark. The book fair was closing down. People were streaming in all directions across the gardens, visitors to the fair, assistants carrying cartons of books.

I picked him up by sheer chance. A waitress had overloaded a tin tray with used cups and saucers from the tables. A few yards past me she lost her balance. The tray tipped forward. The explosive clatter of pyrex coffee cups over a tin table dragged everybody's eyes in her direction. Twenty yards on I saw Antonio Burgos's face as he span round in a second's alarm, before continuing his way to the small exit onto Avenue de Verdun.

I moved after him, cutting at an angle into the surging crowd. The French object to this less than a Red Sox crowd at Fenway Park. There were a few muttered complaints but I was through to where I could see my man before they became serious.

As the sun angled into its setting position out at sea Burgos dropped down from the broad sidewalk of the Promenade des Anglais onto the pebble beach below. He knew where he was going now. There was no killing time. He hustled along the beach at a steady speed, throwing a long, bent shadow from the setting sun.

I kept fifty yards behind him, using the ornate iron rails and the height of the sidewalk above the beach to make myself inconspicuous. Just past the point where I could see the rooftops of Fabius's Palais de Justice a few streets back from the seafront, Burgos came up a beach ramp at the Pointe des Ponchettes, moved quickly across the Quai des Etats Unis and began weaving his way into the narrow streets of the old town.

He was not an easy man to follow but there were hundreds of people about to give cover, Niçois and tourists making the long climb up to the castle where red banners and the *Internationale* announced the Communist party were holding their summer fair.

The deep shadows of the narrow streets and the lamplight of the old town was what, I was sure, Burgos was waiting for. The Rue de la Sourde – the street of the deaf woman – was a narrow cobbled alley with an arched exit at the far end. The clatter of dishes, the steam and cooking smells from half a dozen different cuisines floating from windows thrown wide open, the piled empty cartons and lines of trash bins signalled that the Rue de la Sourde was the back entrance of the restaurants whose fronts faced onto the small but fashionable square we had just crossed.

Antonio Burgos was close to his destination. Several times he checked behind him before he entered the alley. I stayed out of sight in the shadow of parked cars while he made his way about half way down the Rue de la Sourde, turning frequently to see there was no one behind him.

He stopped at one of the restaurant kitchen doors about half way down, said something through an open window to a cook working inside and, with one more glance round, ducked quickly inside.

I could lose him here. He could emerge on the other side of the restaurant, into the square and be lost to me for good. Tense, I waited for two, three minutes. I counted out another full minute, then hurried into the alley, down the thirty or forty yards of cobbled roadway and past the kitchen Burgos had just entered.

I pulled back among two big, evil-smelling dumpsters. From where I stood I had a clear view of Antonio Burgos standing among the frenetic activity of a busy kitchen. Men in smeared white jackets were pushing past him with pans and dishes.

I moved my position to get a better view through the steel shelving that ran across the upper part of the window, but the movement obscured Burgos. The shouts of chefs and waiters came to me from five or six restaurants along the street. Two men came onto the street in long stained kitchen aprons and lit cigarettes. I had lost sight of Burgos for a moment. I came forward between the dumpsters, risking being seen by the two smokers.

A man in light suit had appeared next to Burgos. The man's face was half obscured by the cooking pots on the steel shelf. He was counting out hundred-franc bills into Burgos's clumsy hands.

I needed a phone. If I was quick I'd have time to let Bisset know where I was without losing Burgos. I ran back along the Rue de la Sourde. I looked round to get my bearings. I was in the small square I had passed through earlier. Tall, bright, pastel-coloured house fronts above shops, closed now but with lighted windows. A few trees planted in the sidewalk. Not too many parked cars. In the middle, a fountain, and on my side of the square, a row of restaurants, the kitchens of which backed onto the Rue de la Sourde which I had just left. I walked on past. The Marakesh, the Restaurant Rascasse, the Café du Phare, the Club-bar Odalisque . . .

I stopped dead. Antonio Burgos was collecting his money from the Club Odalisque.

Antonio Burgos was collecting his money from Sébastien Coultard.

# 46

STANDING, I DRANK a quick cognac at the Café de la Phare while I phoned Bisset. His instructions were to wait there at the café, but I couldn't do that. Next door was where the green neon flickered the word Odalisque out onto the tumbling water of the fountain in the square.

I pushed open the door. Inside it was as dark as if it were a room lined with black velvet. There was Eastern music, Arabic perhaps, and Turkish. Sandalwood-scented girls, barely visible, were suddenly on both sides of me and took an arm each. I could feel them swaying to the music but I could only just make out pale shapes in the darkness.

The girl on my right was massaging my hand. '*Monsieur est français? Ou peut-être pas?* Doesn't matter. I speak English. Monsieur must have a good table. Near the stage.'

'No,' I said. 'A little further back.'

'I am Gelda,' the girl said. 'I am here to serve you.'

The other girl had released my arm and silently drifted into the darkness. Now as I sat down and as my eyes became more accustomed to what I'd thought was a total lack of light, I became aware of others in the room. Mostly one or two men with girls sitting at black painted tables. No more, it seemed, than ten or fifteen customers in all at this early hour.

'You will have champagne,' Gelda said and seconds later a boy in black with a fez was serving a bottle of already opened 'champagne' at the table. With glasses poured and toasts drunk, the girl snuggled closer. I could feel and see enough by now to know that she wore a short-cut bolero top and a long diaphanous skirt. 'In a moment,' she said, 'we have two Egyptian dancers. They will dance for you the dance of the odalisque. Do you know what it means, odalisque?'

I could tell by her intonation that she was from Eastern Europe.

'They were girls who worked the harems in the old Turkish Empire,' I said.

'Slaves, remember. They were slaves,' she said primly. 'They had no choice.'

The music had moved out of the background, becoming louder, the rhythms more intense. Something was happening behind the stage. Black curtains were stirring.

'Watch,' Gelda said.

Two dark figures wafted out onto the tiny stage and spotlights hit them in a burst of colour. Two girls, dark-skinned, veiled, their heavy, shapely bodies swaying beneath low cut, sequined skirts and a satin bolero jacket, intermittently open fronted to bare breasts.

With light now borrowed from the spots, I could see that the club was fuller than I had first thought, with at least a half dozen booths occupied by men only along the walls on both sides of me. I could see only one door, other than the entrance behind me. Above it a pale green reflector just allowed me to read *Toilette*.

'I'm hungry,' the girl beside me said. 'You know they have a very good chef here.'

I didn't respond. She snuggled closer and began massaging my thigh. In the act she managed to knock over the bottle of champagne. As the wine ejaculated from the bottle and fizzed across the table, a waiter was on the spot with a cloth. While the girl babbled apologies another waiter was seconds behind with another open bottle. A set performance.

'If I wanted to speak to Sébastien,' I said, 'where would I find him?'

'You *know* Monsieur Coultard?' I could hear the wariness in her voice.

'An old friend.'

She sat away from me. 'I'm sorry about the champagne, Monsieur.'

'Don't be,' I said. 'It's your job to keep it rolling.'

'You want me to see if Monsieur Coultard is here tonight?'

I grabbed her round the waist. 'Not yet.'

She laughed, wriggled, relaxed, pouted and began to give me a running commentary on the inner meaning of the dance. It had a lot to do with doves descending from heaven and taking ruby rings in their beaks to princesses who were in dire trouble.

'Does that not make you feel very sad?' she asked me.

I said no. But it made me feel very American.

I drained my glass of champagne. The Egyptian girls finished their belly dance. The music became more western. Some of the girls at the other tables led their partners onto the dance floor below the stage.

'So,' I said, 'is Sébastien in most nights?'

'Not very many nights,' Gelda said. 'But this time of week, you could be lucky.' She gave me a gross caress. 'Or perhaps you think you're lucky already.'

I finished my champagne. 'Yes,' I said. 'I have all the luck.' I stood up. 'Does he have an office somewhere?'

'Continue past the *toilette*,' she said. 'There is one door only.' She stood beside me swaying to the music. 'You will be back?'

I passed her a five-hundred franc note. 'That, at least,' I told her, 'is the idea.'


It was a corridor fifteen, twenty feet long. Long enough to give me time to wonder if Antonio Burgos was in the office with his boss. I stopped in front of the door. I was, I realised, breathing heavily. My legs felt loose and shaky. Counting to three, I opened it and stepped into the room.

I knew, from the outside of the club that it was an old house, but I was surprised by the rambling size of the office which must have been the old beamed kitchen. Sébastien Coultard was standing alone behind his desk, head down, a blue, wide striped shirt with sleeves rolled back. Without looking up he turned to feed wads of yellow papers from the desk onto a pile of charred paper burning in the wide old Provençal fireplace behind him. I stood for a moment in the doorway as he leaned forward and shuffled the unburnt pages with the toe of his shoe so that the flames leapt high. 'Get out,' he said without looking round. 'I told you I don't want to be disturbed.'

He half-turned to take another wad of papers from the desk, with his free hand loosening his tie. The movement brought his head up. Our eyes locked.

'What's this?' I said. 'Memoir burning? Or are you making a run for it?'

Smoke rose from a Gauloise in an ashtray on the desk and he batted it out of his eyes with the papers in his hand. For a moment he stood, uncertain, lips pursed, trying to figure out what could

340

possibly have emboldened me sufficiently to have allowed me to walk into the lion's den.

His whole manner was different from the ranting bully boy I'd seen before. He dropped the papers back on the desk and leaned forward to pick up the burning cigarette. I stood, back to the door, looking down at the short-dark, wavy hair, the bald spot on the crown that caught the light when he moved his head.

This was a different Sébastien, alarmed by my presence even. Perhaps he guessed that I really wasn't fool enough to come to the Odalisque without some species of protection, whether it was the police outside the door or a gun in my pocket. Either way, that easy confidence had gone.

Then, quite suddenly, he straightened up. That moment of anxiety had passed. Very slowly, as slowly as I have seen anyone, he smiled. Or made those movements of the lips that constitute a smile in most men and women. 'Did you come for the show?' he asked, his lip curling. 'You like these fat Arab bitches rotating their bellies in your face?'

The smile unsettled me. I'd had control before, I could feel it. I had control no longer.

'I'll tell you why I came,' I said, 'when I hear the answers to the questions I have for you.'

He drew on his cigarette, a lazy, swashbuckling movement. 'Get out of my office,' he said, still smiling that smile. 'Get out of my club.' He flicked the cigarette into the fire behind him and started round the desk. I think it was at that moment the balance changed back between us. I had not retreated before his stocky, aggressive bustle. He stopped at the corner of the desk. His eyes were on my right hand reaching back under my jacket.

'I'll put the questions to you,' I said. 'If there's any satisfactory answer, beyond the one I'm expecting, I won't kill you . . . maybe.'

His dark eyes moved from my face and back again to my right hand under my jacket. He was having real difficulty making up his mind. He kept his voice low. 'You're bluffing,' he said.

I took out the Mauser and waggled it in front of him. Very slowly, with my thumb, I pushed off the safety. 'Monsieur Coultard, I want you to understand me. You're talking for your life, here.'

If all this wasn't prime California P.I. stuff, I didn't know what was. But what I did know was that things had changed in the few hours I'd had the gun. I'd been through the first exhilarating power of possession. Through it and out on the other side. I'd aimed at Antonio Burgos and not pulled the trigger. Now, I was quite coolly willing to shoot this man if he couldn't persuade me that he had no connection with the attack on Romilly.

'Burgos,' I said. 'Tell me about him.'

He stood, silent. Unco-operative.

I leaned forward, still keeping the pistol barrel at about stomach level. Then suddenly slammed the butt down on the desk. It was the crack of metal on wood that made him tumble backwards. This was one of General John's tricks when interrogating Austrian black-marketeers just after the war. No man, he said, could trust his life to a pistol not going off accidentally when the butt was slammed down on the table in front of him. He used an empty pistol. Mine was loaded. I crashed the butt down again.

'For Christ's sake,' he said. 'You lunatic. You'll kill me.' He was in the corner now, flinching like mad as the butt threatened to hit the desk top again. 'What is it you want?' he hissed, hands at chest height, his open palms warding off the bullet he was sure was coming.

'You heard the first time. Antonio Burgos.' I was leaning forward, both elbows on the desk, a two handed grip on the pistol, the barrel pointing at his genitals. Another piece of General John's advice – for the most effective intimidation aim at the mouth or the genitals.

'Burgos,' he said, looking down at the pistol. 'He works for me. That's to say he did, until he was arrested this morning for theft.'

'How did you know that?'

'He was allowed one call. He called his boss, me. What's sinister about that?'

'What did you do?'

Slowly he took another cigarette from the pack on the desk and lit it. 'Two things,' he said. 'I got onto my sister's civil rights organisation. And I told him he was fired. I don't put up with thieves in my employ. He was paid off this evening. He left a few minutes ago.'

Claire had sent the lawyer. That was a shock. But then, she was involved with immigrants. Why shouldn't she?

I didn't have time to think that through. Coultard could see I was shaking, the Mauser barrel juddering just a metre in front of him. 'For God's sake,' he said. He pointed at the gun. 'Do you know what you're doing with these things?'

'I know enough to squeeze the trigger,' I said. 'I know enough to make sure the safety catch is off first. What else would I need to know? Antonio Burgos . . . what did he do for you?'

'Let's just sit down, for Christ's sake.'

'What did he do for you?'

'I hired him as a spare hand. A driver, doing collections for the restaurant, relief doorman on Saturday nights . . .'

'Collections for the restaurant?'

'The dancers. Picking them up sometimes. Taking them home after the show.'

'And he was allowed to make private arrangements with the girls – on behalf of a small party of customers, for instance?'

'If he did . . .'

'He did it off his own bat. That's what every club owner says from Baton Rouge to Bombay.'

He scowled at me, less afraid now that the pistol would explode between his legs. 'Look,' he pointed to his desk chair. 'I'm going to sit down.'

I banged down the butt of the pistol on the desk. There was enough force there to make his coffee cup leap from its saucer and roll, dribbling coffee across his papers. Enough force, from his side of the gun-sight, to cause a misfire. He froze. 'You're fucking mad,' he said quietly.

'I'm not going to drag it out of you,' I told him. 'Just start telling me. When, where, how . . .'

'Okay, okay . . .'

I saw, with great pleasure, that he was sweating.

'Antonio came to me early this year,' he said. 'Mid-January. He was an illegal. North African, Spanish background, maybe. No papers, no money but a willingness to work.'

'And out of the kindness of your heart, you arranged papers for him. How?'

He shrugged. 'My sister works for Arab immigrants . . .'

Oh Christ. Claire again. 'She arranged his papers?'

'She endorsed his application.'

'Illegally.'

He looked at me for a long moment, letting the idea sink in. 'Sailing close to the wind, but don't we all in France?'

'If you hate immigrants that much, why get them papers?'

'Same with the girls – Arab trash, but if they work well . . .'

'. . . you're happy to use them. Did you know Nicolle Tresslli?'

'No.'

Fury boiled in me. 'She danced here. She danced here the night she disappeared. You knew that. You *knew* that.'

He nodded stiffly. 'But only afterwards.'

'And when a party of your customers went too far with Nicole, you called on Antonio Burgos to get rid of her body.'

I was blundering on now, throwing unprovable guesswork in all directions. But it seemed to work. Maybe with a pointing gun these things usually do.

'If Burgos was involved it was nothing to do with me,' Coultard said.

I waved the gun at him in a way that seemed crazy even to me. 'Burgos took Nicole's body to dump it up in the hills. You knew that too.'

He nodded stiffly. 'Perhaps. I'm guessing,' he said.

'And I'm guessing Nicole wasn't the first time you had to call on Burgos. It certainly wasn't the last, was it? You called on him, again, you murderous scum, when you found my daughter stood between you and a half share of your father's estate.'

'No!' He shouted the word in a mix of anger and fear. 'There was no time I called on Burgos. Before Tresselli or after. The English killed her, five sado-maniacs who went far too far. The rumours round the club said they'd paid him to take her body up into the hills and dump it there. That's the full story.' He was staring-eyed, sweating heavily. 'I swear to you I had nothing to do with what happened to your daughter, Chapel.'

His manner shocked me momentarily into belief. A sudden emasculating belief. And my stance had changed. I was leaning forward, too far for good balance. Too close to Sébastien Coultard's swinging right hand.

He hit me with enough force to throw me sideways against the wall. Somehow I held on to the gun without pulling the trigger. Jumping the desk he reached the door and pulled it open, roaring for help down the corridor outside.

I fired without thinking. He went down. I jumped across him as he rolled over onto his side.

I made it into the corridor and threw myself into the darkness of the club. In the blackness, the confusion was total. Men blundering about, swearing, shouting. Dancers running for the wings.

Girls screaming. The scent of sandalwood all around me. I followed the pressure to move left, took five or six paces, and banged through the front door. Traffic was snarling past me. I made wild movements with my hands. A taxi pulled to a halt and I got in. 'Gendarmerie,' I said and the cab jumped forward, rear door swinging. Behind me, as I slammed the door, people, girls, men, were spilling out onto the sidewalk. None of them was Sébastien Coultard.

# 47

I FELT DEFLATED, nauseous, totally incapable of knowing exactly what I'd done, or why, at that second, I had done it. We'd passed a few intersections before I pulled myself up in my seat and changed my instructions to the cab driver, told him just to drive around the city.

He was talkative. He offered girls, restaurants, and finally, unable to raise an interest that might profit him, just a bored guided tour. Lights flickered by. We took the boulevard of a hundred names – Verdun – Faure – Baptiste – Gallieni – Lyautey, north to Cimiez where Queen Victoria used to come to swelter in her black bombazine dresses, then the driver worked his way south again through the small streets of the Carabacel district to Centre-Ville and the sea. On the Promenade des Anglais, we stopped. He turned and looked at me. I lay back against the seat, resting on one elbow like a drunk.

'Are you all right, Monsieur?' he said. 'You want me to take you to a hospital?'

'I'm all right.'

'Or the gendarmerie?'

Until I remembered I had asked for the gendarmerie when I first got into the cab, I thought with alarm that he was referring to the gun in my pocket. To me, the stench of powder seemed sharply evident, but the driver's cigarette probably disguised it to him. I shook my head. 'Just drop me at the Ruelle de l'Eau Fraîche, next to the prison. My mind was working that much, at least. I needed to pick up my car.

In my own car, pulled over on a quiet stretch of road between the city and Villefranche, I cleaned the gun with windshield washer fluid. It wouldn't pass any forensic test but a strip of my shirt used as a pull-through cleared the harsh smell from the short barrel. A final rub-over with roadside grass and it was safe to keep in my pocket.

I drove on with the sort of emptiness that I couldn't remember having experienced before. No triumph. No regret. No fear of the consequences of what I had done.

Had I killed him? Or just wounded him? And which did I want it to be? I seemed incapable of thinking. Instinct told me Sébastien Coultard and Antonio Burgos were involved in what had happened to Romilly. But I knew instinct wasn't enough. Worse, I knew instinct could be the most false of friends.

By now I was more at ease with the twisting road up to Villefranche, so that the light did not penetrate my consciousness quite as quickly as it might. But I was still a kilometre or so away when I first saw the flash of blue. Like lightning, was my first thought. Then the moment I was over the switchback I could see that stutter lights were illuminating blue the tops of the tallest trees in the darkness above me. But this is a stretch of road that turns and twists ferociously, where you allow your concentration to slip at your peril and I'm not sure how long it took me to realise where the lights were coming from.

My first thought was the Villefranche gendarmerie station. An image of the building flashed through my mind – a dozen police cars in the market square, flashing blue against the underside of the leaves of the plane trees. But that didn't work. The blue lights weren't in line with the Port du Roi. They were lower, to my left. Sometimes, the mind works slowly. Reluctance perhaps. Of course, I said to myself, well below the square. Some emergency further down. I relaxed at the thought it was someone else's trouble. Sympathetic, but comfortably remote from it all. Then it hit me. 'Oh my good God!'

The words seemed to have been spoken by someone else. An emergency *further down*. That meant Elaine's house, on the road just beyond the old chapel. There were no other houses in that lane. The police cars were at Elaine's house.

I swung the Renault off the highway and cut through the narrow dirt road that would take me below the rocky outcrop on which the house was built, the Laguna bouncing over the uneven ground. Accelerating up the last fifty yards I braked in a fog of dust rising through blue police lights.

The uniformed gendarmes were already running towards the car as I got out. I saw their pace slow before I recognised one of them as young Rodinet. 'Philippe,' I broke into a run towards him. 'What's happening?'

Beneath the peak of his kepi, his face was white, accentuated perhaps by the flash of blue lights from the half dozen police cars.

'Has something happened to Romilly?'

'Let me take you to Monsieur Fabius,' he said. He turned immediately. 'This way.'

Out of the corner of my eye I saw Claire getting out of her Mercedes. 'Tom,' she called. 'I was in the village. *Nom de Dieu* – what's happening?'

She ran across the lane. Quickly, Rodinet turned back. 'This way, Monsieur.' And as Claire took hold of my arm. 'You too, Madame.'

Claire was asking questions. Rodinet was avoiding having to answer anything, walking at a pace, running almost, up the slope towards the house. I was silent. I think I was in shock. The shock of anticipation. Anybody else would have demanded to know what had happened in the house that stood on the rise above us, every single light on. Was it feebleness again that stopped me, the hanging on to one more minute's ignorance of tragedy?

Because I already knew it was tragedy. I could see it in the tense faces of the young gendarmes we hurried past. I could see it in the two ambulances standing among the police cars. I could sense it in Claire's sudden silence beside me as she, too, saw the ambulances.

Fabius came to meet us in the lane. I saw his quick frown as he glanced at Claire, then he turned his attention to me. I stopped before him, breathing hard.

'What the hell's happened?' I found I was grabbing his jacket.

'Come and sit in my car,' he said.

Suddenly he had detached himself from my grasp and was leading me towards his car. Claire came with us without asking.

I sat in front of the car, next to him in the driver's seat. Claire had slipped into the back. As her door slammed, Fabius was unscrewing a flask. He handed it to me.

I brushed it aside. I wanted the balm of ignorance no longer. 'What is it?' I said. 'Tell me now.'

His tongue passed across his lips and I realised he, too, was suffering something. Some sense of shock? I couldn't tell.

'Who is it?' I said. My voice came out as a croak.

'It's your sister,' he said. 'I'm horrified to tell you, Monsieur. But she's dead.'

'My sister . . . ? Margot?' No accident. Fabius wouldn't have been here if it had been an accident. 'Dead? You mean killed?'

He dipped his head. 'Yes.' He paused. 'Murdered. There's no doubt at all about that.'

'And Romilly . . . ?' I said.

His hands lifted to waist height, palms down as if he were trying physically to suppress my ballooning fears.

'She's all right then, yes?' Something like relief and regret were clashing ignobly together. Romilly and Elaine at least had escaped. 'Is that right?' I pressed him. 'She's with her mother?'

'At this moment, I can't give you any final reassurance,' Fabius said.

*Final reassurance?* The ground fell from under me. 'For Christ's sake, how can that be? You mean she's hurt . . . ?'

He raised a hand, perhaps to quieten me. I felt Claire touch my shoulder, rest on my neck.

'Bisset's with Madam Chapel. We're trying to establish the sequence of events.' I could see Fabius's face flushing with the tension. 'Monsieur Chapel . . . Just give us a few minutes . . .'

'Romilly – you don't know where she is?' I said incredulously.

'She's not in the house.'

'You mean disappeared?'

'It's all I can say at the moment, Monsieur. We're searching the garden now. She could have run from the house.'

'She'd have come forward by now,' Claire said from the back seat.

'Perhaps,' Fabius said desperately. 'Unless she tripped, fainted perhaps. She's still weak – and the garden's rocky, uneven ground.'

'She's with Elaine,' I said. 'She's with her mother. She must be.'

'No,' Fabius said, his voice strained. 'The phone here had been ripped out. Her mother ran into the village for help.'

'Leaving Romilly? No. Never.'

I felt close to exploding, close to throwing myself at his throat, shaking him for a complacent, incompetent idiot. 'It's Burgos,' I shouted in his face. 'It's Antonio Burgos for Christ's sake. It's the man you released this afternoon, you fucking idiot.'

He bit on his lip. 'We don't know that, Monsieur. Really, with absolute certainty we don't know that yet.'

'I know it. *You* know it. You're supposed to be guarding them. What about your people guarding the house, for Christ's sake? What the hell were they doing?'

'It was Madame Chapel's wish,' Fabius said. 'More than her wish. She *demanded* the gendarmes should be cleared from the garden. One car at the end of the lane was all she would permit. She said Romilly was not going to get over all that had happened if she was to live her life surrounded by guards.'

'So what has Elaine told Bisset?' I was frantic. I knew I was making little sense. Bisset hadn't yet returned from the village.

I could read it on his face.

'My Christ! She's with him, isn't she? Burgos has taken her?'

'I've already given orders to pull a hundred men in from the departmental reserve,' he said. 'They'll be assembling on the hillside within the hour. They've orders to walk a cordon across the ridge.'

The hillside. Where the bodies of the other girls were found. Where Romilly was found on the road up to the ridge.

'There must be more,' I said. 'There must be more you can do than walk a hundred men with flashlights across the goddam hills.' I was losing it, I knew that. Anger, more than that – rage, frustration, a terrible fear, every one of these emotions had me in their grip.

'We have a helicopter unit just taking off from the Base Aeronavale at Toulon,' Fabius was saying.

I felt Claire's hand on my shoulder but I shook it off. It raced through my mind that she had worked with her brother to bring Burgos in to the country. She didn't have the right to a hand on my shoulder.

A woman gendarme hurried up to the car and bent to the open window. 'A message from gendarmerie headquarters, Nice, Monsieur,' she said, handing Fabius a folded sheet of paper. He opened it on his lap and read it. 'Keep me informed,' he said.

He swivelled round to speak to Claire in the back seat. 'There's been a shooting incident at the Odalisque,' he said.

I held my breath, not knowing what result I wanted.

'Your brother suffered a minor injury. A very minor injury,' Fabius said. 'He has already been treated at St Roche.' He turned back to me. 'It's possible these two incidents are connected, of course.' He was white-faced with tension.

'Then what about doing something positive, for Christ's sake!'

'I don't understand, Monsieur.'

'What about picking up the bastard?' I said. The words had jumped from my mouth, without preceding thought. I had no sense, no awareness of Claire in the car. 'He has to know something. He has to know something about what happened here.'

'Monsieur Coultard is at the gendarmerie now. Answering questions on the incident.'

'Tom . . .' Claire began, but I'd had enough. I turned in my seat.

'This man Burgos, whoever he is, was a gofer,' I exploded words all over her. 'You got him the papers and he did the dirty work for your brother. That tells me your brother's involved in all this.' Frustration and anger blew through my head. 'And, Christ knows,' I said, 'maybe you too. I don't know how and I don't know how much, but you're both in this somehow.'

'Please . . .' she said again, but this time her voice was lower.

I took no notice. I was shouting something in her face. 'Listen.' I was leaning across the back of my seat. I had her by the shoulder of her jacket. 'Listen,' I said again. Then suddenly the energy, the venom, something was flowing from me. I had no words to say.

Fabius was pulling me back. I released her jacket. It was as if air had been let out of my body.

For a moment it was completely silent in the car except for the sound of my breathing, like wings beating air. 'I'm sorry,' I said. 'I don't have reason for saying that. No real reason.' I slumped. 'Except you got Antonio Burgos his *Carte de Séjour* . . .'

She was silent. 'The man who worked for Sébastien,' she said after a moment. 'Yes, last year I helped him get his permit.'

'Why him?'

'Sébastien asked me to. He said there was a job there at the *Odalisque* waiting for him. I wouldn't do it for the girls he employed. But Burgos . . .' She shrugged. 'He seemed to be someone who'd had a poor deal . . .'

'You knew nothing about him except that? And that Sébastien needed him to work for him?'

'What was there to know?'

I looked at her for two, three seconds. Then I swung open the door of the car and got out. For a few minutes they stayed, then Fabius appeared at my shoulder. He said nothing. We stood looking towards the crazy activity surrounding the house.

'I need to see my sister,' I said. 'Before she's packed up, zipped into a black plastic bag, I need to see her.'

Fabius turned his head slowly towards me. 'Better perhaps to see her later.'

I shook my head. I thought of her lying on some mortician's table. Hair brushed and face rouged, artificially dead. I wanted to see her as she was now. Just moments from life. Maybe even with some thread of life still attaching to her.

'No,' I said. 'It's my sister. I'll see her now.'

'Very well.' He turned back for the moment towards the car and said something to Claire, then returned to me. 'The crime scene has to be preserved,' he said. 'The Crime Scene people haven't finished in the *salon* yet. So no further than the doorway. Understood?'

I nodded. I was thinking of how she might look. Would they have covered her with a sheet, arranged her arms and legs?

He looked at me again. 'You're sure this is what you want to do?'

I was calming, more from emotional exhaustion than anything else. 'I can't do anything for Romilly,' I said. 'I can at least say goodbye to my sister.'

'*Je comprends*,' he said gravely.

He touched my shoulder in some sort of gesture of understanding. And for the first time I sensed something genuine in him.

# 48

I WENT UP the path towards the house. I could see the figures of gendarmes searching the garden on both sides of the building. Flashlights glittered among the bushes and trees stretching up the hillside.

Fabius guided me round towards the back door. Now that I had committed myself to seeing Margot I wasn't so sure. Unimportant sounds, sights, grasped my attention: our shoes crunching on the gravel, the light in Elaine's bedroom, the gold thread of the shoulder badge of the gendarme by the door. My mind moved from object to sound with the jerky, mechanical feel of clockwork. I'm not sure if Claire was behind us or not.

Throughout the long walk up to the house, Fabius was silent. I saw him glance at me as we reached the back door. We went in. The corridor took us to the big kitchen. The police already had blue tapes up, marking a passage through to the door of the *salon*. I could see that the big doors overlooking the garden were part open, but there was still a smell coming through from there, from the *salon*, a smell, I suppose, like no other. Have you smelt blood before? In quantities?

A tall woman in white overalls, a wooden spatula in her hand, eased her way past me as I stopped in the doorway. I heard Fabius's voice behind me. 'Keep it short,' he said.

Margot's body lay on the terracotta floor between where I stood at the door and the back of the big sofa that faced out through the open windows into the night. The blue and yellow striped rug had been swept aside by the thrashing of arms or legs. I tried to concentrate on these details to give my seared senses a few seconds' break before I looked down again, really looked again, at Margot.

When I did, all manner of things welled inside, including most bitterly, tears. She was lying on her stomach, right side of her face flat against the tiled floor. Her eyes were open, staring at the base of a bookcase across the room. She wore a yellow tee-shirt and jeans, bare ankles and docksiders. I stood, transfixed. Whatever the recent biological revelations had told us, she was the sister I had spent my childhood with. The woman who had been my closest friend in our young, disturbed adulthood. Who had even, finally, bizarrely, and certainly mistakenly, been my lover.

The tee-shirt was soaked dark red around her upper arms and shoulders. I could just see the matted blonde hair resting on the tiles; the angle of her head mercifully disguised the main wound. But not the blood. A great dark pool had moved out across the tiles like a ghastly halo. I gasped audibly when I realised that across the polished tile surface, the edges of the blood pool were still just moving.

'Steady yourself,' Fabius said behind me.

'Leave me a moment,' I said. I felt the need for a last picture. Elaine had furnished it as a modern room without being fashionably minimalist. Most of the pieces were Danish or Swedish design, probably from the Garden-Habitat Centre on the road leading into Villefranche. Books neatly in rows in the bookcase. A Staffordshire dog and a cream and blue representation of Britannia on a display shelf. Below them, two pieces of furniture overturned, a chair and a small table. Papers scattered. I let my eyes move slowly across the surfaces but I was constantly, mesmerically. drawn to the figure on the floor, the head turned, wrenched almost, as if her neck had been broken, the pain and anguish in her expression, the arms stretched – and that truly sinister pool of blood, bubbling faintly as it crept forward infinitesimally at the edges.

I felt my knees going. I reached for the door jamb. I took a deep breath. Too much of a fucking wimp to perform even a last human rite.

I turned away for a moment and was surprised to see Claire behind me. 'You look as though you're going to pass out,' she said. 'Come away.'

I shook my head. Somehow I didn't care what Claire saw. I didn't know what I thought about Claire any more but I didn't want Fabius to see me like this. With an effort, I turned my head back to the room. Disgust boiled within me, strangling my voice. Unseen, Romilly's cat had slipped into the room. It was crouched, head down, lapping at Margot's blood.

My shout sent it skittering away across the tiles, bloody paw marks gleaming as it raced for the open doors. Claire was holding me. For a few moments she kept her arms round my waist, her face pressed against my back, then slowly she released me, lifted her hand and briefly rubbed the back of my neck. 'I'll see you outside,' she whispered. 'I'll shut the cat out.' Then she turned to head past me for the back door.

I stood alone looking into the room I had come to know well. But it was not *this* room. The same windows onto the terrace, open as they usually were, the night air, the night sounds pouring in, the cicadas and the mating croak of a thousand frogs. But now other noises too. The sound of gendarmes crunching along gravel paths, the slam of car doors – all given that special quality of a tragedy taking place *now* by the flickering blue lights bouncing off every face, every surface.

Cushions on the floor, sofa cushions. Papers, business papers I guessed, multicoloured like those in Sébastien's office. And the doll Sanya had given Elaine, sitting in an armchair, observing, oblivious to the trickle of blood down her cheek.

On the far wall a landscape in oils, and next to it I couldn't miss the blood, the handprints of a falling woman, drawn downwards in streaks of red. I thought of Romilly, just days out of hospital, convalescent, with the weakness of an invalid, running from this monster a second time. Hiding perhaps somewhere in one of the thousand narrow gullies at the back of the house, crouched in one of the outbuildings, in the corner of a garage . . .

I turned violently away from the salon – but it was Bisset, this time who confronted me. There was no sign of Claire. Or Fabius.

'Thank God you're here,' I said. I meant it. I found I had enormous trust in him to do whatever was needed. 'You've seen Elaine. It was Burgos, yes?'

He nodded quickly. 'He burst in. Madame Chapel was knocked down. But your sister fought him. Made time for Romilly to get out.'

'She ran into the garden?'

'He had some sort of club. When your sister went down he set out after Romilly.'

Waves of fear and nausea were passing over me. My heart was jumping like a sack-full of rabbits. 'And Elaine. She followed?'

'She followed him into the garden. Her eyes are not good, she said . . . She called Romilly again and again but there was no answer. That's when she ran back into the house to call the police. And found the line had been cut.'

'Oh my Christ,' I said.

'He can't get far.'

The outbuildings,' I said. 'Have they looked there?'

That calm African intonation seemed to enclose me. 'We have men in every corner of the garden, Tom. We have men in the rocks behind the house – all the way up the hill . . . We'll find them.'

The roar of rotors passing low over the house drowned the rest of his words. Through the open salon windows I could see the naval helicopter up there in the darkness, the beam of its searchlight beginning to describe slow circles round the house. Further up the hillside another beam sprang into sight – from another helicopter high in the darkness.

Bisset had taken my arm and was guiding me away.

'Wait,' I said. I stopped and took one more long look back at the *salon*. Sofa, four club chairs, TV set, Swedish tables, books, magazines, scattered papers, Margot's handbag, car keys on the credenza, framed photographs on the mantel, Elaine at Cannes talking to Clint Eastwood, talking to Sophia Loren, Romilly in America, later pictures of her as a teenager. The doll in the armchair. And Margot, humiliated in death. Or, despite the splayed legs, the blood, the anguished expression, maybe not humiliated. She had saved Elaine, perhaps even Romilly too. No, not humiliated.

Fabius was standing between the police tapes, talking to another man in civilian clothes in the kitchen. The judge made a small signal to me that he was just finishing and I stood to one side and leaned against the cooking surfaces as I had seen Elaine do a hundred times. From here, my angle into the salon mercifully did not enable me to see more than Margot's sprawled legs and about up to her waist. It was enough. I could see the blood spattered cushions and papers on the floor.

The tall woman in the bloodstained white overalls was peeling a white elasticated hat from her head and shaking her short dark hair back into shape. Fabius turned to me. 'This is Dr LaGaillarde, the Medical Examiner.'

'Tom Chapel,' I said.

'Monsieur.' She nodded briskly and dropped a bloody pair of surgical gloves into a plastic bag. Taking her notebook from her breast pocket, she flipped it open and ran the tip of her pencil down the list of points. Suddenly, nobody seemed to be concerned that I was still there.

'A close approximation of the time of death isn't hard to establish,' she said to Fabius. 'If the incident was called in at 22.23 this evening, I would say death took place at approximately that time, no more than fifteen minutes either way.'

'You know there was a third woman in the house.' Fabius glanced at me, then back at the Medical Examiner. 'Monsieur Chapel's daughter.'

She looked at me. 'We won't know until the analysis whether all the bloodstains are from the deceased.'

It had never crossed my mind that those horrific clawing stains on the wall could have belonged to anyone but Margot. The thought that they might be Romilly's I found even more sickening. But I had this need to hear all. I saw Fabius look across at me and I shook my head. 'I'm all right,' I said tensely. 'Just go ahead.'

I gained a moment or two to catch my breath when Bisset came back into the room, shook hands with the Medical Examiner and stood with his back against the door jamb of the salon.

Dr LaGaillarde turned to Fabius, in the process half turning her back on me. 'The cause of death was a blow struck from above. Almost certainly during the course of a violent struggle. She has massive bruises on her upper right arm. I think the assailant had grasped her arm to steady her for the blow. She's a tall woman and I would say fit. Her struggle would account for the size of the bruise – and the fact that under the nails of her left hand there's blood and tissue. I think she raked the nails of her free hand down his face as he hit her.'

We stood in silence watching her consult her notes.

'The blow would have been to the top of the head, probably as she was dragged forward. The point of impact is the join between the left parietal and left occipital bones.'

'And it was certainly the cause of death?' Fabius said.

'Caved in her skull. Death by way of a massive and instant cerebral haemorrhage.'

I'd had all I could take. I nodded to them and headed for the back door. 'I'll be outside if you want me,' I muttered to Fabius as I stumbled past him.

\*     \*     \*

357

I crossed the kitchen and stepped out of the back door into a garden that seemed crowded with men and women, some in civilian clothes, some in blue short-sleeved gendarme uniforms, some in the yellow coveralls of the Crime Scene techs who had just arrived – and every face stained intermittently by the flashing blue lights of the cars in the lane.

Claire was there. She was standing alone, smoking a cigarette. She turned it round and put it to my lips as I stood next to her. That first giddying drag was welcome but not enough. 'A drink is what I really need,' I said.

She smiled, half smiled. 'Me too.' She paused. 'Believe what I told you,' she said suddenly. 'It's important to me that you do, Tom. I helped an immigrant to get work papers. I've done it for hundreds of others. This one was no different. Beyond that I know no more about what's going on here than you.'

'Okay.' I reached out and touched her bare arm.

I tried again to take in the whole scene but it was just too bright and noisy and *mouvementé,* a bedlam overlaid by the thunder of helicopter engines. 'I'm doing no good here,' I said. 'I'm going to look for her.'

'Where, for God's sake?'

*Where, for God's sake?* She was right, of course.

Claire stood for a moment, her eyes not moving from my face. Then she reached out and held my hand tightly. 'If you go, I'll go with you,' she said. 'But there are a hundred men here. With radios and flashlights and helicopter support.'

'You mean there's nothing I can do.'

'Come up to the château, Tom. Fabius and Bisset need to know where you are. You wouldn't want to be out of contact, somewhere on the hillside, when they find her.'

She was right of course. 'Okay.' I was suddenly aware that I was shivering like a madman, although even the down-draught of the helicopter thundering above us was hot on my face. The passage of time is elusive when so much is happening around you. Three or four gendarmes came to ask if I was okay, or more roughly, if they didn't know me, what I was doing there. It was the first time I noticed that all the civilians carried large lapel ID cards, coloured blue, white and red, with photographs and *République Française* stamped across the top.

A few minutes later Fabius appeared out of shadows split by powerful shafts of light. I was becoming disorientated by noise and the relentless activity round me. With an effort I pulled myself together. 'Anything?' I said to him. 'Any sign of her?'

'I'm sorry, Monsieur. Nothing.' He shrugged. 'Not quite nothing. A piece of surgical plaster found just behind the perimeter fence of the property. She still had plaster on her right arm . . . ?'

'Yes.'

'It looks as though she might have knocked it against a rock as she ran from the house.'

'Ran . . .' I had to say it. 'Or was carried from the house.'

He looked at me. 'It would have to be an unusually strong man who could carry a fully grown young woman uphill across broken ground like that.'

'You've seen Burgos, for God's sake. Hands like plates. Shoulders. He spent half his life struggling with young bulls, he told us. Lifting and carrying a girl won't give him a problem. A week ago Bisset was telling me just that, that the man, we didn't know who he was at this time, was strong and sure-footed enough to have carried Nicole Tresselli's body from the road deep into the hills.'

Fabius grunted disapproval at what Bisset had said, but not enough disapproval to indicate disagreement. 'You're going up to the château with Madame Coultard? Good.'

'I'd sooner be out with one of the search teams.'

'It might make you feel better to be out on the hillside,' he said. 'But if I need you tonight, I want to know where you are.'

It was more or less what Claire had said.

'Madame Coultard will be waiting for you.' He was about to turn away. 'In there,' he said, 'in the *salon*. You didn't see anything that you wouldn't have expected? Sometimes it happens . . .'

I could have yelled at him that I hadn't expected to come back and find my sister, my ex-sister in a pool of black blood on the floor, but I knew that would have been worthless histrionics. 'No,' I said. 'Nothing I wasn't expecting.'

We stood in silence for a moment. His face in the blue lights was haggard, defeated. So, I guessed, was mine.

'I have something to say to you, Monsieur,' he said. 'Perhaps this is the time to say it.'

I lifted my head towards him.

'I don't think anything I have done, as a result of what I'm about to tell you, has prejudiced the investigation.'

There he goes again, I thought. These French minds. Even in

the midst of this tragedy I can't understand what he's talking about. This time I asked him directly.

'What are you saying?'

'I took a certain view of this enquiry from the beginning.'

'You insisted Romilly had suffered an accident.'

'Yes.'

'That it had nothing whatsoever to do with Marcel Coultard's will.'

'That's the way I preferred to interpret events, yes.'

'Why? You're going to tell me why?'

'Yes. I owe it to you.' He turned away and stood staring down the lane. 'My father, as I'm sure you know, was the locally notorious Professor Fabius, commandant of the SEC unit in Nice.'

'I know.'

'And doubtless you know he was sentenced in absentia by a military court just after the war to life imprisonment. They caught up with him in Brussels and brought him back to Nice. To prison.'

'Is that where he died? In the prison on the Rue de l'Eau Fraîche?'

He shook his head. 'He was released ten years back. An old, broken man.' He looked at me defiantly. 'You'll say he deserved to be broken. Perhaps. But he was still my father.'

I stared back at him. 'He's not still alive?'

'He's ninety-three. He is as vile and anti-Semitic as he ever was. He shows no remorse, no regret for all he did. The years have taught him nothing. But I still feel I owe him some sort of existence. I was working in Paris when he was released from prison. I felt I had no choice but to move back here.'

'Are you saying he *lives* with you?'

Silently and with what seemed like great effort, he nodded. 'The monster in the attic.'

'Hell . . .' I couldn't think of anything else to say.

He drew a deep breath. 'Marcel Coultard and my father were classic enemies. They fought on different sides of the moral frontier. Marcel the hero – my father the fiend. I knew anything involving Marcel's wartime activities would inevitably involve my father's name. I knew if Marcel's will was involved it would become a journey into the past. I also knew that if it were revealed that I was giving my father shelter, my own position in this region would have become untenable.'

'You knew from the beginning that Romilly was attacked

because of the will? Christ, you're saying that?'

'No.' His voice was raised. 'I swear to you I didn't.' Two gendarmes, waiting by a car nearby, turned their heads towards us. Fabius dropped his voice: 'But I too much wanted to believe it was an accident, to believe she'd fallen from a motorbike. That the boy had not come forward. But that was no longer sustainable when Romilly recovered consciousness. From then on I accepted it was the testament that was motivating events. I accepted we were about to make that journey into the past.'

I stood, waiting for him to say more.

'Now,' he said, 'it's tragically obvious that Antonio Burgos is not just an obsessive, a stalker. Who he's acting for I don't know. Understand I'm not excusing my attitude to the case; I'm not even apologising for being wrong, it's not unusual in an investigation. But I think you have a right to know my story, however it reflects on me.'

I didn't feel him any more likeable. But I felt a cold admiration for the man, for the risk he had just taken for his evil father. And now, putting his career in the hands of a stranger.

'Okay . . .' I said. 'Okay.'

He hesitated, then nodded. 'Thank you,' he said.

'Before I go . . .' I looked down at the gravelled lane, then brought my head up. 'I have a crazy idea.'

He nodded for me to go ahead, the old haughty Fabius again.

It was the idea that had first come to me when Antonio Burgos had turned his eyes towards me through the two way mirror. 'Is it possible Pierre Coultard is not buried up on the hill road to St Juste?'

'Why do you say that?'

I couldn't face telling him Sanya's story. 'I'm asking you – could it be?'

His mouth twisted. He rocked slightly back and forth. 'I should tell you,' he said softly, 'what Pierre Coultard really did in the war. The younger Coultard saw grander opportunities if he turned away from the Resistance. Secretly, he approached the Jewish Commission Police. He was assigned to work for my father. His role was to inform the SEC about the movement of Jewish people trying to escape He was paid, of course.'

'You told Claire this?'

'No.'

'What happened to him?'

'One night he disappeared, that's all my father knew. Like so many other boys my father had working for him. Except in this case, after the war, the Resistance erected a monument on the hill. Pierre Coultard, the informer, had mysteriously become a hero.'

'This never came out at your father's trial? And *you* never told anybody?'

He looked at me coldly. 'Did I ever tell anybody in Villefranche that their local hero was a traitor, a paid Vichy informer? No.' He laughed bitterly. 'Would you, Monsieur?'

I couldn't remember exactly how far down the lane I had left my car. I reached the front gate and began to walk towards the main road through the jumble of police cars and ambulances. Gendarmes surged past me. Dog handlers pulled their dogs tight to their sides. Most blue stutter lights were off by now but head-lights glared at us and smoke from the glowing ends of a dozen cigarettes rose in the light along the lane.

I couldn't get that room out of my head. It was like a colour print. Margot, the scrabbled blood prints on the wall, the sofa cushions scattered on the floor, the overturned chair and table . . . the oil painting of the English Norfolk coast where Elaine had come from, the photographs in chased silver frames of Rom and Elly . . . The blood scattered everywhere, dripping from the face of Sanya's doll, soaking carpets and cushions . . . on papers already soaked rusty brown.

Claire was in the lane, smoking a cigarette and staring up at the house. In one hand she held a styrofoam cup of coffee.

'You go ahead,' I said. 'I have to speak to Elaine.'

She didn't ask me if I was fit to drive myself. That, at least, was good.

'Okay. I'll see you at St Juste.' She took a final sip of her coffee and offered it to me.

'I'll wait for the drink,' I said and she nodded briefly, poured the coffee into the ground and made for her car.

# 49

THEY GAVE ME a radio phone connection to Elaine in the clinic. I sat in the blue gendarmerie Nevada and tried to ask her how she was but she couldn't answer. 'He's got Romilly, Tom,' she said in a strangled, unnatural voice. 'The same man, Burgos.'

For several minutes I could make out nothing more she said, just a terrible wracking sobbing. Then the words broke through. 'This time he's going to kill her, Tom. He's taken her up into the hills to kill her.'

'Elly, please, please, listen to me.' For a few moments the flood of words stopped as she choked tears and mucus from her throat and I took the opportunity. 'Listen to me, Elly,' I said, 'if he'd wanted to kill her, he would have killed her here in the house. He had his chance. Now we have ours. There are hundreds of police out looking . . . there are heat-seeking helicopters, cruisers, everything you can think of. He won't make it, Elly. We'll get him before he can do her any more harm.'

'You think?' She croaked the words through a swollen throat. 'You really think so, Tom?'

I put in all the conviction I could muster. 'I'm sure of it. The man's crazy. He doesn't know what he's up against.'

'It's because of the will, you know that. I was right. It's because of this fucking will.'

'He said so?'

'He was screaming and swearing like a madman. The will, the money . . . Fighting his way past Margot to get to Romilly.'

'What was Margot doing there?'

She went silent. Then she said in a low voice, much more controlled: 'She'd come to tell you – to tell me too, she said – that she was going back home. She was leaving for New York in the morning. She said, her phrase, she said she'd done enough trouble-making in your life.' There was a long pause and I could feel how desperate she was despite doctors and Demerol.

'Go on, Elly,' I said. 'Tell me.'

'She wanted to say goodbye to Rom, wanted to tell me how sorry she was about all trouble she'd made for all of us. She was just leaving when Burgos burst into the house.'

I sat half in the police car listening, imagining.

'She fought him, Tom. She was fantastic. She went for him like a wildcat. She tore his face open with her nails. She was screaming for me to get Rom out of the house. But he had this shepherd's club, a great heavy thing and he was holding her, beating her head . . .'

'Okay . . .' I said. 'No more . . .'

'I wanted you to know, Tom. She was doing it for Romilly.'

I nodded, although Elaine couldn't see. Couldn't see the tears running down my face, either.

I found my car and sat at the bottom of the lane. A line of moonlit cloud seemed to be moving in from the sea, the first time I had seen anything but clear sky since I had arrived here. There was some wind too, less wind perhaps than just a faint movement of the warm heavy air. But I could feel it against my cheek as it rolled slowly through the shattered window,

I was exhausted. Too exhausted for the moment to drive. I closed my eyes and let the horror of it all flood over me. I was terrified for Romilly, beset by images of the creature who had taken her, loping over the hills with my daughter carried like a trussed deer across his shoulders.

Every few seconds, as another image, another wave of anguish hit me, I blew out air, clearing my lungs in a soundless whistle. At the very end, Margot had showed that she had General John's guts. Somehow I owed it to Rom and to her to pull something similar out of my battered self.

My mind slipped back to the time standing with Bisset in the hospital the night I arrived in Nice, the first moment I had registered the idea of a man attacking Rom. Then I had known nothing of him And even when he began to emerge into the light, the cloak of mad priesthood had covered everything. But after the line-up session at the gendarmerie, after following him for a day, I saw him differently.

I knew for sure now that I was on the right track. He was more than just Antonio Burgos, travelling bull-hand, sex-obsessed stalker. Hadn't Elaine said that he had torn his way past Margot screaming about the will?

There were a lot of things still unknown about Antonio Burgos, itinerant stateless worker who could nevertheless pass as a priest. Who shuffled among the lurid fifteen-franc sex books in the market but chose the poems of the medieval French murderer-priest, François Villon.

# 50

O N THE ROAD up to the château a gendarmerie vehicle was
parked every couple of hundred yards; somewhere above, I
could hear the rotors of a helicopter. My car was stopped four
times at roadblocks, ID details recorded, the trunk opened and
examined. They were doing all that could reasonably be hoped
for – but I had seen the photographs of Nicole Tresselli. Despite
what I'd told Elaine, I knew there was every chance it would not
be enough.

I stood with a glass of Scotch in the main hall of the château.
Through the great mullioned windows I could see the lake, its
surface far below us, glinting under a full moon, its sides exposing
the deep band of dried mud. Every few minutes the searchlight
of a helicopter would slowly circle the lake like the tongue of a
huge animal licking the rim of a bowl.

What bears on you at these times is a huge and heavy blanket
of hopelessness, a conviction that you, personally, can do nothing
to avert an inevitable tragedy. It's a hopelessness that has to be
fought against. Something, almost anything, positive has to
replace it. Or you go mad.

I shook my head to try to clear it of the last few hours of
confusion and fear and questions and stutter lights and banging
car doors.

I could feel the tension in Claire in the way she stood, her
shoulders held back, her hands clasped in front of her. 'He called
here a few minutes ago,' she said. 'Antonio Burgos.'

The glass fell from my hand, shattering on the tiled floor.
'Burgos called here? You mean he knew I was on my way up?
He was trying to contact me?'

'No.' She took a long breath. 'It was me he wanted to talk
to.'

'You? Is that what he said?'

'He said, "I've got the girl. I killed the sister and that was a mistake. But don't worry, I've got the girl."'

'*Don't worry!*'

She made a confirming grunt, not even a word.

'Christ. You told the police this?'

'Of course. I called Bisset just before you arrived.'

*But don't worry.* What did that imply? That Claire no longer had *need* to worry. That she would be pleased, obviously. Maybe even that he had done it for her. I said this.

'How in God's name could he be doing something like this for me?'

'For Christ's sake, try! You must have met him three or four times to fix his permit.'

'Just twice.'

'Okay, twice. Did Burgos . . . could it be that he had fallen for you? You know, would do anything for you . . . even this, even all this. We know from Elaine that he knew about your father's will.'

'How could he know anything about that?'

'Sébastien maybe. Why not?' I stopped. A new thought hit me. 'Or wait a minute . . . the break-in,' I said. 'There was a break-in at Mantel, Rolin just after your father died. Nothing was stolen, but somebody went through the files. Maybe the files containing your father's will.'

'But why would he do that?' She closed her eyes. 'Unless Sébastien sent him.'

'When you were helping him with his permit, did you get the idea that he was . . . coming on to you?'

'It would have been ridiculous.'

'All the same, is it possible that he's doing all this for you?'

'How?' she said sharply.

'Two possibilities,' I said slowly. 'He was doing it for you because in some crazy way he was hot for you.'

She flinched.

'Or he was doing it because Sébastien put it to him – or you did.'

Her mouth dropped in shock. 'You bastard!'

'Are you saying Rom's death wouldn't advantage you?'

'Advantage me? What would advantage me? Abducting your daughter? Killing your sister? For Christ's sake . . .' She was shaking with anger, at me, herself . . .

A minute passed and she was talking again. 'I knew from the beginning that Sébastien was afraid of Burgos. I knew he wasn't just an ordinary employee.'

'What does that mean?'

'When Sébastien called me he didn't just ask me to get Burgos a permit. He told me it was something that *had* to be done. We had no choice, he said. It was in my interest as much as his.'

'You didn't ask him what the hell he was talking about?'

'Of course, I did. He told me it was something I'd rather not know. Especially if I was going to continue to live here at St Juste.'

'Are we talking about blackmail of some sort? Is that what Burgos was doing? Blackmail that involved you, too?'

'No.' She hesitated. 'I thought at the time,' she said slowly, 'that we must be talking about something that involves my father. My father's reputation. That's why I put through the permit. A North African peasant, a bull handler, a travelling *corrida* hand.' She paused. 'But he'd only just arrived in the country. What could he know about my father?'

I thought about it before I said it. 'How many North African peasants read François Villon?' I asked her.

She stared at me. 'What?'

I was ready to burst out with the idea that had possessed me since the interrogation at the gendarmerie. Ready to fly it with Claire. The blackmail story was another reinforcement of what had been haunting me. 'There's one more possibility,' I said. 'A crazy idea originally, but it's growing.'

'What is it?'

'That when Antonio Burgos called this evening, he was calling you as a member of the family.'

She looked at me in wide-eyed astonishment. Her mouth opened to deny it.

'Before you say anything, I learnt a shattering fact about your father's brother tonight. Pierre Coultard wasn't a Resistance hero after all – he worked with old Professor Fabius as an SEC informer.'

'That can't be true.'

'It's true, Claire. Nobody would know better than Professor Fabius.'

'Jean-Claude told you that?' When I nodded she stood shaking her head.

'Either the Resistance executed Pierre. Or your father somehow let him go, exiled him.'

'No,' she said. 'No.'

'Either way, the monument on the hillside is a fake.'

She was white-faced with shock. 'When you talk of Burgos as a member of the family, you mean Pierre could be still alive?'

'I'm saying the chances are he's still alive. I'm saying the chances are that Antonio Burgos is the name Pierre Coultard took for the rest of his life. And that fact alone was what he was using to blackmail Sébastien.'

She had run out onto the terrace. I had delivered Sanya's story to her as a series of staccato blows, with no effort to make it easier for her. After a few moments I joined her. I've never seen such turmoil reflected in a face. Somehow, if the face is beautiful, the impact is multiplied.

'You're rewriting history,' she said in a voice not much above a whisper. 'All my life, my father described his brother as a Resistance hero. Now you say that this mad American woman claims that he betrayed the Jewish women my father brought over the mountains – that he even murdered one of them. What does she know about all those years ago? You're mad to believe her. To believe someone who claims to be a reincarnate of one of those Jewish women.'

'Professor Fabius has no reason to invent Pierre's story. What Sanya has to add to it may or may not be the truth. But it *fits*, Claire. It *fits*.'

'Then check New York, or London or Toronto or Sydney . . . Those Jewish women must have gone somewhere. Many of them will still be alive.'

She saw my face. She seemed to fall back a half pace. 'You've checked . . . ?'

'Not me. But somebody has. Spent years on it. He could find none of them.'

'My God . . .'

'I don't understand much. But I think those Jewish women are all dead, Claire. And I think your father and his brother had something to do with it.' I paused. 'And off the wall though it is, I'm damn sure Pierre Coultard is not buried under that stone monument. And never was. And there are old people in this village who have always known that.'

369

She was looking out over the pit that the valley had become. 'Five years ago,' she said quietly, 'the *département* decided the road down to Villefrance needed strengthening in several places to stop it slipping down the valley into the lake. My father and those that remained of the Committee of Seven led a campaign of protest against moving Pierre's grave. I was astonished at the depth of feeling on the Committee's part. But if Pierre is not buried there – then I understand. The road strengthening would have revealed that.'

Suddenly, there were tears on her cheeks. She wasn't crying. Her lips had not puckered or her eyes reddened. She just had tears on her cheeks. 'So if Pierre was not killed by the Vichy police, what happened to him? My father helped him to leave St Juste, you're saying?'

'Looks like it.'

She was crying now. 'Had my father really been involved in betraying those women, too?'

Was this all real, or was it lethal play-acting? I took her shoulders and turned her round to face me. 'Romilly's life could depend on you telling me the truth. Did Sébastien know it was Burgos who attacked Romilly? Did you?'

She shook her head violently, trying to tear herself from me, her hair flying. But I held her.

'Sébastien is a brute, I know that. He lives for himself and his ambition to rise in his appalling party,' she said, breathing heavily.

'But did he know that it was Burgos who had attacked Romilly?'

She was quiet. 'I think he might have known – probably just afterwards, after the attack. Did he put Burgos up to it? I don't know.'

'Okay . . .' I said. I was accepting her story. Her story – and her brother's. 'Which makes him an accessory after the fact. At least.'

'Yes.'

We stood six, maybe eight feet from each other, like actors in a stage production. It seemed to symbolise the point we'd reached in our strange relationship. I had to have the rest out into the open too. 'I was there tonight, at the Odalisque.'

'When Sébastien was wounded?'

'Yes.'

'I asked Fabius if you had been there. He was cautious. But

he said the descriptions Sébastien gave didn't fit you. Deliberately, I assume. He was in no position to press charges.'

'We were struggling. I had a gun. I'm not going to say that if I'd had a chance I wouldn't have aimed it more accurately. I would have.'

She was silent. 'There is something else I have to tell you,' she said. A faint tremor shook her body. 'The auditors began work at Ciné-Coultard today.'

'What's that got to do with anything?'

Her next words took my breath away. 'By now the police will have been informed that the company is criminally bankrupt,' She said.

'Ciné-Coultard is bankrupt? I thought it was worth over twenty-five-million dollars.'

'You must have seen him burning papers at the Odalisque. Didn't you realise he was getting ready to make a run for it? It never occurred to you that Sébastien needed to inherit the company to keep himself out of jail? He was Finance Director. He'd bled the company to promote his party.'

I leaned back against the wall. 'How long have you known this was going on?'

She gestured with a movement of her hand. 'Too long, perhaps,' she said. 'But I didn't know the full extent.'

'If he was expecting to inherit, he was stealing the money from you too.' I couldn't stop saying it. 'If you'd blown the whistle . . .'

'I should have done something about it.' She looked at me with a touch of defiance. 'It still would not have helped Romilly.'

These people down here, this cat's cradle of loyalties! I stared at her for a few seconds longer. Then I walked out.

Claire watched me from the perron as I got into my car. The first streaks of lemon yellow light were appearing in the east. I backed the Renault violently, saw the dust rise between us and turned the wheel. I knew she was there, but without looking up at her, I accelerated down the drive towards the gates.

I went back to Elaine's house. I didn't like the idea one bit, but I needed somewhere to base myself. I could have gone to Marty's place but I wanted to be on hand. I wanted to be ready if anybody wanted to contact me. The thought horrified me, but it had to be Elly's house.

371

I pulled my car onto the parking apron at the end of the lane. In a gendarmerie car on my right, Philippe Rodinet and another young gendarme were guarding the house. When I told Rodinet that I intended living there they cleared it by phone with Bisset and showed me where the off-limits parts of the house were. The kitchen had been thoroughly examined and declared free to use. The *salon* door was locked and sealed. That, I have to admit, was fine with me.

I went upstairs, took a shower and sat on the bed. I hadn't slept last night and the stress of events throbbed in my head. But to sleep now was unthinkable. I couldn't let myself sleep until Romilly had been found.

Or so I told myself.

Five hours later I awoke crumpled across the bed. I had some idea the phone had been ringing downstairs but wasn't sure. I stood up. I was still wearing my linen slacks and docksiders. I picked up a shirt and walked unsteadily downstairs.

Rodinet was making coffee in the kitchen. He lifted the cafetiere to me and I nodded. 'Did you hear the phone?' I asked him. 'Did it ring?'

'I missed it,' he said. 'I was just going off duty, briefing the new shift in the lane. By the time I got here whoever it was had rung off.'

I took the mug of coffee he gave me and felt miserable with guilt. How had I been able to waste five hours when Romilly was in the hands of a lunatic? I walked out with the coffee and sat in the sun by the back door.

The phone rang again.

I set the coffee on the tiled step and went into the house. I lifted the phone preparing myself to start explaining to some business acquaintance or friend of Elaine's what had happened.

But it wasn't a friend or business acquaintance.

A voice said: 'Is that Monsieur Chapel?' A muffled, indistinct voice. I knew immediately it wasn't delivered naturally. Through a cloth perhaps, or wet tissue.

Even so, the accent that came through was local Provençal, sounding more like Italian than French. Easy to imitate. Then it was as if, satisfied that it was me he was talking to, he had removed the cloth from over the phone. The voice changed. Still Provençal, but with a more educated timbre. 'Monsieur Chapel,' the voice said. 'Your daughter is safe. Understand me. Safe.'

I felt the rush of adrenaline hit my voice. 'Safe,' I said. 'Alive? Where is she, for God's sake?'

He brushed the question aside. 'This first call between us will be the longest communication we are ever able to have. After this, your gendarmerie friends will be listening. So everything we say today must carry the fullest meaning. We must be totally, absolutely, honest with each other.'

Was I to say that I knew he was Pierre Coultard? No. If he wanted to me to know he would tell me himself. I agreed his terms. He could trust me, I said. He snorted briefly at that.

I knew now that I was dealing with no ordinary blackmailer. This man was a crazy. Not stupid. But he carried, in his tone of voice, in that earnestness of manner, that knife-sharp certainty of rectitude, the terrible mark of craziness.

I knew it, recognised it from when I had been in the House of Correction. In the US, ordinary people think all the crazies are on the street. But prison is the real place to meet the deranged. For survival you pick up the tone pretty quickly.

'You're telling me that my daughter's safe.' I was speaking slowly, carefully, as I used to speak to men in prison who would break your fingers at the first sign of an offending remark. 'I need you to prove that,' I said. 'How can I be completely honest unless I know she's unharmed?'

'I didn't say she was unharmed, Monsieur,' the voice said coldly. 'I said she was safe. I am attempting to be honest with you. You must appreciate it.'

'Yes . . . yes, I do. Just tell me.' I was just holding on to a semblance of self-control. 'Just tell me how she is.'

He was silent as if thinking.

'She undoubtedly needs medical attention,' he said pedantically. It was like discussing her condition with a doctor.

'Well, for Christ's sake . . .' I began – and stopped dead.

'The conditions here are not suitable for someone who had just been discharged from hospital.'

I had to keep talking. I had to moderate my voice. I had to avoid what every instinct urged: to curse and rage at the man who had brought all this about, the man who had killed Margot and twice brought Romilly to the edge of death.

'Listen,' I said to him. 'Let her get to somewhere, let me take her to somewhere where she can get the treatment she needs. Whatever you're asking, she can be no good to you dead.'

Then he laughed. For the first time. In the soft early morning breezes, I felt suddenly cold enough to shiver. Like a man with a fever.

In my hand the phone went dead.

# 5 1

I KNEW HE was about to call again. But there are times when the mind muddles the body. I was sick with apprehension; sick with hope. I walked the length of the terrace a hundred times. I made coffee and poured it away. I cut bread and cheese and gave up before the first bite. The two gendarmes, now new, unfamiliar faces, were kind but unable to quiet my restless wanderings.

I had spoken to Elaine and I could hear that they had her heavily sedated. I told her I didn't think I should come over to the clinic in case I missed any developments. Half-asleep, she accepted that without protest.

I had not reported the Burgos call to Fabius or Bisset. I'd thought about it over and over, but I felt, as people dealing with ransom demands have always felt, a fear that the police would frighten off the caller. I was using the word ransom to myself, but was a ransom involved? So far there was no demand. No revelation of what he wanted. Simply a phone call. Was I waiting, wasting valuable time for nothing?

I wanted to call Claire. For comfort, for warmth. I'd gone a long way with her last night. I think she had told me the broad truth. She had known her brother was using Ciné-Coultard to support his party, but not that he had been steadily gutting the company. To the point of imminent bankruptcy.

So why didn't I still entirely trust her? I was learning that people down here seemed to develop something approaching a double nature. Physically it was expressed by a shrug of the shoulders, but it had a historical depth. How otherwise, could so many good people have remained so indifferent for so long to the plight of the Riviera's Jews?

Throughout the day I was never too far from the phone. I spent an hour at least sitting on the stairs, the hall table with the phone on it no more than an arm's length away, reading a book I'd found in my bedroom on Archbishop Jules-Gerard Soliège of

Toulouse. It was another book given to Elaine by Marcel Coultard, and on the same subject: the French nation under the government at Vichy.

Archbishop Saliege was, I realised, the man Mother Francesca in Pézenas had mentioned so admiringly. And it's true there was much to admire. Sitting on the stairs, I read of this remarkable prelate, half-paralysed, offering an outspoken and fearless opposition to the savagery the Catholic Field Marshal, Phillippe Pétain, had instituted in Unoccupied France.

When his attention was brought to the inhuman conditions of the transit camps for Jews in his own diocese, Archbishop Saliège had not hesitated. He had drafted a ringing pastoral letter, submitting it to neither Paris nor the Pope, and required all parish priests in his diocese to read it in their own churches on the following Sunday, August 23, 1942: *Children, women, fathers and mothers treated like cattle, members of a family separated from one another and dispatched to an unknown destination – it has been reserved for our own time to see such sad things. The Jews are real men and women. They cannot be allowed to suffer limitlessly – they are part of humanity. They are our brothers.*

It was a clarion call to French Catholics. It told them clearly where their duty lay. It was just in time. Within days, in that hot August, the Vichy police, the fathers of some of these amiable young gendarmes outside the house, were conducting the shockingly brutal great public round-ups or *rafles* of Jews in the towns and villages of the Unoccupied Zone. Without Archbishop Saliège's leadership who knows how many Jewish children would have been dispersed to the safety of convent orphanages while their parents, like cattle, were driven to the abattoirs of the East. Later of course, even the great Archbishop (perversely, it is Pius XII, not Saliège, the church is considering for sainthood) could not save the smallest children from the cattletrucks. *Eight horses / forty men,* the railcars had stencilled on their sides. How many children, I wondered?

I put the book down. I knew from Mother Francesca that this story was my own. And though I had no idea how much of Sanya's strange recountings I could accept, the sign-post pointed inexorably back down that rough time-track that led to the horrors of 1942. How precisely it fitted, *where* it fitted in the mystery of Marcel Coultard's will, in the murder of Margot and the abduction of Romilly, I didn't yet know. But I believed it couldn't be long before I did.

I made another quick phone check with Bisset and discovered that there was no further news. There was a possible sighting of a man up in the hills near St Juste which turned out to be a woodsman on a legitimate errand checking firebreaks, but nothing else.

'We're too late, aren't we?'

'We can't say that when we don't know what he's trying to do, Tom. We don't even know basically why he went after her again. I think he's going to let us know. He's going to be in touch. That's where the hope lies. Stick with it.'

I was sorely tempted to tell him that Burgos had already started the process of letting us know, but I kept it back. I was tempted to tell him that I believed Burgos was a member of the Coultard family, but it would have involved defending my feeble sources, guesswork and the ramblings of Sanya the reincarnate, and I just didn't have the guts to do it.

'How about Sébastien Coultard?'

'He described the shooter as short, fat and French. A customer complaining of overcharging. He's not going to press it. I'd say,' he said with heavy meaning, 'that whoever shot at him is off the hook. Sébastien's got more important problems than a nick in the thigh with a small calibre bullet.'

'Claire tells me he was ransacking the company for his political ambitions.'

'Our fraud unit have already had a provisional report from the auditors. But it won't do any good.'

'He'll walk?'

'He's already walked,' Bisset said. 'The moment he gave his statement here at the gendarmerie. Major political figures in this region get a lot of help taking their long vacations.'

'You mean he's already left the country?'

'We know he flew to Madrid. Where would you choose from there? Argentina? Brazil?' He paused. 'If we'd known a few days before . . .'

I thought of Claire. How many days before had she known? I thought about her, but to Bisset I said nothing.

I rang off and cradled the phone and climbed the stairs to my room. I liked to keep all calls as short as possible. The phone, I assumed, was my only contact with the man who had Romilly. But I was wrong. The next communication arrived unexpectedly.

It was a little before nine and the sun was just going down behind the ox-bow of hills that enclosed Villefranche. There was cloud in the sky now, dark streaks red-braided by the setting sun. From my room I heard a young boy's voice downstairs and the answering voices of the gendarmes in the lane. A few moments later I heard the crunch of boots on gravel and heard my name called.

'A letter for you, Monsieur,' the gendarme said.

I scrambled up and threw the book behind me onto the bed. Half-way down the stairs I saw Rodinet standing in the hall. He was holding out to me a letter in a ten by eight brown envelope.

'Who delivered it? I thought I heard a young boy's voice.'

'You did, Monsieur. Young Henri Beste. He was riding down from the lake, on the far road, when someone stopped him, gave him ten francs to deliver this to you. Condolences, I imagine, Monsieur.'

I took it. I didn't want to seem too curious about it in case the gendarme suddenly felt it necessary to inform a superior officer. 'The boy didn't say who it was?'

'No. Some old fellow, he said.' The middle-aged gendarme sniffed. 'To someone that age that's everybody over thirty-five.'

'Sure. Thanks,' I said.

I walked quickly back inside. At the foot of the stairs I stopped and sat down. I turned over the envelope. In a very elegant French hand it was addressed simply: *Monsieur T. Chapel.* I opened it.

Four photographs slipped out into my hand. Polaroids, the indispensable abductor's tool.

I knew what they were going to show but I was still terrified to look. I lifted the first. A stone room, ill-lit, an iron frame bunk, and Romilly lying on it, a dark blanket covering her body. Conscious, dead – I couldn't tell.

I dropped the picture on the stair and shuffled through the other three. She was alive. Two of them showed her, sitting naked on the bed, holding up a newspaper, *Nice Matin*, with Margot's murder and her abduction making the headlines.

I didn't study the Polaroids for more than a second or two. I remembered afterwards the small crucifix in ivory, perhaps, or plaster above the bed. I remembered a side table with a half bottle of supermarket Scotch and a china beaker. Most of all I remembered the pain of seeing her there like that, with all the fear and defeat and humiliation encapsulated in that last gesture as she lifted the newspaper for the camera to record.

There were three lines written in the same large hand on a card in the brown envelope:

*I will speak to you again at midnight tonight. Take the call at the pay phone on the market square. Your daughter is safe until then. Be wise – tell no one.*

Tell no one. But I had to tell somebody. Not Elly, beyond the bare fact that Rom was alive. Not the police. And Margot was no longer there to talk to. It left Claire – and that, in truth, was probably who I had in mind from the beginning. Despite everything, despite the distrust I felt, I still wanted to speak to her. Come into my parlour, said the spider to the fly.

On my way to St Juste I stopped the car in a lay-by and got out. There had been police cars parked along the road and my identity had been checked just after I left Villefranche. A helicopter clattered across the hills, a searchlight sweeping an area down to my right on the lakeside. But there was a certain hopelessness about a search in this area of steep, deeply creviced, rock-strewn woods. The polaroids had shown a stone building, or at least a stone lined cellar. Up here in the hills there were dozens of old *bergeries*, Philippe Rodinet had told me that first day, half collapsed hovels which the shepherds had used to gather their sheep in, on the long journeys from one high pasture to another. But then the gendarmerie had already passed hundreds of men over this area during last night and found nothing beyond that chip of plaster near the back garden of the house.

In the lavender-scented moonlight, with the faint rumble of distant thunder over the mountains ahead, I walked the narrow animal paths. There were long shadows everywhere, cast by pine trees or jutting rocks. Sometimes there was a pile of cut stones with a few rotten beams sticking out at odd angles, a collapsed *bergerie*. Somewhere in these hills, not so many kilometres from here, I was convinced, there was a habitable or half habitable place. A stone room, a fire grate, and an iron bed with a crucifix hanging over it.

I knew now I should have studied the pictures more closely

back at Elaine's house. But it hurt too much. Instead, I tried to dwell upon the objects I had noticed. The Scotch bottle was just a Scotch bottle. There was nothing I could learn from it. But the crucifix might be something else. He might well have put it up there above the bed himself. I had seen him pray. And a priest's soutane had been part of the case from the beginning. Was it possible, that these items were not conveniences, was it possible that he was genuinely devout? Was it possible that Antonio Burgos or rather Pierre Coultard really was a priest?'

At the very least we knew that this man had an interest in a much earlier murderer-priest. We knew that Burgos admired François Villon.

I shook my head and went back to the car. Several times on the track I heard a heavy rustle of an animal in the rosemary undergrowth; a stoat or a wild boar. There were wolves up here too, I'd heard, crossing over from Italy in the last few years. Once my heart was set racing by the screech of an owl that lifted off a branch not more than a foot or two above my head. But they were sounds that would accompany any solitary walk up here in the woods. Beyond them I heard no footstep of a man, no sound of a girl's cry, no sight of the tracks of this strong and reclusive man as he carried his burden up across the limestone rocks through the sprouting fern fronds and low pine branches.

# 52

WE WERE IN a room I hadn't been in before, with long oak beams and plastered walls, and clothes cupboards and a full-length mirror. Claire's dressing room. In the next room I could see a wide unmade bed through a part-open door. She was barefoot, wearing a dark blue robe, her hair damp from the shower. Very slowly, she handed me back the Polaroids. For a moment she kept the note, glancing at it again before she handed that back to me as well. 'You must call Bisset,' she said.

I shook my head. 'How can I?'

'You must.'

'*Tell no one,* Burgos says. *Be wise.* There can't be any doubt what that means.'

'That Romilly will suffer if you don't do what he says?'

'That Romilly will die if I disobey him.'

'You've already done that.'

'By telling you?'

'Yes.' She got up and walked across the room to pour me coffee. 'You've got an hour to make up your mind about the police,' she said. 'I'll get dressed.'

'What for?'

'I'm coming with you. You can't be completely alone.' She stared at me. 'Don't worry. I'll stay out of the way until he calls.'

I put aside the coffee and stood up. I felt my restlessness almost like a physical itch. I walked to the door and looked across a flagged landing and down stone steps to a gallery overlooking the hall. 'I'll go ahead,' I said. I walked out onto the landing. 'Who knows, he could ring early.' I knew he wouldn't but I had to get to the market square. It was the only place I wanted to be.

She came to the door of the dressing room and stood, like a capital in an illuminated manuscript, her long blue robe and framed by the gothic arch. 'I'll get dressed and follow you down,' she said. She paused. 'But you have to call the police first.'

I shook my head.

'You're mad to think you can do this alone. Is it because you're American?' The sarcasm flowed through her voice. 'Because John Wayne's blood flows in your veins?'

'Nothing like that,' I said. 'I just think of two simple facts. He could have killed Rom.'

'But he hasn't.'

'Because he wants something from me.'

She stood thinking.

'A big batch of money, maybe,' I said. 'If he wants it, I'll get it for him somehow. The police sure as hell won't.'

For a long time she looked at me. Then turned away.

I came down the wide, winding stone steps and stopped in the great arching hall with the tapestries and the huge Géricault. It was lit by the magnificent sparkle of an enormous chandelier. I could feel my heart-rate, fast and, sometimes, even missing a beat. Would it really be money that this man would ask for in his midnight phone call? In Elaine's house, moments before he killed Margot he had screamed something about the will. So he knew the terms, at least the broad terms, of Marcel's last testament. Perhaps he had no idea that Sébastien had bankrupted the company. Perhaps he still thought that Romilly was about to inherit twenty-eight-million dollars? So perhaps it *was* about money. That made it simpler. Made it, to me, more reassuring. Meant that we were dealing with a motive we all understood. Meant that we weren't dealing with a sexually deranged lunatic. Money, I kept repeating to myself. Simple as that.

Yet, as I stood there in the massive hall, I felt far from convinced that what Burgos wanted was something so mundane. In some fashion I knew this man wanted more. Something that went deeper and nastier. I thought of the pathetic polaroids of Romilly in my pocket. Whatever stirred his hate, this man wanted more than money. This man wanted blood.

I parked the Renault by the side of the Resistance Museum and looked out over the market square. Up there in the stone château with its dark, dramatic Géricault, false or not, on the wall and its beautiful woman in the long blue robe, it was easy enough to loose track of reality. Easy enough to think that I could and should handle this by myself. But here, in the village, with the coloured lights strung through the plane trees, the bustle at the Café de la Paix, the bursts of laughter from people drinking pastis in the warm night air, I found myself thinking of the police, of Bisset, of whether I really should be calling him, rather than preparing to cross the square to talk a deal with a lunatic who held my daughter captive.

I checked my watch. It was twelve minutes to midnight. I rested my head on the head-rest and tried to relax the tension in my neck. It didn't work. I closed my eyes but I only saw movie versions of the Polaroids in my pocket. At one of the cafes a woman, with an accompanying guitarist, was trawling the tables singing *Je ne regrette rien* in a harshly convincing imitation of Edith Piaf.

The sudden flash of lightning caused a chorus of aahs from the people drinking on the café terraces. Faces were turned upwards expectantly and the explosion of thunder was fast and sharp. Somewhere in front of me a large drop of water hit the thick dust of the *boules* pitch. A neat depression appeared, the size of a half dollar, darker than the surrounding dust. Then another . . . and another.

I don't know if you can talk of the speed of the storm's arrival when the first premonitory skein of cloud across the moon had appeared out at sea the previous night. But in Villefranche at least, less than half a minute changed the market place from a hot and dusty space ringed by cafes, with relaxed patrons eating and drinking, to a chaos of wind-driven rain, toppling parasols, a panic of people, squealing and laughing, grabbing coats and glasses and crowding under any sort of shelter they could find.

The phone booth stood against the dark church wall. The only light in that corner of the square. Rain thrashed it and poured down the glass sides. If I stayed where I was in the car I'd risk not hearing the phone from there. The laughter and the shouted comments exchanged by the people crowded inside the cafes could easily drown out the sound of the phone ringing. I got out of the car. The rain struck me across the face like a whip. I began to run across the market place, saw how ridiculous it was to hope to keep dry, and slowed to a walk. From the bars they were cheering my foolhardiness.

I reached the shelter of the overhanging stonework of the church wall, paused a moment as water spouted down onto my shoulders and took the last few steps to reach the door of the booth. Inside it was as hot as it had been in the market place a few minutes ago. The little mirror in front of me steamed up. Through the glass wall the lighted cafes opposite quivered through the streaming rain. I stared at the phone, checked that it was working, checked that it sat properly on its hook, and waited. Outside the rain slowed and speeded up again; the wind altered direction and violence; the thunder drifted away and returned. I crooked my arm so that I could see my watch. 11.55 p.m.

Time crawled.

The phone rang at midnight, as the church clock began to strike. I swallowed hard to prepare my throat and picked the grey phone from its hook. 'This is Chapel speaking,' I said into the silence.

I could hear breathing there now.

'Thomas Chapel,' I said. 'Thomas Chapel speaking.' I was fighting to control myself, not to alienate the creature at the other end of the line. 'You've got Romilly there. Put her on. Let me speak to her.'

He laughed. A wet, breathy laugh. And silence.

'For God's sake . . . please. Put her on just so I know she's there.' I swallowed again, had to swallow to speak. 'Just so I know she's . . . she's alive.'

'She's alive,' the voice said, the same slightly muffled, Provençal accented voice. Pierre Coultard's voice.

Perhaps I hoped it would intimidate him that I knew. A feeble weapon against him. 'I know who you are,' I said. 'I know you're not Burgos. I know you're Pierre Coultard.'

'Good.'

I waited through a long pause. Was he laughing there on the other end of the line? Chuckling perhaps at his complete dominion over me. Then, the thunderclap.

'I've had her,' he said.

'Oh my God . . .'

'Just think about it.'

There was a note screaming like a bandsaw in my head.

'Big girl,' he said.

I dropped the phone. Then scrabbled it up like a hopeless drunk. I was shaking with disgust, horror. I could hear him laughing. I wanted to scream and cry and kick and batter the glass side of the booth. Somehow I didn't.

But I was gripping the phone hard enough to crack it. I took long, deep breaths. I put everything I had into controlling the volcano of loathing inside me. 'What must I do? Just tell me.' I heard my voice come out flatly, efficiently. For him to give the orders and me to obey, it seemed the only relationship we could have.

'Please tell me what I must do to get my daughter back,' I knew I was pleading. But at times like this you plead.

Again the laugh.

'One thing,' he said. 'One thing only.'

'And you'll give me her back?'

'One thing only – I swear to God.'

'What is it? I'll do anything in my power.'

A doubting intake of breath. 'Will you?'

'Anything,' I said.

'I wonder.'

'*Anything.*'

A long pause. 'Would you kill yourself?'

It took my breath away.

I don't remember putting down the phone. I don't remember leaving the glass booth. At one moment I was doubled up with pain. I remember Claire running through the rain across the square. And I remember her arms round me, locking us together, and the rain thrashing us as I burst out to her, gasping the words. 'I was right, Claire. He's admitted it.' I gestured towards the booth. 'It's Pierre Coultard. Burgos is Pierre Coultard!' And from the cafés people cheered at this drenched couple locked together in the middle of the square.

But all this in patches. I was mad with grief.

# 53

THE OLD STONES wept water. Long black arrowheads of glistening wetness ran down the walls of the church, broad zinc guttering sagged and poured rainwater at the joins. When the wind rose, the café canopies cracked like gunfire and corner lamps swung wildly on their brackets. Fat plane tree leaves with pieces of twig attached whirled around the market place and along the deserted café terraces. The temperature felt as if it had dropped twenty degrees.

I drove the car close up to the church wall so that the rain no longer burst through the broken window. It wasn't comfortable, sitting in soaking clothes, but it was dry enough for Claire to light a cigarette and hand it to me. From across the market place came sounds of laughter and clinking glasses from inside brightly lit cafés with people moving behind steamed up windows.

Claire brushed away water running from her hair down her forehead. She turned to face me. 'Call Bisset, Tom. It's the only thing to do.'

'What good can the police do now, for God's sake? They've already scoured the hills. In this storm there's no chance of finding anything.'

The wind thundered on the side of the car. I sat back, exhausted. Nothing mattered now but Romilly. What Pierre Coultard had offered me was stark. It was Romilly's life for my own. Unable even to begin to grasp the enormity of the choice before me, my mind slipped away almost as if I were falling asleep. The swirling, comforting fogs were a form of self-protection.

'I can't just sit here,' Claire's voice broke my black reverie. 'I'm going to call Bisset.'

She made a quick movement to get out of the car but I reached out and held her wrist. 'For Christ's sake,' I said. 'What will Bisset be able to do? I've got until dawn – four hours maybe.' I pulled Claire round to face me. I could guess what I looked like, distraught, at the end of my tether but it didn't matter now. 'Four hours,' I said. 'If Romilly's to be saved . . .'

'Are you mad? Are you completely mad? What do you intend to do? Throw yourself under a truck? Crash the car off the autoroute? Drown yourself in the lake? Stop and think about it. He isn't going to let Romilly go. He's not arranging an exchange, you fool. He's arranging your *death*!'

She looked so strange. Haunted. Guilty. She was holding back, I was sure of it. 'You know something, for Christ's sake,' I yelled at her. The door was swinging open, the rain bursting in, but I still held onto her wrist.

'I know nothing I haven't told you, Tom. But I have my own stake in all this. I've always believed my father lived and died a man of honour. One of those who behaved like a human being during the war years. But now I'm swamped with doubt. He became a rich man during those years. How did he pull that off? Was he a bounty hunter like the mad American woman says his brother was? Was he selling Jews, too?'

I touched the accelerator and the engine noise swelled.

'Let me out of the car,' she said. 'I'm not going to let you go ahead with it. It's the act of a man as crazy as he is. As crazy as Pierre.' She said the name slowly but firmly. Then her voice dropped but there was no tenderness in it. 'And also, as a matter of fact, I'm not going to let you go ahead with it because I love you. Did you hear me say that? It won't lead to anything. It won't go anywhere. It has nowhere to go. But I love you.' She stopped, her eyes dark as slate. 'Whatever you say, I'm calling Bisset, now,' she said. 'Because I love you.'

I was too shocked to resist as she twisted free and got out of the car. I watched her to the corner of the church. Through the rain streaming down the windshield I could see her standing in the lighted France Telecom booth, punching the buttons. In my head, that swirling fog was returning again, offering me escape, offering me the release of my responsibility onto others, Claire, the police.

But I shook it away. Four hours. Less now. Could Antonio Burgos, Pierre Coultard, imagine any man would do it? Could he know that only a man who saw his life as worthless, as I did, could even think of doing what he demanded?

A man who, in some sense, had been looking for a sacrifice to make.

In the booth Claire was speaking on the phone. She had, I guessed, made contact with Bisset. I sat back in the car and closed my eyes. I suppose it's a thought all parents consider at some time: what would they really give to save a child. An arm, a leg, an organ, an eye. A life?

Could Bisset really do anything more than he had? I imagined convoys of police cars racing through the night. More helicopter searchlight beams raking the broken hillsides. I imagined examinations and tests on the photographs *he* had sent me of Romilly. But I knew none of this would be any good. Certainly not by the dawn which was only a few hours away.

Claire hooked up the phone. The door of the booth squeaked as she backed against it. She held it with the flat of one hand as she stepped out – and let it swing as she turned towards me. Her shoulders and back were soaked, her shirt sticking to her. She paused to run both hands through her wet hair. It was fifteen paces from the phone booth to the car. Fifteen seconds to decide.

She was reaching for the car door as I put the Laguna in drive. I saw bewilderment change to horror in her expression as the car surged past her. Then she was behind me as I gunned the engine and pointed the Renault across the square.

A wasted life doesn't flash across your mind. I'd discovered that sitting in that jet over San Francisco. But some highlights of my earlier life were playing now. The humiliation of that Massachusetts courtroom where my own defence lawyer had described me as 'an addict, a hopeless, pathetic youth quite incapable of rising to the opportunities his family had provided'. Youth! Then the even worse humiliation of prison, the orange coveralls, stamped in blue across the back, and the beatings for refusing the unmentionable favours demanded by block leaders and their hangers on. And on my release my subjugation by Margot and the price I paid . . . the loss of Elaine, and the afternoon in Manhattan when I lost Romilly.

Had I made my mind up? I think so. I took the road out of Villefranche, up past Madame Noyer's house which Auguste Martin had just left on his bicycle when he came across Romilly spread-eagled in the road . . . up past Marty Pearson's rented villa, up the twisting, steeply climbing road towards St Juste. Gendarmerie vans passed me in a steady flow. Then at about two kilometres out of Villefranche I was forced to scream to a stop by a mass of flashing blue lights from a roadblock of police vehicles.

My first thought was that Bisset had made radio contact with them. But among hills and in rain like this radios are far from reliable. This was a routine examination. The inside of the car was examined. The trunk opened. The captain in charge of the operation on the hillside, hunched in a black rain slicker, came over and was handed my driving licence. He apologised and handed it back. 'I saw you with Monsieur Fabius at the murder house, Monsieur Chapel,' he said.

I stood, drenched in front of him. 'Then I can go.'

'*Sûrement.*' He was about to turn away.

'Captain. You're still looking. You haven't given up?' I gestured to the gendarmerie vans passing on their way down to Villefranche as I was standing here. I was pretty sure they were pulling out.

'We're keeping some units up here, Monsieur,' he said. 'Although whether your daughter's still in the area . . .' He shrugged his doubts. 'And in any case, *franchement* . . .' he gestured to the falling rain, 'until it lets up there's not much we can do . . .' His moustache hung wet and heavy. 'Even then, to tell you truth, Monsieur, when this rain stops the ground mist will rise like a smoke screen across these hills. It's going to be mid morning before we can do anything. I'm sorry.'

I got back into the Renault confirmed in my decision to do what Pierre Coultard wanted. The captain had unwittingly made it clear – I was on my own.

I sat for another minute or two as I watched the gendarmerie Nevadas and Citroën vans form up and pull away down towards Villefranche in a tight convoy, leaving a dark, rain-lashed hillside. Then I put the Renault in drive and began to climb the hill.

We pretend we make decisions. Was I really going to do it? Nothing like the rationality we like to think plays its part in our decisions entered my head. But in the next two minutes of spurting rain and skidding wheels, rain so dense the headlights just reflected back on themselves, I seized some moment of transient certainty.

I made up my mind.

Every now and again as the road bent the right way, I could see the distant outline of the Château St Juste, a dark hulk except for the lights flickering from its top floors. Once or twice a police car passed me, the last in the procession making its way back to the coast.

Raw rock hemmed the roadside on the left. On the valley side, the ground dropped away in a steep slope of stunted umbrella pines and jagged limestone rock. In every flash of lightning, I could see the black lake below and the rooftop outline of the drowned village at its centre. Another half kilometre and I would have reached the spot Antonio Burgos, Pierre Coultard as I was just beginning to think of him, had selected.

There were two bends before the monument his brother had had erected to him. I swept round the first. Somewhere down there he was waiting for me. For a second I held an image of the man, not tall but powerful, rain streaming down his face as he crouched expectantly among the bushes. No longer the half-articulate Antonio Burgos but now Pierre Coultard, the infinitely cunning auto-didact. Melodrama even gave him a priest's soutane.

The last bend flashed by. The road stretched before me straight for three or four hundred yards. I was following precise instructions. I gave it gas and the Renault seemed to lift forward. Trees, mostly thin, reedy pines and thick rosemary bushes lined the valley side of the road here. I don't think I had a single thought in my head as I jerked the wheel. As the car left the road I heard small trees crack, I felt rocks clatter against the underside of the car. Eyes tight closed, I felt the explosive impact of sideswiping the carved stone of Pierre Coultard's monument. Doors burst open. I was moving through air now, flung free of the car. Suddenly my eyes were open. I was tumbling through the dark. For seconds I seemed to float in the air as the back of the car came up over my head and the twin beams of the headlights suddenly flared full in my face.

In that moment I saw my chances of life as infinitesimal. But if I died now I had done all I could possibly do for Romilly. And if I lived, I still had the gun.

# 54

HIS POLICE SLICKER dripping water, Polydore Bisset stood on the patch of gravel in front of the shattered monument to Pierre Coultard. The air was damp, heavy with humidity. Every leaf in the woods in front of him seem to drip water. For the first time in weeks he could feel a chill on his face. The headstone flanked by columns wound with stone-carved vine leaves had been cracked in two, but the inscription could be clearly read across the six centimetre gap: *Pierre Coultard. Héro de la Resistance. Tué le 2 Novembre, 1942. Mort pour la France.* Bisset read the words out loud.

Claire Coultard stood behind him, her arms folded across her breast. In jeans and the dark blue puff jacket she had been lent by one of the gendarmes, she was still cold. 'In ten minutes this valley will be covered in mist,' she said. 'The only way to locate him is to get some men down there.'

Bisset turned from the monument. 'We'll have some lights up in a moment. And equipment. I can't send men down there in these conditions.'

Claire came forward and looked down at the tyre marks and the snapped and scarred pine trees where the Renault had burst off the road. Beyond that, the drop disappeared into a mist-laden nothingness. 'Is it possible he's down there, still alive?' she said.

Bisset faced her. 'You know these hills better than I do, Madame,' he said sombrely. 'But I'd say the rocks are too sharp, the drop here just too steep for there to be any real chance.'

Claire nodded and felt in her jeans pocket for cigarettes. Lighting one, she offered the packet to Bisset as an afterthought. He shook his head.

'Did you become friends, you and Tom Chapel?'

She nodded.

'Strange,' he said. 'In the circumstances.'

She smiled briefly. 'Less than friends. Lovers. Of a sort.' She drew deeply on her cigarette and exhaled into the mist. 'I don't think he'd decided who he loved. Me . . . Romilly's mother, the Englishwoman . . .'

'Not the sister, the ex-sister?'

'You know about all that?'

Bisset nodded.

'Who can tell?' Claire said. 'Maybe her too. I think he was one of those men who could love any number of women. But he wouldn't have killed himself for any of them. For Romilly, it was different. Perhaps because she was innocent.'

Behind them a convoy of police cars approached. Claire stood away as the line of vehicles pulled to a halt and uniformed gendarmes swarmed out carrying ropes and climbing equipment. Generators were set up on the roadside and started with string pulls. The lieutenant in charge came over and shook hands with Bisset and they both went forward to examine the drop. After a few moments' discussion, the lieutenant took over the preparations for the climb down into the valley. Electric cables were laid from the generators to powerful lights fixed to trees above the point at which the Renault had been driven over.

Bisset walked back slowly to where Claire stood. 'Won't you go back? This could take some time.'

'You mean I might not want to be here when they bring him up.'

'That could be.'

'I'll stay.'

He nodded and they stood in silence watching the half dozen gendarmes in coveralls and climbing boots as they prepared to abseil down. The mist had thickened to a point where the monument to Pierre Coultard was no more than a shape rising like a Gothic ruin in the mist.

'Did your father ever talk about him?' Bisset asked, gesturing to the monument.

'Very little. I hadn't really thought about it before,' she said. 'When I think about it now I realise he was anxious that we didn't grow up worshipping our dead uncle.' She paused. 'Just things he said – "a monument doesn't necessarily make a hero . . ." a careful disparagement of Pierre's hero status.'

'And yet it was Marcel who organised the monument.'

'Yes,' she said. 'It was Marcel. I can understand why. There was honour to be preserved. The honour of France was not an empty idea in 1945, Monsieur. Such dreadful things had been done. Heroic things too, of course. Many of them. But France was desperately in need of any honour she could get.'

As they watched, the first two gendarmes took the strain on the ropes then, on the lieutenant's signal, pushed off backwards into the rolling mist.

# 55

NEEDLE SHARP LIMESTONE rocks had stripped away the side of the Laguna. The second or third bounce before it wedged between two rocks had snapped the chassis. The engine spat out a thin stream of steam and water. One wheel, trailing shredded rubber, was lodged in an umbrella pine; the grey leather driver's seat sat, incongruously upright, upon a flat rock surface.

It seemed to me that I opened my eyes a half dozen times and slipped back happily enough into a dreamy sleep. When I finally held my eyes open for more than a few seconds I found that I lay propped up, my back supported by a thick rosemary bush, about thirty yards from the car. The rain, its driving force abated by the projections of rock, streamed comfortingly down my face. *I feel, therefore I am.*

Above me, a hundred or hundred-and-fifty feet at least, I could see in the mist the faintest smudge of a car's headlights. That would be roughly at the monument to Pierre Coultard. Hero of the Resistance. The monument that commemorated not his death, but his removal from the life he knew, from friends and family. All this, it seemed, with the connivance, maybe even at the behest of, his elder brother. And where Pierre Coultard, in his way, had departed this life, he clearly envisaged I would depart this life too.

I vaguely thought of police cars, gendarmerie patrols, the helicopters from Toulon Aeronavale. But, of course, even in my half-reverie, I knew that all but a token force had been withdrawn. They believed Romilly had been taken out of the area. The captain had said as much on the road. All this I contemplated in an eerily relaxed state of mind, as if these issues weren't matters of life and death to Romilly.

Very slowly the pressure within the cracked radiator diminished and the hissing fell away. Equally slowly, I emerged from my dream state. The patter of rain on rock and leaf urged me gently back to reality. Then, above me, and somewhere in front of me, a sound that brought the world back with a frightening immediacy: a man's low curse. Spoken in Spanish.

I reached down to check the Mauser pistol had not been thrown clear during my fall. At least it felt as though I was reaching down – but a numbness from my right hand to my shoulder seemed to hold the arm like a dead weight. Panic flared in me. I tried to move the other arm. The pain in my left hand made me gasp, but the arm moved. I looked down. There was no blood, but the fingers seemed at all angles, broken or perhaps dislocated. Certainly incapable of pulling a tightly bound pistol from my belt, aiming it and pulling the trigger.

Above me Pierre Coultard emitted a series of simian grunts as he worked his way down the rockside towards the wreck of the Laguna. I could see him now, a dark blob appearing for moments at a time against a background of pale, wet limestone rock. I tried my legs, first right, then left and both seemed to work without more pain than might be bad bruising. I turned my head from one side to another and felt no pain at all. I bent forward at the waist and all those muscles, ligaments and joints seemed to be functioning normally. So I had come away from the wreck with a paralysed right arm and a shattered left hand. And a gun strapped to my waist which I was incapable of using.

I could no longer see him. Could hear nothing but the wind as it rose and swept down the valley. The thinner stems of trees and bushes thrashed around me; huge sheets of rain curtained myself, the Renault and the man coming for me from anybody who might have been passing on the road far above. I was on the point of surrender. I knew that longing for some sort of cowardly quietus.

But then, somewhere deep inside my head, the tune changed. I saw that my idiot gamble with the crash had left Romilly more isolated from help than ever. Pierre Coultard, motivated by whatever hatred born of madness or imagined revenge, was bound to find me. From then it would be a matter of moments for him to cut my throat or batter my brains out with his shepherd's club.

Or I could fight back. Of course, I wasn't used to fighting back. But I wasn't incapable. I had a gun. I could feel a faint tingling down my paralysed arm. Perhaps I could do something about my left hand before he found me. The words I heard in my muddled head were my own, but the voice seemed to be the voice of General John. No surrender, he seemed to say. Take it all the way. As you die, at least know that you have done everything you could possibly do for Romilly. At least know you have not died as you've lived. That last sentence was in a different voice. My mother's, prompting.

I was aware that I was fading in and out of full consciousness. I took deep breaths. I shook my head to banish the dizziness from my brain, blinked to clear the double vision from my sight. Now it was up to me alone. I didn't think he had seen me. I pushed back into the rosemary bush. I lay on my back, the rain falling directly onto my face. I placed my left hand on my chest and winced with fear at the angles in which the broken fingers pointed. My right hand was buzzing with returning life. I tried flexing the hand and the fingers moved. Slowly but not in response to the messages my brain was sending. I did it again and again but I could only move all four fingers in unison. I would need my other hand, battered though it was. I brought my left hand to my right. I could hear Coultard close by now. Muttering to himself in French now, '*Où est-ce que tu t'es caché, mon petit Juif?* Where've you hidden yourself, my little Jew?' poking at the bushes, clambering over slippery rocks. I took the thumb and all four fingers of my left hand, closed my eyes and pulled. The pain forced a shout, a sort of honking noise through the back of my throat. He must have heard it. I held up my hand. The two middle fingers were clearly broken, already misshapen and swelling. But the thumb moved and the index finger seemed to have been wrenched back into its joint. I was as battle-worthy as I was going to get.

I could see him now, drawn towards me by my shout, sure-footed even on the wet rocks, swinging and sliding down. In one hand he carried a club, a big, heavy tree root and, hanging from his belt, a length of cord.

With a tropical suddenness it had stopped raining. I felt the shield of obscurity, a fragile insubstantial shield but the only one I had, had been withdrawn from me. And he had seen me. I was certain of that now. Moments later he had disappeared behind the flailing branches of a stunted oak. When I heard him again, he was behind me. The paralysed right hand would never have gripped and pointed a gun. With my left, I fumbled for the Mauser but a powerful arm was hooked round my neck. I smelt an earthy wetness, a tobacco breath, a soap and sweat combination. The arm tightened in a series of powerful movements. I tore at it with my broken hand. Hopelessly. The pain burnt like an electric surge.

I passed out.

# 56

I WAS ON my knees next to him. My arms roped. A cord looped round my neck. I was crouching by the water's edge. Like a dog beside its master.

My left hand throbbed pain. My right arm was numb as if wrapped in a thick sleeve. I had a vague sense that I had been moving, stumbling forward in response to the rope, but had no idea how far we had come from the crashed Renault.

I turned my head to the man beside me. He was facing the lake, thumbs hooked into the waistband of his jeans. His rough shirt stuck to his broad shoulders. Sparse grey hair was drying tight to his scalp and his ears, naturally flat to the sides of his head, gave him a demonic look.

There was still cloud, silver-black strips running in parallels across the sky. The moon, just past full, sought gaps in the cloud cover to shoot sharp rays toward the earth. The silence now that the rain had stopped was broken by the gush and trickle of new streams. All around me the hillside was steaming. Mist rose from the surface of the lake. I could still see the village knee-deep in water, still see the winking lights of the château up at the far end of the valley. But up on my left, where the road ran, the side of the valley was obscured by a droplet-laden white fog, already folding in on itself and tumbling silently down the hillside.

'Pierre Coultard,' I said.

He turned unhurriedly. His eyes were deep sunk, the lines on his face emphasised by the glister of water on his cheeks. The change in him since I had followed him through Nice was more the change in my view of him. Certainly he was no longer the mixed race North African peasant I had seen in the gendarmerie interview room. What I saw in his face now was a monkish, ascetic quality. But with the addition of a cruel contempt.

If I dare to think, I see that I have never felt such intense fear. His presence, his silence is totally commanding. I want to ask him a hundred questions, but I'm afraid of what a question might precipitate. What does he plan to do with me, with Romilly? I admit even to myself the answers to both questions are too obvious for words. Claire was right. But I need other answers. *Why* should he want to kill two people, Americans, strangers to him? To make sure that the Coultard estate goes to Claire and Sébastien? I don't think so. He never even knew Claire and her brother as children or adolescents. He hasn't returned from North Africa or Spain or wherever for their sakes.

He seems to sense that I am about to ask him a question. The lips turn down; the lines from nose to the corners of his mouth deepen. Can you be an aesthete and a sensualist at the same time? I think of him looking at Romilly like this and my stomach lurches in fear for us both.

'All right, you can do what you like to me,' I say though I don't for a moment mean it. 'But you promised me my daughter's life. You swore to God.'

I push myself to my feet. Stand rocking before him.

'One thing, Jew . . .' he says. 'Crashing that car . . . it took courage.' The words emerge with reluctance. He turns away. 'Your mother had courage, too.' He spoke out towards the lake.

*Jew!* Is that how he sees me? Is that single fact the focus of his hatred, that I am Jewish, or part Jewish? Part Jewish and related to him as his brother's son? Does he believe my Jewishness taints the Coultard line? Are these the mad thoughts that inspire him to murder?

'My mother,' I say. 'I never knew my mother.'

His eyes rest on me, his lower lip turned down. 'Isobel Berne,' he says, ruminatively. 'The bitch.'

He bends and takes up the cord which binds my arms and is looped round my neck. The mist, steaming from the hillside, is whiter where it rises from the lake and thick enough to reduce the outlines of the half-drowned village to an impressionist's arrangement of roof planes of the village. The cloud breaks to allow passing shafts of moonlight. The church spire stands above the roofs wavering in the enclosing greyness.

I am stunned by the realisation that Sanya's story is true. Wherever she found it, however she traced it, she has arrived at the truth. Isobel Berne was my mother, a Jewish girl whose father had owned the Château St Juste at the beginning of the war.

Up on the road, a misty vehicle headlight passes through the rolling mist. And another. Have the police resumed the search? Coultard's head follows the movement of the lights. I think of shouting. I try to guess whether the mist will muffle the sound. I stand listening but I can hear no sound of the engines as the headlights pass in an arc across the treetops. As they fade, he tugs hard on the cord and I jerk forward with the first clumsy, uncertain steps of a laden pack animal.

He leads me towards the edge of the lake and splashes into the shallows. I'm two or three yards behind him. He drags me forward till I stumble and trip. I am on my knees again as he turns on me. He kicks me high in the shoulder so that so that I lose my balance and roll over, fighting to keep my mouth above the water level. He presses my head down with his boot. I see the grey surface line of the water just above my eyes. I am gulping, choking water. Is he going to drown me here?

Then he pulls my head upright with a jerk on the cord. Kicks me again and growls at me to get to my feet. I splutter water, try to clear it from my lungs. There's no fight left in me. Every torturer knows that water is the best weapon. I try to stand but the strength's just not there. He takes the noose round my neck and hauls on it. The cord cuts into my neck and I gag and choke but I stumble upright, coughing, spitting water. Pathetic even in my own eyes.

He looks at me with a sort of blank hatred. Contempt. Then we set out again, the white cord over his shoulder as he wades through the thigh-deep water with me, reeling, gasping, barely on my feet, splashing up great quantities of white water as the mist closes round us.

# 57

ON THE TOP road, Fabius had joined them. He stood close to Claire in his light grey trenchcoat, trying to be official and protective at the same time. For a few moments they watched as the gendarmerie sergeant, who had led the second team down, was hauled back over the edge of the drop. He unbuckled himself quickly and crossed towards where Bisset stood next to Fabius.

'*Monsieur le Juge*,' he said to Fabius, shaking hands with him while he unhooked the strap of his climbing helmet. All around him men stopped what they were doing in the hope of hearing the result of the search above the roar of the generators.

'So?' Fabius said, his chin rising.

'No sign of a body, Monsieur,' the sergeant reported briefly. He rubbed at the tree scratches on his face and turned to Bisset. 'The car was a Laguna, *oui*? Alpes Maritimes registration.'

Bisset nodded briskly. 'How is it?'

'Torn to pieces of course. But no fire.'

'And no sign of Chapel.'

'Correct.'

'He couldn't have been thrown clear higher up?' Bisset said.

'Could have been. The vehicle struck the hillside at least twice on its way down. There are broken trees, pieces of bodywork trapped among the rocks. At two distinct points before you get to the wreck itself.'

'You checked all around those two points?' Fabius said.

'We did, Monsieur. But we're not going to find him there. Lower down, perhaps twenty metres from the wreck of the vehicle, there are several strips of clothing.'

'Strips of clothing?' Claire said.

The sergeant looked at her. 'Torn pieces of a shirt probably, Madame. Caught in a tree.'

'But absolutely no sign of him,' Fabius said.

'Absolutely is not a word you can use down there until we get twenty men searching in daylight, Monsieur. There are hundreds of cracks in the rock. Crevasses anything from a metre to ten metres deep. Trees and bushes growing all over them. It's not a parking lot.'

'Quite,' Fabius said. 'I understand the difficulties.'

Bisset stood, his arms folded in front of his chest, thinking hard. 'You said the torn pieces of material were near the car.'

'A few metres above the car. But there's something like a trail leading from there down towards the edge of the lake.'

'A trail?'

'Scraps of cloth . . . a shoe . . . It's not much. Maybe he saw our lights up here and was trying to get to somewhere where he'd be seen.'

Bisset shook his head. 'He'd sit tight and try to call out to your men as they came down.'

'Makes sense,' the sergeant said. 'But he's not down there, lieutenant. At least he's not down there trying to attract our attention.'

Bisset nodded. 'So either he's lying unconscious among the rocks somewhere. Or he was carried away by someone.'

'Dead or alive,' Fabius added.

Claire stared hard at him, then turned her attention back to the sergeant.

'What do you think?' Bisset asked her. But she just shook her head, unable to answer.

'So he, or they . . .' Fabius stared down into the white mist-filled bowl of the valley. 'He, or they, could be anything from a half kilometre to a kilometre away by now.'

'At least, Monsieur,' the sergeant said.

Bisset stood thinking. '*Bien*,' he said. '*Très bien*. Then I think we have to make the announcement.'

# 58

Mist whirled around us stirred by our own movement. Water birds croaked, disturbed by our heavy splashing steps. I had little ability to keep my balance as I dragged my feet from the clinging mud and my legs were torn by broken branches or stones or rusting cart wheels or oil drums, all invisible under the dark water.

From time to time there was a dip in the bed of the lake and we were both pushing forward at chest height. I knew instinctively that if I lost my footing at this depth he would not turn back to pull me up. I knew that any one of the next fifty steps could mark my end.

Then suddenly the bed of the lake became hard and strangely flat. There were still obstacles, stones, pieces of timber, but they were easier to negotiate when my feet weren't sucked down by mud. Better still, the water was getting shallower and I realised we were following the rising line of the old submerged road into the village.

Now Pierre Coultard wasn't turning and shouting and pulling on the rope every few seconds. Instead I had worked myself into a rhythm: if I kept a rough eight paces behind him, didn't move up too close or drag back so much that he would give a tug which jerked me forward choking for air, he would keep moving without turning. And I could use the seconds, never more than half a minute at a time, to work my left hand up, under the cords, towards my waistband where, almost miraculously, I could still feel the gun pressing into the hollow of my hip.

For five minutes we splashed forward through the mist. From the man in front of me came a stream of mingled madness, curses of obscene ferocity, scraps of Spanish, snatches of the old Latin Mass, Villon's *Ballad of the Hanged Men*, a French marching song, the *Sambre et Meuse*. Then, rising above it the mad voice bawling: *Who would wish harm to the Kingdom of France?*

Enclosed in the mist, he seemed to have no thought that others, police, searchers up on the hillside, might hear him.

Straining, I found I could just touch the gun butt. I could reach out and try to grip the pistol. But what if my fingers weren't yet strong enough? If these broken fingers slipped, if I lost grip on the butt, the Mauser would fall from my waistband and be lost forever in the waters of the lake.

I was increasing in exhaustion yet gaining strength. I could feel this strange physical paradox in my leg muscles, in my shoulders and neck. If I ever got free enough, with or without the gun, I could summon up the strength to tackle him. The exhaustion could be thrown aside, it always can. And I was impelled by the thought of Romilly held somewhere, probably in an upper room of one of the village houses that had been emerging slowly over the past weeks from the flooded lake. The return of anger was another sign of life. Ten minutes ago, when he had first dragged me like a roped animal into the water, I had not the strength to feel anything but fear. I still felt fear, but it was fear for Romilly as well as myself. And it was not unmixed by a determination to do anything I had to, to destroy this creature in front of me.

We approached the village. A village that was given a weird normality by the mist. From this distance, a hundred yards or so from the first house, the fact that the church and every dwelling stood in several feel of water was obscured. The absence of lights or movement reminded me of those mournful French villages in the north of the country where every inhabitant is long a-bed and even streetlights are extinguished by midnight.

There was one final stretch to go before we reached what must have been the St Juste village square. If I was going to use the gun, this was the time to use it. I struggled with both hands. If I stretched, the broken fingers made me want to scream with pain but I was able to use my right hand to push the Mauser slightly closer my left. I reached for it, my eyes on the back of the laughing, shouting maniac leading me. I found the butt, gripped it hard, or hard as my damaged hand could hold it, and drew it from my waistband. I fumbled the safety catch, struggling to insert my index finger into the trigger guard before it slipped away from me. My arms were still bound and I would have to turn side on towards Coultard to train the barrel on him. I brought my right forearm up to lift the gun high enough to hit him. Pain surged through the broken hand as I tightened my grip.

Fearful of losing my hold, my reaction was to squeeze harder. Pain lacerated my fingers – and the pistol squeezed out of my hand and splashed into the water. I cried out in frustration and Coultard jerked on the rope, taking my cry for pain, and I splashed forward two or three paces from where the gun had fallen, lost forever.

He turned towards me and stared without asking why I had cried out. Mist rolled around the buildings around us, a moving presence all its own, lit from above by the watching moon.

Then suddenly a voice spoke with a vast valley-filling volume and an echo and re-echo that was nothing short of terrifying:

'Monsieur Chapel . . . Monsieur Chapel. This is Judge Fabius. I have a message for you.' Even amplified so that it rolled like the mist across the hills, I could recognise his academic English accent. 'Monsieur Chapel, your daughter Romilly is safe. She was found barely conscious in the hills just half an hour ago. She is suffering from exposure but no major physical injury. She is being treated now.'

There followed several clicks and another voice, it was Bisset's, speaking in French. 'We don't know your situation, Tom. And we don't know for sure whether Pierre Coultard is holding you. If so, this is a message for you both. We know from the position of the Renault roughly where you started from. We have already several hundred men assembling at each end of the valley. We're coming in to get you.'

Pierre Coultard's head lifted towards the hills. 'You'll be too late, Messieurs. Far too late.'

'I'm talking to Pierre Coultard now,' Bisset's amplified voice said. 'You will have one single chance to give yourself up. And only one.' The voice rolled and echoed away along the valley. 'One and only one.' The echo reminded me that the warning applied to me too.

Coultard and I stood not ten feet from each other. His face was set, drawn tight across the cheeks by the drying silt in the water.

'She beat you,' I said, relief whirling through me. 'She got away.'

'No . . . I showed mercy. It can give intense pleasure to the donor. Your girl couldn't believe she was free. She crept away like an animal. All that female pride frightened out of her. And what does it matter now if she lives? My fool nephew Sébastien has made sure there's no Coultard money to inherit. And your daughter is welcome to that pile of stones up on the hill. Without money to hold it up, it'll collapse like the Saracen Tower in a year or two.'

He looked down and stirred the water with the end of the rope. His head came up slowly with infinite menace. 'And as I said, what does it all matter now? Now that I have the one I wanted. I have you.'

# 59

A M I PREPARED to die? I'd been prepared to crash the car into the valley, and into near certain death less than an hour ago. But I am not going to die now. Now that Romilly is safe. The fact that her life is no longer a bargaining counter gives me a determination to live, or at least to make sure Pierre Coultard dies with me.

We had reached the old village market square. Where the original ground level has dropped here, perhaps from centuries of usage, the water level is correspondingly higher. At times I am wading at waist level; once or twice water flows across my shoulders as I'm dragged forward. He could drown me here, I realise, with a mere twitch on the rope.

The stink of rotting timber, of floorboards and dead trees is all around us. We cross a square which must have been once not unlike the market place at Villefranche. The ancient church with its added spire rises before us. The Romanesque stone doorway, its oak door leaning at an angle where its rusted lower hinges have snapped, is the entrance I floated through with Sanya the night before. Now, as he drags me up the stone steps into the church, the water falls away to about knee level. But there are no lights, no candlelight to indicate Sanya was there, no sign of the boat tied up anywhere. She is in Villefranche perhaps, or one of the remote *bergeries* around the lake, sheltering from the storm with her goats.

Irreligious as I am, I'm struck again by the desolation of the place. A sudden white shaft of moonlight shows stone effigies chipped away, pews and ancient brasswork stripped from the grey cavern of the nave. Epitaphs have been prised from the walls and coffins removed from the niche behind. The timber pulpit appears to have been attacked with axes and the solid stone altar table has lost its decorative carving. Where the grey walls rise, enormous areas of plaster have peeled way. The glass in every window of the clerestory has been smashed, yet most of the roof remains, and only above the altar is a large area of moonlit sky visible where the hammer-beams have collapsed.

Down here, the smell is of wet plaster. Even the water we trudge through as we walk the length of the nave swirls up in whitish eddies as our feet stir the bottom. We are heading toward the altar, two or three steps above the level of the nave. Coultard is dragging on the rope so hard now that I have to splash behind him, gasping for breath. When he stops, I stumble the last few steps, grateful to be out of the water, and collapse on the stone paving, green with dry algae. It is only then that I have a moment to register that the altar is draped with strangely old fashioned clothes that I immediately recognise as the styles Sanya wears. And open on the altar and scattered beside it, four or five old-fashioned suitcases. More clothes stream from them, all women's coats and dresses of another age. Print frocks and trailing silk stockings, silk ball gowns, straw hats and a scatter of 1940s shoes. But the women Marcel Coultard had brought over the mountains were not all rich and fashionable. There are other sets of clothing, from other suitcases, the dresses or coats of patched, cheaper cloth, the shoes scuffed and down at heel. The possessions of the forty women who had made it no further than St Juste in their bid for life.

'The mad woman found them,' Pierre says. 'After forty-five years hidden in a priest-hole on the hillside that dated back to the Wars of Religion, the madwoman found them. Clothes like that suited her fantasy.'

He glances down at the scattered clothes with contempt. But he says nothing more as he tethers me to the altar rail. For a few moments we look at each other. I am willing him to talk. If I'm to die, first I want to *know*. I sit up, my back supported against a stone pillar. He watches me with an eerie lack of expression, as if he is examining my features for the first time.

I know I have to ask. 'Why bring me here?' I say.

He sits back against the altar rail and for a moment I think there'll be no answer. Then he nods to himself. 'It's true,' he says, 'that I could have cut your throat in the hospital parking lot any time in the last two weeks.'

'But you chose not to.'

'Yes. I chose not to.' He pauses. 'In your case, I think a certain formality is called for.'

*A certain formality is called for.* No, not the words of an itinerant feria-worker.

'Are you a really priest? Or a seminary reject perhaps?'

He peers at me under his heavy eyebrows. The eyes have that dark, fixed quality of Picasso's eyes. 'I was a lay brother for forty years in a Spanish monastery. The servant of servants of God. Their cook, their woodcutter, their grave-digger when the time came. You must forgive me if I've absorbed something of the manner of priests.'

'Is that why you wore the soutane?'

'Mostly because it offered a form of invisibility. Uniforms do.'

'What sort of believer are you, to do what you've done?'

'I pray to God direct. At the monastery I saw enough to know that no man needs the intervention of priests and monks.'

'If you hated life at the monastery that much, why didn't you leave?'

'Return to France? My own brother would have had me hunted down. It was made clear what would happen to me if I tried to come back. But the lust for life is stronger than the fear of death.' He looked at me and smiled. 'I was growing old. I had barely known a woman. Though when I was young I had known a good dozen monks. So what, I thought, if my brother had me hunted down. So what if his ageing Resistance comrades took a contract in my name. I'd have a year or two of life.' There is a savagery about his eyes now, about his expression. For a chilling moment I can see what life means to him. For Pierre Coultard life means violence. Life means death.

We stared at each other for a long moment.

'I talk too much. My life has been a life of restraint, of isolation, of few daily words, rationed like wine . . . You with your bright colourful life of the American streets, the neon, gasoline in the nostrils, the scent of women . . . For a normal man, an average man, an *homme moyen sensuel*, you can't imagine the deprivation of the monkish world.'

'But I can see why you read François Villon.'

He lifted his head in surprise, appreciation even. 'Yes. The hypocrisy of priesthood was too much for him, too. He needed the streets, the whores, the buzz you Americans call it, of everyday life. But certain dreams, certain beliefs. A belief in France.'

'It's one of his refrains, isn't it? *Who would wish harm to the Kingdom of France?*'

'I don't have to tell you who. The English in Villon's day. The Jews in mine.'

I looked across at the sad tumble of dresses and shoes spread across the altar. The church was full of creaks and the sound of dripping water. 'What harm could these women have brought to France?'

He looked down at the clothes and shrugged. 'They themselves? None. But they would have children and their children's children.' He dismissed the subject with a wave of his hand. 'So my life has made me ache to talk, Monsieur Chapel. Even to you. Let's see, what shall I tell you, now? Not that I'm going to kill you. You already know that. But, as I said, revenge should have a form of ceremony to it.' His eyes closed on my face. 'Know that I've suffered a lifetime because of you.' He was staring down at me. 'Know that I'm not prepared for you to leave the world relatively painlessly, victim of a quick thrust to the gut.'

I let him talk. No interruption that might remind him that the gendarmerie knew more or less where we were and would surely be here within minutes.

'You sit there, staring. Face as white as it was when you were a child.' The Provençal accent was still strong but the cadences were from his other world. 'Eyes as frightened as they were the first time I saw you.'

'You knew me?' I asked him. 'You knew me when I was a child?'

'I knew your mother.' He spoke each word separately, deliberately. Significantly.

A new thought made me tremble. Had I made a mistake about Marcel Coultard? It made sense now. The child he'd hidden away in the orphanage at Pézenas was Isobel's child, certainly. But not Marcel's?

The possibility rushed at me. I almost retched at the idea. 'You knew my mother,' I said, dreading his next words. 'You knew her well?'

'Of course.' He allowed a long pause. 'We grew up together,' he said. 'Of course we knew each other well. Except Isobel was the daughter of the château and I was the son of the laundress.'

'Tell me,' I urged him.

He looked around him, out through the broken windows to the dark hillsides. I'd no doubt he was looking for gendarmerie lights – but there were none. 'Your mother wasn't just one of the old Jewesses who came down humping their suitcases full of clothes from Paris.' He gestured to the suitcases behind him. 'Her

410

family owned the château – until old Joseph Berne was turfed out.'

'He was interned by the Vichy police.'

'Of course, as a Jew. Films were one of the first businesses banned to them. Ciné-Berne as it was called then. A few cinemas, fleapits along the coast. One decent size place in Nice, I remember, the Roxy.'

'So Marcel worked for Monsieur Berne . . .' I was bizarrely aware that I was talking about my grandfather. 'And you too?'

'I was too young. Not as clever as Marcel, the Jew said. Not fit to scrub the floors in the offices old Berne had downstairs under the fake Géricault. Marcel worked for him, not me.'

'And you're saying Marcel stole the business from him? Legally, under the Vichy anti-Semitic Laws? Made Ciné-Berne into Ciné-Coultard?'

His face tightened.

'Marcel lived the life of a rich bourgeois. An aristo almost . . .' He breathed deeply.

'While you were a servant of the servants of God. Is that it? Are you asking for pity?'

He moved quickly. His foot lashed out and caught me on the shoulder. I rolled over and lay face down. His boot hit me in the lower back and I shouted in pain.

'You're not going to inherit, Monsieur. I am not going to see a Israelite inherit. Even the wreckage that Sébastien left . . . Not the Israelite whose one single cry in the night betrayed me. If I'd only got to you first . . .' He stopped.

As I turned my head towards him I saw he was listening. His head was cocked. Whatever it was I had not heard it over my shout of pain. I moved and he gestured to me to be silent.

I rolled over to look up at the gallery. I could hear it now, the sound of shuffling in the planked loft above us. And the bleat of a goat, muffled.

'Marcel never stole from *anyone*,' Sanya's voice came from the darkness on the gallery above us. There was a compact fury in the words. 'How dare you, of all people, call Marcel a thief.'

We were both looking up as she came forward. Her hair hung lank. She was dripping water. Mud streaked the yellow silk ballgown she wore. The skirt was stained brown mud to her thighs, the bodice dark with wetness. She held my Mauser out in front of her, the barrel pointing down at Pierre Coultard. Had she been there, just behind us in the mist. Had she seen me drop the gun and recovered it from the water?

'It's here,' she said. From the table next to the gallery rail, she lifted a thin leather bound book and thumbed it open. 'The truth is here.'

Pierre began to say something but she shook her head for silence.

The Mauser in her other hand remained steadily on Coultard. In what, I suppose, she imagined was Isobel's voice, she made to read, although I could see that she could have spoken the words by heart: '*August 6, 1941. Papa and Marcel have come to an arrangement which they hope will preserve Ciné-Berne intact until Vichy is overthrown. Funds are to be transferred to Marcel to buy the company from the Vichy Administrators. Today, the prices of seized Jewish property are rock bottom. There are enough profiteers for Marcel to look as if he's simply doing what so many others are doing, exploiting the new anti-Jewish laws. But his promise is to hand it back to the family when the war is over. And it's a promise I know he will keep.*'

Sanya glanced up and rested the gun hand on the bannister rail. '*If it were Pierre, of course, he would never keep his promise. The good work he does for the Resistance is to impress Marcel. Not because he hates the terrible injustice he sees around him. I am afraid of Pierre. I am convinced he is an anti-Semite at heart . . .*'

I glanced at Pierre. There was an ugly expression on his face, a smile of anger.

Holding the journal in one hand and the gun steadily in the other, Sanya moved along the gallery to the narrow staircase, descending very slowly step by step until she was over half-way down. The goat, I noticed, stood at the top.

I was trying to work out which persona Sanya was inhabiting. The rich California out-of-time hippie, the woman Dave of Stop Mountain had cynically abandoned and persuaded to search for an alter ego somewhere here in the South of France, or the woman she had found among the clothes and the diary hidden in the church priest-hole, my mother, Isobel Berne.

'Release him,' Sanya ordered Pierre. And when Pierre stood, unmoving, she raised the Mauser.

He came forward slowly. From his pocket he took the long-handled Opinel, the knife that had featured in his list of possessions in the Nice gendarmerie. Pulling out the blade until it clicked into place he rolled me onto my front and made three or four expert cutting movements. I felt the cords loosen.

'Throw down the knife,' Sanya ordered.

With a movement of his wrist, he flicked the Opinel so that it arced slowly through the air and landed at her feet, point down on the wooden stair, the handle quivering on the long blade.

'You don't deserve to live,' she said.

'Who does? God's choices remain a mystery.'

'You are the man who murdered Isobel.'

His lips turned down. 'I looked after her. Didn't I hide her in the hills with the other Jewish women when the police came from Nice?' His tone taunted her. He was not defending himself.

Sanya tapped the journal on the bannister rail. 'You were in love with her. You told her that. You thought the dangers of war would eliminate the differences between you. Peasant and haute bourgeoisie. But she rejected you. And you murdered her.'

'No, no,' he said, his anger billowing. 'That's not at all what happened.'

In his banal phrase I realised they were both arguing an event that could have taken place last week. For both of them, for reasons vastly different, it was the central event in their lives. And in mine.

'She was safe with me,' he said. 'Even after she turned me away. But I didn't know about her then.'

'What didn't you know?' I said and he cut me a dismissive glance and turned back to Sanya. 'I didn't know what a whore she was at heart.'

'She was no whore,' Sanya said.

'She was sleeping with Marcel. One of the women told me. At night she used to leave the other women in the hills and slip down into the château. She'd stay there, sometimes till dawn. Until that moment I loved Marcel as my elder brother, admired him, looked up to him.'

He took a huge breath and I could almost feel the division in his life that moment marked. As great as the division his words tonight marked in my own life. I was the son of Marcel Coultard and Isobel Berne. I was the half brother of Claire.

Pierre shook his head. Baffled even after half a lifetime. 'He was twenty years older than her. He didn't have looks, he had a withered arm – but he was now the *patron* of Ciné Coultard. He had money.' He paused. 'So if Marcel had made money stealing from the Jews, why not me too?'

'This is why you made contact with Professor Fabius?' I said. 'For money.'

He glanced down at me, then back at Sanya. He shrugged awkwardly, suddenly like a small boy, guilty. 'Not just money.'

She understood better than I. 'What did he offer you?' she said.

'Treatment like I'd never had before.' It was Sanya he answered, his voice slow as he regurgitated the memory. 'There was a big round-up of undesirables that week. I went to see Professor Fabius in his office in Nice. I offered him the next batch of women and children I was supposed to escort down to the Spanish border. I remember it well. In that moment we became comrades. A slap on the back, his arm round my shoulder. He called in his secretary. Cognac all round to clinch the deal. "You've joined the National Revolution," he said. "The true France!" And for a few days I thought I had. Arrangements were made that very afternoon. For a few months it all went smooth as clockwork. The Professor's Jewish Affairs police unit would pick the women up as we crossed the hills on our way to Spain. We always stayed away from the main coast road. It was easy. He'd wait till we were camping for the night and his squad would surround us, whooping out of the dark. You should have heard the women's screams.'

A handful of dollars for a life.

'But your blood money did you no good with Isobel,' Sanya said. 'She may have put off her departure three or four times, but it was not for love of *you*. She makes that clear.' Sanya came down another step. The goat, less sure-footed on a staircase than in the hills, moved down a level behind her.

'The book,' Pierre said. 'Where did you find it?'

'In the false bottom of her suitcase,' Sanya. 'Did you never think to look?' There was a fine touch of contempt about the way she spoke to him. None of the craven fear I'd felt. But then she was holding the gun.

'In the book,' Pierre said, 'what does she say about me?'

I wondered how this disparate trio, a murderer, a reincarnate and a tongue-tied newcomer to their world like me, might look to anyone else as we all three used each other to recreate the past of nearly a half-century ago.

'She says she already suspected you,' Sanya said triumphantly. She rested the journal on the banister rail and thumbed through the page: '*October 26, 1942. Last night, the appalling news that all the men in my father's internment camp have been transported East. God knows what awaits them in Poland where Marcel believes they are bound. But the rumours of the last few months are too ghastly to even think about.*

'*I know now I must leave. I should not stay longer now that I can do nothing more to help my father. The temptation, after this terrifying news, is to delay my journey to stay an extra week with the man I love. But there is also the baby's safety to consider. Everything argues for the earliest possible departure for Spain. All these things are true. But there is another which I can't raise with M or with any of the brave men who take their orders from him.*

'*It is this. I fear Pierre. I have asked two girls with whom I became friendly in the last two consignments to write me a post-card to the château when they reached safety across the Spanish border. We devised a crude code – a request for Ciné-Coultard to sell them second-hand spare parts for a cinema projector. But no request has arrived from either convoy. This despite the fact that Pierre swears that both groups passed safely into Spain. And Pierre, suddenly, has money. He is trying to buy me things. Of course I refuse. But should I risk myself and the child on this next trip? Should I speak to M and accuse his brother of treachery? Or should I confront Pierre myself?*'

'She confronted you,' I said. 'The night her convoy was to leave. She confronted you. And you murdered her.'

'What else?' he said calmly.

'You murdered *her*,' I said, 'but not the child. What happened to Isobel's child?'

'The child . . . ?' he said, his dark eyes on me. 'The child betrayed me.'

## 60

ON THE HILLSIDE, through the thick mist, Claire was leading. It was twelve years since had taken this path down from the château to St Juste village, twelve years in which, until the drought, strange underwater vegetation had flourished, in which old bicycle frames and mattress springs had been hurled into the lake and settled here. But it was still a path of sorts. Quicker by far to bring a gendarmerie column down this way than to try to descend through the sharp slimy rocks and leafless dead trees. Quicker, but with every step she took, she asked herself was it quick enough?

Bisset was at her shoulder. Like her he carried a powerful flashlight that cut through the fog for perhaps a yard or two before being reflected back as a series of looming shapeless shadows. From time to time they stopped and each gendarme flashed his light behind him to signal a pause while Claire tried to pierce the haze ahead.

It was the instability of the mist that confused her. One moment it would be at its thickest on her right. A dense wall. Then it would lift and flounce away like a dancer's skirts and fifty yards of the water's edge would be revealed with perhaps a piece of a village building appearing to float off into the lake.

On one such moment when the mist rolled away, she was certain she had seen two men wading through the water towards the village. She had thought to turn to point them out to Bisset but they had disappeared before she could point. Disappeared before she was certain they really were men and not simply the shapes, the figures, which her tired eyes were forcing out of the mist.

Bisset held a compass which gave them their general direction but it was Claire who guided their steps, fighting to recapture memories of the shape of the village, the *mairie*, the market place, the church square . . .

They reached the water's edge with a sudden alarming splashing underfoot. Further back down the column men were carrying deflated rubber boats and Bisset signalled them forward. In the greyness Claire cluctched her arms about her and leaned against a rock while she watched the uniformed men lay out the boats and fit the compressed air cylinders. It was the first time she had felt terror on someone else's behalf. Standing there, against the rock, she was shaken by brief tremors. Bisset standing beside her, moved his eyes from the men inflating the boats, to her face. She dropped her head and stared at the ground, biting her lip.

Aware he was watching her she lit a cigarette, pluming the smoke into the mist. Tears were running down her cheeks.

'We'll find him,' he said. 'More often than not hostage situations work out.'

She nodded.

'Will you stay with him? Would you want to stay with him?'

She shrugged and threw her cigarette. It was a gesture of hopelessness. 'That's not even a question for me,' she said. 'I have another commitment.'

He seemed to understand.

'A husband.'

'I know. In Paris, I heard him lecture once,' was all he said.

## 61

IN THE LONG pause I swallowed hard, tasting the thick odour of vegetable corruption around me.

'The child . . .' I knew I was talking about me. 'The child betrayed you to Marcel? How could that be? He was too young to talk.'

'Not too young to cry out.'

Sanya was listening intently now. This was the part Isobel's journal could never have covered. By then she was dead.

'She'd hidden the child,' he said. 'Moses in the bullrushes. She took a beating from me that night – but she wouldn't tell me where. I tried to tell Marcel I had already put her on the road to Spain, but he didn't believe me for a moment. He and Rolin started searching.' He looked at me. 'At dawn they heard your screams coming from a ruin, a pile of stones where she'd hidden you. It wasn't difficult for Marcel to guess that Isobel Berne had never left St Juste. He knew she was not the mother to abandon a child.' He paused, then shrugged his shoulders. 'The Committee put me on trial for murder. It was done up here in the woods. November 1st, 1942. There was snow that night. They sat on logs in a circle around me in the big cave. Just one shaded lamp for old Jean Rolin to write the record.'

'They knew you were guilty.'

'They were all looking to Marcel for guidance. But his face was like a stone. Find him guilty if that's what you think, he was saying, But he never uttered a word. He got up and left when they began asking about the other women.'

'So they found you guilty of the murder of Isobel Berne,' I said with a dry throat.

He laughed a laugh beyond bitterness. 'But that wasn't the problem for them. The problem was their reputation as a Resistance unit. How could they have harboured the viper who sold the women they were supposed to save?'

'And who had murdered one of them.'

He made a sort of smile. 'The way our writers talk today you'd think the French always saw the Resistance as heroes. Not so, Monsieur. As often, villagers saw us as scrounging bandits, demanding food and shelter, calling a Vichy police unit down on a village. That could mean plunder, arrests. So support for the Resistance was finely balanced. No . . . in those days no Resistance Brigade could afford to allow my story to get out. I was confident. I was young. I was sure my brother would find a way to save me. Even when his friend Rolin produced the idea of a hero's death.'

'A hero's death. A monument. How old were you?'

'I was seventeen. Due to be eighteen the very day the execution was to take place.'

'But Marcel intervened.'

'Only because my mother pleaded. That night Marcel asked the judges for a concession. He asked that his old friend Jean Rolin should take me into the woods and shoot me. And that Rolin and himself should be allowed to bury me.'

'Instead they let you escape.'

'Escape?' He spat anger. 'No. Instead they took it on themselves to sentence me to life in exile. They took me across the Pyrenees. To Ascobar, the monastery there. And when I began to make trouble and demanded to return to France, I was sent on to another monastery in Spanish Morocco. It was made clear to me that if ever I tried to return to France the Resistance would hunt me down, even though the war was over. They threatened this to a boy not yet twenty . . . It was my own brother did that.'

I didn't try to remind him that his own brother had kept him from being shot. 'How long did you stay?'

'Until Franco died and Spain began to change. I thought the new Spain would give me papers. I would become Spanish . . . Instead, I became Antonio Burgos, without papers, without identity. I was the lowest of the low. A stateless North African refugee with no claim to be Spanish and no claim at all to be French.' He paused and then repeated: 'My own brother did that.'

'But you had your revenge,' I said.

He shook his head. 'I swear I wouldn't have killed him if he hadn't left his money to the Jews,' he said. 'I went back to make my peace with him. An old man. But even after forty years he wouldn't have it. He babbled on about Jews and wills and obligations. We parted as enemies. But I knew I had to see the will he'd written. I broke in to Mantel Rolin's office. Went through the files. Even then I wasn't prepared for what Marcel intended to do. To leave it all to the Israelites.' He straightened up. 'I knew then there had been a purpose in my life. All the years of hardening my body and soul as a monastery lackey had not been in vain. I was called to right wrong. I was called to deny the Israelites their triumph in the end.'

'And to kill your brother?'

'You can't talk to a deaf man.'

Sanya had been listening so intently that the gun had lowered in her hand. I saw it in the corner of my eye but Coultard was already moving. For such a square built man he was fast on his feet. He was across the space to where the stairs rose before she could re-sight the pistol. He had already snatched up the Opinel from the stair as she screamed at him to stay back.

She brought the gun up and fired, point blank. I saw a stone chip explode from a verdigris saint's kneecap and then the long bladed Opinel flew through the air towards her. She tried to turn away but the sound was like the gentle slamming of a car door as the blade buried itself deep in her groin. She screamed, sharper and higher than I have ever heard a human scream. The goat leapt back in fear, its hooves pattering on the bare boards of the gallery. A red stain welled quickly where her dress was pinned to her body. I shouted to her not to, but, gasping with pain and shock, she clasped the wooden hilt and dragged the knife from her flesh. The blood geysered. The gun only now flew from her hand.

I had moved. Without thought, I threw myself across the floor. To grasp the gun was an agony I had never before experienced. My right forearm was bent oddly. As I stretched for the gun I saw a great lump, which was probably broken bone, pushing at the skin a few inches above my wrist. Bringing my left hand over, with my damaged fingers I gripped hard on the butt. Close to fainting, I rolled onto my back. Coultard stopped dead, just three feet away. Very slowly he stepped back. He had no idea that my gun hand was all splintered bones. To him, he was faced by an aimed gun. Nothing less.

For me it was very different. None of the fingers seemed to have the strength to point and fire the gun. But I had pushed myself up onto one knee. Using my damaged forearm to steady the weapon, I held it trained it on him.

Behind me I could hear Sanya's breath coming in gasps of terror as the blood gushed from her. Coultard crouched poised in front of me. I think he was beginning to realise that my strength was failing. There was no way in which I could take control of the situation, issue orders to Pierre Coultard, get medical help for Sanya. Her blood was dripping fast over the edge of the stair beside me.

If the gendarmerie were coming, they were still too far away to save Sanya. Through the gaping church doorway, I could see no sign of flashlights on the hillside, hear no sound of men's voices. I had to decide. A course of action. There's no one more dangerous than a frightened wimp.

I shot him. To kill him was the only way to save Sanya from bleeding to death, wasn't it? Afterwards I'd tell myself I'd also done it for what he'd done to Romilly, or Margot. Or even my true mother, Isobel Berne. But perhaps I don't have the savagery necessary to be motivated by vengeance. I could, however, pretend.

He had fallen back in a clumsy cartwheel across the altar steps into the two feet of water in the nave beyond, wounded but not stopped. For a moment he faced me just six or seven yards away. Perhaps I could have killed him then. Perhaps I just had the strength to aim and pull the trigger. But now, I hesitated.

And Pierre Coultard turned and walked, *walked*, away from me, expecting the bullet in the back any second. But walked with an Islamic resignation towards the church doorway.

Firing a handgun to stop a man is twenty times more difficult than any film or television show depicts. With my arm shaking, trying to support one damaged hand with a damaged arm, my chance of hitting Pierre Coultard, was just that, nothing but pure chance.

I knew that. I fired without the expectation of hitting him. I fired twice more, maybe even with the hope that I would miss. It's only afterwards we make sense of our motives.

I closed my eyes. I've no idea whether I'd have tried harder if my fingers had been strong enough. For a moment I lay back against the staircase while he wallowed through the water, his course veering from one side to another. He was singing, low-voiced but clear enough, the great François Villon ballad, put to music by Georges Brassens, *Où sont les neiges d'antan?* Where are the snows of yesteryear? That sad salute to an unrecoverable youth, to a golden age that never was.

At one moment he stopped and rested his shoulder against a stone pillar, looking back at me, then he turned and waded on again, splashing like a dying seabird.

He passed through the door and down the church steps into deeper water. It seemed to me certain that he would drown out there in the mist of the market square when I heard a voice. A young man's voice which called his name: 'Coultard . . . Pierre Coultard.'

And almost immediately two shots, not sharp cracks like a rifle, but the big, loose explosions of a shotgun – and bits of the shattered glass on the edge of the oriel window flew across the nave and spattered on the water.

It was no more than a glimpse through the broken window, but enough to show me two figures, two men, one young, one older, wading into the deep obscurity of the mist.

The square at St Juste was filled with lights and people as it had not been since the day the Paris government had released the floodwaters into the valley. Gendarmes, up to their thighs in water, fished damp cigarettes from their pockets and handed them around. A loudspeaker system was issuing orders for the removal of the body of Pierre Coultard, then further orders on the treatment of the crime scene inside the church and additional instructions on where guard duty gendarmes would find coffee and croissants in the dry upper floor of the old *mairie*.

Sanya's inert body was carried out of the church by two gendarmes. But her life was saved by an Aeronavale helicopter pilot who risked his own life to drop his craft through the mist and hover over the square of St Juste while the gendarmerie fought the waves thrashed up by the rotors and lifted her and a twirling paramedic aboard.

The pain in my hand ebbed and flowed, bringing me close to fainting. Claire and I sat together on the base of a statue which had been long removed. She held one arm round me and a cigarette to my mouth while Bisset's men brought up a rubber boat to take us across the lake to where an ambulance was waiting.

We sat in the bow of the boat unable to speak above the roar of the outboard motor. At the lake's edge the gendarme in charge of the boat helped us ashore and flicked his flashlight to receive an answering signal from the ambulance higher up the hillside.

My left hand had by now swollen to the size of a baseball mitt, the fingers pushing against each other, throbbing as if jolts of electric current were being passed through them. The right arm seemed mostly numb.

We stood together for a few moments, baffled at where the last month of our lives had led us, our faces streaked with mud and grit and water in the headlights of the gendarmerie vehicles grouped around us. The medics were ready to help me into the back of the 4x4 ambulance. There was no room for Claire, even if she'd intended to come with me. A medic opened the back door and looked toward me. 'Monsieur . . .'

'*Un moment*,' Claire called to the paramedic. '*Il vient, le Monsieur*.' She stood before me, resting both hands on my shoulders and glanced up to where I had driven the Renault off the road. 'Not so much of a wimp after all, it appears,' she said. Then she slowly leaned forward and kissed me. I felt her open lips at first cold on mine, then the warmth and the grit in her mouth. For all its wonderful imperfection, I knew she meant it as a kiss goodbye.

# 62

T HE DISMANTLING OF Pierre Coultard's monument was never intended to be a big ceremony. The surviving members of the Committee of Seven were to be present, naturally, and some old folks from the original village of St Juste who had known Pierre. And, of course, a few people like me with a special interest. Romilly and Elaine were back in England, never, I suspect, to return here.

As the hour approached, people drifted up from the village by bicycle or on foot, and cars were parked all the way along the roadside where Romilly had jumped from the blue van and all this had started.

I wasn't at all sure how the village was going to accept the removal of a monument many had known and pointed out to strangers since it was first erected after the war. What was happening today, was, after all, to be the acknowledged destruction of an important part of the local myth. The myth that described a wartime France divided between a few Frenchmen like Professor Fabius who had backed and collaborated with the Nazis, the *collabos* – and an ever-growing groundswell of popular Resistance as France recovered its soul. It wasn't, of course, the story that Pierre Coultard's life had to tell. The past, I'd learnt, is seldom that clean-cut.

Bisset joined me. He was wearing a dark blue suit and striped tie. His height and the pale colour of his skin gave him a special elegance. I saw he also wore the discreet strip of the *Légion d'honneur* ribbon in his buttonhole.

But the most surprising visitor was Jean-Claude Fabius. He arrived with Claire and wore a tricolour sash over his impeccably cut business suit. I inclined my head to him. I needed to acknowledge that it took courage for the son of Professor Fabius to arrive at today's ceremony.

I tried to catch Claire's eye, but though I'm sure she had seen me, she seemed to have no wish for us to meet. Bisset, I saw, had noticed my efforts.

'Don't even think about it,' he said. 'She's got a husband. She won't risk it with you. She won't risk it getting that serious.'

Shortly before the dismantling of the monument was about to begin, a Nice Airport taxi drew up. Marty Pearson got out and stood for a moment adjusting his sunglasses. He was wearing a tie and a linen suit and carrying an expensive leather briefcase and suddenly I saw him as the man who had served as a Hallmark executive in his other life, his life with the attractive American wife and the two successful children. Among the crowd a few people turned to see who the late arrival was. From behind his dark glasses Marty made contact with someone and made an almost imperceptible movement of the head, a nod of complicity, of greeting. I looked for the recipient.

Luc Rolin stood looking at Marty from maybe fifteen yards away. He too, inclined his head, then turned back to the event taking place in front of him. And in that moment, linking the two together, an image hit me of two figures, one shorter, older, stockier, the other tall and younger, wading through the shallow water, like duck shooters, to be swallowed up by the mist in the flooded old square of St Juste.

I walked slowly over and shook Marty's hand. 'You were planning to leave without saying goodbye?' I said, trying to keep an accusatory note out of my voice. He shrugged.

'Or perhaps you figured we'd said goodbye down there in the water.'

He raised his eyebrows. 'That could be.'

'Either way, I want to say thanks a lot.'

He knew what I was thanking him for. 'It was for both of us, pal,' he said. 'You and me. And for her. Isobel. But the orders came from the Committee of Seven.'

'It still exists?'

'It runs Villefranche. Mantel's the head. Young Luc and Philippe Rodinet have been elected in their fathers' place. It's the Committee for the defence of the interests of Villefranche sur Bol. I'm like I was before. An honorary member.' He gestured towards Pierre Coultard's monument. 'Young Luc and I were entrusted with making sure that this time he really did die. No one wanted a trial. You understand what I'm saying.'

'Perfectly. In the mist down there, I saw nothing. No one. Is that right?'

He nodded. 'It had to be done that way. No trial. It's about preserving the community's self-respect, Tom.'

'Preserving it from reality?'

'Adjusting the scales a little, maybe. In the early years forty million Frenchmen supported the old Marshal. In the end everybody was a resister, or claimed to be. Except the real fascists like Professor Fabius. The Resistance played its part – but they didn't liberate France. The Allied armies did that. So if some of Resistance history is a little shaky, okay, we don't have to go there. Meantime the myth has served France well. Her post-war recovery of self-respect depended on it.'

We stood there in the sunlight. 'I still need one more answer,' I said. 'Pierre told me in the church that Isobel used to go to Marcel every night.'

'She went to the château, yes.'

'She'd begun an affair with him before Switzerland? So it was Marcel who made her pregnant.'

He looked at me and took off his sunglasses. 'It was me she was meeting at Marcel's,' he said carefully. 'He arranged it so that we could be together.'

'*You* were Isobel's lover.' I waited without speaking, the question poised between us.

'Yes.' His eyes were locked into mine. 'But I wasn't the father of her child. Isobel was pregnant before I even met her, Tom.'

There was a long moment's silence.'No,' I said. 'Oh Christ, no.'

He nodded slowly. 'Your mother and Pierre had an adolescent roll in the hay,' he said. 'Call it what you like, a couple of kids, it didn't mean anything at the time.'

'You mean it didn't seem to.'

'She was barely eighteen. I arrived in the area a month later, not much more than a kid myself. Within weeks she and I were storybook lovers. So it was a hell of a shock to find she was already pregnant. Her father, old Berne, sent her to Switzerland. It was the way things were done then. I didn't expect to see her again.'

'But in Switzerland she heard her father had been arrested. Interned.'

'She refused to surrender you for adoption. Instead she brought you back to St Juste. It was too dangerous for her to stay in her own home, in the château. She lived up here in the woods with the other women, waiting for a chance to get down to the camp where they were holding her father. She'd come over to the château after dark and Marcel would allow me in to spend the nights with her. From then on, Isobel and I both thought of you as ours. Fatally, now I look back on it, she made this clear to Pierre.'

'Were you here the night Pierre . . . ?'

'I was pulled out a week earlier, just before the Allies invaded North Africa. I never knew what happened to her.' Slowly he put back his sunglasses. 'There it is.'

'I don't even know where to contact you,' I said.

'Think about it first,' he said. 'Then if you want to . . . I've left a forwarding address with Lieutenant Bisset. I figured if you wanted contact you could follow it up. If not . . .' He spread his hands. 'Maybe what we've had together here, is a sort of compression of the years. Maybe it's as good an adoptive father-son relationship as it gets.'

We both smiled.

'I've got a flight to catch,' he said. He checked his watch. 'Look, I'm going to have to miss the ceremony.' He reached back towards the taxi door. 'Listen Tom, I'm feeling that all this . . .' he waved his arm at the people grouped around the monument . . . 'It's one book closed. I'm going to be looking for a change of lifestyle.'

'I'm not surprised.'

'I mean I'm out of Mission Hills, Kansas City. I'm planning to take an apartment in Manhattan. To spend my last days in wine, women and song. It'll shock my family, my other family. But you might like to swing by from time to time.' He picked up his bag. 'As the more reprobate part of my brood.'

'I'll do that,' I said. 'If I ever get back to the US.'

He raised his eyebrows and smiled. 'Maybe see you in New York, then,' he said. 'I hope so.'

We shook hands. He pulled open the car door and slid into the passenger seat. He lifted his hand as the taxi pulled away. To all intents and purposes, Mr Ordinary.

The mayor of Villefranche, the old *notaire*, Maître Hercule Mantel, was helped onto the back of a flat-back truck on which had been set up a crude lectern decorated with a tricolour. The crowd hushed.

'Today's newspapermen,' Mantel began, 'describe what happened here in November 1942, and what is about to happen today, as a blow to the myth of Resistance France. But the

Resistance is no myth, however much besmirched by people like Pierre Coultard. That is something, difficult as it was to admit in the past, that we are strong enough as a French community to acknowledge today. We had bandits, thieves, murderers and cowards among us. But even they don't affect the thousand genuine monuments to young men erected in woods and by road-sides in every corner of France.

'I speak now as a friend of Marcel Coultard – and, most of all, as the voice of the past. They were days like no other. France was on her knees. Marshal Pétain was our only possible leader – who had heard of the obscure General de Gaulle in London? But our Marshal led us down an unworthy road. He began by persecuting foreign Jews seeking refuge among us. Before long he extended his vile persecution to all Jews, French and foreign. Men and women. And finally, children too.

'It's painful, but it's right that all these facts should come to light, that we should cease sheltering as Frenchmen, under the convenient myth that we were forced to these things by a brutal occupying army. We all know that until November 1942 there was no occupying army. Marcel's brother Pierre showed a weakness of character widely apparent in the France of those days. It led him to the betrayal of innocent women. And finally to murder. It's right that today, in a recovered France, we stare the past honestly in the face. It's right that in this village we honour the name of one Coultard – Marcel – and execrate the name of his brother Pierre. But it's also right that we recognise that, if the Resistance didn't save France militarily, it did, nevertheless, save its soul. It saved France for you others today.'

He turned abruptly to the bulldozer standing by, its engine turning over, and nodded to the driver. As the steel bucket bit into the stone-carved vine leaves of the monument, there was a shuffling of feet among the people present as they all turned their backs. Very few watched as the bulldozer ground the monument into dust. I looked round for Claire, but she was already getting into a car with Fabius.

There were four big removal trucks in the courtyard when I got back to the château. Pale blue monsters with *Déménagements Picard, Nice* inscribed on the sides. Maybe six or seven men were carrying chairs, boxes, sewing tables out to the vans. Two men struggled with the fake Gericault, wrestling it down the perron, and headed towards the nearest truck. Bernadette, the old retainer, told me Madame Claire had already left for Paris. To live with her husband. 'What she should have done years ago.' She glared contempt. 'Then she wouldn't have had so many of you men hanging around her, putting temptation in her way.'

*Put temptation in her way . . . That's what you did then, was it?* I said to myself as the first removal truck pulled past me, kicking dust in my face to reinforce the old woman's disapproval. The sort of dust that stays in your mouth as sharp little pieces of grit. I know.

# EPILOGUE

I see a lot of Romilly and Elaine in London. Romilly has every appearance of having pulled through some of the most terrifying and humiliating experiences a young woman can suffer without visible scars – but I guess she has dark dreams and it'll take years to be sure she's healed. Elaine's scars are more visible. The tension builds whenever Romilly is late home. But perhaps a new job, a new life will handle that in time, too.

I have dark dreams, too. Mostly when I'm in London, which I find strange. I see a group of women struggling down a path that twists through the rocks on a bleak hillside. They are bundled in thick coats and scarves against the cold, barely able to manage the heavy suitcases they carry. On the narrow track the snow banks up on either side of them. Their guide walks easily, a light knapsack on his shoulder. He is a young man in a dark blouson and black beret, a staff in his right hand. I can't see his face clearly but I know he's Pierre Coultard. The head of the column is just a few yards away from a battered truck parked just off the track when there is a sharp blast of a whistle. Then another and another from the woods around them. There are shouts, men's voices shouting in French, but I can't make out a word, and screams of terror from the women. They drop the cases and try to run in different directions, scrambling among the rocks and pines, rolling across the snowbanks as members of Professor Fabius's Jewish Affairs Police Unit come running from the woods, flashlight beams raking the path. There is no firing, only the shouts of the men and the screams of the women.

Moments later, it seems, it's all over. The women are pinned down on the path. Chains are roped round their waists. The suitcases are thrown onto Pierre Coultard's old truck, the spoils of war, and the women are led away sobbing to the dull green painted military vehicles that have been brought up the track.

The tall, distinguished-looking man in the broad brimmed hat counts out money into Pierre Coultard's hand. I wake up to the revving of engines, the sound of sobbing women and a song, I don't recognise it, sung by the members of Professor Fabius's squad. A song about youth and hope and the freedom of the fields.

Despite my dreams, I like London. A few days spent there every couple of months is part of the pattern of my life. I keep it to a few days because Elaine has another man – and because late teenage girls can easily grow tired of their father's company.

I've been back to Villefranche a few times. I've sat at Madame Beste's Café de la Paix and watched the strange copper and iron engine with the big brass taps, its boiler like an old locomotive, dragged into the Place Frédéric Mistral. As a head of steam is worked up, the peasants line up with their barrels and galvanised bins of rotten pears or grape crushings. I've learnt this is the *alembique*, the travelling State distillery which converts rotten fruit to the powerful alcohol which warms the tongues of story tellers round their hearths on winter nights.

I've also learnt who Frédéric Mistral was. One of those early figures vainly fighting to preserve the language of the past, the Provençal Occitan which everybody in Villefranche spoke not thirty years ago, but which only the very old speak any longer.

My visits here are to sell up Elaine's house for her. I see Bisset whenever I'm visiting, but he's expecting a new posting soon and whether we see more of each other will depend on the whim of gendarmerie headquarters in Paris. With his easy smile he tells me he could be sent to Chad or Réunion, in the middle of the Pacific, as easily as to Avignon or Angoulême.

Once I drove up the hill, past the flat patch of gravel which was Pierre Coultard's monument and visited the old château but, already, even after just the first few months, it was too full of ghosts and rats and crumbling ceilings to make me want to stay. Sanya has said she'd like to camp there next summer when she returns.

Wills and testaments continue to figure importantly in our lives. My former mother, Margaret Bannerman Chapel, died last month. She left her entire estate, not as big as I thought, but big enough, to Romilly. Her trustees were specifically warned to watch for any attempts to exert an undue influence

432

by the girl's father, Thomas Berne, formerly Chapel. She always had faith.

Romilly's legacy was surprise enough. But, to my reeling astonishment, Margot had amassed enough to leave her one-time brother her all, fifty thousand dollars a year for life. That Margot.

The money has been enough to maintain a small apartment in Paris, off the Boulevard St Michel. Where Claire spends one night a week with me and breakfast the following morning before she hurries off to her new job with Amnesty International.

It was all her doing. One day, some two months after she had left for Paris, I was at Elaine's house. It was empty of any sign of Elaine or Romilly, and Margot's blood, thank God, had been cleaned from the *salon* wall. When the phone rang I was expecting the real estate woman, Madame Boretti.

But it was Claire.

There were no formalities. 'Why should it happen that I feel I can't live without you?' were her first words.

There was no furniture left in the house. I sat down on the stairs.

'I don't have much to offer you,' she said. 'Nothing full time.'

'It's in Paris, at least. I like the city.'

'I suppose that's something. Will you take it?'

I said I couldn't think of anything that would stop me.

'Then get here, for God's sake, Tom. Get here as soon as you can!'

So that's how it started. Her husband knows about us. She insisted on telling him. And he's one of those French intellectuals who claims he believes wives *should* have lovers. For him, poor man, it's a claim he has to believe. For me, it makes for another of these half-life entanglements, not so different, in some ways, from my life with Margot. Or maybe not, if I really think about it. For one thing, we don't play games. The time with Claire is short and intense. Each Monday is a scrabble to eat dinner, to tell each other about latest developments in our work, to tumble into bed and to lie gasping, locked in each other. Then the rest of the week I live the life of an *homme seul*. I write. I dine in small corner cafés off the Boulevard St Michel. Some nights I get a little drunk and ring Elly to see how Romilly's liking Cambridge. From time to time I cross the city to have dinner at Boulevard

433

Malsherbes where Claire has her other home with her husband. From his wheelchair Jean Philippe greets me as he greets the other guests, like old friends. We talk (or rather *they* talk, because I'm completely out of my depth) about French philosophers, and the Death of the Author and the significance for literary theory of Picasso's *Les Demoiselles d'Avignon*. And I mutter deprecatingly about the novel I'm secretly proud to be publishing in London and New York next month – then bid goodnight to the guests, who must wonder why I'm invited at all, and I take my leave, longing for the weekend to be over and Claire's return home to me to come round again.

Yes, I know what you think. I know what it looks like. But I'm not sitting here on the Left Bank waiting for an invalid to die. I've learnt enough from Margot's death and Romilly's narrowest of escapes to realise that the first called aren't necessarily the first to be taken. I'm happy with what I have now, the life I have now, even if it is only a life of sorts. It won't last for ever, of course. But then, shockingly, life doesn't, does it?